"It is written!" said Margrove.

"Where?" Sari asked. "It doesn't make any sense. Aren't there are least two? A master and an apprentice?"

Margrove affected a merry chuckle. "Isn't she charming? Have some wine, Princess. Now, where were we?"

A servant in highly ornamented livery appeared from behind a screen. "This is Reginald," said Margrove. "He is my most trusted servant. He will show you to the library. You may ask of him anything that you require. When I am gone, and one of you is master in my place, Reginald will serve you also." Reginald, who stood behind Margrove, distinctly grimaced. He stepped forward and made a small bow. Sari recognized him from the hostile takeover at DataMagics. He'd been the one grimly walking down the corridor of cubicles handing out pink slips. Sari shuddered.

"What happens to the other?" said Ivan. "The one who doesn't solve the proof?"

Lord Margrove shook his head sadly. "I'm afraid you must publish or perish."

—from "The Apprentice"
by Catherine H. Shaffer

HEROES IN TRAINING

EDITED BY

Martin H. Greenberg
and Jim C. Hines

DAW BOOKS, INC.

DONALD A. WOLLHEIM, FOUNDER

375 Hudson Street, New York, NY 10014

ELIZABETH R. WOLLHEIM
SHEILA E. GILBERT
PUBLISHERS

http://www.dawbooks.com

First Printing, September 2007

1 2 3 4 5 6 7 8 9

DAW TRADEMARK REGISTERED
U.S. PAT. AND TM. OFF. AND FOREIGN COUNTRIES
—MARCA REGISTRADA
HECHO EN U.S.A.

PRINTED IN THE U.S.A.

ACKNOWLEDGMENTS

CONTENTS

INTRODUCTION

Jim C. Hines

Greetings, dear reader, and welcome to *Heroes in Training*.

If you're standing in a bookstore, please stop reading this introduction right now. Skip ahead and read through some of the thirteen stories contained in these pages. If these wonderful tales don't make you run to the nearest cashier, nothing I say is likely to change your mind.

Okay, so now you've bought the anthology.[1] (Either that, or you're still reading this introduction in the bookstore, blatantly ignoring my advice. I swear, you're as bad as my kids.) Regardless, it's time for me to tell a quick story.

When I was younger, I went through a phase where I read nothing but Star Trek novels.[2] After a few years and more than a hundred books crammed onto my sagging shelves, my parents finally snapped. They picked up a new novel by an author named Raymond E. Feist and pushed it into my hands.

Magician: Apprentice told the tale of two boys, des-

---

[1]Checking the book out of the library is also acceptable.
[2]Not that there's anything wrong with that.

tined to become the most powerful wizard and warrior in their world. I devoured the book and the sequel, then waited impatiently for the next two in the series.

There were more books, but those first four remain my favorites to this day. The scene when the magician Pug first challenges a full arena of wizards still gives me chills. Time and again I've followed these ordinary boys as they discover their destinies and struggle with the choices and responsibilities that come with their newfound power.

There's a special sense of wonder that comes from such stories. As readers, we want to relate to our heroes. We put ourselves in the place of Luke Skywalker, Paul Atreides, Frodo Baggins, and all the rest. I can't even begin to count the number of Harry Potter-inspired costumes we saw last Halloween, including my own daughter "Hermione." When we care about the heroes, we feel their struggles like our own. If the hero loses a loved one, we grieve with them. When a writer kills off one of our favorite heroes,[3] the blow is almost as painful as if we'd lost a real friend.

It can sometimes be difficult to relate to the full-grown hero. But the hero in training, the man or woman who starts out as ordinary as you or me: these are characters we can identify with. Take the new student in Esther Friesner's "Roomies," arriving for her first day at the Royal Academy of Damsels' Arts. We've all been there. We've had dreams of showing up unprepared for a test, or finding ourselves clad in nothing but our underwear in the middle of our social studies presentation.[4]

Then there's the power of watching these characters grow throughout the story. I cheered as I read Robin

---

[3]Curse you, Joss Whedon!
[4]Do you think Harry Potter has nightmares about showing up for potions class in his boxers?

Bailey's "The Children's Crusade," following young Ari as he pushed the limits of his special gifts. Gifted or not, in many ways, Ari and his friends are ordinary kids, determined to accomplish the extraordinary. That determination gives the story its true magic.

We love to see ordinary people become heroes. Whether it's Kimet's quiet courage in Sherwood Smith's "The Princess, the Page, and the Master Cook's Son," or the bumbling luck of poor Jack in G. Scott Huggins's "Giantkiller," these stories inspire us.

For some of the authors, this anthology also provides the opportunity to share a bit of background about their established characters. Mike Jasper has published a number of stories about his mysterious aliens, the Wannoshay. For the first time, we learn why the Wannoshay left their world, and we meet the lowly Drinker Iyannoloway who led the way. Julie Czerneda invites us to join her shape shifting alien Esen-alit-Quar as she embarks on her first visit to another world in the delightful tale "A Touch of Blue." And those of you who are familiar with Peter David's famous antihero Sir Apropos will appreciate the unique lessons he shares with his successor in "Sir Apropos of Nothing and the Adventure of the Receding Heir."[5]

What ties all of these stories together is that central theme of growth and discovery, the wonder of watching people push themselves beyond their limits, and the inspiration that stays with us long after we've closed the book. I'm honored to be the one presenting these stories, and I hope they bring you as much pleasure as they've brought me.

---

[5] Yes, I groaned too.

ROOMIES

Esther M. Friesner

Auriana was sobbing, her face so deeply buried in a huge goosedown pillow that she wasn't aware she had a visitor until a heavy hand fell on her shoulder and an unfamiliar voice demanded, "Are you all right? Why are you making that noise?"

Auriana bolted upright on her bed. "Who are you? When did you get here? Who let you into my room?"

Her uninvited caller took a step back and held up her hands, fending off the flurry of questions. "I'm a new student. My mother left me at the castle gate; then a sharp-faced woman came out and squawked, 'Why are you here, you miserable creature? This is the Royal Academy of Damsels' Arts, not a training center for trolls!' I finally gave her the smallest box Mother sent along. Once that woman saw the gold, she got *much* nicer. She begged my pardon and told me that the light was bad, so it was no wonder she'd mistaken me for a troll instead of a damsel of quality. She brought me inside, called for a porter to fetch my trunk, and told me to go on ahead up to the topmost room in the eastern tower. Is this it? I'm not used to places this big and bustling."

Auriana wiped her eyes on the back of one hand,

smiling for the first time all day. "That sounds like our headmistress, Lady Florinda. Was it a *lot* of gold?"

The new girl made awkward gestures to describe the dimensions of the box. It was a big box and as such would have contained a lot of gold indeed. Auriana was puzzled. "*That* much? I'm surprised she sent you up here. By rights you should have one of the big suites on a lower floor. You certainly shouldn't be forced to split this cramped little nest with a roommate."

The girl shrugged. "I don't mind. Mother said that what I'll learn in the classroom won't be half as useful as what I'll pick up from mingling with people. Will *you* be comfortable, sharing a room with me?"

Auriana looked a little wistful. "You're the first person who ever asked about my comfort, and this is my third year at the Academy. For that alone, I'm overjoyed to have you here."

"Really?" The girl's plain face lit with joy. "Then please, don't worry; this room is more than good enough for me. I like heights. At home, I always climbed as high as I could go, just to enjoy the view." She crossed the floor to the turret room's lone window. It was little more than an arrow-slit, but the girl looked out over the landscape below in rapture. "I can be happy here," she said.

Can you? Auriana thought. The longer she looked at her new roommate, the more she understood why this girl had been sent to the smallest, most out-of-the-way room in the entire Academy, and why she would most likely spend her term of study being treated like a jewel-encrusted chamber pot—highly valued but forever stowed out of sight. Through no fault of her own she was that most unfortunate phenomenon, a damsel-in-training with all the glamour and charm of a mud fence.

Auriana sized up the newcomer's appearance with a compassionate but honest eye. Where she herself was tall and willowy, with the creamy skin, golden hair and brilliant blue eyes most desirable in trainee damsels, the other was short, brunette, and built like a block of granite. Her face was square and as brown as if it belonged to a peasant wench who'd spent her life laboring in the fields. With wide lips, a pug nose, and a round, fleshy chin, she distinctly lacked that ethereal delicacy eternally touted as a maiden's *beau idéal* by the instructors at the Royal Academy of Damsels' Arts. It was as if some waggish god had opened Lady Pandecora's immortal *Ye Parfaite Gentylle Demoiselle* to the chapter on "Fairenesse of Ye Face & Phyzyque" and then set about creating a being who embodied the opposite of every attribute on Ye Olde Cheque-Liste of Manifold Maidenly Beauties. The newcomer's only striking feature was a burning emerald gaze so wide, so clear, so brilliant that the effect was stunning.

But eyes alone did not a beauteous damsel make. Auriana had been at the Academy long enough to know the way of things. Gold would open the gates, but once inside, grace and beauty were what counted with both faculty and students alike. If you didn't have both, *plus* riches, your time within the castle walls was a daily dollop of hell.

And don't I know it, Auriana thought. *I'm sick and tired of the nasty remarks, the jibes, the way the other girl treat me like an old rag just because I haven't got their clothes or jewels or family connections. But all that's nothing compared to what* this *poor lass will have to endure. She might as well go to class with an archery target strapped to her back. It's not fair, but that's how it is.*

A fresh realization struck her: *That's how it is, but it's not the way I'll let it be.*

She extended a hand in welcome. "My name is Auriana of Kestrel's Keep. I hope we can be friends."

The newcomer made no move to take Auriana's hand in her own stubby paws. She seemed entirely bewildered about how to reciprocate the companionable gesture, though she was more than eager to say, "Call me Brandella." She paused, then added, "When I came in, why were you doing that?" She did a peculiar imitation of Auriana's earlier bout of weeping.

That's odd, Auriana thought. *Hasn't she seen people cry? I know that some of the girls here come from distant, exotic lands with strange customs, but still—* Aloud she said, "I'm sorry you had to see that, Brandella. It wasn't much of a welcome for you. I was crying because I was feeling very lonely and sorry for myself."

"Lonely . . ." Brandella seemed to try on the word for size. "There are so many people in this castle, how can you be lonely?"

"There's no trick to that, given our fellow students," Auriana said bitterly. "I told Mother that this place would be crammed with snobs, but she said I was spinning tales just because I didn't want to come here. And that's true, I didn't; she made me."

"You too?" Brandella's astonishing eyes filled with surprise and sympathy.

Auriana nodded. "My family's fallen on hard times. Mother's convinced that the only way for us to recoup our fortunes is for me to make a great marriage."

"Then why did she send you here?" Brandella asked. "Isn't this where you learn to be a–a–a damsel in distraught?"

"Distress," Auriana corrected her automatically.

She folded her hands in Attitude # 23A from the *Manual of Applied Demureness* and recited: " 'Ladies, pay no heed to those who claim that the full glory of the quest fulfilled, the peril overcome, the monster slain needs must go to the warrior, knight, or prince whose sword achieves the goal. Were it not for the presence of a suitably distressed damsel, these adventurings would be only so many boyish jaunts through the countryside, with or without attendant mayhem and property damage. It is the addition of the damsel that confers legitimacy upon all these somewhat rowdy endeavors. Ladies, they need *us* far more than we need *them*. No man may deem himself a hero unless his record boasts the rescue of at least one lady fair, and he who would seal his claim to the highest accolades of valor will do the done thing by the rescued maiden at his exploit's end.' "

She finished speaking, made a perfunctory curtsey, then added: "That was from *Queen Nicolette's First Admonition to Her Unmarried Daughters*. I used it for my piece in the declamation contest last spring."

"I don't get it," said Brandella. "What's the 'done thing' the warrior's supposed to do once he rescues you?"

"Marriage, of course," Auriana replied. "What else is there, for a damsel? According to Mother, I must devote every ounce of effort, drive and focus to the business of landing a rich, powerful husband. His wealth and influence will save my family's future, and he'll be hailed as a great hero for his part in delivering me from whatever dire peril I can get myself into. The more dire the peril, the greater the heroic reputation to be won and the higher the class of would-be heroes vying for the honor of rescuing me."

"So that's what you learn here? How to get in trouble?"

"How to get into the *right kind* of trouble. The kind that attracts princes. As a matter of fact, the Royal Academy of Damsels' Arts has such a fine reputation for producing rescue-fodder that sometimes princes come directly here to pick brides. When people hear a prince's wife attended the Academy, they simply *presume* heroics were involved in how he met her. And *she'll* never reveal the truth, not when her meal-ticket depends on keeping mum." She sighed. "So yes, it's all about marriage, marriage, marriage. Why? What did you *think* you're supposed to learn at the Royal Academy of Damsels' Arts?"

The plain girl didn't answer. She looked so miserable that Auriana's heart went out to her. "Don't fret, Brandella," she said, putting one arm around her roommate's bulky shoulders. "You don't *have* to marry the first warrior who rescues you. Lady Violetta gives a very handy senior seminar on *The Art of Refusing with Apparent Reluctance*. We girls call it *Welcome to Dumpshire, Population: You*." She giggled, but Brandella remained uncomforted.

"I don't think Mother knew about any of this when she told me to come here," she said. "She said that I'm supposed to use my time getting to learn about people. It's very hard to do that, where we're from. Our land is in the heart of the Bestbegone Mountains, desolate and lonely, yet I was happy there. I liked things the way they were, but Mother kept hearing so many strange and frightening reports about what people were doing in the wide world beyond the mountains that she decided we must know the truth. She says that anyone who ignores danger just because it hasn't reached them is a fool who doesn't know the meaning of the word *yet*."

"What sort of reports did your mother hear?"

"Dreadful ones." Brandella shuddered. "Maidens

carried off by dragons every time you blinked, over and over, and it never seemed to stop no matter how many dragons were slain."

"Did your mother think that you were in danger of dragon-capture?" Auriana asked. "Is that why she sent you here, to learn how to survive the experience?"

"That wasn't exactly how she put it." Brandella shook her head. "I know she never expected all this talk of *marriage*."

"Marriage? *You*?" A nasty snicker sounded from the doorway. While Auriana and Brandella had been speaking, three eavesdroppers had materialized on the landing outside the cramped turret room. One of these was the porter, back bent under the weight of Brandella's trunk. The other two were twin maidens, sumptuously dressed, each mirroring the other's loveliness. Their violet eyes glittered with gleeful cruelty.

Auriana gave the twins an icy look. "Who sent for *you* two?" she snapped. "This is *my* room. You're not welcome here."

"We're not *in* your precious room." One twin turned to the other and added: "You must be blind as well as poor. We're on the landing. Would you ever *want* to cross this grubby threshold, Bellira?"

"Not in my worst nightmares, Lirabel," her sister replied haughtily. "Poverty had such a ghastly stink, I wouldn't want to risk it rubbing off on me."

"Ugly stinks worse," said Lirabel, giving Brandella a long, meaningful stare. "There isn't enough gold in the world to make it go away, but I hear that there are some warriors—jumped-up third sons of minor nobility, or the occasional enchanted swineherd—who're willing to pinch their noses shut long enough to make it through the wedding, if the price is right. Gold buys a lot of blindfolds."

Auriana reached under her bed and pulled out an ancient sword in an unadorned but serviceable scabbard. Without unsheathing it, she advanced on the twins, holding it high in a menacing manner. "If you brace of harpies don't walk down those stairs under your own power right now, I'm going to teach you how to *fly* down them."

"You wouldn't *dare*," said Bellira. But she was already backing away from the door.

"We'll tell Lady Florinda that you threatened us," Lirabel added, scuttling into retreat alongside her sister. "Everyone knows you're here solely on her charity, because she was your mother's classmate, but there's only so far you can stretch *that* tie. If it comes down to a choice between two full tuition-paying students and one paltry charity rat, I know which one Lady Florinda will pick!"

"Pick this, you hags-in-training!" Auriana shouted, and swung the sword. Lirabel managed to dodge, but the flat of the sheathed blade caught Bellira on her rump and sent her stumbling down the turret steps. She collided with her more agile sister and the pair of them had to sit down hard on the stone stairs or risk taking a corkscrew spill all the way to the bottom of the tower. They were wailing and moaning about their bruises and broken fingernails when Auriana turned to the nonplussed porter and said, "Thank you for your trouble, Wat. Just put that down anywhere that Lady Brandella says."

Old Wat did as he was told and was about to leave when Brandella stopped him with a hasty, "Oh, don't go just yet! I think—I think I might need you to take that downstairs again."

The porter turned, his face a page on which a low, exasperated opinion of the nobility and their whelps was writ large. But all he said was: "As y'r ladyship likes." He trudged back to the trunk and made as if to haul it back onto his bowed shoulders.

"Wat, *no*." Auriana laid one hand on the trunk. "This is *not* going back downstairs and Lady Brandella is *not* leaving the Academy just because two unmannerly cows tried to give her a hard time. She is *not* going to take their stupidity seriously. She's going to stay here, be my roommate, learn everything there is to know about the Damsels' Arts, and graduate with full honors. And when she is carried off by the biggest, fiercest, most powerful dragon in all the land, she will come back to the Academy after her spectacular rescue by the world's handsomest hero and she will rub the twins' snippy little noses in it. Understood?"

The porter straightened up slowly and regarded the damsel with a bilious, long-suffering eye. "So yer sayin' she'll be wantin' clean undies fer all that? Fine." He shuffled for the door, pausing only when Brandella grabbed him by the wrist and pressed a heavy gold piece into his callused hand.

Once the porter was gone, Brandella turned a shy, grateful face to Auriana. "Did you mean that?" she asked.

"Of course I did." Auriana straightened her spine. "A proper damsel is worthy of trust. If we ever resort to deception, it is only for the sake of our own survival. Even so, we take care that our words always contain a grain of truth. For instance, when we have our supper tonight, Lady Florinda will call me forward to answer the twins' complaint against me, and they *will* complain. Being an honorable damsel, I will swear on the Academy's most sacred relic that I never raised my father's sword against either of those highborn bitches."

"But—but I saw—" Brandella stammered, gesturing at the sword that was still in Auriana's hands.

The golden-haired maiden smiled and pulled the blade a finger-span out of its sheath so that her roommate could see the faint line of letters etched just below the crosspiece.

" 'To my darling daughter on her twelfth birthday,' " Brandella read. She looked up suddenly. "This is *your* sword."

"It is, though I wish I knew how to use it better. Daddy gave it to me on the day that he was finally able to afford a new one for himself. Mother insisted that the lord of Kestrel's Keep shouldn't disgrace himself by going off to war with an old blade. His new one was much shinier, with a jewel-encrusted hilt and a gold-inlaid scabbard." Her face fell. "He should have held onto this one; old or not, it's trustworthy. The new sword snapped against another man's blade and Daddy—" Her voice caught for a moment, but then she pulled back her shoulders and regained her composure. "Never mind. A damsel must be brave."

"So if you swear you never raised your *father's* sword to the twins—?" Brandella began.

"—it's all true, because the blade I used is *mine*. Am I to blame for what other people presume?" Auriana smiled. "No one knows the truth but me, and now you. Will you tell?"

Brandella managed a wobbly smile back. "If anyone asks me, I'll try to be as clever as you in how I give my answer. My father too was killed in battle. We're half-orphans, roommates, and I think we'd both like to see those twins devoured by a dragon with bad breath."

"In other words, we've got so much in common, we *have* to stick together?" Auriana raised one eyebrow in amusement. "I'm agreeable, though I wouldn't wish the twins on any dragon. The poor beast would die of indigestion."

"Oh, I *do* like you, Auriana!" Brandella cried. She ran to her trunk, flung open the lid, and removed a sizeable ivory box. When she opened it, a golden glow filled the turret room. It was jam-packed with more jewelry than Auriana had seen in a lifetime. She watched, fascinated, while Brandella took out strand after strand of gold, gems, and pearls beyond price, laying them out on her bed. Heavy bracelets clattered and rang against intricately fashioned pins, earrings, and even a queenly diadem. A few of the pieces were in the latest fashion, but most carried the grace of age. Auriana found herself drawn toward the miniature treasure trove, her hands reaching out as though to warm herself with the jewels' fire. An extraordinary sapphire necklace caught her eye. She couldn't help but hold it up to the light, spellbound by the dancing blue stars.

"Good, you like it!" Brandella exclaimed happily. "That's exactly the piece I wanted to give you." She began scooping the other baubles back into the box.

Auriana gasped. "Are you crazy? I can't accept this!" She tried to stuff it in with the rest of Brandella's treasures, but the squat girl stopped her. She was far stronger than she looked; she immobilized Auriana with one hand while continuing to repack the jewels with the other.

"You can and you will," she said calmly. "Or I'll tell the twins about whose sword you've *really* got."

"You're bluffing."

Brandella turned a complacent face to her roommate. "A proper damsel speaks the truth," she said with mock primness.

Auriana waited until Brandella turned her back while

unloading her trunk, then hit her with the goose-down pillow.

At dusk, a fanfare of silver trumpets summoned everyone to enter the great hall and take their places for dinner. The special table reserved for the headmistress, the senior faculty members, and honored guests stood at the front of the hall on a low platform. Above it hung a stained glass window depicting a damsel triumphant, one hand upon the head of a docile dragon, the other holding a golden chain encircling the neck of an adoring knight.

"See that open space between the head table and the rest?" Auriana whispered to her roommate as they sought places at the long, white-napered tables. "That's where the bards perform when we get entertainment. Too bad it only happens once in donkey's years. But that's also where you've got to stand and wait if Lady Florinda's got something . . . special in mind for you."

"Special?" Brandella repeated nervously. "You mean, if you're to get an award?"

Auriana chuckled. "I suppose getting your head handed to you could be called getting an award, even if the prize is your own noggin. We're both going to be called up there tonight, but *you've* got nothing to worry about."

As if on cue, the headmistress' assistant, Lady Delicia, yanked Auriana and Brandella from their places before their bottoms hit the bench. She herded them into the open space, then bustled back among the students until she likewise chivvied up the twins. As a solemn better-you-than-me hush fell over the hall, Lirabel leaned just a hair towards Auriana, grinned, and whispered, "*Now* you're going to get it."

"Don't hold your breath," Auriana whispered back.

"Or better yet, do, and spare the rest of us from the stench."

According to Academy procedure, the twins' complaint against Auriana was part of the official announcements always given before the meal was served. A wise stratagem, for it meant that the hungry masses of faculty and students would pay attention, process all needful matters swiftly, and not engage in any dilly-dallying or ego-flaunting as might further delay them from getting fed.

Lady Florinda heard Auriana's disclaimer with an icy attitude, but she dealt with the twins' complaint exactly as foretold, dismissing the whole matter as inconsequential and informing all of the parties involved that they would lose dessert privileges for the evening. This was to serve them as a lesson on the subject of not bothering their beloved headmistress with trivialities.

"Now then, to *important* affairs," she said. "Girls, you have a new schoolmate, the lady Brandella of the Bestbegone Mountains." She waved her hand in the new girl's general direction.

"Th—thank you, Lady Florinda," Brandella said. "It's a great honor to be—"

But the headmistress had already moved on to the next item on the agenda that stood between her and her dinner. "In addition, we are this night privileged to enjoy the presence of his most gracious Highness, Prince Torgal of the Northeastern Wastes. Prince Torgal is en route home after a long and wondrous quest for the Phoenix dagger of Destinia, but the reputation of our humble Academy has proved too great a lure for him. He will be with us for a fortnight. Ladies, I charge you, make him welcome."

At her words, a handsome, blond, brawny specimen of manhood stood up from the place of honor at Lady

Florinda's right hand. He bowed and waved graciously to the girls.

"What did I tell you?" Auriana whispered to Brandella, unnoticed in the upsurge of flirtatious giggling. "A pre-peril bride-shopper. Come on, let's sit down and eat."

To Brandella's discomfiture, the only four seats left vacant at the student tables were all together, which meant that she and Auriana would perforce have Lirabel and Bellira for their dining companions.

"Nice speech, Lady Loathsome," Bellira hissed as she passed Brandella the rolls. "*So* eloquent. I'm sure Prince Torgal is even now planning to ask for your hand in marriage."

"Hunh! I'm surprised Lady Florinda let her talk even *that* long," her sister put in. "But at least she had the good sense to make the toad invisible as soon as she could manage it."

"Invisible?" Brandella reduced her roll to crumbs on the plate.

"Not *really* invisible, stupid," Lirabel said. "Just acting like you're not there. Which is exactly how everyone else in this school's going to treat you, wait and see."

"Tsk. Don't count your basilisks before your mother hatches them," Auriana said, reaching for the butter. "Not everyone here is a mossbrain like you two."

"Well, of course *you'll* talk to her," Bellira said with a scornful lift of her lip. She flicked out her spoon, handle first, and gave Auriana's new necklace a saucy flip. "Bought and paid for, aren't you?"

"Oops," said Auriana, and the butter dish somehow wound up squashed down hard on Bellira's head.

This time there was no hope of getting around the headmistress' stern judgment. There had been too many witnesses to Auriana's breach of decorum, including the visiting prince. She was sentenced to perform menial labor in the Academy kitchens for ten days when she wasn't attending classes. She found herself forced to tiptoe out of her room well before dawn each morning and return long past lights-out at night. She never saw her roommate during waking hours, for as a newcomer, Brandella was enrolled in far less advanced classes than she.

On the last day of her sentence, as Auriana was headfirst and hip-deep into a particularly tall pot, excavating a thick layer of dried oatmeal from the bottom, she was surprised by a familiar voice inquiring, "Can I help?" Emerging from whole-grain hell, she saw her roommate standing before her.

"What are you doing here?" Auriana asked.

"I didn't have anywhere else to be," Brandella replied. "And I've missed you. The twins were right: everyone in my classes treats me like I'm not there, even some of the teachers. I suppose I shouldn't be surprised." She stuck a perfect Attitude #23-A and intoned: " 'A damsel must be possessed of many virtues, but above all, beauty. For it is a truth well-attested to by all natural philosophers, that dragons do be kin to magpies, and as such are drawn to those objects most dazzling to the eye. Among these may be counted gold, silver, all manner of precious stones, and also that scintillating glamour which has its heart in female loveliness.' " She let her hands drop to her sides and concluded: "That was today's lesson."

"Oh, so you're up to *Ye Mirror of Maidenhood* already?" Auriana remarked. "Watch out: Lady Rosemary's a bear for giving pop quizzes."

"She can pop herself silly," Brandella said. "I won't be here to take them. Auriana, I've come to say goodbye. I've learned all I need to know, plus some lessons I could have lived happily without."

"Brandella, you can't let them drive you away without a fight," Auriana said. "You're my friend, I'll stand by you, I'll—"

Brandella only shook her head. "No, Auriana. It's time I was gone. I've learned enough; Mother will be pleased. That recitation I did from today's lesson will satisfy her. The two of us often passed the winter's nights debating *why* dragons bothered to abduct damsels in the first place. It couldn't be for food—a sheep's fatter fare—though if it was, why aren't the damsels devoured the instant they're brought to the dragon's lair? Why keep them alive until some blowhard warrior comes along with slaughter on his mind? It's just because you pretty girls all *glitter* so."

"But that's not all of it." As upset as she was by her roommate's declared departure, Auriana was too diligent a scholar to let an error pass uncorrected. "In second semester, when they let you read Lady Otillia's *I Was a Dragon's Love Slave*—it sounds better in Latin—you'll learn the whole story: dragons *capture* us for our beauty, but they *keep* us for our conversation."

"Our . . . what?"

"You heard me. You see, it's male dragons who do all the abducting—"

"Indeed," Brandella said grimly.

"—and they've got a reputation for being solitary, *silent* beasts. In the distant past, other maidens just screamed and screamed when they were captured, until the dragons devoured them just to regain a little peace and quiet. Lady Otillia was the first who tried *talking* to her abductor. She hoped her prattle would distract the wyrm from thoughts of gobbling her up on the spot, but soon she learned that the creature was actually quite garrulous. Centuries old, and all that time he'd been *perishing* for the chance to talk about himself! Which he did when Sir Vingardo the Violent finally showed up and sliced his head off, whereupon Lady Otillia thanked him, turned down his proposal, wrote her book and married her publisher. It was a bestseller, of course, and soon all damsels began applying Lady Otillia's method, with great success."

"Getting dragons to talk?" Brandella was astounded. "*That's* what damsels do?"

"That's what we're taught." Auriana waved her oatmeal-sticky hands. "Male dragons have volumes to say about everything: sociology, economics, philosophy, the sorry state of the world these days, what a shame it is that lady dragons never *listen*. Apparently the female of the species can't be bothered to exchange two civil words with the male, unless it's mating season, and then it's a quick please-and-thank-you."

Brandella's brow furrowed. "*That's* what they're after? *Conversation?* *That's* why they keep losing their lives to muscle-bound sword-oafs? Augh! And *this* place keeps churning out bunches of butter-mouthed ladies fair, trained to coax those scale-skulled fools to talk themselves to death? Someone should burn these walls to the ground, and if I stay here any longer, I'll do it myself." She turned on her heel and stalked toward the door.

"Brandella, wait!" Auriana detained her with a grimy hand. "You can't leave now. It's after dark, and the forest paths are—"

"I can deal with whatever the forest throws my way," Brandella declared. "I'm going back to the room to fetch my treasure trove—Mother would slay me if I came home without it—then I'm gone."

"You mean that ivory box? But it weighs the earth! I know how heavy *this* is, and if you multiply that by all that the box holds—" She touched the necklace Brandella had given her.

"You're wearing that?" Brandella's eyebrows rose. "Now? While you work in the kitchen?"

"I never take it off except to sleep," Auriana replied. "Even then, I keep it safe beneath my pillow. Some of our classmates have rather . . . opportunistic ideas about 'private' property. If you weren't such a sound sleeper, you'd know how many girls came down with a bad case of sleepwalking as soon as word got 'round about this necklace." She grinned. "Luckily I sleep lightly, and command a wonderful cure for somnambulism. It's called a boot to the behind."

"You didn't have to do that, Auriana," Brandella said. "I could've given you another."

"No," Auriana said. "This gift sealed our friendship; it's irreplaceable." She wiped her hands on her apron. "I know we haven't known each other long, but in my three years here, you've been the only soul who's been kind to me, the only person who's thought of me as *Auriana,* not as *Lady Florinda's charity rat*. I can't stop you from going, but I won't let you go alone."

The woods surrounding the Academy were dark and deep. The two girls trudged along with only one small lantern to guide their footsteps. "You know, you didn't have to do this," Brandella said for perhaps the fifteenth time since they'd sneaked out by the tradesmen's door near the castle kitchen. "I can get home on my own. All I have to do is get word to Mother and—"

"But you can't get word to anyone until you reach the king's highway and a decent inn, with couriers," Auriana repeated, also for the fifteenth time. "And you can't do that if you don't know the right path. I do. I travel it every year when the Academy closes for the summer holiday. I always walk to the Bellman's Knuckle and buy a place on the eastbound cart from there. Now you're going to want the *north*bound cart, and—"

Brandella sat down in a pile of dead leaves. She made a mighty crunch, all the mightier for the weight of the ivory box she carried. "Now I know why male dragons are so desperate to get someone to *listen* when they speak. I told you, I don't need to go through all that! Once we reach a clearing of sufficient size, I only have to hold *this* up to the moonlight and call for Mother." She fished down the front of her gown and reeled up a huge, luminous pearl on a silver chain. It glowed with a misty, greenish light that fairly screamed *Magic*!

Auriana was impressed. "I didn't know your mother was a sorceress. How exciting! Does she travel by flying carpet, or cauldron, or—?"

"Don't be silly, she's— Oh, what does it matter? What counts is she'll come when I call. She just needs a big enough landing spot. Now will you *please* leave me? You haven't thought this through. If you come with me any farther, you'll have to go all the way back to the Academy *alone*. It wouldn't be safe."

"That's why I brought *this*." Auriana patted her sword, tied at her waist as best she'd been able. "I'll be fine on my own, but how safe would *you* be, trying to find your way to the inn *or* a clearing? You don't know these woods like I do, and you've got your hands full with that treasure box. You need me to carry *this*." She held the lantern high. "Unless you can see in the dark?"

"What makes you think I can't?" Brandella gave her friend a half-joking, half-daring look.

"Because if you could," said a deep, resonant voice from among the trees, "you would have seen me." Prince Torgal stepped into the little islet of lantern light and bowed deeply to Auriana. "Fair lady, you are in luck. I've come in time to rescue you from a monster." He leered at Brandella and added: "A troll, by the look of her. And see, she's stolen your jewels!" He drew his sword slowly, meaningly, and leveled it at the ivory box in Brandella's lap.

Auriana swiftly set down the lantern and drew her own sword. She held the heavy weapon in a firm, two-handed grip, but her action only evoked a slow, superior smile from the prince. He made no move to engage her in combat, merely waited until he saw the blade begin to waver under its own weight, then lower just a finger-span. At that, his own sword licked out and neatly knocked Auriana's weapon from her shaking hands.

"Whoever gave you that toy should've given you the training that goes with it," he remarked nastily. "I'll give you more ladylike playthings once we're wed."

"Wed?" Auriana cried, aghast. "Are you mad?"

"No more than you, if you think you've got a choice," the prince countered. "Luck put me in the kitchen shadows when you two made your escape, curiosity made me follow, but opportunity held my interest once you spoke of treasure." His eyes slewed lazily in Brandella's direction. "Open the box, troll."

Brandella obeyed in grim silence. The dazzle of gold and gems made Torgal grin like a hungry wolf. "A fine dowry, Lady Auriana."

"You mean Lady Brandella," Auriana said. "That's *her* treasure. Except she won't marry you, either."

"Why would I want to marry *her*? She's ugly. You, on the other hand, are not, and gold can belong to a beautiful maiden just as easily as to an ugly one, especially once the ugly one is dead." He took a menacing step toward Brandella.

"Stop!" Brandella leaped to her feet with unexpected speed, sending treasure spilling everywhere. "Good sir prince, noble and handsome lord, stay your mighty hand! Have pity upon a maiden who is helpless before your valor and male beauty." She wrung her hands prettily.

That's Attitude #43, Beseechment Level IV, Auriana realized with a start. *What's she up to?*

Before such a startling display of flattery and abasement, Torgal paused in his murderous course. "I'm afraid I can't do that, milady. It's unwise to leave a witness."

"Dear sir, I prithee, grant me ransom of my life." Brandella held out the glowing pearl. "Behold, my *mother's* gift, compact of greatest sorcery."

"So you're a witch's whelp? That accounts for your repulsive looks, I suppose." Torgal held out his hand. "Give me the pearl and I'll think about it."

"Brandella, don't!" Auriana cried. "He's a treacherous beast. He'll take it and kill you anyway."

"Oh, surely not!" Brandella cried. She lavished a languishing look on the prince. "For I have heard this noble man speak of his many awesome deeds, and by my mother's life—yes, my own *mother!*—can heroism exist without honor? Sweet Prince Torgal, if I must die, so be it, but will that same honor not allow you to grant me one last wish?"

"What?" the prince asked, suspicious.

Brandella did a simper that a fourth year Academy student might envy. "Will you not recount for me yet once again the wondrous tale of how you achieved the Phoenix dagger of Destinia? After that, I can die content."

Torgal couldn't help but puff out his chest a bit at Brandella's words. "Well, I don't like to brag, but—" he began. As he rambled on, a light breeze came up, riffling the treetops. By the time he was done, the breeze had become a wind that moaned through the branches. It kicked up spurts of dust and debris from the forest floor until at last Prince Torgal had to stop his story on account of how much he was coughing.

"By heaven, what's this unholy weather?" he protested, wiping grit from his eyes. He looked at Brandella and said, "You're a good listener, troll, but I'm afraid I can't waste any more time on you."

"Oh, but dear, brave, handsome, noble sir—!"

"Oh, but *nothing*," the prince replied, and grabbed the pearl, snapping it from Brandella's neck. He raised his sword and coldly said, "Die."

Brandella smiled. "After you."

That was when the dragon came.

She plunged down through the forest canopy, breaking branches like strands of spiderweb. Five stout oak trees were reduced to splinters when she landed on them. "Is *this* where you summon me? Does *this* look a clear landing spot to you?" she thundered. "I've got pinecones up my—" Suddenly she paused, her head swinging slowly from side to side, taking in the scene. Her eyes narrowed to slits of baleful green fire when she saw the prince, sword raised and ready to strike.

"Not *my* daughter, you don't!" she roared, and incinerated him with a gout of flame so elegantly accurate that it didn't even singe the surrounding foliage.

Auriana was still staring at the pile of ash that had been Torgal when Brandella said, "Auriana, dear, I'd like you to meet Mother." With that, the girl's plain face and ungainly body shattered like an eggshell and the glorious form of a gold-scaled dragon emerged.

*   *   *

"Hatchlings, it matters not how wide her wingspan or how bright her scales, no self-respecting female wyrm may hope to find a worthy mate without the proper education. To that end have you come to Auriana's Academy of Draconic Arts, in the heart of the Bestbegone Mountains. Welcome." Brandella stretched out her sinuous neck, peering toward the back of the huge cavern, crammed wall-to-wall with young female dragons. "Yes, question?"

"I'm only here because Mother made me," came a querulous growl from the last row. "What do we have to do to graduate and get out?"

The great golden dragon chuckled. "You'll find that our course of study is short but sufficient, my impatient little Egg, consisting of Elementary Listening, Intermediate Listening, Advanced Listening, and *How to Pretend You Are Listening to a Male Dragon Go On and On About Whatever the Hell He's Been Yammering Over for the Past Twelve Hours*. (Thus, in our school catalog, but more popularly known as *Sleeping With Your Eyes Open* among you students.) It's usually taught by Lady Auriana herself, though this year I will be assuming all her teaching duties so that she may enjoy a lengthy honeymoon with the chosen of her heart. He's only a poor swineherd, and he didn't turn out to be in the least enchanted, but she loves him and that's what matters. Yes, another question?"

The same ill-tempered voice echoed among the stalactites: "*Lady* Auriana? You mean she's *human*? We dragons are powerful, ageless, and wise. What could *we* ever learn from one of *them*?"

"Hmm, how about how to save our stupid males—and thus ourselves—from gradual but inexorable extinction? Or how to open our eyes to the fact that true friendship doesn't care about dress or dazzle,

dragon or damsel? Or how about *this*?" Brandella
spread her wings and soared to the rear of the cavern.
The she-dragons in the front row strained to see what
she was doing back there, but before their keen eyes
could pierce the gloom, they heard the startled yelp
of their petulant school-chum followed by Brandella's
voice declaring: "My dear *human* friend and former
roommate calls *that* Ye Olde Boote to Ye Uppity
Backsyde. Make a note of it, Hatchlings; it *will* be on
the final exam."

She flew back to her place at the front of the cavern.
"Any more questions?" Silence answered her. She
smiled. "Class dismissed."

THREE NAMES OF THE HIDDEN GOD

Vera Nazarian

The world holds as many gods as there are directions radiating outward from the heart of the Compass Rose.

There are gods who must blaze across the spheres in pure glorious light. There are gods who prefer to remain in the shadows, folded cleverly upon themselves like feathers in a dove's gray wing, doling out tiny motes of grace to the famished worshippers. There are gods who choose to be submerged in the lowest places of darkness, with forms huge and heavy and malleable, containing so many possibilities that they may not remain in any other shape than primeval clay.

And then, it is said, there is the one god who hides and can be found in none of the divine places.

For the most part, the god—he, she, or it—stays hidden so well that nothing is known about it, her, or him. Indeed, it is a fair question whether the Hidden God exists at all.

When Ruogo the youngest birdcatcher found the dead bird, it was too late for it. It was lying cold and tiny on the ground, partially hidden by the fallen leaves of the great backyard tree. A miracle that the household cats had not gotten to it—or maybe they had, and this was just an abandoned victim of a feline game.

There was something particularly sad about the remains. The boy picked up the little bird and examined it, seeing that it had been but a hatchling, its tawny feathers consisting of fluff and bits of its rosy-gray tiny body stained with newborn moisture. Then he put it in the front of his apron and carried it inside the house, only to be scolded by the elders.

"Why do you waste your time with hopeless things? Make yourself useful instead by returning with a net filled with the living, not the dead," said an old master birdcatcher as he bound together bark and twigs in the workroom. He was the one who made the most intricate cages in the shape of great buildings and houses and temples, for the nobles' fancy.

The dark-haired boy listened to the reprimand, the olive skin of his face showing no discoloration brought about by shame. His gray eyes were blank, concealing any possible cleverness, and he merely lowered his gaze when the elder was finished speaking. And that gaze continued to observe the dead bird.

When excused, Ruogo took the bird's corpse, still in the folds of his apron, to the rear of the house and out into the back yard, where the old trash pit made itself known by its thick stench from many paces away. Just at the edges of the hole he paused, considering— while others constantly walked past him and threw in various rubbish, since this was a busy household.

"Either do your business or move aside, boy," they told him, and yet he remained, frozen.

It would take but a moment to toss in the little corpse, and forget it, forever. Do this and go on with the course of his life.

But the gods had other plans for Ruogo.

And the boy wrinkled his brow in a profound gesture of resignation, and eventually turned away from the edge of the pit. He returned to the house, the dead bird still with him.

In his tiny closet of a room that he shared with four other child apprentices, there had been an old wooden box. His grandmother, who'd died two summers ago, left Ruogo very little in the way of possessions, and this was his one most prized object. It was hardly larger than a tobacco box, and possibly once held someone's small jewelry pouch. Delicate patterns of varicolored wood inlay covered its top, which swung up on twin hinges. Inside, lined with soft fabric, Ruogo stored his treasures. One was a pendant of carved jade, shaped like a bird—the symbol of his apprenticeship, given to him when he was brought to the Birdcatcher House. Another was a small knife for fingernail grooming that he found on the street, and a couple of other pretty trinket stones also discovered on the ground.

Ruogo did not think twice but opened the box and emptied its contents on the worn blanket of his pallet. Reaching into his apron, he put the small corpse of the bird on top of the fabric, then covered the box once again with a soundless movement.

And then Ruogo put the box away where it always sat, gathered his other treasures and stuck them under his blanket and went back to his ordinary chores.

Thus, from this one simple action, his story becomes important.

Many years later, in a great desert *qalifate* that lies sprawled along the shores of Lake Veil, the salt-rich waters of which stand in grim solitude among the boundless sands, people woke up one morning to a miracle.

The Qalif himself witnessed the miracle from the windows of his bedchamber as he stood to stretch and squint as he always did at the rising sun that would be reflected in blinding persimmon glory upon the eastern shores of the lake.

Rubbing his eyes, the Qalif stared out of the window, then called his First Wife. The plump-breasted Qalifa replied with a lazy moan, then rose from the perfumed silk and stood at his side.

"Oh!" exclaimed the Qalifa, coming fully awake, and putting her smooth hand upon her lord's shoulder. "The lake! Where is it?"

For indeed, the lake called Veil was gone.

In its place stretched a dull brownish quagmire of mud and sand, ugly and already drying solid in the sun, revealing underwater growth and occasional puddles filled with squirming water creatures and flapping fish. The sun would fry them alive in a matter of hours.

The water from the lake had drained away somewhere—where? how?—as though overnight a god breathed upon the lake and swallowed it in one divine gulp—either from above or below.

All that remained was this mud and desolation.

And one other thing. In the center of the former lake, in the deepest part of the bed, was a mud-covered bulky shape, vaguely resembling a structure.

At first, no one paid any attention to it, so shocked and terrified they had been by the disappearance of the lake. The residents of the *qalifate* congregated along its shores, bewailing the loss of water to the skies—never mind that it had always been useless and salty, and the meager wildlife it housed made for poor fishing. Some dared to walk the mud, carefully venturing deeper from the shoreline, afraid that any moment the water might return and drown them.

Priests of all the gods from all the temples were called, and they stood chanting, incense and burning sacrifices wafting up through the rapidly heating air, while the tops of their shaven heads cooked likewise in the sun. . . .

Until someone pointed to the strange thing of mud, a great mound rising in the middle of the lake. At first glance it appeared to be a natural growth, a rock formation. But then a sharp-eyed priest noticed the regularity of its slopes and the angular stairs cut into the muddy rock, indicating a structure. The priest counted the number of stairs, observed their placement, and found a repeating pattern of threes, the highest of all divine groupings.

Awe and terror filled him at the implications of the discovery. The priest whispered his suspicions into the ear of his superior who heard him out and then raised his staff to acknowledge the truth revealed to them. The pronouncement was made, and immediately a cry went up from all the shores.

The legendary temple of the Hidden God was found. It had to be it and none other, for here all things came in threes and such was the number consecrated only to the Hidden God. Indeed, suddenly they could think back and remember that the lake itself had been called "Veil" for a reason—it hid something.

And now, the answer was before them, covered by hundreds of pounds of sand and mud.

The Qalif ordered a rapid excavation of the structure in the center of the lake bed. All day, humans lined up like ants to carry buckets filled with hardening sand and clay away from the structure, and to dump it onto the neighboring shores. Artisans worked with shovels and fine tools to chip away at the solidifying reddish-ocher mud—for the sun was baking it even as they worked—and soon enough they had cleared an ancient stone building of large rose granite bricks piled in ziggurat-stair formation, with a perfect square base of several hundred meters, and with four sealed entrances on each of the sides.

The Qalif himself, his royal feet bound in many layers of protective cotton, walked carefully through the mud and stood to observe the discovery. Flanked by bodyguards that never left his side—for he was a careful man—he paced the perimeter of the ancient structure from all sides, and noted the designs on the entrances, etched symbols of ancient writing.

On the eastern side, the entrance bore the outline of a bird. On the western side, there was a human hand, its five fingers splayed in greeting . . . or caution. On the southern side the doorway revealed a heavy-lidded eye. Finally, on the northern side, there was something that resembled a gaping mouth with teeth, and then—as the artisans chiseled and chipped away the layers of clay—it took on the final shape of a serpent, and the teeth were but the regularly spaced scales along its ringed hide.

"What are these symbols? What significance? What language? I must know!" the Qalif muttered—a curious man by nature—and scholars were sent to observe and copy down the shapes onto scrolls.

At the same time, messengers were sent out into the wide expanses of the *qalifate* to find experts who might be able to reveal more about the nature of these hieroglyphs. Snake charmers and birdcatchers and palm readers and eye physicians were called from the

markets and the trade caravans, and with promises of
rich reward they converged upon the drying mud of
the missing lake.

In their midst was a young man, a foreigner, who
had come with one southbound caravan and was
stopped along with the rest of his mercantile fellows,
all trading in exotic species of birds.

The birdcatcher, Ruogo, had grown into a slim,
quiet youth, and his master's rich wagons carried cages
of sparrows and canaries, parrots and nightingales,
pheasants and peacocks. All of the creatures were
under his gentle care, for Ruogo had skilled hands
where it came to handling the animals. He was also
adept at binding and weaving nets and lures, and at
catching the wild birds after lying in wait in patient
silence.

"What exactly does the Qalif want from all of us?"
Ruogo said to the bearded man next to him, a snake
handler by the look of his work basket and charming
pipe. They stood in line at the shores of the former
lake, to be questioned and allowed past the guards
into the lake bed.

"And what do you think you can do for the Qalif?"
retorted a beautiful youth just behind him, with dis-
dainful and fierce eyes, wearing fine noble clothing
and a prominent sword at his side.

Ruogo turned to consider the peculiar challenge.
But before he could reply, the bearded snake charmer
muttered, "Be careful, say nothing to him, birdcatcher.
He is likely one of the local princely sons. The nobles
in this land are known to take their boredom out on
foreigners like us."

Ruogo understood. And as the line advanced forward, he merely threw the noble youth a polite nod,
and then looked away, intent on his own business.

Behind him the youth laughed.

Soon enough they moved up to the edge of the shoreline, where Ruogo was questioned, when his turn came.

"Do you know many species of birds? Will you be able to recognize a bird and its habits from an ancient picture in stone?"

"I know all the species in which men trade," replied Ruogo humbly. "As far as images in stone, what I would know depends on the nature of the image itself."

The Qalif's scribe seemed to like the answer. "Come forward then," he said. "If you render good services, you will be well-rewarded." And while many others had been turned away, Ruogo was allowed to step forward into the drying mud.

They were made to walk in the soft, slippery lake bed without any foot protection beyond what they already had, and many men slipped and fell, or found their footwear rendered useless. After about ten steps, Ruogo decided to remove his poor ruined sandals, tied them together, slung them over his shoulders and walked barefoot in the sinking sludge.

Ruogo noticed that the bearded snake-man and the angry noble youth were among those who had been allowed to continue, and they ended up in the same order in which they had stood in line. The snake charmer was poor and barefoot already, but the youth had on a fine pair of boots, and they were now encrusted with drying dirt.

The excavated structure grew in size as they approached, taking on grandiose proportions, newly cleared marble stone shining polished and clean in places, and in others still caked with mud. At the walls, they were stopped again by soldiers and guards of the *qalifate,* and Ruogo was directed to follow a head scribe to the eastern-facing wall, and its sealed doorway with the bird shape.

"See this symbol?" said the head scribe to their group of birdcatchers and other fowl handlers, as they gathered near the entrance, "What do you make of it? What does it mean?"

"A great hawk!" said someone from the crowd. "I've seen such in the royal cages, and caught many myself."

"No, surely it is a falcon! A fierce and noble creature of the air, appropriate to the god's abode."

"An eagle! It is the ruler of the air, the greatest bird of all."

"But how can you tell?" Ruogo spoke up. "The image shows no wingspan, no grand tail. If anything, it looks like a simple northern field sparrow or a finch."

Several other birdcatchers and vendors, older and more distinguished looking, glared at him. "What kind of nonsense? Who would put a lowly bird's image upon a great temple?"

"I only suggest what I see," Ruogo said, his brow furrowing in intensity.

The head scribe turned to him. "It is useful what you say. We need to know if this is a simple or dangerous symbol, and whether its presence indicates that the entrance is not to be tampered with. The last thing our Qalif wants is to insult the Hidden God whose abode this must be."

"I understand, my lord." Ruogo inclined his head in politeness to the scribe. "Then I might add that the bird is shown in profile, and its beak is neither overly long nor short, and its feet show three claws. Its tail is slim and medium-long, and there is no eye but a dot, which suggests a symbolic representation—it could be a number of ordinary birds, for no dramatic markings are emphasized. Maybe this is supposed to be a general image, that of any bird?"

In that moment there was a noisy commotion on

the opposite side of the structure, where the entrance depicted a hand. Whatever the recommendations of the palmists and occult line readers had been, some-one had attempted to open the sealed door, and now black thick smoke poured up into the heavens, for the insolent one had been struck by an unknown force and burned to ashes. There were screams of awe, ser-vants and scribes scattering like rats, and the Qalif himself approached with his retinue of guards to ob-serve the incident.

Ruogo and the bird specialists were forgotten, pushed aside by the flow of the crowd as all attention was focused on the western wall.

"Who dared to open the sacred door without my permission?" the Qalif cried. "No one is to touch any-thing; simply learn and then inform me!"

The scribe in charge of the palm readers came for-ward and then fell to lie flat before the Qalif, in obei-sance. "No one, oh great one, no one alive . . ." he muttered. "The insolent one has been struck by the Hidden God himself, it is no doubt—behold, his ashes alone remain!"

In that moment, two more explosions of smoke and brightness came from the two remaining sides, north and south, with the entrances decorated by a serpent and the eye.

"In the name of all the great gods of this world, cease and desist!" the Qalif cried, his voice cracking in outrage. "No one is to approach the entrances again until we learn what has been attempted!" And then he pointed his finger to the prostrate head scribe. "You! What exactly was done before the divine pun-ishment came?"

"My father, I can tell you exactly what came to pass," said a bright young voice. And Ruogo recognized the intense noble-clad youth who carried a sword.

"Ah! It is the Qali!" someone hissed.

But the youth stepped forward and removed his head covering. Long raven-black hair spilled around the shoulders and covered the sword and the back, down to the youth's ankles.

"Not the Qali, but the young brash Qalia, the lord's daughter!" retorted someone else in the crowd near Ruogo.

Ruogo stared in curiosity, for he had never seen a woman in the clothes of a man before, nor one with such fierce manners or with such glorious long hair.

"What are you doing here, Lealla, my child?" said the Qalif, his voice growing soft and befuddled—for he was a doting father.

"The same thing all the rest of these people are doing," she replied. "I am here to solve the mysteries of this ancient place."

"But—" the Qalif said. "This is no place for my daughter."

In the bright sun the maiden suddenly inclined her head so that her mane of hair which caught and swallowed all light falling upon it, rained to the mud at their feet. She remained bowed, heedless of its ends lying in the dirt.

"My sweet lord, father," she said. "My place is ever at your side."

"And what of Khoiram? Where is my son while his sister takes his place?" continued the Qalif with reproach which was quickly dissipating.

Lealla raised her face and swept her hair behind her and out of her way, while her eyes took on a living brightness. "Khoiram walks in the gardens, deep in esoteric thought. But he will come to you soon enough with the true answer to this mystery. There is no other, and you know it. None can match the brightness of thought of your son."

"That remains to be seen . . ." the Qalif muttered. "Very well," he continued. "Join me, my daughter, for I can use your fair company. But take care. This is a deceptive and dangerous place, and I will not have you fall into any harm. Therefore, touch nothing here without my consent!"

And then the Qalif returned his attention to the man wallowing in the dirt before him, the head scribe.

But the indomitable Qalia was not to be put aside. "As I was saying, my lord father," the maiden continued, resuming her willful tone, "I can tell you exactly what happened. These fool overseers of your men gave the command to force open the doors all at once, so that men who were struck by the god had no time to exclaim, much less warn the others. They touched the doors near the sealed edges. I saw them all move to it, heedless of your own wise warning, and—"

"How did you see them all," Ruogo interrupted suddenly, "when they were all on different sides of this structure?"

The Qalia turned to him and there was icy cold in her expression, ice over anger. "What?"

But Ruogo was undaunted. Wind swept tendrils of his equally dark hair into his face and he squinted against the sun, but not against the sudden inexplicable hatred he saw in her expression.

"You dare speak back to me, birdcatcher?"

Ruogo watched her and did not blink. "With respect, I simply ask a reasonable question. How could you, standing only steps away from me, see what happened on the opposite side of these walls?"

"It is not of your concern." If her words could cut him, they would have used dull, lingering blades to cause additional torment.

"What?" the Qalif interrupted.

"My lord . . ." On the muddy ground, the head

scribe continued to grovel. "I can explain, in truth! I was ordered by—"

But in that peculiar moment Lealla, fierce daughter of the Qalif, drew steel, the cool blade hanging at her side. With one smooth motion it left the sheath and in a moment its tip was resting at the back of the scribe's neck.

"Silence!" she said, and the man on the ground stilled. "Do not befoul the air with your lies—for it will be lies that will come forth from you. And as far as this one—"

And then the Qalia stepped away and sheathed her sword, and suddenly Ruogo found himself facing two cool, intense eyes—and it seemed there was nothing in the world but those eyes, no face, no crowd, no heat of sun, nothing.

"This one," repeated Lealla, boring into him with inexplicable fury. "He is clever and has a smooth tongue but not enough judgment to keep him out of trouble. Well, what do you say now, birdcatcher?"

Ruogo looked down at the mud at his feet. "Whatever I say now," he replied quietly, "will be misconstrued."

The bizarre tension was dispelled by the Qalif himself, his laughter.

"Why pick on this poor youth, my dear child?" said the Qalif. "He did ask you a reasonable—as he insists—question. And now I too am curious. How came you to be aware of each of the different places at once, when walls separated you from them?"

The maiden blanched, but did not lose a moment in answering. "As soon as the edges of the walls were cleared of mud, I had mirrors installed, my lord father. Knowing ahead that miracles might befall us, I wanted to witness all and miss nothing."

"Mirrors?"

She pointed to the corners of the structure where indeed something white blazed in the sun, a spot of reflected fire. "Angled mirrors that show what is on the other side and around the corner. My own conceit, father. How do you think I can spy so well on my lazy serving maids?"

The Qalif's mouth parted in surprise. "But—how can you see anything from the distance? These mirrors are tiny."

Lealla touched her right hand to her throat and brought out a tiny golden device on a chain. "It is a magnifying lens of glass carved in such a manner that allows me to see from a distance. The same kind that your physicians use to look at tiny objects."

"Amazing!" the Qalif exclaimed. "You are a wonder, my daughter. If only my son had half of your wits and vision—"

Something terrible and bright settled in the Qalia's eyes at the mention of the son. She said nothing, only lowered her gaze.

"Enough interruptions, then," said the Qalif. "I want to know how to open those doors safely without incurring the wrath of the Hidden God."

"Forgive me for speaking one last time, my lord," Ruogo said. "But from where we stand, there are only two mirrors, enough to show two other sides, not the very opposite third. In addition, even if equipped with a clever spying glass, it is impossible for one man or woman to see two things that are happening simultaneously in different places, much less three."

The Qalif frowned. "An excellent observation, young man," he said. "You are clever."

The Qalia was staring at Ruogo with a look that intended to kill. But her father was quite taken with him, and he said, "Come forward, tell me, what is your name, birdcatcher? For I see you are among their group."

"I am Ruogo," he replied, with a deep bow.

"Tell me, Ruogo," the Qalif said, "What do you think of this door closest to us?"

Ruogo hesitated only a moment. "I am not sure, my lord. But it seems this is a symbolic representation. The bird indicates either all birds in general, or it is a character symbol for something else. Something that your scribes might know better than any of us in the bird trade."

This earned him some angry looks from the other birdcatchers.

In that moment, the Qalif's daughter, who had been glancing around them peculiarly all this time, exclaimed, "Khoiram! My lord father, your son comes!"

Everyone turned to see a slender young man approach with a small retinue of bodyguards. He was elegant and dressed in silk, and his head was covered with a small turban. All of him shone in the sun, especially the fine gilded scabbard of his long sword. The lines of his face converged into beauty that was almost feminine, and he walked through the mud with an odd lightness, as though he were floating over it in the air—even his footwear appeared unstained.

"Greetings, my father." His voice carried on the wind, more virile than could be expected out of such a delicate frame. "After much pondering, I am here to solve the mystery for you and to open the gates of this temple."

Lealla watched her brother with proud adulation.

The Qalif was somewhat less impressed. "You've decided to join us, my son—good." His words were guarded and there was no change in his expression.

The Qali stopped before his father and gave him

an impeccable bow which by its perfection somehow managed to be insulting. He straightened, saying, "Tell all your men to rise out of the mud and step fifty feet away from the temple. It is for their safety."

The Qalif motioned to the prostrate head scribe and all the rest of them, including the guards, to rise and step back. "What will you do?" he asked his son.

Ruogo backed away with the rest of the crowd and watched in curiosity. The heat of the day beat down upon them, and there was a moment of expectant silence.

"Well?" the Qalif said.

The handsome Qali smiled. "This," he said. And with a flowing movement he drew his long sword and ran his father through with the blade.

The crowd screamed. For a moment there was shock, then panic; guards lunging forward too late, scribes and birdcatchers and snake charmers and palm readers scattering in every direction. But the parricide held his father in a last embrace, and as the older man's lifeblood ran scarlet upon silk, spattered on the mud and their mingled clothing, the daughter of the Qalif drew her hands up and cried, "Silence! Fall back! No one dare lay hands upon the new Qalif of this realm!"

Her words held such furious power that once again everyone froze.

Her father, blood pouring from his lips, stared in disbelief at his daughter's betrayal. "Not you . . . Lealla," he whispered. "No, not you." He slumped, released from Khoiram's hold, and sank on his knees in the mud.

"All this time, father, you wasted your love on the wrong child," Lealla hissed. "If you'd only loved your son and not your daughter, you would still be alive now. But you disdained him, since childhood. All his

learning, his grace and wisdom, all in vain! And so we
have arranged your downfall through occult means—
Khoiram drained the lake by means of sorcery so that
you would come unguarded and bound only with curiosity. At my orders, explosive powder was sprinkled.
Not some forgotten god, it was I—my will was carried
out when they forced the doors, so that you would
know terror, so that you would feel weak. For it's
what you are, weak and impotent, an old blind fool.
But enough! Now my brother will rule, and I will rule
at his side. All these years of waiting, all these endless
days . . . it is only him I loved."

The Qalif was in his last moments. "I have loved
you *both* . . . my children," he said on his final breath.
"My son chose not to see it, chose the path of darkness." He gasped, a whole-body shudder passing
through him. And then he raised his gaze and he said,
"I do not curse you, my son, my daughter, though it
is within my right. Instead, I ask that you see the truth
of what you have done. May the sun never set for you
until you do."

And with these words the old Qalif fell motionless
into the drying mud of Lake Veil.

Ruogo had been squeezed back by the movement
of the crowd together with all the others, and he was
now pressed from all sides by terrified men. He
watched as brother and sister stood above the body of
their slain patriarch, both radiant in wicked, unearthly
beauty. And something made him draw his gaze for a
moment upon the closest gate of the temple, the one
with the carved bird image.

It was softly moving.

The doors fell inward in silence, placing the shapes
of the Qali and Qalia in silhouette against the gaping
darkness revealed. Then gasps came from the crowd
on all directions of the structure. All four doors had

opened, and the crowd noticed that the dark within was like a void, an infinite nothingness that pulled to itself.

Out of that nothingness sounded a voice.

A wrongful death, it said from all the four entrances, rumbling in deep echoes that sent shudders and raised hair along the skin of everyone in the crowd. *One must now come forth and be punished, or you will all be.*

A pause and then there were cries among the multitude. "The Hidden God speaks!"

The young Qali who stood before his father's slain body went still. His sister turned to stare at the gaping entrance, while the Qali's and the late Qalif's mingled bodyguards still had not reacted, restrained with indecision and split loyalties.

But Lealla quickly searched the crowd, and her gaze rested on Ruogo. She pointed at him suddenly, saying "You!" And then, to the nearest guards, "This one, this birdcatcher—quickly, take him inside the temple to satisfy the God!"

Ruogo had no time to protest. He found himself alone as the crowd parted on both sides of him. And then two burly warriors of the *qalifate* took hold of his arms and bodily carried him to the temple.

The doorway gaped, and then he was pushed inside the ancient structure. And in the next moment, doors shut behind him.

Absolute darkness came like an ocean, and he felt like a speck of seaweed floating many fathoms deep.

And then the voice of the deity sounded, this time soft and intimate. *You are not the one.*

Ruogo blinked, and somehow his stifling terror vanished, effaced by the cavernous peace of what was around him. Although his eyes were not acclimated to the night, he could almost perceive an outline of *someone,* a silhouette of a lesser degree of darkness among the perfect void.

Ruogo stood, and it never occurred to him to kneel or make any mortal gestures of obeisance. This was a different, *true* place, requiring no ritual, no superfluous layers of meaning between man and god.

"I'm not the one—indeed, a no one," Ruogo said to the god. "I was forced against my will to come before you. Not a hero, just the wrong man at the wrong time."

As soon as you made the choice to open your mouth and speak out in defense of what is real, you were noticed and you became someone, said the Hidden God. *Now, go back outside and bring me the dead body of the victim and the living body of the true murderer.*

"But," Ruogo said, "there are guards! They will not allow me! What can I, a poor birdcatcher, do?"

Go!

A thousand needles of pain and excitement hit him simultaneously, and Ruogo could do nothing but obey as he turned around in the darkness and sprinted to where he last remembered the door.

He pushed it open with a feather-touch. Remarkable, considering its weight.

On the other side, there was sunlight and . . . *birds*. The world was filled with them.

The birds blackened the sky like bees from a disturbed hive and covered the mud of the lake bed in varicolored speckled dots. They flew, rose, circled, sat and preened, fluttered around, pecked each other in anger, sped in pursuit, teemed in madness. Sparrows, hawks, canaries, falcons, finches, eagles, pheasants, magpies, hummingbirds, parrots, jays, peacocks— Ruogo recognized these breeds and others with his practiced eye.

There were no people.

Ruogo stood petrified at the entrance of the temple and considered what was to be done, and what miracle the Hidden God had wrought. His glance slid to the place where he had last seen the murderer brother and sister and the fallen Qalif's body.

Amid the swirling madness of the flying and roosting fowl, he noticed two crows sitting very still, and between them, a fallen third.

And somehow without a doubt Ruogo knew who they were.

But—how to catch them?

Ruogo thought of the lures and ropes in his belt pouch. He thought of seed and bread crumbs in the other pouch, of dried worms and netting.

And then he thought, *These are not true birds.*

Ruogo took out a knife from his belt, and he used it to cut the palm of his left hand. And then he stepped forward, moving very slowly, and stretched his hand forth, palm down, so that his blood dripped on the mud in a trail of scarlet crumbs.

One of the crows, a raven, rotated its eye, then its head, to stare. And the next instant it hopped forward, drawn by the spilled blood, by the smell of life-death, and began to peck at the earth.

Ruogo pulled out his net and threw, so that it landed over the raven, and then he tightened it. Too late the raven flapped its wings, for it was now caught.

The other crow screamed in fury, and Ruogo knew exactly what she would do. Not blood here, but love was the lure, love for her brother, no matter how twisted.

And the crow came at him, beating her wings, flying up to peck at his eyes and hands that held her brother captive in the net.

But Ruogo was a master of his trade. With his one free hand he threw a length of rope with a loop, and it caught around her neck, past the beak. He lassoed it, pulled tight, then quickly bound her feet, which was how one secured fowl, and the crow was his prisoner just like her brother.

After the two living crows were secured at his belt, struggling in futility, Ruogo stepped toward the third. He bent over the dead body of the old raven, while the multitudes of birds screamed and roiled around him in the sky, occluding the sun.

With sorrow and care he picked up the dead bird and then carried all three back into the temple.

Darkness returned all around, the captured crows screamed in fear, and the dim shape of the god shimmered before him.

You have done well, birdcatcher, sounded the intimate voice. *And now I will reward you with three of my names. They are Mercy, Wonder, and Fulfillment. I have many other names, but in this world of three dimensions I may only be known by a sequence of three.*

"What must I do with your three names, O Great One?" Ruogo whispered.

Knowing them, you must now observe the world with different eyes. You will now look for my names in all things.

And immediately Ruogo felt the crows disappear from his grasp. Instead, they were back in human form, somewhere nearby in the darkness. Ruogo knew, in that instant, true wonder.

Lealla screamed, and her brother Khoiram's cry also sounded, the lingering echo of a thwarted hunting bird. They were to go unpunished by the god, Ruogo sensed, and with a wrenching in his heart he knew pity and mercy.

Finally, a gasp of divine breath. The dead Qalif's body shuddered. And in the darkness he arose and was a corpse no longer.

The god's voice filled the temple. *And thus you know fulfillment.*

In the world outside, birds returned to human form—or had they ever been otherwise? The Qalif came forth from the temple and was greeted with cries of exultation, for in this *qalifate* he was a man well-loved and his death was deemed a thing of regret and sorrow. Now, his resurrection was a thing of wonder.

Khoiram and Lealla, protected by their father's mercy, made their way unhindered through the angry crowds, compelled somehow to keep walking west in the direction of the setting sun. A curious punishment was upon them, for they were driven by no one yet they were in exile. Those who saw them pass later, in other places, other lands, claimed that it always happened at sunset. It was as though they were rushing to catch the sun at the end of its journey across the vault of heaven; indeed, the grim shadow-forms of trudging brother and sister became the stuff of hearsay and legend.

As for Ruogo, he was favored by the Qalif, feasted for a day and then—since the Qalif was grieving the loss of his son and daughter, and would grieve for the rest of his days—allowed to go on his own way in the world.

Before Ruogo left this land, he made one last stroll across the dry mud of the former lake into the silent temple of the Hidden God, which now sat unattended by all but a few devout priests. Ruogo carried with him an old box of carved wood, with an ancient thing inside it, a desiccated body of a tiny hatchling that he had kept all these years. At the altar in the shadowy cavern within the temple, he placed the dead thing of bones, and he implored the Hidden God one last time.

And in his mind, the God answered. *What's this?*

You bring me a tiny lost bit of my heart. And for that reason I grant you a tiny bit in return.

There was a breath of fire, a wash of air and power, and the tiny creature came alive. A fragile running pulse, and it beat its newborn wings, and then, as Ruogo watched in awe, it managed to take flight, and sped forth into the daylight outside.

You give it a second chance—the greatest gift. And the chance to have made such a gift was my gift to you, so many years ago. For you found a small worthless thing yet recognized significance while most others in your place would not. And it opened the spaces within you for other things to come. Now, be on your way, go reap these things, all the infinity of things that you will find.

"But I have so many questions left!" Ruogo said. "Why did this poor creature die so young before it even had a chance to live? Why do any of us die? What of the symbols upon the gates of your temple? What of my own place and the burden of knowing your three names? What must I do now?"

May you spend the rest of your life finding these answers. From this moment onward you begin to know. And it is what makes you.

Ruogo bowed with his soul before the invisible Hidden God, and left the temple with a fevered mind but an easy heart.

Hours later, long after he had clambered out of the lake bed and resumed the caravan route on his own life's journey, the waters of Lake Veil returned.

It was said they came rushing out of nowhere, allowing the priests and worshippers of the temple only moments to escape with their lives before they closed in and flooded the place, covering once again the ancient temple under a smooth mirror surface.

What is hidden will remain.

THE PRINCESS, THE PAGE, AND THE MASTER COOK'S SON

Sherwood Smith

Kimet opened her eyes. Her dream vanished in the strong morning light slanting through the row of tiny attic windows. It was so cozy in her warm nest of blankets with the sun on her cheek—

The sun! She threw off her blankets and reached for her livery.

It was the first time she had ever woken up to sunlight in the dismal attic where the pages slept. Her shoulders hunched, braced against the anticipated sting of Steward Greb's stick as she yanked her tunic straight and fumbled her sash into place.

She dashed out of her cloth-hung cubicle, glanced into the sleeping spaces directly opposite hers, and stopped when she realized that she was not alone. Blanket-covered bumps in the three she could peer into meant at least three of the other pages stuck on extra duty late the night before, when the Queen decided to have a midnight supper, were still asleep. Such a thing had never happened before.

"Sun!" she cried, not wanting anyone else getting into trouble.

Tousle-haired girls popped their faces out of the

cubicles, and heavy eyes widened to round-eyed surprise and dismay when they saw one another.

"It's late!"

"Why weren't we called, Kimet?"

"Is this a Greb trick, Kimet?"

"I don't know," she said in a low voice, peering fearfully down the ladder. "But I do know I was supposed to be on duty in the Queen's chamber at sun-up."

At the word *Queen* all the faces blanched. Kimet scrambled down the ladder, leaving shrill, anxious voices behind her, everyone asking questions that no one listened to.

She hesitated at the narrow door used by the servants. This route was long, dark, and often crowded, and being only a page, and not yet under an order, she'd have to give way to everyone else pushing slow carts of dishes or bed-linens, dashing with royal messages, or bringing up silver trays with steaming food from the kitchens. *Besides, if the Queen's spies see that I'm late, they'll blab to Steward Greb.* She tiptoed away, and up to the carved door opening onto the upper landing of the royals' residence. You weren't supposed to use that door unless you had to deliver something directly beyond it, then you had to come right back.

It would mean a terrible beating if she were caught wandering the royals' halls, unless she could convince someone she had an errand. On the other hand, the royals' hallway was less than half the length of the servants' as it did not have to wind around and up and down and behind all the huge rooms, and it was never crowded.

The stick if caught here, the stick if caught late—but if she used this shortcut and wasn't seen, she might avoid both punishments.

Yes. Worth a try.

She opened the door and sped soundlessly down the marble hall.

Usually she gazed hungrily at the age-darkened tapestries on the walls, each time garnering some new detail of stitchery, design, color, and longing for the day to arrive when she'd have her place restoring them. That is, if the Queen didn't get her way and use her daughter's marriage to a neighboring prince— or the new war—as an excuse for burning them all.

On her way to the Queen's suite, which lay all across the entire length of the castle front, she sped by the newly decorated corner wing where Princess Zarja had moved just before the visit from King Orthan's son last winter. Last time Kimet was in this hall the door to the afternoon parlor had been open and she'd glimpsed the Princess sitting with the other noble girls on the terrace outside, their drawling voices carrying as they sat decorously, eating fruit from golden bowls and making fun of the customs of the other kingdom. The same noble girls who flattered the Princess to her face, but maligned her behind her back, overheard by the pages who were regarded as furniture. The Princess wore a gown of crimson and gold that day, her skirt spilling in rich silken folds all round her chair. Kimet had longed to feel that fabric, to smooth it against her cheek, and to examine the embroidery. . . .

The Princess! Kimet ran faster. The pages assigned to her all said Zarja's temper was growing more like the Queen's every day, particularly since the recent declaration of war against King Orthan—whose son had spent the entire winter here, dining and dancing and hunting and hawking. Kimet did not want to be seen by the Princess, for Steward Greb's beating would have to be severe indeed. The Queen would watch to make certain of it, and the Princess's narrow, sour face would be right at her shoulder.

Voices echoing down a side hall—voices and sword clanks and the ringing ching of chain mail—caused her to skid to a stop and duck under a mighty sideboard. Cowering there, she clapped her hands over her face. The laughter and voices resolved into familiar ones: four of the guardsmen from the castle walls.

What were they doing inside the residence? The Queen had forbidden the guards to enter wearing anything but livery and the other servants' silent wool-slippers, their weapons hidden, and decently muffled.

The voices diminished abruptly, as if the speakers had gone into a room and shut a door. Kimet climbed out and was about to run when she heard a muffled, gulping cry. It wasn't very loud, but it reminded Kimet of the way the pages sounded after one of Steward Greb's beatings, and her guts tightened with pangs of sympathy. She hoped it was no one she knew.

She sidled to the doorway from which the weeping had come, and peered in to discover no page, but Princess Zarja herself. Surprised, Kimet was about to retreat when the Princess, who was staring out the window at something in the rose garden, sucked in her breath on a shuddering sob, then put her hands over her face.

Kimet's surprise sharpened into amazement—and a hot, burning-ember glee. See how the royal snit liked feeling that way!

Then loud voices echoed down from the corridor round the corner: "The Princess is not in her sleeping chambers! Find her—now!"

"The Wizard wants a matched set, eh?" someone else said, and this was followed by harsh laughter.

The Princess jerked round to face the doorway—

and she and Kimet stared into one another's eyes for a long, painful heartbeat.

The Princess's eyes were red from weeping, and her narrow face was drawn—not the usual anger or haughtiness, but terror.

The same terror to be seen in the faces of the pages when Steward Greb loomed up, tapping his switch against his palm.

Kimet didn't think. She just acted. This room was the smallest of the reception chambers, with the service door on the opposite wall from the entryway. Kimet sprang to it and pushed the catch. The door opened silently. She beckoned to the Princess, who ran inside, stumbling over her hem, and Kimet pulled the door shut. Moments later they both heard heavy boots tromp into the reception chamber; Zarja's breathing was harsh. She had obviously never run in her life, and was further encumbered by her heavy, brocaded-silk dressing gown with its voluminous, dragging skirts.

When the sound of the boots diminished again, the Princess said, "Get me away from here."

Kimet obeyed, of course, as good pages are trained to do. She led the Princess down the service corridor—strangely empty—and at the landing, paused and said, "Where to, your highness?"

"Anywhere," the Princess snapped, though her voice shook. "Anywhere secret. Don't let them find me."

Hide from the King's guards? The Princess choked on a sob. Kimet shook her head as she led the way up the stairs.

"Are you in trouble, your highness?" she asked as they started up another flight of stairs. She could imagine the Royal Heralds wanting to beat the Princess—but she couldn't imagine them being allowed to any more than the Royal Tutors had been, when the Princess was small, and had thrown her shoes, her dishes, and her toys at them. From all accounts she didn't throw shoes any more, but she ignored the Heralds just the same, though she was supposed to be learning statecraft. And there was nothing they could do but smile.

"You're not supposed to ask questions," the Princess scolded. That sounded more like her usual self, and though Kimet felt a stab of the old annoyance, she realized she was also somewhat reassured. At least one thing was back to normal. She might not like it, but she was used to it. This being allowed to sleep late, the Guard in the royal chambers, above all the distant laughter and, close by, the Princess's weeping—those things were frightening because they were so strange.

They climbed in silence, stopping midway up one of the towers. They were on a seldom-used service landing. The main rooms in this tower were crammed with old-fashioned royal furnishings and ancient trunks. Before Steward Greb came into control, the pages had sometimes retreated there to play during their rare free time. Kimet had always liked to sit perched on a pile of ancient baskets next to one of the old-fashioned arrow-slit openings, and practice her more difficult stitches on rags and scraps as she chatted with friends.

She led the Princess into this tiny room now. Morning sunlight streamed in through the two slit-windows, sending narrow shafts of light in parallel lines on the stone floor. As the two girls moved, dust swirled in and out of the light, brief-lit then dimming.

"This is disgusting," the Princess snapped, arms crossed, hands tightened into fists.

"It's storage, your highness," Kimet said.

"At least it could be clean."

Kimet didn't know how to answer that without earning a beating, so she just bowed, hands folded before her the way the Queen required, her head meekly lowered.

"Don't just stand there, dolt! Dust something off so I can sit down," the Princess commanded, but her voice was still breathless, still too high.

Kimet obeyed, using the edge of her own clothing to clear off a place on one of the trunks. She spied a new addition to the clutter, yet another of the ancient tapestries, this one from the formal audience chamber, now junked in a bundle on top of a basket by careless hands.

As the Princess glanced at the dusted trunk, sniffed, and lowered herself daintily to the very edge, Kimet lovingly lifted the tapestry and smoothed it onto an old table.

There were only two tapestry restorers now. Both aging, appointed by the previous queen as the present queen hated old tapestries, which was why the tapestries themselves were currently relegated to the hallways. The Queen had stated at Kimet's promotion interview, "This stitchery of yours is all very well, but I want to be rid of those dirty, ugly things. When my daughter marries, I will have the castle walls redone in gold-flecked velvet. Begin a new fashion. In the meantime, I require pages. Errand runners are useful. Stitchers on old rubbish are not."

Remembering that remark about Zarja's marriage, Kimet looked down at the Princess's face and saw dried tear tracks on her cheeks.

There was silence for a time, Kimet standing there, hands folded, watching the Princess, who picked at the lacing on her gown. Finally Zarja jerked her chin up. "You could at least get me something to eat."

"What if someone asks after you, your highness?"

"You don't know where I am. Unless it's—" The Princess bit her lip, and her shoulders hunched up sharply. "No. I don't know who I can trust. I'd thought Master Elcan was a friend, and Captain Dormar . . ."

Kimet was puzzled. She pictured Master Elcan's face, bony—the nobles said ugly—but always interesting to Kimet as he performed little tricks to entertain the staff. "The Master Wizard? Not a friend?"

Princess Zarja sniffed again, but it wasn't the sharp hissy sniff of anger, it was the gulping sniff of someone on the verge of tears. She raised her blotched face and rubbed her pointy nose. It was red from her crying, almost as red as her eyes. "He—he turned my parents into statues. In the royal garden. And Captain Dormar . . . he always bowed so low whenever he saw me, and his guards were always so polite . . . H–he laughed when he saw them. Laughed, and said, 'They'll make royal bird perches!' "

"Statues, your highness?" Kimet repeated, horrified.

Zarja jerked her chin up and down, looking horribly like a bobbing wooden toy for that moment. "I saw it. And then the First Scribe came out, and she too was laughing—" The Princess's mouth quivered, and she buried her face in her hands.

"Statues?" Kimet said again, and moved to the nearest slit window. She could see the royal garden from this tower. Yes. There, right in the middle of the roses, stood two new statues, marble-veined white. One was tall and fat, the frosty white crown spiked exactly like the King's golden crown, and the other figure was short, arrogant of stance even in stone, chin up at a haughty angle, the folds of her long brocade dressing gown now hardened into smooth marble.

Guards ringed the two statues, and other servants as well.

Nobody stood at attention, the guards straight with their weapons held just so, the servants with bowed heads and meek attitudes. They all looked like they were on holiday, guards chatting with servants, and the sound of an occasional laugh echoed up the stone wall as a plump laundry woman poured out what looked like wine and passed the glasses. Three or four servants and guards lifted the glasses, sometimes to the King, mostly to the Queen, their laughter sharp and triumphant. With violent motions they tossed off their drinks and then poured again from dusty bottles Kimet recognized from the royal wine cellar.

Behind them several servants stood, shoulders hunched, faces twitching from side to side, as if they didn't know what to do, and they were seeking hints—or orders.

Kimet turned away. "I don't understand."

"Don't you see, you thick-witted lump?" Zarja retorted. "The Master Wizard, the Captain of the Guard—all of them are evil traitors. They've taken over the kingdom. And they want to find me so he can put me out there in the garden too."

Kimet looked out again, struggling to understand why. Family loyalty forced the words out, though even as she spoke her shoulders tightened against the expected whack. "Master Elcan's so kind," she said. "And wise."

"Was so kind," the Princess corrected, her voice trembling again.

They were both startled by the sound of the Wizard's voice outside. Kimet joined Zarja at the window, and for a moment the two stood side by side, staring down into the garden.

"Come, come," the Wizard said briskly, clapping his hands. "Why are you all standing about? There is work to be done! Beginning with finding the Princess. Bring her directly to me."

The crowd began to disperse, some of them talking in low voices, others glancing back at the sun-touched statues, their expressions varying from worried to smug.

Zarja sniffed again—her mother's hissy sniff this time, through a similar long, pointy nose. "Who could ever have thought Master Elcan could be so evil underneath?"

"Evil?" Kimet repeated.

"Will you stop being an echo?" the Princess demanded, dashing her tears away with an imperious gesture. "If you have to talk, say something that will help—or better, make yourself useful and get me something to eat."

Kimet returned to her first question. "And if they ask if I have seen you?"

"You tell them you haven't, of course," the Princess said impatiently.

"But that would be lying. We get the stick if we lie."

"You're not lying, you're doing what you're told. By me. Princess Zarja—Queen Zarja now. I'm the queen now, and—" The Princess's mouth opened, and her red, puffy eyes filled again with tears.

Kimet paused, uncertain whether to go or to stay. As she looked down at Zarja, whose face was now buried in handfuls of her brocade skirts, she thought about the Master Wizard. His intent face with the wild fringe of silver hair fluffing round his bald pate, his willingness to do little things to make the servants laugh, did not match in her mind with an evil man. However, turning the King and Queen into statues did seem an evil act. Was he now going to go through the kingdom turning people into statues and potted plants right and left?

Kimet thought of her parents, night guard and laundrywoman respectively at the palace of the Duke and Duchess of Rivarand. Mama's cousin had married Master Elcan's sister, and it was the Master Wizard himself who had made it possible for Kimet to get the royal palace job. Every poor family in the kingdom wanted to get their children out of a grim future of poverty and into the royal palace. The work was hard, but after five years, if you were dependable and diligent, and practiced your chosen craft, you could interview for places in your craft. If they liked your work, you waited only for a place to open up. If you were lazy, careless, or disobedient, Steward Greb would still get you your interview if your parents were important, but the Wizard only got your interview if you were good at your job. No matter who you were. And his word had always counted more.

Except if the Queen decided she didn't want you promoted.

"Greb!"

Kimet started, looking wildly around, then realized the voice had come from outside.

"Get him!"

"Catch him! We want our own statue!"

"Go round the other path—stop him there!"

Zarja and Kimet jumped to the window. Below a tall, spare man ran, his golden chain of office bouncing on his chest. The broad face that to Kimet had seemed to have only two expressions—a frown of threat, or the smirk of anticipation as he hefted his stick—was now blanched with fear.

"Go find the Wizard," howled one of the mob of servants chasing him. "He can set him up to decorate the midden heap!"

The man vanished round a shrub, his voice diminishing. The posse pelted after him, most of them yelling Greb's name, or threats, or both.

"Who was that they were chasing?" Princess Zarja asked.

Kimet said in surprise, "Steward Greb."

"What does he do?"

"Beat us."

The Princess frowned, then her brow cleared. "Oh! Steward in charge of you servants. I never knew his name."

Kimet shook her head, feeling the burn of anger and fear that the sight, or sound, or even thought of Greb always sparked. "No. That is, the Queen put him in charge, but he never looked out for us. All he was interested in was his stick, and any excuse to use it."

Faintly, from the direction of the service end of the castle, came a shout of triumph from many voices.

"They got him," the Princess observed, sinking back down onto the trunk. "Is the Wizard going to make statues of everyone in authority?"

Kimet still could not believe that of Master Elcan. "Or just those who—" She met the Princess's gaze, and closed her mouth.

Zarja flushed. "Why not just say it? Or just my family?"

Kimet shook her head impatiently. "I wasn't thinking that. I wasn't thinking *who* so much as *why*."

"What do you mean?" the Princess demanded.

Kimet turned away from the window and faced the Princess. "The Master Wizard—the statues. Could it be like with the Master Cook's son?"

Zarja looked up. "What?"

"The Master Cook's son. You didn't know about him?"

"What would I know about a cook's son? I don't even know who the cook is, much less his or her son!"

"I think maybe I should tell you about him—"

"I don't want to hear about any stupid cook's son," Princess Zarja snapped. "Go get me something to eat!"

Kimet's heart started thumping, even faster than it had when she'd woken up and found out how late it was, and knew she was going to get a beating. "I think I should tell you," she said, trying to keep her own voice steady. "And there's no one to order to beat me, because the servants are capturing Steward Greb, or drinking wine, or standing in the garden laughing at those statues."

Zarja's lips pressed together into a white line.

Kimet felt suddenly that she had to sit down, even though that was a serious breach of proper behavior, to sit in the presence of the Princess. But so many rules had already been broken so far that morning she wasn't going to worry about this one. She plopped onto a barrel labeled *Worn List Slippers*.

"The Master Cook's son," she said, "never wanted to learn anything. When the Head Carver would say, *Here's how your mother wishes us to carve the meats,* he'd go away, saying, *I don't have to know that. I'm the Master Cook's son.* And if the Head Pastry Maker said, *Here's my secret recipe for the finest crust in all the kingdom* the Cook's son would say, *I don't have to know that boring stuff—I'm the Master Cook's son!* But then one day the Master Wizard came in when he was telling the Head Vintner that he didn't have to learn how to choose wines because he was the Master Cook's son, and the Master Wizard didn't say anything, but the next day we saw the Master Cook's son mucking out the royal stables."

The Princess was still staring, her eyes wide and dark and her mouth pressed in that thin line.

"So anyway," Kimet finished lamely, "he's not a cook's apprentice anymore, he's a stable sweep."

The Princess stated, her sharp cheekbones dark red, "If you're daring to say that I belong in a stable—"

"I didn't say that," Kimet stated. "I told you the story of the Master Cook's—"

"—son. Yes. I think I managed to gather that much."

Silence. Zarja turned away, her chin on her hands.

Kimet's thoughts swirled around like the dust motes in the light.

"Or," Zarja's voice snapped, "are you hinting that I ought to sweeping the stables because I skimped my studies in order to go dancing or boating or riding?"

"I think," Kimet said, "they are still searching for you."

To make you a statue.

She didn't say it, but she knew from the Princess's short intake of breath that she was thinking it as well.

Zarja's chin jerked up, and she glared at Kimet for a long, nasty moment. "The war is to save my honor," Zarja finally said, and rubbed her eyes with hands that shook. "Prince Emik broke the marriage alliance our parents made when we were born. After spending all last winter here, and all the parties we gave him! He was so handsome, everyone wanted him, but he was supposed to court *me*!"

She clamped her jaw, and tightened her fists again.

Kimet said, "What happened?"

"He wouldn't kiss me. Even though I gave him gifts every day, and had all his favorite foods cooked, and ordered the musicians to learn that tweedle-tweedle music they like over there. I wore a new gown every day. After the masquerade on New Year's, at the midnight masking, he refused to kiss me. He said it didn't show proper respect. And I believed him. I believed his smiles and pretty words right up until he got home, after being escorted by Papa's army to keep him safe from brigands, and Mama's sister at their court sent a secret letter along with the official one breaking the alliance. It said that he entered King Orthan's throne room and straight away declared in front of all their nobility that he wouldn't marry me even to combine both kingdoms. Don't you comprehend that that's a royal insult? An insult to me is an insult to our entire kingdom, don't you see?"

"No," Kimet said. "Of course I don't know anything about kings and princesses feel about things, but I know how other people feel. Even the Master Wizard, a little, for he's kin. And I don't think he'd like to go over to another kingdom and turn them all into frogs. I don't think Captain Dormar and the guards would like going over to thrash up their kingdom—especially when a lot of the guards have family over there. Nobody would want to end up fighting his brother or cousin. And what happens after? If you feel royally insulted because Prince Emik doesn't like you, their king is going to feel even more royally insulted if we do all those things to them."

"As well he should!"

"So what if he sends a bigger army over here to smash up our houses, and his court wizard comes to turn the rest of us into scorpions? Then everybody would be miserable."

"Except me. I'm really miserable now." Zarja pointed at the window. "And so are my parents. That is, before they were turned into stone. Now they can't feel. Or even breathe."

Kimet didn't say anything.

Zarja sighed. "I can see that Papa might not have

considered the consequences of a war. But that's because he's used to relying on the Master Wizard for—" She stopped, and frowned.

"For ruling?" Kimet said.

Zarja stood up, then sat down again, quite suddenly. She turned away, turned back, wrung her hands, then stared down at the rings on her fingers.

Kimet watched, her body poised to turn. To leave. The Princess could not stop her. In fact, Kimet just had to go to the door or window and yell, and the Guard would come pounding up to take the Princess.

Zarja trembled, the diamonds on her rings glimmering like sunlight on water. She began speaking to those diamonds in a high, breathless voice.

"When I was small, he told me stories, sometimes weaving magical illusions to make them exciting. Stories about my ancestors, and the great things they had done. Sometimes he'd get terribly boring and preachy about 'responsibilities' and 'duties'—as if I don't know the royal schedule better than anyone!—but I was used to ignoring that from the Royal Tutors. And then on my tenth birthday, he made me a magic carpet. *Fly, see the kingdom,* he said to me. *Really see it, Zarja, see all that you will one day be responsible for.* I flew up nearly to the clouds, and looked down at everything that will be mine one day, and I never once felt scared. His magic was good magic, I thought. It made me safe—it made the whole kingdom safe. Why, my father trusted him! Whenever the least problem came along, he always said, right in front of the court, that he relied on Master Elcan's great wisdom!"

Kimet shook her head. *Leave that for the wizard,* was what the King actually shouted, after a jovial laugh. Kimet remembered hearing that many times, when she had throne room duty. Whether it was a famine in River Valley, or a squabble between the Fishers

Guild and the Boatwrights, the King genially called for the Wizard to fix it, and he'd go back to his games or his hunting. Kimet had been right there when the official news came from the returning escort that King Olivan's son wished to break the marriage alliance. The King had laughed before calling out to the Master Wizard, *Go find Olivan, and turn his royal court into frogs.*

He'd been joking. But the Queen had added in a sharp, cruel voice, *And send the army to burn their border towns. That'll teach them to insult our daughter!* She'd laughed, the King had shrugged and laughed, as he always did after the Queen's words, and the court also laughed. And that's how the war declaration came to be.

"Ruling," Zarja said, her eyes narrow. "So you think Master Elcan wanted to be king all along?"

Kimet shook her head again. "I don't know what he wanted, or wants now. I didn't know about that." She pointed at the window. "But it seemed to me— when I had duty—well, he was doing the real ruling. Then came this order to go to war."

Zarja's face flushed again. When she spoke, she said, "I wonder what this conversation would be like if you were the princess and I the page."

Kimet was silent.

"Or," sardonically, "the Master Cook's son."

"I don't know," Kimet said slowly.

"Sure you do," Zarja retorted, though her voice still trembled, and tears gleamed along her lower eyelids. "You are a page-princess now. For you can get me killed in a heartbeat, by just giving a single shout out that window. *Zarja's here!* What kind of reward do you think you'll get? Rank? Gold? You say you're kin to the Wizard, maybe he'll crown you as princess."

Kimet said in a low voice, "Don't want to be any princess."

Zarja gave her bitter, angry laugh. "Because I'm eeeee-vil?"

Kimet was on sure ground now. "Because it's boring," she said. "I'd like the fancy clothes, but I wouldn't like sitting around all day with those false-faced noble girls who smile when you can see them, but as soon as your back is turned they start the whispering."

Zarja jerked upright. "They whispered about me?"

"All the time."

"What did they say?"

Kimet felt uncomfortable, wishing she hadn't spoken. This conversation would have been easier with the angry, arrogant Zarja, but this tearstained face, puckered in confusion, was harder to address. "That you're mean," she said finally, leaving out all the rest about her looks, taste, and lack of success with Prince Emik. "Mean and . . . not knowledgeable, despite all those tutors."

"Stupid," Princess Zarja stated wryly. "Stupid and what else? Ugly, of course."

To avoid having to answer, Kimet returned to the original subject. "Second reason I don't want to be a princess—or a queen—is that it's dangerous. You wake up with a bellyache or you get angry with someone, throw out an order, and people die."

Zarja was silent.

Kimet said, "Kings and queens come and go. If they aren't respected, they're forgotten, except when children have to recite long strings of rulers for their tutors. What I want to do—restore tapestries—well, look." She turned to the table, and carefully lifted a corner of the tapestry, where an embroidered patch, long faded, could just be made out. "A thousand years ago this was woven by the hands of Ulda Nim. Her name—right there on the old writing, her work—right here. And if I get my way, a thousand years from today, if someone lifts this corner, there will be another patch above that one, saying 'This tapestry was restored by the hands of Kimet Darjabee.' I will be remembered for my work."

Below the tower a man hollered, "The Princess is still missing! Search the grounds! A reward for whoever finds her and brings her to the Wizard!"

Zarja's eyes met Kimet's. "My mother always told me I was ugly," the Princess whispered. "She said I had to make myself feared. If you were beautiful people loved you, but then you had to give them gifts to keep their love as you aged, and jolly them, and eventually give in. If they feared you, no one ever dared to demand gifts, or place. They obeyed you and respected you."

Obeyed and hated, Kimet thought. She didn't say the words aloud. But she saw Zarja's acute gaze, and suspected she knew it anyway.

Zarja gave her a crooked almost-smile. "It's beginning to sound like your Master Cook's son was following the royal example, isn't it?"

Kimet shrugged, feeling very awkward.

Zarja rose up and paced about the room. Kimet watched, her gut growling, her head aching. But she waited, though right then she could not have said why.

Finally Zarja looked up. "What do you think— Kimet? Are you going to shout out that window?"

Kimet sighed, wishing with sudden intensity that she had left. Of course she could leave now. There was no one to stop her. She knew the back ways. She could just turn her back on the Princess, slink down the servant ways, and pretend nothing had ever happened. Act surprised when she saw the other pages and someone mentioned the statues. Let life return to normal.

Except it wasn't going to return to normal. For bad or good, everything had changed. She still did not know how—the Wizard could be busy making statues of all the nobles, or all the Stewards. It was even conceivable he would make a statue of a page who had dared to hide a princess.

Meanwhile right in front of her were those eyes, not angry, or arrogant. The Princess had asked her a question—because she wanted, perhaps for the first time, to hear what a page might say.

Not just a page. She had used her name.

"No," she said. "I won't."

Silence. From outside a faint cry, "She's not in the wood!"

"Queens," Zarja said in a low voice, "are expected to risk others' lives. I never thought it might be my own. But it should be, shouldn't it, if I am the Queen, even for one day?"

She got to her feet, marched to the door, and yanked it open.

For the last time the two stared at one another. Princess Zarja shook out her skirts, smoothed her hair with trembling fingers, then gave an odd, crackling laugh that betrayed far more pain than humor. The sun in the window shone full on her red nose, her puffy eyes, her dust-spattered dressing gown and disarrayed hair. "I believe—if he gives me the chance to speak—I'll ask him to put me in the stable with the Master Cook's son. Maybe I'll learn what I wouldn't learn in the royal rooms."

Kimet had always admired the Princess's clothes, her possessions, the ease of her life. Now for the first time, she admired the girl inside them.

No, she respected her.

Yes, things had changed. For bad or good Kimet did not know, nor could she predict. The Wizard might turn them both into statues, or he might listen, but Kimet had decided her own first step in this new life, and it seemed right and true.

"If he does, I'll come and help you," she promised.

And she held out her hand.

Zarja took it.

Together they walked down the stairs.

THE CHILDREN'S CRUSADE

Robin Wayne Bailey

Aryamand knelt at prayer in his small room and, with eyes closed and head bowed, tried to contemplate the nature of God. The words he whispered, though, were mere recitations, rote verses without enthusiasm, and his knees hurt. He wanted to be devout, but his mind churned with too many questions and too many doubts about the things they made him do.

His stomach rumbled with hunger, and he hesitated in his prayers until the sensation passed. Then, listening for any sound in the hallway outside his door, he bit his lip. He could go to the market, pick up a bit of fruit and be back before anyone knew he was gone. Everyone else was at prayer; nobody would miss him. But he pressed his head to the floor again. Hunger was no great burden.

A stern voice grumbled from his doorway, startling him. "Get up, Ari. I need you to do something for me."

Aryamand squeezed his eyes shut briefly, then rose and turned to face his uncle. No smile or hint of warmth brightened the weathered, dark-bearded face that stared from the shadowed arch, and his uncle's dirty fatigues made him almost invisible in the poor lighting. Ari's gaze went to the pistol belt his uncle wore and to the brown paper wrapped box he held.

"Not at prayer, Uncle Abad?" Ari bit his lip, regretting the note of sarcasm.

Abad's eyes narrowed to dangerous slits as he looked down on his nephew. "Take this to the Khafafin Mosque. Wait for your opportunity and place it behind the minbar. Then come right back. Someone will be watching."

Ari's heart sank. "A mosque?" he protested. "Are we making war on our own people now?"

Abad clenched his teeth, but he knelt down and took Ari by the shoulders. "We do what we must," he answered. "Our people will blame the Americans and take to the street demanding revenge. You have to do this. We are the Hands of God."

Ari looked down at his scuffed shoes. Was it blasphemy, he wondered, to think that God's hands had a lot of blood on them? He had no love for Americans; their bombs had killed his mother and his two young sisters. Remembering, he took the package from his uncle.

"The timer is short . . ."

Ari didn't wait to hear any more. No warning and no sermon would make him feel better or ease his conscience. He obeyed his uncle because Abad had taken him in and given him a home, and he would do this job as he had done all the others Abad had given him. He glanced at his prayer rug, thinking that he should roll it up, but there was no time.

In the space of a heartbeat, he shifted. His small room faded in a brief flash of blackness, and when the blackness dissolved he stood in a shadowy alley across the street from the Khafafin Mosque. The street was filled with activity, and four armed Shia guards stood outside the entrance to the mosque. The open vesti-

bule beyond, however, appeared empty, and Ari
shifted again.

The silence inside the mosque startled him. Even
the street sounds seemed reluctant to enter through
the ancient, arched doorway. Mindful of his package,
he crouched low, hoping no one had seen him, but as
far as he could tell he was alone. At prayer time, the
mosque would be full.

Wetting his lips, Ari spotted the minbar at the far
side of the inner chamber and shifted once again. Still
crouching, he reappeared behind the cloth-covered
altar. His pulse raced, and he breathed faster as he
dared to look around the altar's edge. A sound caught
his ear; a door opened on the north side of the chamber. A bearded imam paced across the tiled floor with
a Qu'ran in the crook of one arm and vanished into
still another room. Ari heard voices.

Out of sight behind the minbar, he sat down and
stared at the brown paper wrapped box. A deep sadness came over him as he thought of his mother and
two little sisters. He missed them so much! *This is for
you,* he told himself as he pushed the box beneath the
minbar's overhanging cloth. Yet he knew that wasn't
true. This was for his uncle Abad.

Ari heard the imam's voice again as a door opened, and
he shifted once more. Empty-handed, his package delivered, he leaned from a rooftop parapet above the alley
where he had first appeared. If he was too close, he didn't
care. Staring toward the mosque, he began to count.

The bomb blast shook the air. Pressure cracks frac-
tured the mosque's façade. A great cloud of dust and
plaster roiled into the street and up through a newly
gaping hole in the roof. Struck by fragments of stone or
blown off their feet with bloody ears and noses, pas-
sersby screamed.

Gunfire sounded, random staccato shooting that

caused Ari to look further down the street toward another building—the Saladeen School. Shia militia protected it, too, but they abandoned their posts and ran to defend the mosque.

Then, unexpectedly, a second blast more powerful than the first followed. On his rooftop perch, Ari felt the shock wave like a fist against his face and chest. He staggered backward and fell with his hands pressed to his head. Eyes stinging, filled with outrage, he got painfully to his feet again.

A black cloud of dust and fire shot upward from what remained of the Saladeen School. Rubble fell like rain. For an instant after the blast, absolute silence hung over the neighborhood, and the few people still on their feet in the roadway gaped, too stunned to seek shelter or protection. Then came the wailing and screaming.

Ari pressed himself against the parapet and strained to see through the smoke. The school's entire eastern wall was gone. As he watched, a huge section of its roof collapsed, and the building next to it groaned and sank inward in a shower of brick and mortar.

Ari's attention returned to the school's main entrance as a pair of burned and ragged young boys stumbled out. Another boy came behind them, too much in shock to cry. No more than seven or eight years old, he tripped on a piece of debris and didn't get back up.

The mosque, Ari realized, had only been a diversion to lure the militiamen away while another bomber got into the school, which had been the real target! Not clerics and imams, but children! It made no sense! Squeezing his eyes shut, he pounded clenched fists on the stone parapet and cursed himself over and over again, not knowing which was greater, his anger or his shame.

Then he snapped his eyes open. More children with bloody hands and faces staggered from the devastated structure, and he knew there must still be more inside. Without a thought for himself, he shifted, leaving his rooftop to reappear at the school's entrance. He didn't care who saw or who witnessed. He swept up the fallen seven-year-old in one arm, and gathered the first two boys in the other, and then shifted again.

He'd only seen the hospital on the American base near Baghdad Airport from a distance, but he knew it well enough. Pain flashed through his body as he materialized with his charges on its doorstep. He'd never shifted so quickly and with so much weight before.

A tall, uniformed American opened the door and nearly fell on top of him. "What the hell . . . ?"

Ari looked up and answered in his poor English. "Please! Take care of them! There's more!"

Denying the fire in his muscles and brain, he shifted back to the school. This time, he ran through the entrance, ignoring the cascades of crumbling stone, the choking dust and the angry shouts of confused Shia. A boy his own age lay unconscious under a broken beam. As gently as he could, Ari hugged the boy, but a splintering and cracking drew his attention upward as a piece of the roof fell. Wide-eyed with panic, Ari drew a sharp breath and shifted barely in time.

A crowd of soldiers and medics were waiting around the American hospital entrance. A few jumped away as Ari appeared in their midst with his passenger. Some reached for their weapons. "If you're really here to help Iraqis," Ari shouted angrily, "start with this one!"

Without waiting for a reaction, he shifted back to the Saladeen School. His brain burned as if on fire, the cost of so many shifts. But as he looked down at the body of a boy half-buried in the rubble he knew his pain was nothing. In the shadows nearby, another child groped about, blinded, bleeding and whimpering.

Ari couldn't help himself. He began to cry even as he reached out for the sightless boy. "I'm so sorry!" he muttered as he wrapped the boy in his arms. He glanced back at the dead child in the rubble, but all he saw were his two sisters. That was how he remembered them after the bombs had fallen on their home in the night. A great sob shook him, and he shifted to the hospital again.

"Stop! Wait!"

Ari looked up as he set the blind boy carefully on his feet. The man who spoke was the same one who had nearly fallen on him before. A single star shone on the man's collar. Ari didn't know what it meant, and he didn't care. He wiped a sleeve over his moist eyes and swallowed as a ring of soldiers cocked their guns. "I don't listen to your orders!" he answered, tight-lipped. "I won't ever take orders from gunmen and thugs again!"

And he shifted. He wasn't sure to where, just somewhere warm and familiar. Safe was too much to ask. No place in the world was safe. He collapsed immediately, weak and aching as if he'd taken a beating, and when he hit the floor he wept until exhaustion overcame him.

It was night when he awoke, but he knew where he was. A faint smile with a hint of sadness turned up the corners of his lips. Even in the gloom he knew the shape of the room and its broken roof. He imagined he heard his mother's soft footsteps, and some echo of his sisters' voices still wafted among the shattered walls. The moon poured in through an unshuttered window, filling the small house with ghosts and shadows.

He'd come home. Or to what was left of home. Some unconscious thought had brought him here before he passed out. He sat up in the empty corner where his old bed once had been. Some scavenger had carried it off. It had been a good bed, and he hoped someone was getting use of it.

He felt strong again, his pain gone, but in its place he found an emptiness, a loss that felt even worse. He shuffled through the ruins that once had been his house, remembering, saying goodbye to things that were already gone.

"You're too predictable, Aryamand. I told you to come right back."

His uncle had found him. He turned toward the silhouette in the crooked doorway and noted the two restless shapes standing a few steps behind. "I'm not coming back," he answered with calm resolve.

Abad put a hand on his pistol butt. "It had to be done," he growled. "You're not old enough to understand the way of God yet."

Ari resisted the urge to laugh as he kicked at a bit of rubble. Old enough? Did his uncle even remember what day it was? While Ari had slept on the broken floor of his bombed-out home, he had turned fourteen.

"You let outsiders see you today," his uncle chided. "That was foolish."

Barely listening, Ari turned his back on his Uncle Abad. In a flat voice he said, "I renounce God. Particularly your God, and especially any God that would justify what we did today."

One of the men behind Abad hissed. "His mouth is filthy!"

Abad's footsteps stirred the debris as he moved toward Ari. "He's confused," his uncle argued. "I'll see to his punishment."

Ari closed his eyes and thought of someplace far

away, a favorite place he'd only recently come to know. "You wrapped a present today, Uncle," he said over his shoulder, "but you forgot to wish me a happy birthday."

Darkness flashed around him, neither cold nor warm. He felt no sense of falling or flying, no sense of movement at all. One moment, he stood in a stray beam of moonlight in the ruins of his home, and the next he stood under a full moon on a hillside overlooking quiet Bethlehem.

With a soft smile on his lips, he sat down in the grass and folded his arms around his knees to study the faint, beautiful lights below. It wasn't his first time on this hillside. He'd been pushing his limits, testing his abilities, shifting farther and farther in secret. It was like lifting weights, he'd discovered, like building muscle. The more he tried, the more he achieved.

To the north lay Jerusalem, another city in conflict. Always there was fighting and war. It seemed to make the world go around. No matter how far he shifted, he wondered if he could ever escape it, if he could ever feel safe.

"Ari! Is that you?"

Ari grinned as he leaned back on one hand and twisted around. "Abraham!" he answered in a low, excited voice. His only friend in the world walked down the slope. Abraham was tall, rail-thin for thirteen years and possessed of the biggest ears Ari had ever seen. "What are you doing here?"

Abraham disappeared in mid-step and reappeared at Ari's side. With gawkish grace, he folded his legs and sat down, too. "I've been coming here every night." Reaching into a hip pocket of his trousers, he drew out a page from a magazine and unfolded it. "Since you showed me this." In the moonlight it was hard to see, but Ari knew it showed the hillside upon which they sat. "I've been practicing and hoping you'd turn up," Abraham continued. He clapped Ari's shoulder. "Your English is getting better!"

Ari blushed at the compliment. "How many shifts did you take to get here?"

Abraham inclined his curly head. "Just one."

Ari's eyebrows shot up. "From Tel Aviv?"

Abraham nodded. "Thirty-two minutes, three seconds north; thirty-four minutes, forty-six seconds east. It's easy with your picture, and easier when you know the longitude and latitude." He looked at Ari from the corners of his eyes. "How many jumps to get here from Baghdad?"

"Just one," Ari admitted. He tried to cover up as Abraham elbowed him in the ribs.

For a long time they were silent. Both boys folded their hands behind their heads and stretched out on the grass. Ari watched the stars parade overhead, naming the ones he knew, wondering at the others. He hadn't had much of an education.

Not like Abraham. The Jewish boy was bright, well-schooled and well-traveled. He knew lots of things that Ari didn't, like the longitude trick, and he learned quickly. Ari let go a long, deep sigh as he remembered. Only four years had passed since he'd found Abraham with some other captives, members of an international peace group, in a terrorist camp in northern Afghanistan.

Abraham's parents had been killed. Like Ari, he was an orphan, and without understanding quite why, Ari had shifted his new friend to freedom. He frowned as he remembered how Uncle Abad had beaten him for days.

But that one shift had tripped a switch in Abraham's brain. He'd tried to describe it to Ari. He saw patterns, he said, where he hadn't before. Interstices, he called them. Small spaces between things that he could slip through.

Abraham was educated. Ari had never tried to analyze what he did. He'd just always been able to do it. As a baby, he'd sometimes turned up inexplicably in his mother's bed, or so he'd been told.

He couldn't teach it to everyone, though. He'd shifted his uncle numerous times with no result to see if Abad could learn.

"They're going to start looking for us," Ari said. "A lot of people saw me shift today." He sat up and looked at Abraham's feet. "Where are your shoes?"

The Jewish boy made a face. "I can teleport farther than ever," he said, "but I still have trouble with *things*. I'm lucky to get here with my clothes on!"

Ari lay back again and studied the moon as it sank lower in the sky. Thoughts of the Saladeen School crept into his mind, along with thoughts of the mosque bombing. That wasn't the first package he'd delivered, and guilt gnawed at him.

His entire life had been filled with bombs. Bombs in shoeboxes and bombs from jet planes. Roadside bombs and guided missiles. What was the difference when the only result was indiscriminate death?

Tears leaked from his eyes, but he wiped them away before Abraham could see. "It's my birthday," he blurted.

Abraham sat up. "Really? That's great!" He squeezed Ari's knee. "I bet you didn't get a present yet. What can I get you?"

Ari thought for a moment as silly answers danced through his head. But then he turned quite serious. "A better world, Abraham." He sat up and looked his only friend in the eyes. "I want a better world."

Abraham didn't blink. "Can you wait until morning when the stores open?"

*   *   *

Morning found them in the suburbs of Tel Aviv. Abraham's foster parents were well-off, if not rich, and their pantry was stocked. While Ari stuffed a backpack with edibles and changed into some of Abraham's clean clothes, his friend struggled with a note of explanation to leave behind. When that was done, Abraham went to a bookshelf and pulled down a world atlas.

"We're taking this, too," he said. "Now where do you want to go? Where do we hatch this grand plot?"

Ari scratched his chin. He'd seen magazines that some American soldiers had traded or given away in his country and remembered the beautiful pictures they often contained. He nodded to himself as he recalled a favorite, a place of monuments and memorials and architecture more grand than anything he'd ever seen.

"Washington," he whispered, speaking the name as his uncle had pronounced it.

Abraham wasted no time as he flipped through the atlas. "Thirty-eight minutes, fifty seconds north; seventy-seven minutes west." Closing the book, he looked up with a worried expression. "Ari, I've never teleported that far!"

Ari bit his lip, and then put his hands on his friend's shoulders. "We'll take it slow in as many small shifts as you need," he said. "I'll carry you whenever you need me to, and you'll learn along the way." He winked. "Just don't lose your shoes!"

Sunset of the next day found them on the lawn of the White House. It looked exactly like a photograph Ari had seen in a soldier's magazine, and he grinned, pleased with himself for making his longest shift ever. "London to Washington!" he murmured.

"Probably not a good spot," Abraham said as a pair

of uniformed men ran toward them. He looked pale and near exhaustion.

Ari wrapped his friend in his arms and shifted. Instantly, they were outside the fence among a crowd of tourists on Pennsylvania Avenue. A group of nuns flung up their arms like startled penguins, and a jogger took a tumble on the pavement. Ari shifted again, moving farther down the street and stared in confusion. He was used to crowded, war-torn Baghdad with its narrow streets and alleys, not to such wide-open space!

"Let me!" Abraham said. "I was here a long time ago with my parents." Darkness flashed around them, and the scene changed. The street was wide, but busy with honking cars and noisy pedestrians. For a dangerous moment, Ari froze, too stunned to move, until Abraham dragged him out of the traffic to the safety of a sidewalk.

"Georgetown," Abraham explained. "I think."

Ari stared at the shops and glittering window displays, the bright lights and neon. He'd never seen anything like it. Abraham tugged at his elbow.

They found an alley and, taking shelter behind a dumpster, searched their backpack for something to eat. The sky was growing darker as night came on, but Ari couldn't resist peeking into the street. He found the city lights almost dizzying. Yet finally, exhaustion overcame him. Crawling back behind the dumpster, he curled up around his friend. Abraham was already asleep.

For days they lived on the street in alleys and crannies. When their supplies ran out, they engaged in minor thievery, taking apples and candy bars, cartons of milk and loaves of bread from supermarkets and convenience stores and shifting away before they were caught.

Under Ari's tutelage, Abraham began to shift faster and with increasingly heavier objects. They made up games to pass the time and impress each other. Sometimes, they played pranks. Once, as they wandered through Georgetown, Ari paused to admire a parked Mercedes SL 500.

"You like it?" Abraham asked.

Breathless, Ari nodded. With a chuckle, Abraham leaned against the expensive vehicle. An instant later, car and boy vanished. A dumpster reappeared in the space where the Mercedes had been parked, and Abraham sat perched like a gnome on top of it.

Ari gasped. "What did you do with the car?"

"The Barnes and Noble Bookstore," he answered, grinning as he jumped down and hurried Ari away. "I left it on the rooftop. Let the owner figure that out!"

But there were serious moments, too. One night, as they slept beneath the loading dock of a business in Dupont Circle, an explosion shook them awake. Filled with the old terrors of his past and his homeland, Ari sprang to his feet. He knew the sound a bomb made. Running around the corner with Abraham quick on his heels, he stared as smoke and flames poured from the ruins of a bar. Car horns activated by the blast raised a cacophony. Shards of glass sparkled on the sidewalk, in the street. A young man, his clothing in tatters, staggered through the wreckage of the door and fell.

Ari cursed. For the first time in his life, he'd begun to feel safe. He'd begun to sleep without listening for the sounds of bombs and missiles and gunfire. Yet not even here could he find such a thing as safety!

Clenching his fists, he shifted to the front of the bar. The flames from inside scorched his skin, and he sucked smoke. Still, he dropped to his knees and put his arms around the fallen man in the doorway. A once-handsome face turned to look up, and Ari gazed into eyes filled with pain and tears and confusion. Ari knew the look too well.

"It's all right," Ari said, coughing, "I'll get you somewhere away!" He stared around, but shattered cars blocked his view.

Abraham appeared at his side. "The park across the street!" the Jewish boy suggested. "Take him there! I'm going inside!"

Ari stood up to get a look at the park. Then he touched the injured man's shoulder and shifted him to a bench near the sidewalk, startling onlookers who had gathered to watch the excitement. "Don't move!" Ari urged. "We'll get help!" He stabbed a finger at a young couple watching close by. "You!" he shouted. "Call your authorities!"

Abraham appeared with another young man whose neck and shirtless back were bleeding from multiple lacerations. "Ari, they don't speak Farsi," he reminded his friend. Then he shouted in English at the growing crowd. "Don't just stand there! Who's got a cell phone? Someone call for help!"

"I've already called it in." The voice came from a stranger who stepped out of the crowd. He held a cell phone, and. As he bent over one of the victims, his gaze met Ari's. The Iraqi boy felt a jolt of surprise. Though the man now wore the plain suit of a western businessman, only a few weeks ago he had worn the uniform of an American soldier with a gold star on his collar!

"Ari, come on!" Abraham called.

Ari barely heard. His attention was focused on the hint of a pistol beneath the stranger's left armpit as his jacket gaped open. It couldn't be coincidence that this soldier was here in Washington. Ari's heart hammered, and he thought about shifting away to a far, far place. Instead, he calmed himself and met the soldier's gaze again with a defiant look of acknowledgement. "I have work to do," he said, and before the soldier could respond, Ari shifted.

The flames inside the bar were intense. *An incendiary device,* Ari realized as he shielded his eyes from the heat. He knew his bombs and their types. This one had been designed for maximum damage. He shot a look around, spotting a half-conscious man beneath an overturned table, and on the floor near that one, lay another. Dead or alive, Ari couldn't tell, but he grasped the hands of both and shifted them to the park. Abraham appeared a split-second later with the bartender, whose arms were burned and broken.

Ari cast a glance around for the soldier as an ambulance arrived screeching at the curb. "Why here?" he said to Abraham. "Why now?"

Smoke and grime smudged Abraham's face. He wiped an arm over his eyes before answering. "Even America has its religious fanatics," he shouted. Then he vanished again.

The flames crackled as a brisk wind swept down the street. Choking smoke sent onlookers scattering, but the soldier returned with a pair of dark-suited men. Used to command, he shouted at the ambulance drivers as they hurried with their equipment. "Where the hell is the fire truck?" he demanded. "This entire block could go up!"

The paramedics rushed toward the park bench and the victims on the ground. "It's stuck in traffic," one of them answered gruffly. "Two blocks back. Now get out of the way!"

Once again, the soldier turned toward Ari. There was something challenging in the tall man's gaze, and

Ari stiffened, sensing trouble. Abraham reappeared with yet another unconscious victim as Ari walked toward the soldier. "Who are you, American soldier?" he demanded.

Even out of uniform, the man could not conceal his military bearing. He looked down at Ari as if studying him. "General David Piper," he answered. "Brigadier General."

Ari lifted his head higher. Far down the block, he could see the distant flashing of red lights. "Keep the street clear, General." He couldn't quite keep the sneer out of his voice.

The general reached out as if to grab him, but Ari shifted. Darkness flashed, and he reappeared in front of the stranded fire truck. The noise from the siren, combined with the ear splitting honking and shouting of angry drivers, momentarily disoriented him. *Surely,* he thought, *Americans are the loudest people on earth*!

One of the firemen leaned out of the truck and waved an arm. "You stupid kid! Get out of the way! Get out of the way!"

Taking a deep breath, Ari put his hands on the fire truck's bumper. With some instinct he couldn't explain, he sensed the sheer mass of the truck, its equipment, and its passengers. It was a new and interesting sensation.

The fireman waved again. "Get out of the . . . !"

Ari shifted. Not just himself, but the entire fire truck.

"What the holy hell?" The waving fireman stared dumbfounded at the burning bar right beside the truck, and leaned so far out of the window that he nearly fell before another fireman caught him. The rest of the fire team jumped down from their stations with their hands at their sides, jaws gaping and eyes wide.

The general ran into the middle of the street. "Get

some water on it!" he shouted, giving one of the firemen a purposeful shove. "There are still people in
there! Move!"

Shocked into action, the fire team got busy.

Ari uncurled his fingers from the chrome bumper
and straightened up. He felt strained, as if he'd run a
race, but there was none of the pain and burning that
had wracked him when he'd moved heavy objects only
a few weeks before. He turned to look at the flames
and the coils of thick hoses and the jets of streaming
water, then bit his lip and smiled, knowing he'd done
something great.

The general stepped into his field of view. "I want
you to come with me, son," he said in perfect Farsi.

Common sense told Ari to shift away, but the general intrigued him. "I knew that somebody would
come after me," he answered in his own language.
"But how did you find me so quickly?"

The general's lips drew into a tight line before he
answered. "Surveillance cameras," he explained.
"After Baghdad Airport, we formed a task force to
locate you. We drew a blank the first few days, but
then you turned up in London. The Brits have cameras on every corner. It's Orwell's *Nineteen Eighty-
four* everyday over there, and half a dozen of them
got your image." He blinked, and then knelt down to
address Ari eye to eye. "Same thing here, really, although Americans aren't aware of it. When you
turned up on the White House lawn, the cameras
kicked in. And every time you stole an apple from
a supermarket or a convenience store? Same thing.
Surveillance cameras. We've had entire teams sweeping the neighborhood for you, knowing it was just a
matter of time until you turned up again."

Ari's eyes narrowed with suspicion. He looked at

the destruction across the street, and then back to the general. "You set this bomb to lure me."

General Piper shook his head. "We're the good guys, son," he said. "We don't operate that way."

Ari sneered, remembering the nights when American planes had streaked over Baghdad raining bombs. "It's a matter of perspective," he answered.

The general sighed. "I'm not inclined to argue politics with a kid," he replied. "But we need to know how you do this amazing thing that you do." He ran a hand along the side of the fire truck, and when he looked back, Ari thought his face was not so friendly. "The applications are infinite."

Something small and sharp struck Ari in the side of his neck, something that burned like chemical fire. Ari clapped a hand to the wound, detecting a tiny needle, and whirled to see where it had come from. The general's powerful arms locked around his waist.

Panic overcame Ari. Kicking and scratching, knowing that he'd been drugged, he fought to get free. The fire spreading through his veins turned to cold, freezing. "No!" he protested, half delirious. "No, Uncle Abad! You won't use me again!"

The two suited figures he'd seen earlier rushed out of the park's shadows. One of them raised a tranquilizer pistol to fire again. Ari kicked out once more, driving his heel against the general's knee.

At the same time, darkness flashed. Barely conscious, Ari shifted to freedom, leaving his captor behind.

He reappeared in the home of his Uncle Abad and sank to his knees. Two dirty figures in fatigues spun toward him, pistols whipping from holsters. At a desk in the corner of the room, his uncle bent over the workings of another bomb. Abad's eyes widened, and he shouted Ari's name.

Reflexively, Ari shifted again, to the Khafafin Mosque this time. The rubble had been cleared, but the hot sun streamed down through a giant hole in the mosque's roof. The Call to Prayer rang in his ears, mixed with shouts of outrage and fear. Despite the damage, the mosque was full of worshippers, and hands reached to seize him.

He couldn't think, couldn't even lift his head, but his power reacted, shifting him away yet again to a house in Tel Aviv where Abraham's foster mother screamed at the sudden sight of him; to the middle of a busy street in Georgetown where a taxi nearly ran over him. Barely in time, he shifted from beneath the onrushing tires.

In an alley, behind yet another dumpster, he finally found shelter. Though filthy, the place had a familiar smell. It was night, he realized, and cool. Unable to keep his eyes open, he clutched at a plastic bag full of garbage and dragged it closer to make his pillow, and then curled up like an injured kitten, shivering until the drug in his system carried him to sleep.

An insistent tapping on his shoulder brought Ari awake. His body felt heavy, and at first he couldn't seem to open his eyes. He ached in every muscle and joint, and his head throbbed as it never had before. Yet, he knew that it wasn't from the shifting, but the aftereffects of the sedative.

The tapping continued, and an urgent voice spoke his name. "Ari, wake up! Aryamand! It's me, Abraham!"

Ari fought through the thick fog that filled his brain. Slowly, he peeled his eyes open and focused on the Jewish boy's face. "You're safe," he muttered as he clutched at Abraham's arm. "I didn't mean to leave you."

"Safe may be too optimistic," Abraham whispered. He pressed a bottle of water against Ari's lips. "People are looking for us. They seem to be everywhere."

Ari sipped and pushed the water bottle away. "Looking for us?" he said with a puzzled expression.

"Those men tried to grab you!" Abraham reminded. "I teleported back into the park just as they shot you, but you vanished. So they took a shot at me, too, but I teleported the hell out of there!"

Ari sat up and leaned against the dumpster. He smelled of rotten lettuce and his clothes felt damp. As he rubbed his temples, he remembered some of the places he'd shifted to in his delirious escape. There might have been others; he couldn't remember. He glanced at Abraham. "Where did you go?"

Abraham pulled at the lobe of one oversized ear. "Darfur in the Sudan," he said with a sheepish frown. "I've been holding out on you, Ari. I have another friend—my best friend until I met you. Her name's Suleima, and I've known her for a long time, since my parents worked as peacekeepers in that region." He looked askance, and then offered the water bottle to Ari again. "I've been teaching her for the past few months the way you taught me."

Ari took a long pull from the bottle and sat up straighter. The drug aftereffects were wearing off. "What can she do?" Ari asked. The idea of a third shifter excited him.

"She can't move heavy objects yet, but she's getting better," Abraham answered. "And her range is terrific. I had nowhere else to go after you disappeared in the park. So I went to her."

Ari chewed his lip as he nodded his head. "Do her parents know?"

"She's an orphan like us," Abraham answered. "Her parents were government workers, but they were killed by Janjaweed rebels. She lives with an aunt now." He shrugged and looked thoughtful. "I don't think her aunt knows, but she has to wonder how I showed up."

"How old is your friend?" Ari asked. "Do you think she'd join us here?"

Abraham let out a long, slow breath. "She's four-teen, and she's already here. While I've been checking the alleys and parks and places where we slept or hung out, she's been in a downtown library using the computers to track news stories about us and maybe turn up a clue about where you went. She's good with computers." A grin spread across his face, and his eyes twinkled. "We're a bit of a news item. Maybe even celebrities. When you teleported that fire truck, some tourist with a video camera caught it. The pictures have been all over the television and newspapers. They even got film of the guys who shot you. That's caused a real row. The government's calling us a threat, but a lot of people think we're heroes."

Ari closed his eyes and rubbed the side of his neck as a slow anger began to build. "We saved a lot of lives," he grumbled, "and they still shot me!" He opened his eyes again and, with a shock, discovered that he was alone.

Not for long, though. Abraham reappeared a mo-ment later with a girl hand-in-hand at his side. She was tall as a reed and nearly as thin with an impossible tangle of curly hair that spilled past her shoulders in a bushy ponytail. Her eyes were wide and dark, and gold earrings pierced both her ears. Her skin was black as coffee. It seemed to shine with captured light. She wore American blue jeans and Nikes with a white, embroidered blouse.

Her fresh-scrubbed look reminded Ari of how dirty and ragged he felt.

Abraham made introductions. Suleima extended her hand. "Abe tells me that you want to make a better world," she said in accented English. Her expression was deeply serious. "I want to help."

Ari stared at Suleima's hand. Her fingers were beautiful, delicate, like the rest of her. He took her hand as if it were a flower and then smiled at Abraham. He felt lucky to have two friends now.

They were all hungry. Abraham had repacked his backpack with supplies from the kitchen of Suleima's aunt. Ari found some of the food strange, but he smacked his lips as he ate. When they were finished, he stood and walked to the end of the alley to look out. The afternoon sky was beginning to darken with storm clouds, and a brisk wind propelled a newspaper down the street. The air smelled of rain.

He felt a sudden concern for Suleima. He and Abraham were boys and tough, but it didn't seem right that she should sleep in the street. "There are plenty of abandoned buildings and empty apartments around here," he said as he scanned the skyline. "It's time we put a roof over our heads."

Abraham leaned took a step outside the alley, too, and quickly backed up. "Forget the roof," he said as he pulled the Iraqi boy back into the shadows. "It's time we got out of here. That black van on the corner and the two men coming this way—I'm sure they're looking for us. I've seen a lot of black vans today."

"Two of them and three of us," Suleima said as she shouldered the backpack. "Let's give them a bath in the river."

Ari grinned. "It's tempting," he admitted. "But I'm the one who needs the bath, and I know where." Taking Suleima and Abraham by the hands, he shifted all three of them to the Reflecting Pool before the Lincoln Memorial.

In the late hour and with a brewing storm, they found themselves alone except for a pair of homeless figures on a nearby park bench. The old men stared with blank, disinterested gazes, oblivious to the sudden appearance of the children. Ari noticed their clothes—old fatigues and army jackets. They were soldiers once, veterans of other wars.

He turned toward the memorial. He'd seen it the first time in the pages of a soldier's magazine, and he'd never forgotten it. He only wished that he could read the words carved in the stone, but while he could speak some English, he could read none of it.

Abraham read for him. "Great words," he said when he had finished. "A pity they're so little honored."

"I don't know," Ari said. He frowned and stepped back to stare at the great stone figure with its beard and stern expression. "They seem to glorify war, the righteousness and the heroicism of it. But even honored dead are still dead."

Suleima's eyes flashed with hidden anger. She turned her back on the monument and walked the edge of the pool. "And their children are left parentless," she added, "or worse."

Abraham and Suleima fell into a brooding silence, each wandering to opposite sides of the water, each lost in their own thoughts. Ari stripped off his shirt and trousers and washed them in the pool. His gaze constantly swept the park for signs of security police, and when his clothes were done, he pulled off his shoes and socks and bathed in the cool water. When he was clean, he donned his wet garments and hugged himself. The wind was turning chill.

He gazed toward the trees at the park's edge as Abraham and Suleima joined him again. He suspected they contained security cameras, but he wasn't ready to go. He looked toward the far end of the park where the illuminated Washington Monument loomed in the deepening dusk.

"I want to fill this park with children," he said in a low voice. "It's time to send a message."

Abraham tilted his head. "A message to whom?"

With his friends following, Ari began to walk along the pool's edge. The Washington Monument drew closer, and beyond that, over the long expanse of the Mall, he could see the Capitol Building. On another quiet night with Abraham at his side, he had stood on its stone steps. But another structure beside the capitol interested him more—the Peace Monument.

"You've got a peculiar look, Ari," Abraham said when Ari didn't answer. "What are you thinking?"

"I'm thinking of a new Peace Monument," he said. Stopping, he lifted his nose and sniffed. The smell of rain was strong. The coming storm was only minutes away.

"Do you really want to fill this park with children?" Suleima asked. "I know how to do that." Ari and Abraham turned toward her at the same time. "With computers," she continued. "Chat rooms and message boards to start. Then the word will spread. We'll use the celebrity Abe says we have now."

Abraham gave a thoughtful nod. "One month from today," he said half to himself. "We use the time to plan and work and grow stronger." Then he spun toward Ari. "But why? I still don't see . . ."

"I do," Suleima interrupted. Her face was grim, yet excited as she reached out and took Ari's hand.

A black van cruised along the western park perimeter and slowed down as it approached their position. Ari could feel the eyes trained upon him. "Let's go," he whispered as the first heavy drops of rain began to fall.

* * *

They found shelter on the north side of Franklin Park in a vacant hotel that was up for sale. Their rooms were musty and without utilities, but dry and secure. A neighborhood library just a block away allowed Suleima to work her magic for a few hours each day. She spread the word across the Internet, organized children into units, and promised those who could come to the mall a chance to change the world. With the rest of her time, she trained and grew stronger.

For their parts, Ari and Abraham followed fire trucks, police cars and emergency vehicles and made heroes of themselves in the eyes of the public, appearing long enough to save lives, then disappearing again. When an old man suffered a heart attack on the Capitol steps, a slight figure in a hooded sweatshirt shifted him to a hospital. When a train jumped track on the Baltimore-Washington corridor, a gawky young boy in a stocking cap teleported the injured to safety.

They didn't restrict their activities just to Washington. In midwestern Kansas when a chemical spill threatened a small town, three children popped up to help with evacuations. In London, when terrorist bombs exploded in the subways, three small figures with camouflaged features arrived to shift the victims to emergency rooms and rescue stations.

In short time, they dominated the headlines and news programs, and speculation spread that they were more than just two or three.

Then in cities large and small, flyers began to appear announcing a call to children everywhere, not just in America, but around the world, to participate in a gathering on the Washington Mall. Governments and officials countered with dire warnings only to meet resistance from churches, service organizations and humanitarian groups.

Ari, Abraham and Suleima watched in amazement as a movement grew from their efforts. When a senator broke ranks with his party and came forward to fight for a park permit, Suleima flung her arms around Ari and cried.

On the night before the gathering, the three sat together in a dark hotel room nursing sodas and hamburgers that some grateful paramedics had given them. Abraham trembled, his voice nervous. "Are we ready for this?" he asked. "We're just three kids, Aryamand." Not *Ari,* but *Aryamand.* He dropped his gaze to the dusty floor.

Suleima shook her head. "We're more than that, Abe," she answered in a whisper. "We're an army now. Somewhere among all those children we're reaching out to will be others capable of doing what we can do."

Ari listened, but his thoughts were elsewhere, back in his homeland. While Abraham and Suleima talked, he remembered his mother and sisters, the long nights when American bombs fell from the dark skies. His ears rang with remembered gunfire, missiles, mortar rounds and bursting shells.

But worse, he remembered things he had done and packages he had carried. He remembered the hidden camps and hideouts his uncle had shown him, and all the murders he had done. He was more than a child. He was a terrorist.

And he had one more act of terrorism to commit before he could make atonement. Setting aside his sandwich, he arose and picked up a brown paper wrapped box from the dusty top of a dresser. "Stay inside tonight and rest," he told his companions. "I have an errand, an offering to place in the Hand of God."

Before Abraham or Suleima could protest, he shifted. Distances meant nothing to him anymore. With effortless ease he crossed the world, and for the first time in a long while he wondered why he'd been given such a gift. When he shifted, he almost believed in God again, but a different God that no book or text or sermon could ever contain.

He arrived in Baghdad at dawn by his uncle's bed. Abad lay sleeping with a thin gray coverlet drawn up to his waist. An AK-47 rifle leaned against the head of his bed, and a .45 automatic lay within reach on a table beside a copy of Islam's Holy Book. Ari stood silently, watching his uncle in repose. Then, bending low, he pushed the paper-wrapped box beneath the bed's edge.

Perhaps it was the soft scrape of the paper on the floor, or maybe it was Ari's quiet breathing that disturbed his uncle, but Abad's eyelids peeled open. "So you've come home," he said in a soft, deep voice as he rose up on one elbow. He looked his nephew up and down, and then his gaze drifted toward the automatic.

Ari shook his head. "This isn't my home," he answered, "and before you pick that up you should look beneath your bed."

Abad's eyes narrowed, but he leaned over and felt with one hand until he found the box. Fear flashed across his face. Cautiously, he slid the box into view.

"It's just a box," Ari said with cold emotion. "There's nothing in it this time. But find another way to settle your differences, Uncle. If you ever explode another bomb, if you ever injure another child, look for me in the shadows and check under your bed." He picked up the Qu'ran and dropped it on the coverlet. "Find another way."

Droplets of sweat beaded on Abad's temples as he

placed a hand on his Holy Book. He trembled, though he tried to hide it, and he spoke with false bluster. "So you think you've become a man, Aryamand?"

Again, Ari shook his head, and he wondered if his uncle could ever change. "I'm just a boy," he answered as he picked up the automatic and set it back on the table again. "A boy who hopes to respect his uncle again someday."

With that, he shifted away, back to America and to a dirty hotel room where night had closed in. Abraham and Suleima were asleep, curled up around each other on one of the creaky old beds. Flyers and leaflets announcing the gathering on the mall lay scattered on the floor with food cartons and empty soda bottles and napkins. Like a protective big brother, Ari sat down in a chair to watch over his two friends and to count the hours until morning.

At dawn, he woke them, and they stretched, rubbing their eyes with fists and yawning. They dressed in clean clothes, not new ones, but donations from a supportive Salvation Army worker, and they combed their hair and washed their faces with bottle water.

For a few moments, they stood together, their hands joined, each thinking private thoughts. Ari felt small and inadequate, and his friends looked so confident. He drew a deep breath. "Let's go," he said at last.

Still holding hands, they shifted to the mall, and appeared in the morning shadow of the Washington Monument. Suleima gasped. Her fingers tightened around Ari's hand as she looked out upon the crowd already gathered—children alone and with their parents, teenagers and adults, reporters and news crews. Someone had prepared an elaborate stage.

"These are your lists," she said as she reached into the hip pocket of her jeans and drew out several pages of printed coordinates. "Be quick as you can."

Ari took his list and glanced at the first coordinate. He'd studied pictures of each destination and knew the numbers. Nodding to Suleima, he shifted.

On a street corner in Belfast, he found twelve children waiting with a priest and a minister. They cheered and waved familiar flyers as he appeared among them. "Join hands," he called, and when all had joined hands, he shifted them across the Atlantic to the mall.

In front of a school in Manila, he found 40 children waiting with five teachers. He shifted, leaving them beside the Belfast group. In Kyoto, on the Bridge of Dreams, 130 students greeted him. Over a thousand youngsters with their parents waited in Trafalgar Square. Ari shifted them in two groups, and his heart soared.

Not to be outdone, Abraham raced with a similar purpose. From Tel Aviv, he teleported seventy-five children with their rabbis, and from Jerusalem, another hundred. In Oman, Jordan, a throng of 200 waited with eager faces. From Nairobi, three hundred and twenty-six students came, and from Buenos Aires another three hundred.

Suleima worked her own list, collecting groups from Los Angeles, Seattle, Albuquerque, and Mexico City, from Wichita, Kansas City, Atlanta and Bangor, Maine. Her course took her across the continent and into Canada, to Vancouver, Montreal and Toronto.

The crowd on the mall swelled, and as news crews spread the word, still more people came from around the city and the suburbs.

On the perimeters, black vans drove slowly, and dark-suited figures prowled among the gathering.

When the long lists were completed, Ari and Abraham and Suleima reconnoitered in the shadow of the Washington Monument once again. Suleima looked pale and tired, but her large eyes burned with determination. Abraham was flushed with excitement. The Jewish boy who once couldn't keep his shoes on beamed with pride as he looked out at the crowd. His gaze fastened on the stage and the banks of microphones. "This is what you wanted for your birthday," Abraham said. "It's months late, but your *better* world starts here. Just talk to them. They're ready to listen."

Ari began to tremble, and he felt sick in his stomach. A flood of doubts washed over him as he gazed outward. So many people! He didn't know what to say. Abraham and Suleima were educated; they were the smart ones. He was only a boy from the Iraqi streets. "I don't . . ."

Suleima put a hand on his shoulder. "Yes, you do," she said. "Speak for your sisters. Say what they can't say." She leaned close and kissed his cheek.

Ari blushed with embarrassment as he touched the place where her lips had made contact. "We started this together," he said finally. "Let's finish it the same way." Laying hands on the shoulders of his friends, he shifted to the stage.

A profound silence fell over the sea of children as expectant faces turned upward. The depth of that silence stunned Ari. His throat went dry. The microphones loomed before him like a metallic forest, and he took a step backward. Suleima slipped her fingers into his. Abraham did the same, and as one they stepped forward again.

Ari swallowed. "We have one message to bring, and it's a simple message." The microphones picked up his voice, magnified it and sent it outward with startling power. "We hope you'll speak that message with us." He swallowed again as he spied the dour face of General Piper near the stage. Ari looked to Abraham for support.

Abraham leaned forward. "Ari is from Iraq," he announced. "Suleima is from Sudan, and I am from Israel." He waved a hand over the crowd. "You are from many places. We want to say to our parents and our leaders—we want a better world."

Suleima leaned forward with stern confidence. "Stop making war on the children!" she demanded.

A loud cheer went up from the masses, and young voices echoed her demand, turned it into a chant that rolled across the mall in endless waves.

Emboldened, Ari looked directly at General Piper as he shouted into the microphones. "And if you won't stop"—he thrust a finger at the general—"then we'll stop you! We'll take away your toys the same way you take away ours! Wherever you send your planes, we'll send them back. Wherever you send tanks, we'll send them back. You raise us to be responsible! Now we have to teach you responsibility!"

The crowd fell silent once again, and Ari hesitated. He wasn't a speaker. He was just a boy. An orphan. He didn't know what else to say to so many people. But somewhere down among all those children were others with a power inside them that only needed to be awakened and nurtured. It would take time to find them. Maybe he wasn't a speaker. But he could be a teacher.

"I only have one more thing to say," he said, finding strength and resolve again. "One month ago, I promised my friends that I'd build a new peace monument on this mall. I mean to keep that promise now."

Without another word, Ari shifted, reappearing on an airfield in Hamedan, Iran. Startled soldiers scrambled as he placed a hand on the fuselage of a Shafaq jet fighter, but they were too slow to stop him. He deposited the aircraft at the feet of Lincoln's statue and, without a pause, shifted again, this time to another airbase at Heliopolis outside of Cairo, Egypt. He touched the wheel of a French-made Mirage 2000 fighter. It was a tremendous weight to shift even for him, and the effort left him panting.

But he wasn't finished. With Suleima's help and a library computer, along with lessons his uncle had taught him, he'd made his plans. His next shift took him to Israel's Southern Infantry Base in Shomryyi. With a wave to a crew of maintenance mechanics, he leaned against one of their prized Merkava Mark IV tanks and shifted.

Ari's head began to throb, and as he set the heavy tank on the lawn at Lincoln's feet, he sucked a deep breath. Television crews were closing in, but he beckoned them away. "Stay back!" he shouted. "Leave me room!" Then, despite the growing strain, he shifted yet again.

He reappeared at a U.S. base in Asadabad, Afghanistan in Kumar Province. For a brief moment, he thought of a secret jihadist camp not a hundred miles away in the mountains where he'd found and rescued Abraham, but that wasn't his target this time. Reaching out, he touched an American Stryker fighting vehicle. Someone shouted, and a bullet ricocheted on the pavement. Ari smiled and shifted away.

Back on the mall, the crowds were running to see as people took note of what was happening near the Lincoln Memorial, but Abraham and Suleima were warning them back, and a huge ring was quickly beginning to form.

Sweat poured down Ari's face, and he cried out with pain as he shifted yet again. An instant later, senses reeling, he fell to his knees on hard-packed earth. "Home," he murmured. Weary and aching, he looked up and searched the gloom for the ghosts of his mother and sisters. He heard their whispers in the shadows, and echoes of old laughter, and smelled half-remembered cook-smells over the lingering acrid stench of smoke and fire.

Stubbornly determined, Ari got to his feet and placed one hand against a wall. He sensed its mass just as he had sensed the mass of the fire truck. Then, moving to a corner where the bombs had done the least damage, he stretched out his arms and touched two walls at the same time. With a grimace, squeezing his eyes shut tightly, he shifted.

A warm beam of sunlight on his face caused him to open his eyes again, and he gazed up through the great hole in the roof to the blue sky beyond. Shadows and ghosts were gone. So was his headache and pain. Wiping the sweat from his face, he went to the shattered threshold and stepped out into bright day. A vast ring of silent people and cameras to numerous to count greeted him. Beyond, ominous black vans sat parked, motionless.

The imposing Merkava sat in front of his door, and the sleek fighter jets on either side. Pursing his lips in satisfaction, he walked a few paces over the green grass and turned to see the Stryker in the rear. Finally, he gazed up at Lincoln, all white marble and glittering in the sunlight, then back at his own handiwork.

Four mighty weapons with guns all trained on his small home. It was not an attractive sculpture, Ari thought, but it made his point.

THE APPRENTICE

Catherine H. Shaffer

As Princess Sari stood bound to a wooden post, with a dragon staring her down across a moonlit clearing, she realized it was time to change her major. She'd had a lot of time to think, waiting for the dragon to eat her. Damsel in Distress was not at all an improvement upon Ugly Stepsister. She was running out of departments that would accept females. She had been assured that Damsel was a respectable degree, not just a place to wait for Prince Charming (or at least Prince Inoffensive) to rescue her. But as far as Sari was concerned, being recruited for post duty by a scruffy Alchemy geek was the last straw.

Sari leaned sideways as far as her bonds would allow to peer up the hill at her "rescuer," Ivan Quickblade. He sat in a desultory heap on the ground surreptitiously munching on cookies. "Are you about ready?" she called. "It's five to twelve!"

This dragon was a large one, probably a full ten feet long, with a lovely fringe framing a well-proportioned head. Ivan had assured her there would be no danger whatsoever. It was part of some kind of alchemy experiment for his master's thesis, and he'd promised her six silver hobs in exchange. That was equal to a week's pay at the grog kiosk.

But there was the very small fact that normally harmless dragons would eat young women like herself at midnight on the night of a full moon, and Quickblade's dragon-slaying sword, the Roury Super-slasher 9000, seemed to have malfunctioned. Sari's boredom had gradually developed into apprehension, with vague signs around the edges that might soon develop into stark terror, the likes of which would do her Intro to Distress professor proud.

At the stroke of midnight, the dragon moved forward, its snout even with her face, and deeply inhaled. Then, with a quizzical look on its face, it said, "The deal's off, Quickblade. You'll just have to get the secrets of dragon magic from some other sucker."

Ivan trotted up the hill and glared at Sari. "I thought you said you were a virgin."

"I am!" Sari said indignantly. She looked at the dragon. "Of course I am! Unless . . . well you can't possibly be counting that!"

The dragon shook its head. "What a disappointment." It scampered downhill, then spread its wings and took off.

Sari was fuming. "You made a deal? With that thing? You were going to let it eat me? In exchange for teaching you about dragon magic?"

Ivan shook his head. "Of course not. No, I was just stalling for time. The Roury was malfunctioning, you know." He was definitely lying.

Ivan untied Sari's ropes, and she shook them off angrily. Ivan opened his mouth to say something.

"Don't talk to me." Sari stomped off down the hill, heading for her dormitory.

* * *

More than a year later, Sari sat tapping her quill glumly on the edge of her desk. Partitions set her off from hundreds of other workers, all huddled in the sunless depths of DataMagics Incorporated. She was working on a document describing how to turn a turtle into a cat, but feeling uninspired. A crystal ball the size of a prize-winning pumpkin sat on her desk, and blinking icons floated inside it, alerting her of users who had forgotten their wizardnet passwords. Sari was studiously ignoring a series of increasingly urgent pleas for help removing popup windows advertising enhancement enchantments from the VP's ball.

"May I have a word with you, Miss Royalanishka?" the boss said, poking his head around the corner of her partition. He was a middle-aged man with a round, red face and a fringe of wildly curly hair framing a bald head.

"Of course, Stu," Sari said. "What is it?"

"It's this change request, Your High—I mean, Miss." Sari had asked him not to use any titles or honorifics in the workplace. He was a slow learner.

"Is something wrong with it? I tested my bug fix, and it worked perfectly. You see, I noticed that the numbering went from line one thirty-three to one thirty-five. Skipping one thirty-four caused the spell to go into a loop at line four hundred, here." Sari pointed to the relevant spot in the scroll Stu held in his hands.

"It's wonderful. Very good," Stu said. "Exceptional. But there's a problem. You see, we don't make *changes* here. It disrupts the work flow." He said the last part quietly, as if afraid that the delicate work flow of the surrounding cubicles might be disrupted right at that moment. "You're not supposed to proactively make a change without buy-in from upper management. If you want to renumber the lines of a spell,

you need to fill out a 'Request for Line Number Reas-·
signment Form.' " Stu pulled a scroll from the bundle
under his arm.

Sari took it. "I suppose I could do that . . ." she
said.

Stu handed her two more scrolls, one goldenrod and
one pink. "In triplicate, please."

Sari blinked. "And what happens then?"

"Oh, we'll have a change review meeting to see if
the whole team is on board—that only takes about
a fortnight, and then we'll assign you a new set of
line numbers."

"But I don't need a new set of numbers. I know
which numbers to use."

"I'm sure you do, Your—I mean, Miss Royalanishka," said Stu. "Thank you for your patience. We
have a certain way of doing things here that we like."

"Who likes it?" Sari said, glancing around at the
cubicles filled with sullen, long-faced workers who
barely lifted their heads unless it was for free food.
But Stu had already turned and was waddling away,
pretending not to hear.

Sari slumped into her chair and sighed, tossing the
three scrolls into the pile on her cluttered desk.

An hour later, she was still sitting with her head in
her hands, thinking of different ways to torment her
politely incompetent boss, when a murmur rippled
across the hall, passing from one cubicle to the next.
Chains clanked as workers moved from one end of
their cubes to another to tell each other the secret.
(Sari had asked to be chained to her desk, just like
everyone else, but Stu kept "forgetting.")

Soon, a head popped up over the wall to her left.
"Hostile takeover," whispered Fafnir. He had a mop
of red hair and skin marked by acne scars and freckles.
He looked like he was twelve years old, but Sari knew

he'd be promoted ahead of her. They always were. She'd been working on Stu, trying to convince him that she wasn't going to run off and get rescued by Prince Inoffensive, scared off by a ferret, or discouraged by a mayonnaise jar that she couldn't open.

"You don't say?" said Sari. She peered over the wall behind him, trying to see as far as the main doors. Sure enough, there was a faint banging. "Battering ram?"

"Yep," said Fafnir. "D'you reckon they'll kill us or sell us into slavery?"

"Worse," said a voice from the other side of the cubicle. Morris was an older man, nearing retirement. "They'll downsize us. Mark my words."

"No!" cried Fafnir. He threw himself to the floor of his cubicle in dismay. "I'm too young to be downsized."

"And I'm too old," Morris said.

Sari sat down with a slight smile on her face. She tore the Request for Line Number Reassignment Form into tiny pieces.

Morris had been right. They downsized the entire department. Fafnir had found a job shoveling pig manure for a fraction of his former salary. Morris had hanged himself.

Sari stood in her best traveling silks, disconsolately waiting for her carriage. This was the end. *The end.* Of course, it wasn't as bad as the time two of her older brothers made her climb down the highest tower in the castle on a rope made out of bed sheets. And it wasn't anywhere near as humiliating as the time her sister Patsy had slipped tincture of trotwort into her mulled wine on the Eve of the Solstice Festival.

But still, she'd have to go home to her father's castle and let him find a husband for her. He'd gloat, saying that he knew a woman could never make it out in the real world, then he'd offer to open a mayonnaise jar for her, and eat all the cookies that were supposed to be saved for later.

"Are you staying for the melee?" said Fafnir.

"What melee?" Sari asked.

"You didn't know? Old Augustine Margrove is hosting a magical melee later today. The winner will get a chance at a job in the new company."

"Why wasn't I told about this?" Sari demanded.

Fafnir shrugged and looked away. "Maybe you were powderin' your nose."

Sari fumed. She knew that Stu had probably passed the word down to the workers, and had most certainly left her out of the loop deliberately. Stu was getting downsized, too, but the look on his face when he saw Sari dressed for travel was one of naked triumph. He had never believed that Sari belonged there.

"*Will* I be here for the melee?" Sari muttered. She took off her gloves and threw them on the ground. "I'm going to be *in* the melee."

Sari stood at the edge of the crowd, waiting for the magical melee to start. She wanted to stay away from the center, and keep her rivals from getting behind her, at the very least.

A robed wizard in a conical cap lit a firecracker to start the contest, and Sari dove in. Most of the other competitors were ordinary magic users. Sari had been called in numerous times to reset their lost passwords, perform administrative rites on their systems, and remove viruses and spyware from their crystal balls that they'd stupidly installed on their own. She mowed them down disdainfully, deflecting their petty charms with a flick of the wrist.

The fallen were carried off and fanned back into consciousness. As the field narrowed, Sari edged into the heart of the fray, challenging stronger opponents already tired from fighting each other. Too angry for chivalry, she took many of them from behind. Stu saw her, and his eyes widened. He had another man in a headlock, and was muttering some kind of chant. Sari blasted both of them with a love spell. She barely had time to watch their eyes fill with stars as they slid to the ground before another opponent was on her. The fighting became more intense, and Sari was twice almost eliminated by stray bolts intended for others. One huge magician they called the Brick kept rushing her bodily, grappling for her even as she tried to weave complicated spells. She dodged him again and again, trying to land a stunner on him before he knocked her flat. When she finally got him, he keeled over slowly, like a tree felled by a lumberjack. She turned to face the next opponent, and found herself alone.

The crowd roared her name. She could see Fafnir waving his hat. Sari tossed her hair back and held up her arms, throwing kisses to the people. She was a princess. She knew how to work a crowd.

Sari's next few days passed in a whirlwind as a team of handlers whisked her away to Margrove Tower for the final confrontation between the DataMagics champion and the Margrove Champion.

"Who is he?" Sari asked one woman who was stitching seed pearls into the hem of her dress. "Is he a great wizard?"

The woman shrugged. "He's . . . inoffensive," she said.

Another woman stood behind Sari, braiding her

hair. "You won't beat him, you know. He's got all of Margrove behind him. Don't worry, though. It's an honor just to be nominated."

"Of course I can beat him," Sari said. "As a woman coming up through the university, I had to work twice as hard as any man just to make passing grades. No one ever gave me a break, no one ever accepted any of my excuses. It was always ridiculous old stereotypes like 'Women are all afraid of ferrets,' and 'Women can breathe under water like fish.' " Sari's words were bold, but there was a knot of uncertainty in her stomach. When Sari had sent word to her father that she wasn't coming home after all, he had sent word back for her not to bother. Really. She had been disowned. It wasn't a game anymore. If she didn't win this competition, she could end up like Fafnir. Or Morris.

"Those aren't stereotypes," volunteered the seamstress. "I'm truly afraid of ferrets. Horrible, toothy creatures." She shuddered.

Sari turned to look over her shoulder at the hairdresser. "What about you? Are you afraid of ferrets?" she asked.

"Where?" the woman cried out in alarm. She grabbed her skirts and jumped up onto a nearby settee, peering at the floor suspiciously.

When Sari finally stepped into Margrove's banquet hall on the eve of the competition, it was lit up with thousands of candles. The guests were already seated, awaiting her arrival. In their brightly colored silks and finery, they looked like a flock of birds. Frescoes decorated the gold-trimmed walls. It was far more sumptuous than Sari's father's hall, where the youngest royal siblings were often wrestling with the dogs over leftover scraps of food.

And at the head of the table, the Lord of Margrove

Castle, Inc. presided. "Princess Sarinalova, welcome to our table!" he boomed. A smattering of applause followed his remarks as the courtiers sensed that Margrove was pleased about something and that they ought to follow his lead. Margrove had the appearance of an older wizard who had used his craft to maintain the illusion of youth. His voluminous blond curls were a jarring contrast to his pasty skin—thinly covered with actor's face paint to conceal the lines of age. He had a jocular appearance, and a waistline that was surreptitiously attempting to escape from his tightly belted tunic.

Sari's stomach growled at the sight of so much food laid out on the table. There was roast fowl, leg of lamb, beef, turtle, tureens brimming with hot soup, crusty bread, creamy cheeses, and dainty fruits— enough to serve hundreds of guests.

"And welcome, also, my beloved shareholders and investors. You are about to witness an historic competition. I have searched the land far and wide for the most able young wizards (and witches)," he gallantly nodded to Sari, "to compete for the privilege of becoming my apprentice. Now, here before you I present Princess Sarinalova of the most noble nation of Shgvsmx . . ." he glanced at Sari. "Have I pronounced that quite correctly, my dear?"

"The x is silent, my Lord."

"–Aha! And here, ladies and gentlemen, is Margrove's own champion, Sir Ivan Quickblade."

Sari felt her jaw drop as she turned and saw Ivan standing behind her. "You?" she said.

Ivan offered her a slight bow, and a smile as if they shared a hilarious secret.

Sari wanted to kick him in the shins. He was ruining her fun. A moment's reflection, though, made her realize that it would be eminently satisfying to defeat him in Margrove's competition. Sari returned his smile tightly and curtsied. Then they both were seated for the banquet.

Sari was eager to begin the competition, but it seemed that it was to be delayed until after the banquet, and all of the business thereof. First all of the courtiers at the banquet, who were shareholders, voted to give themselves more dividends. Then followed presentations by the board of directors.

While the shareholders applauded, Sari whispered to Ivan, "What are you doing here?"

"What are *you* doing here?" Ivan said. "Last time I saw you, you were a clueless undergrad."

"Last time I saw you, you had made a bargain with a dragon involving *my life*."

"You really hold a grudge, don't you? Listen, I've changed. I left the university with my Master of Magic degree and have been working for Buzz ever since."

"Buzz?"

"Oh, yes. He likes his friends to call him Buzz."

"Don't think for a minute I'm going to take it easy on you because you're a friend or something," Sari said. "Because you're not."

"Now," said Lord Margrove, his voice rising above the excited chatter that had followed the last presentation, "For the main attraction of the evening, I give you Lady Sari and Lord Ivan, the two finalists for Apprentice!"

Sari and Ivan stood up while the courtiers applauded. Sari smiled widely, feeling as if her cheeks were going to seize up. Ivan looked genuinely pleased and relaxed.

"The two of you will now retire to my library. It is the largest library in the known world. You will have ample resources there to write a proof of my latest mathemagical theorem—" Margrove pulled two scrolls from the front of his tunic and handed one each to Ivan and Sari. "The first one to present me with the completed proof will receive the antidote to the poison you have just taken."

Sari jumped back, spilling her wine and throwing her plate away from her.

Ivan tipped up his empty wine chalice and stared into the bottom of it, as if it contained some mystery only he could perceive. Then he set it down and turned to Margrove.

"How long?"

"You have until dawn," he said. "I apologize for the inconvenience—"

"Like hell!" Sari shouted at him.

"—but it was the only way. There can *be* only One. For the winning contestant, your proof will be copied by hundreds of calligraphers and sent to every wizard in the land. Your fame will spread far and wide, and you will be wealthy beyond imagining. You will become my apprentice, and co-owner of intellectual property on my new theorem, which we will use to spinoff a new company, go IPO, and then reacquire it, plunder the technology, fire all the employees, outsource everything to Hindutania, and achieve world domination!" Margrove pumped his fist.

"What do you mean by 'there can be only One?' " Sari asked.

"It is written!" said Margrove.

"Where?" Sari asked. "It doesn't make any sense. Aren't there are least two? A master and an apprentice?"

Margrove affected a merry chuckle. "Isn't she charming? Have some wine, Princess. Now, where were we?"

A servant in highly ornamented livery appeared from behind a screen. "This is Reginald," said Margrove. "He is my most trusted servant. He will show you to the library. You may ask of him anything that you require. When I am gone, and one of you is master in my place, Reginald will serve you also." Reginald, who stood behind Margrove, distinctly grimaced. He stepped forward and made a small bow. Sari recognized him from the hostile takeover at DataMagics. He'd been the one grimly walking down the corridor of cubicles handing out pink slips. Sari shuddered.

"What happens to the other?" said Ivan. "The one who doesn't solve the proof?"

Lord Margrove shook his head sadly. "I'm afraid you must publish or perish."

Margrove's library was a circular chamber six stories tall, lined on all sides with shelves of books that stretched up to the ceiling. In the center of the room stood a round marble table. A chandelier hung over the table, on a chain that stretched all the way up to the ceiling. Two ladders ran up opposite sides of the chamber.

Sari paced around the table, her arms crossed over her chest and her mind racing. The shelves at her shoulder were loaded with texts in all of the classic hard sciences—alchemy, thaumaturgy, astrology, necromancy, and herblore. Many of them were in ancient languages, and had leather bindings so old they were cracked and powdery.

The door they had entered through was locked. Sari looked up. "Is that glass at the top of the room?" Sari asked. "I think I see stars."

Ivan craned his neck, staring up as if out of the bottom of a well. He glanced at the chandelier, then back at the ceiling. "It's a mirror. That's light reflected from these candles. See how they sway? The 'stars' are swaying, too. Lumifiber cables run through the chain that supports this chandelier. Sunlight comes in through the side windows, and then is reflected by the mirrors onto a collector, and runs down this chain. In the daytime, this room will light up like the prairie at high noon."

Sari squinted up, then rubbed her chin. "Someone's covered the windows. They're completely black. The moon was full last night. There should be moonlight. This place should be full of moonlight."

"Why would anyone cover up the only windows in a room like this?" said Ivan.

"Dark wizards like a dark fortress," Sari speculated. With a thoughtful frown, she said, "Do you think it's symbolic?"

"What?" Ivan said.

"The glass ceiling."

"I don't know what you're talking about," Ivan said.

"The glass ceiling?" Sari said, with emphasis. "You know, the invisible barrier that keeps women from being promoted to positions of authority in an organization? Tool of the patriarchy?"

Ivan rolled his eyes. "That's a myth. If there were such a thing, someone would have told me about it."

Sari huffed. "You're just another male chauvinist, blind to the oppression in the system." She plopped down in a chair, unrolled a fresh piece of parchment and began to scribble on it.

Sari crumpled her sheet of parchment and threw it on the floor with her previous false starts. Ivan was sitting opposite, studying the theorem. "It has something to do with the elemental superiority of air over water," he said.

"It's fire over water, water over air, air over earth. Look it up," Sari shoved a heavy volume across the table.

Ivan cursed and scribbled out his page, then wadded it up and threw it on the floor with the rest. He looked up at Sari. "Thanks."

"I'm not helping you," she said. "I just told you that because you're hopelessly stupid." Sari answered. "Wait. Look at me, Ivan."

"What?" Ivan looked up. His skin was sallow and the whites of his eyes were yellow.

"You're jaundiced!" Sari said. "You're turning yellow!"

"What?" Ivan said, clearly alarmed. "Where?"

"All over. How about me? Do I look yellow?"

Ivan squinted at her. "Kind of hard to tell . . . yes, you do look a little yellow."

Sari stood up excitedly. "That means we took a poison that unbalances the bile humors . . ." She walked clockwise around the table, muttering, "Bile, bile, bile . . ."

"I don't feel so good," Ivan said. "Feel my forehead. Am I hot?"

Sari ignored him. She was trying to remember all of her herblore. Was it wolfsbane or snowdrop that cured chest pains? Oil of armadillo or hair of hyena for the bloody flux? Somewhere there was a cure for this poison, if she could only remember.

Sari put a hand to her head. She was feeling dizzy. She leaned on the table, trying to regain her balance, and belatedly noticed that Ivan was snooping in her proof. "Stop that!" she barked. She grabbed her parchments and hugged them to her chest.

"I think there's something wrong with this theorem," Ivan said.

Sari slumped into a chair. Her head was pounding. "Me, too," she said. She glanced sideways at Ivan. She was uncomfortable admitting any weakness to her competitor, but she, too, had grown certain that the theorem was wrong. "I can't seem to solve it. It's like there's something missing."

Ivan got out a fresh sheet of parchment and started working. "Maybe we should work together on it, just until we can figure out what the error is. Then we'll finish on our own and may the best man, er, person win."

Sari shook her head. "I don't know. How can I trust you?"

Ivan returned her gaze for a long moment. "You can't," he admitted. "But I'm not the one who poisoned us and locked us in this room with a phony theorem. If we don't figure out what's going on, we could both end up dead."

Sari sighed. "Okay, but once we get the theorem straightened out, it's every man, er, person, for himself. Er, herself."

"It's a deal," Ivan said. He held out his hand.

Sari gingerly took it and shook.

"Tell me something, Ivan," Sari said. "You don't seem very upset about all this. The kidnapping, the beating, the poisoning . . . don't you care about anything?"

"I guess I got used to it in graduate school," Ivan said. "My roommate got thrown into a pit with live alligators while he was writing his dissertation."

"I fell into a pit with alligators once," Sari said. "My little sister pricked my horse with a hatpin."

Ivan nodded. "And my friend Gary had two of his fingers chopped off while taking qualifiers. That's just the way the world works, Princess. Like it or not."

"Is that why you're so morally bankrupt?" Sari asked. "Is it why you were ready to sacrifice me to save your career?"

Ivan closed his eyes. "You'd have done the same thing," he muttered. "And it's not moral bankruptcy.

It's more of a . . . flexibility. I'll bet you would have done the same thing."

"Really?" Sari said. "No, I don't think so . . . I believe people should succeed or fail on their merits, not their station or their good looks, or who they know, or their . . ." her voice trailed off, then she finished quietly, ". . . sex."

"I agree," Ivan said. "No one should get special treatment because of their sex. I mean, I think it's great that you're here and all, but—"

"What?" Sari cried. "That's not what I meant!"

"Don't take offense, now," Ivan said. "If you want my honest opinion, I'd say you're very nearly as qualified as the men that were passed over so you could be here."

Sari fumed. "I'm here because I earned my way here, fair and square," she said coldly.

"Sure you did," Ivan scoffed. "Look! What's that behind you! It's a ferret!"

Sari jumped. "What? I am *not* afraid of ferrets," she said.

"Are too."

Sari grunted in fury, too incensed to even respond. She crumpled up her latest parchment and threw it on the floor. "Why don't we work on saving our lives before we kill each other, shall we?" She unrolled the scroll with Margrove's theorem on it and studied it closely.

"Toadswallop!" she cursed.

"What?" said Ivan.

"Someone *has* tampered with the theorem," Sari said. "Changed Dirscheim's coefficient for Melgaster's, which means the symbol for starlight here should be sunlight instead. Sunlight!" She looked up at the dark glass windows far above. "Sunlight!"

"But I need Dirscheim's to describe the flow of energy through the ether, so I can carry the nine, here,"

Ivan answered, pointing to the page filled with his scribblings.

Sari grabbed the quill from his hand. "No, you don't," she said. She drew a line through Ivan's entire second page. "You can get straight from here—" she tapped the bottom of the first page, "To here—" she flipped to the top of the third page "—with Zakalik's theorem."

"Yes!" Ivan said. He scrawled a few lines at the bottom of his third page. "You integrate over infinity, and . . . voila!" he pushed back his chair, tipping it up on two legs, and promptly fell over.

"Someone is trying to kill us," Sari said, "But it's not Lord Margrove."

"How can that be?"

"We're both turning yellow. That means the poison is unbalancing our bile humors. Sunlight is the cure for poisons of the bile," Sari said. "Margrove never meant for us to die. Remember what he said."

" 'You have until dawn,' " Ivan recited. He slapped his head. "Dawn!"

"Right," said Sari. "The sun comes up and this room fills with light. We're both healed of our poison, and one of us becomes the Apprentice."

"And the other receives a consolation prize and a trip back to Shgvsmx." Ivan thumped the table. "I knew it!"

"Except that someone boarded up the windows, and threw us off the trail by changing the theorem, making it unsolvable. When the sun rises, we really will be dead because this room is going to stay dark," Sari said. She paced a circle around the table, looking up at the black windows far above.

"Who would do that?" Ivan said.

"Who would want us both dead?" Sari said. "A loyal servant who has been Margrove's go-to man for about a hundred years, who doesn't want to step aside while Margrove elevates some whippersnapper above him."

"There must be dozens of jealous young wizards in Margrove's household . . ."

"But only one with access to these scrolls, *and* those windows," Sari said.

"Reginald!" they both said simultaneously.

"I think I can get us out of here." Ivan emptied his pockets and sorted through the various wires, bolts, and small metal parts.

"Where did all of that come from?" Sari said.

"Left over after I fixed my sword," Ivan answered. He climbed up on the white table and walked to the middle of it, where he could just barely reach the chandelier. The light from its hundreds of candles quivered as Ivan fiddled with it, twisting wires together and screwing on some of the extra parts.

"What are you doing?" Sari asked.

"Light cures the poison, right?"

"Only sunlight," Sari said.

"Right. Candlelight doesn't have enough colors in it. Well, I can use the capacitor from the Superslasher to bypass the lumifiber uptake cable, here, and ensorcell this crystal oscillator to produce a very bright, full-spectrum light. A man-made sun!"

Sari watched while Ivan jury-rigged the chandelier.

"There!" Ivan said. He jumped down from the table and pulled a small, square box from his shirt pocket.

"What's that?" Sari asked.

"Remote. Cover your eyes!"

Before Ivan could activate his sun, the library door burst open. Half a dozen armed men spilled into the room. One of them pointed a hand-held immolator at Ivan and fired. Ivan jumped out of the way of the flames, and his remote control went flying. The pile of crumpled parchments on the floor burst into flames.

The other guards came around the table at Sari. She jumped up onto the table, then leapt for the chandelier. Candles tumbled off of it and rolled down to ignite more parchments on the floor. She swung wildly around the room, catching an upside-down glance at Ivan grappling with two of the guards, until she finally clawed her way up on top of it, her skirts billowing beneath her. Ivan was making his way around the room to his remote control device. To distract the guards, Sari grabbed some more burning candles from the chandelier and threw them. Most of the guards scurried to put out the flames on the floor and on their clothes. But one ignored the flying candles and tackled Ivan, who fell with his hand stretched out just inches away from the remote device.

Another guard jumped at the chandelier, and Sari pulled a wand from her bodice and hit him with a stunner spell. The recoil from the spell sent the chandelier into a mad spin, and Sari held on tightly, unable to focus on any of the figures below. As the spin slowed, Sari finally spotted Ivan just as he reached for a four-inch thick volume on herbology from the bottommost shelf and whacked his attacker in the head. "Hurry, Ivan!" she screamed.

"Shut your eyes!" Ivan yelled. The remote was in his hand. Sari shut her eyes and put her arm up over them just in time to avoid being blinded by the sun that burst out beneath her feet. The guards screamed and fell, clutching their eyes. A burning sensation ran through Sari's veins and exploded inside her head. The poison was being burnt out of her system by the bright light.

When it dimmed, Sari heard a dull slapping, rhythmic slapping. It picked up in speed and was joined by dozens of other slapping sounds. She cautiously opened her eyes to see that one entire wall of the library had disappeared and Lord Margrove and his shareholders were on the other side of it, reclining in couches and on pillows, with crystal balls on pedestals all around the room. They were all clapping.

"Bravo!" cried Lord Margrove. "That was excellent! Excellent!" He was laughing so hard his face was red. The shareholders tittered politely.

"Someone help that young lady down!" Margrove said, and one of the guards, who was blinking very hard and obviously having a lot of trouble with his vision, climbed up onto the table and offered Sari a hand down from the chandelier.

Sari mustered her dignity and let him lift her down by the waist.

"What is the meaning of this, sir?" she demanded.

"Yeah," Ivan supplied.

"My new entertainment," Margrove answered. "This has been stupendous. Ever since Reginald invented the crystal spy-eye, we've been having a wonderful time setting up zany situations with unsuspecting guests." Margrove took a handkerchief from his pocket and dabbed at his eyes. "Haven't we, Reggie?"

Reginald stepped forward and made a small bow. "Indeed, sir."

"What's a crystal spy eye?" Ivan asked.

"You're familiar with a standard crystal ball, I assume?" Reginald said.

"Of course," Ivan said.

"Well the crystal ball can be tuned to act as a receiver, and the crystal spy eye, which is really just a miniature crystal ball, is programmed as a transmitter. The ball then displays everything the spy eye sees."

"The chandelier!" Sari cried. "You were watching us through the chandelier. There are hundreds of tiny crystal balls on it." She felt herself flush recalling her desperate upside-down-swinging scramble up onto the light fixture. A rotund man in a ruffled shirt winked at Sari and raised his glass to her. Someone else gave a low whistle.

"You mean this whole thing was a sham?" Ivan crossed his arms. "There was never going to be an apprentice?"

"On the contrary, my boy, that was the only thing that wasn't a sham. And now . . . it's time for me to *choose* my apprentice."

Sari opened her mouth in surprise, but found herself speechless. Her thumped in her chest. The contest was over, and she had either won, or would be sent back to Shgvsmx penniless and in disgrace.

"Thank you, sir," Ivan said, pumping Margrove's hand. "I just want to thank you for giving me this opportunity and I want you to know that I'm a great match for your organization and have a lot of great skills to bring to the table."

Sari gaped at Ivan. He released Margrove's hand and ran his fingers nervously through his hair, straightened his collar, and smoothed his tunic. He flashed a bright smile at Margrove and the assembled shareholders. Sari silently fumed at him. It was obvious that Sari had been the one to crack the mystery of the theorem, and that she'd taken a proactive approach to the problem, while demonstrating decisive leadership skills.

Margrove walked up to Sari, favored her with a stern, fatherly gaze, and pointed an index finger at her casually. Sari felt a flush rising to her cheeks. "Princess Sarinalova," said Margrove. "You lose."

"What?" Sari said.

"I said, 'You lose,' " Margrove answered. "It's my new catchphrase. I made it up for the competition? Isn't it catchy? I like to say it while I flourish my forefinger, like so," he flourished his forefinger. "You lose!"

"You didn't invent, 'You lose!' " Sari replied. "People have been saying 'You lose' for centuries! There's nothing clever or original about that."

"See, that's the kind of negative attitude I don't want around my organization," Margrove answered.

Ivan's face lit up and he stepped forward to pump Margrove's hand. "I can't believe it," he said, beaming.

Lord Margrove slapped him on the back, and began to lead him out of the room. "Let me show you your dungeon," he said. "I think you'll really like it. And we have cookies."

Sari was pressing a seal into hot wax when the crystal ball in the corner winked. "Yes?" she said.

It was Ivan. "Guess what? I presented our proof to the shareholders and it was a huge success."

"No kidding," Sari answered. "I'm happy for you."

"Are you filing papers for your dad?" Ivan asked, squinting into his crystal.

"No," Sari said patiently. "My dad disowned me. I'm stuffing scrolls. My witch's group is having a rally next fortnight, for witch's rights."

Ivan sighed. "You're not still going on about—"

"Yes," Sari said. "I am *still* going on about your old boys' network and your glass ceilings. I realized that what I really want to do is to work for equal rights for witches. That's why I went back to school to major in Witch's Studies. And I'm volunteering all my extra time for the N, double A, W, P."

"You have a real gift for mathemagics," Ivan said.

"I was hoping you'd join us at Margrove Tower. I've almost convinced Lord Margrove that there need not only be One. There could be Two. I'm writing a theorem."

"Tell me, why is it that when a woman makes a good soup, you call her a cook, but when a man does it, he's a chef?"

"Um, I don't know?" Ivan said.

"And why is it that a witch is good enough to make a love potion or cure hemorrhoids, but when you want a ring of power, you go to a wizard?"

"I think my jailer is calling me . . ." Ivan said, glancing to the side.

"I'll tell you why," Sari answered. "Witch's power is not respected. Witch's work is women's work. Wizard's work is man's work. A witch could make you a damn fine ring of power, and a bracelet to match!"

"You're breaking up, Sari. I can barely hear you. Hello? Are you there?" The ball went dark.

"Figures," Sari muttered. "Some men just can't handle a real witch, eh, Gertrude?"

Gertrude the ferret yawned and scratched her ear, then went back to sleep in Sari's lap.

BENEATH THE SKIN

James Lowder

With each blow of the hammer, the wolf pelt shuddered like a still-living thing and gave up a little more of its stolen human shape. The iron nails holding the skin fast to the cottage door seemed to rob it of its unnatural power. Where once the thing had possessed features combining man's and beast's, the final spikes left the pelt looking like any other hunter's trophy, save for its unusual size.

Simon Synge stepped back from his handiwork and, after a moment, handed the coal hammer to the boy at his side. Adjusting the revolver holstered at his hip, he turned to the satchel on the ground. It resembled a cricketing bag, but its contents were intended for anything but sport. Knives, metal flasks, and wooden stakes—all gifts from his mentor, the renowned occultist, Arkady Grin—clattered together as he reached past them to a velvet-wrapped item nestled at the bottom. He whispered a prayer as he unfolded the red cloth, revealing a simple silver cross.

"The final step," he said as he turned back toward the cottage door. "The Lord's mark to—"

Synge's sun-browned hand clamped down on the boy's fingers, crushing them. The boy whimpered in pain as the scholar pulled him back from the pelt. The whimper became a gasp when the child saw the skin straining against the nails where, an instant earlier, his fingers had almost touched it.

"Don't mistake this cursed thing for harmless, Lukas," Synge said sternly, his German tainted by a faint Cornish drawl. "Now go, lad. Get your mother."

As Lukas ran off around the cottage, a mangy dog sprang up from its resting place in the shade and raced after him. Hunger had left both boy and hound sickly thin, and their flight reminded Simon Synge of skeletons on the move. It was not a pleasant image, and the memories it sparked—a nightmarish whirl of all the unnatural things he'd witnessed in his travels with Professor Grin through Asia Minor and North Africa—were more unpleasant still. But Synge did not dwell upon those ghastly thoughts, returning instead to the rite the boy's intemperate curiosity had interrupted. He repeated the prayer and hung the cross's chain on the topmost nail, which he had left jutting from the wood for this very purpose.

Where the silver symbol fell upon the dirty yellow-gray pelt, from the tip of what had been the creature's nose to the space between its eyes, the hair sizzled and burned. Foul-smelling smoke drifted up. The skin bucked and spasmed. One of the iron nails slipped a little and the door groaned, but after a moment the struggle ended, with the wolf pelt still securely splayed.

"So long as the cross remains in place, we've robbed the thing of movement," the scholar explained to Lukas and his mother, when the two arrived a moment later. He glanced at the dirt on the woman's dress, caked from where she'd knelt beside her husband's grave. "You noticed nothing odd about the earth over his body, Frau Metzger?"

The young widow shook her head, the movement slow and mechanical.

Synge nodded. "Then we're in control. So long as the wolf skin—"

"Wait," Frau Metzger interrupted, then scowled at the sound of the small voice keening pitifully within the cabin. "How long has she been crying?"

The scholar's thick eyebrows knit in consternation. "Crying, you say? Who—? Ah, the infant. I have no idea. I hadn't noticed. . . ."

"I'll see to her, Mama." Lukas hesitated when he got to the door, uncertain if he should touch even the wood upon which the pelt was hung, until Synge pushed it open for him. "Thank you," the boy murmured, then slipped past.

"So long as the wolf skin remains as I've arranged it," the scholar continued, "your husband will rest easy. Unlikely as it may sound, had we not fixed it with iron nails and a cross, the cursed thing would have called out for someone else to wear it. And if the skin didn't find someone among the living with a weak enough will, it would have beckoned your husband's corpse from the ground."

Sudden fear dissipated the grief clouding the woman's face, and for the first time since she had witnessed her husband's death at Synge's hands, she met the scholar's cold blue eyes. "You said that you saved him." Tears streamed down her hollow cheeks. "You said that his soul—"

"Is now in God's hands. Yes, that's so. But the flesh is the devil's realm, even after the heart stops and the spirit flees." He waited for the widow's sobbing to subside before he concluded: "You must be strong, Frau Metzger, and ready to do whatever the Lord requires of you. The first victory is ours, but there may be other battles yet to fight."

Lukas came meekly to the door, the squalling infant cradled in his arms. "She's hungry, Mama."

"Excuse me, Herr Professor," the young mother said. She cupped her son's face with her hand. "Thank you for being so kind to your sister." Then she took the baby from him and went inside.

Synge did not correct the woman; he was no professor, merely a disciple trying to carry on the work of his dead mentor. He owed Grin that much after Tunis, when the night things exploited his inexperience and his youthful sentimentality, and got their claws into the old man. He could still hear the professor's agonized screams if he listened closely at any mirror or highly polished metal surface.

Synge put the boy to work leashing the hound to a tree near his father's grave. It would be three days before the skin, robbed of a human host, was feeble enough to be destroyed, and they must take every precaution while they waited. The skin itself remained dangerous, of course, but there were even greater threats. The dead man had not been the only lycanthrope in the isolated little valley. The clues that had led the scholar to Metzger suggested at least two more of the hell-touched creatures in the vicinity.

As night descended upon the valley's blighted vineyards and twisted woods, Synge checked the pelt one final time, secured the door from the inside, then settled into a chair by the grimy hearth. At a table nearby, Frau Metzger and her son hunched over the food he had given them from his travel pack. They tore into the bread and cheese as if they had not eaten in weeks, though Synge knew otherwise. True, they'd suffered the usual deprivations plaguing the Rhineland since the Armistice. But for a few days, at least, Metzger had provided them with more than enough food. That, surely, was the lure with which the were-

beasts' pack leader had tempted the idle vineyard
hand: become like us, and you will find enough to
eat for you and your family, no matter how long
the blight withers the vines or how many occupying
soldiers descend upon our land. Metzger had been
passionately devoted to his wife and children. Synge
had recognized that even in the brief time he'd spent
with the man, before the terrible secret was revealed
and the brief battle begun. Such strong emotion was
easy to pervert; Grin used to say passion was the
gateway through which the devil invaded a man's
flesh.

Synge studied the woman and her son. In time, Metzger would have turned them from the righteous path,
too, or devoured them when they resisted. The woman
might have fought him. She knew right and wrong, at
least. Otherwise, she wouldn't have insisted they inter
what remained of her husband's soul-bought bounty
alongside him. Perhaps that was why they ate so eagerly now; they knew this would be the last food to
grace their table for some time.

Frau Metzger noticed the eyes upon her. "Are you
not eating, Herr Professor?" she asked, wiping crumbs
from her face.

"Water will be enough for me tonight," he replied.

Synge continued to watch as the woman cleared off
the table and ushered Lukas to bed. She discovered a
chunk of sausage hidden in his little fist. After chiding
him for his greed, she knelt beside him and together
they prayed. Though he was not listening closely, the
scholar still heard his name among their murmured
reverences.

He nodded in satisfaction. Frau Metzger understood
what was required of them. She would raise her children to do their duty to God, to reap the proper lesson
from her husband's mistakes. She was the sort of wife

Synge might have wished for, had the demands of the Lightbringer's Path, as Grin had called their work, not precluded such attachments. She was less educated than he would have deserved, of course, but that flaw could be corrected.

The boy reminded Synge of his own nephew. The two shared a gentleness of demeanor and could have been friends, had Christopher not fallen prey to the night things. Had Synge not helped put him in the ground four years past, much as he had buried the hunter that very morning. Only this time there had been no hesitation, no revulsion at the blood on his hands.

If these thoughts troubled the scholar as he sat by the cooling hearth, he hid the disquiet well. His breathing was calm, his sleep, when he let it overtake him, appeared to be untroubled by nightmares. His hand remained steady upon Grin's old Webley .455 service revolver cradled in his lap.

Only the soft creak of the front door opening disturbed Synge's rest. At the sound he leapt to his feet and leveled the pistol at the small shape on the threshold, but it slipped outside before he could fire. He hurried to the door, then paused, wary of an ambush. The moon shone brightly, and in its cold white light he could see that the pelt hung quiescent. The locking bar lay next to the door, carefully placed there by someone inside, not shaken from its duty by a would-be intruder. A theory formed in his mind, one confirmed an instant later by the happy barking that rang out behind the cottage.

Synge hurried into the night. He found Lukas, as he had expected to, standing near his father's grave. The tethered hound eagerly nudged the boy, even as it licked its chops in anticipation of another stolen morsel. Fortunately, neither the child nor the dog had dislodged the sword standing as a marker—a moonlight-touched metal cross—at one end of the fresh-turned earth. No damage had been done.

"Inside," the scholar said coldly.

"I thought Shutz would guard Papa better if I fed him," Lukas started to explain, but stammered to a stop when his mother came around the cottage's corner. She had her infant crushed to her chest with her left hand, a hunting knife clutched in her right. The baby, jarred from sleep and shocked by the chill air, began to wail piteously. The rise and fall of the child's cry filled the night.

"We need to go back inside," Synge said. He raked the tree line with his gaze. "The pelt on the door will keep the other night things from invading the house, but we're unsafe out here."

The scholar's concern was borne out a moment later by the hound's ferocious growl and the appearance of a pair of horrible shapes at the wood's edge. It was as if they had coalesced from the air, so abrupt was their arrival. They stood still for an instant only— huge, animal-headed things, part man, part wolf. Their razor-clawed hands flexed in anticipation, and they swayed on two massively muscled legs with knees that bent the wrong way. Then they attacked.

Their footfalls were silent, their movements so incredibly quick they were revealed only in their results. One moment the beast-men stood at the clearing's limit, the next the hound's tether snapped and the animal tumbled broken-backed through the air. Lukas flew off the ground, trapped in the arms of the larger of the two monsters. The beast threw back its wolf-jawed head and howled.

Synge took aim at that gaping, screaming maw and fired. The bullet did not find its mark, though. In the same instant the scholar pulled the trigger, a blur passed between him and his target. The second were-beast jerked to a stop, its unseen charge halted. The creature's right arm hung limp at its side, dangling from a shoulder torn open by a silver bullet. The wolf hide was peeled back from the wound like tattered cloth to reveal bloody human flesh beneath. Shock twisted the monster's face. The expression was almost pathetic.

Before the sound of the pistol's report had died away, the two creatures were gone, vanished as abruptly as they had appeared. Only Lukas's cries for help, growing more distant with each passing second, made it clear that the air had not swallowed them up. Soon those cries were gone, and the only sound to be heard was the shrieking of the infant girl still clutched to Frau Metzger's breast.

"No," Synge said as the woman started toward the woods. She ignored him and staggered on, uttering her son's name in a choked gasp every few steps.

The scholar wasn't surprised by her mad bravery. Some mothers would march into hell itself for their children. Certainly his own sister had done nearly that, in hopes of saving her cursed son, and paid for that impulsiveness still. Her fate—like that of Arkady Grin—was a reminder to Synge that he must count on reason alone to guide his actions against the night things.

He stepped between the young widow and the forest, and leveled the Webley at her face. "No," he repeated.

Frau Metzger's eyes grew wide. "You doom him, then! Damn him as his father was damned!"

"I'll kill him before I allow that to happen," the scholar said. "But that may not be necessary." He lowered the pistol. "If the monsters had intended murder, they would have carried out that grim work here. No, they have other uses in mind for your son. That means we have time to act. . . ."

As Frau Metzger sat sobbing in the dirt with her crying infant, Synge weighed his options, laid them out as Professor Grin had taught him—as if they were elements of an experiment, items to be assessed and valued with a passionless eye. "We must be soldiers in this," he said at last, more to himself than to the weeping woman. "And if we tempt the devil with our flesh, it's no more than we do every day we walk upon God's earth."

He took up the hunting knife from where Frau Metzger had dropped it, studied its edge for a moment to be certain it was sharp enough for the task at hand. Then, satisfied, he methodically set about his work, drawing out the iron nails with which he had fixed the wolf pelt to the cottage door.

His feet did not touch the ground as he ran, and the vines and bushes and trees shrank back from his touch, clearing the way for his pursuit. It was as if his unnatural form repulsed the natural world. Synge took comfort in that, just as he found solace in the clarity of his thoughts and the dispassionate way in which he could regard his new, hideous body.

The transformation had been agonizing, a twisting of sinew and warping of bone that threatened to blot out his consciousness. He had refused to allow the pain to overwhelm his mind, though. To do so would have been as dire a sin as welcoming the newfound power of his limbs or reveling in his heightened senses. Synge did neither. Instead he focused on the undamaged sanctity of his intellect. The wolf pelt had claimed his flesh, left him a hybrid of man and animal, but it had not touched his soul. He felt no more connected to his body now than he felt at one with the passenger car when riding a train. It was a vehicle, a tool for him to wield in his work.

He took in the landscape with his inhuman senses. The tracks left by the monsters—the sights and sounds and smells of their passing—were leading him toward the Rhine. This was as he had expected. Local legends had drawn him here, and all the stories ended with the accused lycanthrope, like the infamous Stubbe Peeter, tossing away the belt or skin that granted him the power to take on a beast's shape. And the place where the cursed pelt was hidden away on the eve of the sinner's execution was always near the Rhine.

Why the evil should rear its head now was no mystery to Synge. The Rhine was beset by the same chaos wracking Middle Europe in the aftermath of the Great War. While the downtrodden starved in the countryside and the conquering armies scrambled to claim whatever arms the Kaiser's defeated troops had abandoned in their retreat, rich industrialists rebuilt shattered castles into palaces overlooking the river, just as Bismarck and his bloody-minded confederates had done fifty years earlier. Then, as now, the warlords preached the need for order but refused to see that their strivings only furrowed the field for the hell-born. They erected their temples to intrigue, wrath, and greed, while the humble houses of God shattered by their wars remained in shambles, to be overtaken by the wild.

Such was the ruin to which the were-beasts' trail led Synge. Huddled on a ledge high above the Rhine, near the moldering corpse of a barrage balloon escaped from Cologne during an air raid, the holy place was now little more than the unsteady arch of a doorway and four low, tumbled walls. The roof had col-

lapsed long ago and the slate carried off for other
buildings or buried beneath the weeds that had
claimed the once-hallowed ground. Human bones lay
tangled in the undergrowth. Certain bones had been
gnawed, others left untouched. Synge recognized the
pattern instantly; the right was the arm with which
men made the Sign of the Cross, so those bones were
left to decay. The skulls, too, were spared the lycan-
thropes' hunger, because the Holy Chism of Baptism
made them unpalatable. A midden stench hung over
all, a rank odor of offal and rotted meat that made
Synge, with his wolf's sense of smell, wrinkle his snout
in disgust as he approached.

In the center of the ruin, near where the altar had
once stood, crouched one of the monsters. Alert to
the newcomer's scent even over the stink of its sur-
roundings, the guard moved forward. Its right arm still
dangled useless at its side, and its wounded shoulder
gaped black and blasted in the moonlight. As Synge
came through the door arch, the creature growled,
though the sound was more question than threat. The
guard recognized the markings of its pack mate, saw
the confident stride as a sign that the newcomer was
at ease. Yet the smell was wrong somehow. The guard
growled again. This time fear and alarm edged the
angry rumble.

Synge did not hesitate. Capitalizing on the monster's
confusion and alarm, he closed the distance between
them until he was near enough for the other to see
the cross burned upside-down along his snout. Then,
just as the guard opened its jaws to bark a warning,
Synge lunged and drove the thumb of his left hand
into the beast's gaping shoulder wound. The cry of
alarm became a yelp of pain, one silenced an instant
later by razor-clawed fingers. The blow was as precise,

as emotionless, as any surgeon's cut. The were-beast collapsed, its throat torn out, its warning undelivered.

The trail snaked through the fallen church to a rocky slope beyond, where a rift split the stone like a slashed wrist. Synge moved with steady, certain steps to the cave entrance. This had been a hiding place for the priests in other times of trouble. What lurked within the cave now surely had no holiness about it.

For the first time Synge wished he'd brought a weapon. But that simply hadn't been possible. His fingers could no longer grip a pistol or operate a trigger with any dexterity. He might have been able to wield a sword. He was a skilled duelist, as Metzger had learned that morning, and the blade now planted in the hunter's grave had been created for just such battles—forged decades past from a cross by a hunchbacked scholar and a former Prussian soldier devoted to the destruction of the devil's pawns. Yet Synge didn't dare risk taking the blade with him; its presence was all that was keeping the dead man in the ground until the cursed pelt was destroyed.

No, the only weapons available were his wits and the teeth and claws afforded him by his inhuman guise. He prayed they would be sufficient.

The cave's ceiling was low enough that Synge had to crawl a short way before the passage opened up to a wide, tall chamber and he could stand again. No sooner had he entered than he was greeted by the low whines and yips of infant wolves, and the deeper, wavering yowl of warning from a hybrid she-wolf. As his eyes adjusted to the faint light bleeding in from the entryway, he saw the three cubs suckling at the engorged breasts of a were-beast. Farther back in the cave, Lukas Metzger crouched in speechless horror.

Synge edged along the perimeter, closer to the boy.

The cubs seemed to recognize him, their noises happy greetings for their sire, but the she-beast rolled ponderously to her feet and regarded him with baleful yellow eyes. Positioning herself between Synge and her young, she crouched upon her backward-bending legs and snarled until slather dripped from her black lips.

The scholar understood it all. The pups were hers, the product of her coupling with Metzger in beast form. That was why the young mistook him for their sire; they recognized the pelt's scent. But they had no trace of humanity in them, or not enough that they appeared as more than simple animals. To give them the ability to take on a more human shape, to resemble their gruesome parents, they needed a human's skin to wear. As with so many of the blackest rites, the skin of an innocent child would serve the monsters best.

He continued to edge along the cave's wall, giving the she-beast as wide a berth as possible. If he did not menace the cubs directly, he might be able to get Lukas out of the cave. She would not fight unless absolutely necessary, not when a battle might leave the young unprotected.

Lukas cowered as Synge approached; fear had robbed the boy of any other response. The scholar leaned close, reached down with one clawed hand in hopes of turning the child's face toward him so that Lukas might see the cross on his face and understand, but he did not get the chance. The pups whimpered in fear, even as Synge caught the scent of the last of the monsters—the pack leader—entering the cave. The creature crawled into the cavern and rose up, a foot taller than Synge and muscled like a circus strongman. Around this creature's waist hung a belt braided from the skins of wolves and the faces peeled from thirteen hanged men.

Before he charged into battle, Synge willed himself to speak: "Close your eyes, boy," he rumbled to Lukas, "and lift your voice to God."

Spoken by that monstrous, lupine mouth, the words sounded obscene.

"From the age of the belt I recovered from their leader, it might well be the token of Stubbe Peeter himself." Simon Synge waited for his listener to react. Though she did not, he continued anyway: "I suspect it had been passed from damned soul to damned soul since that infamous man's death in 1590. My dear Katharine, it's likely I've destroyed the last of their kind—in the Rhine Valley, at least."

The scholar's sister seemed not to hear him. Her eyes followed a pair of sparrows flitting among the topiary and statues of the autumn-hued garden. She watched the birds dart and swoop through the gathering English dusk, until they settled on the outstretched wings of a granite angel. "And the boy?" she asked in a sweet voice.

"As I explained, he's safe. He helped me burn the monsters' skins after enough time passed for them to be destroyed."

A frown tugged at the corners of the woman's small, heart-shaped mouth. "No, Simon, not that boy," she said, turning her sad eyes upon her brother. "Christopher. My son. Your nephew. Did you save him yet?"

She had posed the same question to him for four years. But Christopher was dead. Katharine had seen the child's life ended, watched Professor Grin and her brother destroy him as one of the undead. The boy

had been beyond Grin's help, beyond even the help
of the experts he'd consulted—Edward Janus, a fellow
ex-Army officer and scholar of the supernatural, and
a young theologian by the name of Anton Phibes, renowned for his research into curses.

"You know Christopher is gone," Synge said after
an unpleasant pause. "I can't change that. But I swore
to fight the night things in his name, and I have
done so."

"Then you remain dead, too." She leaned away
from him, slid to the far end of the bench, into the
shadow of the stone angel. "I can prove it, you know.
You've no marks on you, Simon. Not even from the
fight with the monsters on the Rhine."

Poisoned with the first hints of hysteria, her voice
rose and grew shrill. The other inmates loitering in
the garden echoed her excitement, and soon the quiet
courtyard rang with the same raucous screams that
filled the cells of the massive, gray-walled asylum surrounding them on all sides.

Synge spoke to his sister calmly, but she refused to
be comforted. "Living things have scars," she sneered.
Curling her blunt-nailed fingers on one hand into
claws, she lunged forward and raked the air before
the scholar's face. He did not blink, did not flinch.
"You see," Katharine screamed, retreating, "you've
no fear of being hurt."

Hysteria gripped her fully now, and a tall, loose-
limbed attendant appeared at her side. "King Laugh
has come to visit, eh? Have you been telling her those
stories again, Mister Synge?"

"Not stories, lessons," the scholar said flatly. "Ex-
amples of how order can triumph over chaos." He did
not explain that the stories were true; he'd learned
long ago that evil's greatest strength was the doubting
minds of even the wisest men.

"Order over chaos?" The attendant snorted a laugh more genial than swinish. "I've not seen it here, even with the flowers and the neat little paths. I've not seen those things cure anyone—though a patient bashes his skull open now and then on one of the statues. That's a cure, after a fashion."

The discord in the courtyard grew, so that the attendant could barely be heard above the cacophony. One of the inmates had begun to burrow into a flowerbed like a mole, while another plucked and ate the leaves from a topiary deer. Laughter continued to pour from Katharine Rowley, a shrieking noise that had no joy or humor in it, just the raucous bray of madness. The sound was multiplied a hundredfold by the madmen crying out through the barred windows surrounding the garden.

Through it all, Simon Synge sat silent and unmoving, his square chin thrust out, his mouth a hard line.

The attendant blew a whistle to summon assistance. "I don't know how you can ignore this riot," he said to the scholar as other white-coated men arrived to gather up the rowdiest of the patients.

"Our reason, properly trained, allows us to conquer all disorder."

The attendant shook his head. "Mine must not be properly trained, then. When they get to howling like this—" he gestured at Katharine, who had drawn her knees up to her chest; she rocked back and forth on the bench, still spewing laughter "—I sometimes throw back my head and howl right along with them."

"We must never give in to that urge," Synge said. His tone was a combination of the scholar's practiced pedantry and the soldier's blunt expectation of authority. "We must make the world inhospitable for the things that feast upon bedlam. We must give the unfortunate victims of madness a light of reason toward which they should move, even as the righteous moves day by day toward the radiance of the City of God. We must heed His voice—"

"Pretender!" Katharine screamed. The hysteria had fled, leaving her sad eyes bright with pain. "God wouldn't speak to you!"

She crawled along the bench on hands and knees, until she was inches away from her brother's face. Seen side by side, so close together, it was clear the weight of the past four years had fallen on the two quite unevenly. The scholar's hair was still the brown of fresh-turned earth, his blue eyes clear, his face tanned and unblemished. His sister looked three decades his senior, instead of a meager three years. Her skin had grown sallow and transparent, where time had not creased it with wrinkles.

"You know nothing of the Lord's will," she whispered.

As the attendant placed a surprisingly gentle hand on Katharine's shoulder and pulled her away from her brother, she tore back the long sleeves of her dress, revealing thickly bandaged arms. "He wills us to take on suffering," she said, her voice a throaty growl. "He wills us to accept pain. . . ."

The attendant tried to stop her when she reached down to pull away her bandages, but she knocked him aside with the strength known only to the mad. With trembling fingers she peeled away the wrappings. Self-inflicted scars crisscrossed her arms, scabbed gouges and ragged tears blotched her flesh. "Even your pain, Simon," she said. "Even yours."

Synge heard the attendant call for a straitjacket, saw him rise up to restrain Katharine. He saw, too, his sister close her right hand over her left arm and grit her teeth against the anticipated pain. The attendants would not reach her in time. There was nothing else to do.

He balled his hand into a fist and struck her in the face.

There was no anger in the blow. The act had been fueled by no more passion than the killing of the bestial guard at the ruined church. It was the action reason demanded.

The attendant checked Katharine's breathing and made certain the blow had only split her lip and knocked her unconscious. To a chorus of screeches and barks from the inmates crowded at the barred windows, the warders lifted her from the dirt. The attendant handed Synge a handkerchief to wipe the blood from his knuckles. The spatter of gore came away as if it had never touched his hand.

"Don't worry, sir," the attendant said. "No one will blame you for what happened."

Synge regarded him with blue eyes as cold and hard as the deepest winter ice. "Blame? To deal with unreason, we must be strong enough to do harsh, even terrible things with a pure heart and clear conscience. When God calls upon us—"

The words died in the scholar's throat when he saw the attendant's eyes dart toward Katharine. Then he heard the Lord's name from a dozen windows, spoken by madmen with fervor equal to his sister's. Equal to his own.

"In any case," the attendant said, "we know you did her a kindness, knocking her out before she could do herself worse harm. That's how we tell the real voice of God from the one these lunatics hear, eh? It's the voice of kindness. . . ."

When he got no answer, the attendant muttered something about having to shepherd the last of the inmates out of the garden and close up the asylum for the coming night. Before he disappeared into the madhouse, he paused and waved with forced politeness to Synge.

"Kindness isn't for us," the scholar whispered into the gloom as the door clanged shut behind the attendant. "It's what we must hope for from God when we're finished with His work."

He suddenly wanted to feel the howling enough that he, too, would howl, that the pain would grieve him so keenly it would batter his heart. It had once, not so long ago. But Simon Synge knew he could no longer allow that weakness—not now, with what he knew about the world—and chastised himself for even that fleeting desire. To put his mind aright, he withdrew a small metal mirror from his pocket and pressed his ear to its brightly polished surface. After a moment he replaced it and, standing alone in the empty garden, listened to the shutters slam closed over the barred cell windows, each one muffling another mad cry, until he was once more like the wide-winged granite angel at whose feet he stood—untouched by suffering and insensible to the sounds of the night closing in.

GIANTKILLER

G. Scott Huggins

*It is presumed by the simple that we legends know no
fear, that we are born into our roles, and take to them
as easily as stud bulls; leaping to duty knowing only
boundless energy and excitement. Those who know
only the Giantkiller's record may be pardoned, of
course. But before there was the Giantkiller, there was
a man called Jack . . .*

From Chapter 1: "The Map's Greatest Legend."
A Man Called Jack: The Early Years. With Cleave Custer.
Singing Harp Press: Happy Valley, MDCXVIII.

And you best not get taken, boy! You hear me?
You just best not!" The shrieks of Jack's mother
followed him up the road with the rising sun. Briefly,
Jack's brow creased in puzzlement; he gazed at the
rope in his hand. To his utter lack of surprise, it
looped around the neck of their cow, Milky-White.
Milky-White stared back at him with an arch look of
contempt.[1] Yes, he was taking the cow to market. The

---

[1]It did not occur to Jack then that arch looks of contempt were
things that cows rarely possessed, and thus seldom gave away.

cow was behind him; he was not behind the cow. Therefore, Jack was doing the taking.

Dismissing his mother's worry, Jack continued along the road to town. Milky-White had stopped living up to the first half of her name earlier in the week, so Jack was taking her to market. It was all very simple: a lovely day's walk in the sun. Trade the cow for some money. A lovely day's walk back. It was all very simple until, just a mile from their door, they ran into Jack and his cow.

Meeting a double of myself on the road was the first inkling I had that things had gone wrong. Wrong? All my instincts were screaming betrayal. In the King's Necessary Anti-Villainy Executive, we are taught over and over again that there are no such things as coincidences. The fact that there are such things as colossal blunders, we're left to learn in the field. There, at the beginning of my career, I was to see what such mistakes could cost. I stepped forward, using every ounce of the cold-steel nerves the gods had granted me to stand there with a dumbfounded expression on my face and greet my double as if I hadn't noticed a thing out of the ordinary.

From Chapter 2: "The K.N.A.V.E. Naïve."
A Man Called Jack

"Howdy, strangers," Jack called out, glad of company on the road. It was a lawful kingdom, of course, but you never knew who you might meet. He stuck his hand in his pouch. There was some cheese with hardly any mold on it, and it cost nothing to be generous, did it? Or was it, it costs nothing to be friendly? Jack often got the two confused. The strangers looked awfully familiar, but Jack couldn't place them. The cow especially looked as if he should know it. Suddenly, he realized what it was.

"Hey," he said to the man. "We're wearing the same clothes!"

The stranger gaped at him for a moment, and then said, in a kind of sad tone, "Most people do, Jack. Roughspun is pretty much roughspun, no matter how you tailor it." He looked behind Jack at Milky-White. "All right, Bulganova, we've found you. Are you going to come quietly?"

Jack looked at the man hard. He'd heard of people talking to cows, or even walls when they were drunk, but those people tended to fall down a lot more. "Who are you talking to? Say, did you notice we're the same height, too?"

"Just your cow, Jack." The stranger smiled reassuringly. "Bulganova there is an excellent cow, and I'd really like her to have this fine cowbell." He pulled a cowbell from his pouch. It was attached to a silver mesh collar. It *was* a very fine cowbell, and the stranger moved past Jack with it. Milky-White backed away from him. Tugging Jack. Jack set his heels in the dirt, but Milky-White tugged harder, pulling him off the road.

This struck Jack as very strange. Normally, people did not stop strangers on the highway and give presents to their cows.

Milky-White is pulling me now. She's taking me off the road. I'm getting taken by a cow. In the desperate terror that can only be produced by abject poverty and drastically upset mothers, Jack called on all his strength and heaved on the rope. Abruptly, Milky-White changed tactics. She cannoned forward past Jack, lunging at the stranger with her horns. He howled in pain.

Jack reacted with the speed of a farmer. "Bad cow!"

he cried and hit Milky-White in the shoulder with his
full weight. She staggered away from the bleeding
stranger. He picked up the silver mesh bell in one
hand, never letting go of the rope. "All he wanted to
do was to give you a present." In one smooth motion
he fastened the bell around Milky-White's neck. She
gave a bellow of protest and jerked to her feet, lunging
at him with a horn, and then suddenly stood looking
blankly behind him, completely motionless.

Jack turned to the stranger, kneeling beside him,
and found his path blocked by the other cow. Who,
now that he could see them together, looked exactly
the same as Milky-White. But this cow was looking
up at him in a fury. "Haven't you done enough?"
she said.

Before Jack could react, another voice said, "I think
you've all done rather enough."

Emerging from the hedge was a dwarf. A dwarf
with a wicked-looking hand crossbow. It was pointed
straight at Jack. Jack had never had a weapon pointed
at him before. Jack had never even seen a weapon
before.[2]

"Don't move, boy," said the dwarf. He looked down
at the stranger with Jack's clothes. "So, the great
James Nulsieben. At last, defenseless. Bulganova
fought well, did she not? One of our side's greatest
agents. I don't know who your double is, but I con-
gratulate him; I've never seen Bulganova enspelled
before, though many tried. Almost fooled us. I hoped
I'd be the one to kill you." He looked from Jack to
his double, grin widening. "But I never dreamed I'd
be so lucky as to get to do it twice."

The stranger—James—was breathing in labored

---

[2]Which nevertheless failed to prevent his testicles from trying to
crawl up his spine with the gratifying speed of seasoned experts.

gasps, blood staining the road. "The boy knows nothing," he got out. "Do you, boy? I knew you were our enemy, Rumpel. But I never thought you'd betray your own kind by siding with giants."

"Really?" said the dwarf. "And why do you think they call me the Stilts' kin? The Giants will make me taller than any of you dream. But enough of this." He turned, pointing the bow at Jack's heart. "Will you die honorably, as your master does, or will you further insult my intelligence by pleading that you know nothing?"

"Oh, no," said Jack. "I've learned that pleading isn't much use in nightmares, and that must be what this is, because I can't see how there could be two Milky-Whites, and even if there could, I don't reckon there's ever been a hedge by this crossroad in real life."

The dwarf turned in surprise. At that moment vines looped from the hedge and gripped the bow, his hand, and his neck. There was a brief contraction of foliage, and the dwarf dropped limp. The hedge contracted, collapsed in on itself and became a dark green figure with long, flowing hair.

Jack stepped forward on quaking feet and addressed the dryad. "Thank you, Miss."

"What do you mean, miss?" the figure said in a brassy tenor. He knelt by James. "Sorry, Jim. Didn't see it coming." He gave the cows a glance. "Well, well. Bulganova. So nice to see you. When were you going to lose the spare, here?" His chin gave a jerk toward Jack.

Milky-White simply mooed.

"Don't play dumb with me!" He picked up the lead and looped a tendril of vine over the cow's neck. "I know that little enchanted bell won't let you move much, but you can talk just fine."

"What are we going to do?" asked the other cow.

"Oh, she's too valuable for hamburger, don't worry. We'll find out everything she knows. We don't often get a chance to interrogate a deep-cover cow."

"Not her," said the other cow, "the mission!"

"What mission?"

"That's on a Things Man Was Not Meant To Know basis!" the cow snapped.

"James is a man. I'm not," replied the green man.

"You can't replace him," she sneered. "Our contact is expecting something that looks vaguely human, not a half-a-dryad."

"That's 'hamadryad,' " said the green man, his voice going cold. "And look who's talking about human."

James coughed and both their eyes fell on him. "I believe that the watchword of the agency," he labored, his own eyes falling on Jack, "has always been 'improvisation.' "

No one would have believed in the last years of the XVIIth century that this world was being watched keenly and closely by intelligences tinier than man and yet with bodies twice the size of a bull elephant; that as men busied themselves about their various concerns they were scrutinized and studied, perhaps almost as curiously as a drooling toddler might scrutinize maggots squirming on a heap of garbage and wonder if they would be fun to eat. Or, failing that, to step on.

From Chapter 3: "The Lore of the Worlds."
A Man Called Jack

"But why," said Jack, as the hamadryad and Milky-White, with James groaning softly from his perch atop her, vanished into the distance, "did we have to trade your Milky-White for real Milky-White?"

"Bulganova," corrected the cow. "We traded me for Bulganova, because she's working for the Giants. Plus, she's quite a deadly fighter. Hey, keep your hand out of that pouch."

Jack had traded pouches with James as well as cows. It was no improvement. James had not packed any cheese.

The cow went on. "We saved your life back there, in case you hadn't noticed. So stay out of the pouch until I tell you."

Jack said nothing, partly because the cow was right, but partly because he was trying to think whether pointing out that he had captured Bulganova would be a good idea.

"All right, other Milky-White."

"And stop that," the cow snorted. "I have a name. It's Philomila." At the sight of Jack screwing up his mouth to perform hitherto unimagined feats of polysyllabic speech, she said, "Phil will do."

"All right, Phil." After a pause, Jack said, "How much do you suppose the butcher will pay for a cow like you, Phil?"

Phil looked at him. "You know," she finally said, "just about any other man, discovering himself to be in the company of a talking cow, would be saying something along the lines of, 'How does a cow learn to talk?' or 'I wonder how much the circus would pay for a talking cow?' Yet you're thinking of the butcher. Why do you suppose that is?"

"Because my mum said to sell the cow to the butcher." Faintly, Jack also thought, *and Mum also said not to get taken, and there's Phil ahead of me*.

"We're not selling me to the butcher," said Phil.

"Then how much will the circus . . ."

"Or the circus."

"How much then?" asked Jack finally.

"Four beans. Haggle. Try to make it five. We don't want him to be suspicious."

"I should take five beans from the man we sell you to," repeated Jack. "And then he will not be suspicious?"

"Not if Bulganova's intercepted reports are any indication," sighed Phil. "Five, four, three, two . . ."

"What giants?" said Jack. "And why were you counting backwards?"

"Never mind, Jack," said Phil. "Have you ever noticed how, on most days, there are great white clouds in the sky that look like castles on the top of mountains, floating above the valley?"

"Yes!" said Jack, pleased that the conversation had taken such an interesting turn. "They look like towers, and hills, and houses . . ."

"And have you ever wondered why that is?"

Jack wrinkled his head in thought. It seemed an easy question. "That's where the giants live?"

Phil stopped dead in the street. "Yes, Jack. It is." She cocked her head, a difficult thing for a cow. "Our local half-a-dryad, pain though he is, did help us stop Bulganova from contacting her agent."

"Why do you call him a half-a-dryad?" asked Jack.

"Because he is," said Phil. "Mom was a dryad; Dad was a man who didn't mind splinters. Cross a tree and a man, and you get a hedge. He's a bit sensitive about it."

"Oh," said Jack. "Are you sensitive about being a cow?"

"No," said Phil. "It's not that much different from life as a princess. Men still drool at the sight of you, of course. On the plus side, it's in the fresh air, and if they do catch you, it's a much shorter and less painful way to go."

"Oh, good," said Jack.

"Irony is just the taste of nails in your mouth to you, isn't it, Jack?" asked Phil. "Anyway, we don't know why Bulganova was meeting her contact, but he's sure to figure out that I'm not her the second we're alone. That'll be the dangerous part, but I can take him. Hopefully, you'll be away with the beans by then; you won't get hurt."

Until I bring Mum home five beans in trade for the cow, Jack thought.

"Oh, hell," said Phil. They were rounding the corner and the village lay before them. "I'm not sure it matters anyway. The giants may invade no matter what we do. Sure as hell we'd invade them if we thought we had a chance."

"Why?"

"Jack," Phil sighed. "You know those mountains in the sky we were discussing?"

"Yes?"

"When the sun sets, what color do they turn?"

"Gold," said Jack. "Oh."

"Just as well we can't get up there. It would be easier for the giants to get down than for us to get up."

"But you can get there, can't you?" Jack said. "Mum told me how a cow jumped over the moon!"

Phil gave him a withering look. "No, Jack."

"No?"

"That was a prototype model, and she burned up on re-entry anyway."

"Where were you princess of, then?" asked Jack.

Phil looked up at him. "You know, Jack, just when I think you're going to forget how the breathing thing works and topple over in the road in front of me, you say something that makes me suspect there's a brain working in there." She sighed. "It was an enchantment a long time ago and it makes an even longer story. Besides, the witch is dead. And we don't have the time. We have a mission to accomplish, which means trading me for these beans: that's the only thing we know about this man Bulganova was meeting. He has beans. Unless . . . ?" she looked up at Jack expectantly.

"Unless what?" he asked.

"Jack," Phil said in a low tone. "You're standing in the lane with an princess who's been bewitched into the form of a cow, who likes strong young guys with a lot of learning potential, and who doesn't particularly want to finish a mission that could well result in her being turned into prime rib." Phil paused. "Princess. Enchantment. Transformation. Happily ever after." She stuck her muzzle up into his face and whispered, "Does that suggest a course of action to you?"

Jack leaned down, his lips moving towards hers.

"Like what?" he whispered back.

I knew that kissing her would have broken the enchantment right then, of course. Had I known Phil then as I know her now—the half-elf assassin acrobat; the agent with nerves of mithril and skin of alabaster; the woman with enough sheer sexual magnetism that you can track her in a city simply by looking which way the statues of the local fertility gods are pointing—I might have done it. But right then, I needed her as a cow. The mission needed her. For only as a cow could she impersonate Bulganova and fool the Bean Man.

From Chapter 5: "Cow of the Wild." *A Man Called Jack.*

"If you don't mind," said Jack, "I'd like to have a few words with my cow before we part."

"Sssure, kid," said the man. His face was completely obscured by the hood of his cloak, and the voice seemed to come out of darkness. The beans he'd handed Jack were large and gave off a heady green smell; he kept feeling like they ought to move when he touched them. Jack led Phil a slight distance away. He knelt down to talk to her.

"Good work, Jack," she said. "Now slip one of those beans inside my collar. We'll get the Technical Section to work on it after I've escaped."

Jack did so. "Will you be all right?"

"Oh," Phil tossed off lightly, "sure, Jack. I've been in lots of worse places than this. Well, at least once."

"What do I do with the rest of the beans?" he asked.

Phil shrugged, insofar as that was possible for a cow. "Just hide them where no one will find them," she said. "Whatever they are, I'm certain they're dangerous."

"Are you sure you'll be all right?" Jack asked. "I don't like the Bean Man. I can't see his face, there. Are you sure he isn't one of those Things That Man Was Not Meant To Know?"

Phil glanced under Jack's arm at the Bean Man. "I doubt it," she finally said. "Probably he's just an engineer who's selling company secrets. They don't get out much. Now, Jack, you're well clear of this. Go home and Forget That Any Of This Ever Happened." Those last words seemed to take on a special resonance, as if they'd been spoken in a large and invisible cave that enclosed just the two of them. He nodded, and handed Phil's lead over to the Bean Man, and then he went home. He felt a bit uneasy at leaving Phil with the Bean Man. But even if he was a Thing Man Was Not Meant To Know, Jack supposed Phil wasn't a man, and there probably weren't many Things Cow Was Not Meant To Know,[3] so Phil was unlikely to come to harm.

The walk home was a blur. It seemed to him that the morning had been a dream. There was something very important he had to remember, and he did eventually remember it, but that was because being beaten systematically and thoroughly by an enraged farmwife who has just discovered that you have traded her only cow for four really odd-looking beans had a way of focusing even Jack's attention.

He did remember that he was supposed to hide the beans where no one would ever find them. So, reasoning that only an idiot would plant crops slap up against the side of the house, he buried them there. When he was done, Jack was sure even he wouldn't be able to find them again. Sore and aching, his mind even blurrier than usual, Jack went to sleep.

I can truly say that the planting of the Beanstalk is the foundation on which my career—no, my entire character as an operative—rests. Those who accuse me of rashness or (and this only shows the depths of jealousy to which mediocre minds can sink) being under the influence of some enchantment have simply failed to think the matter through. An agent like Bulganova would never put her masters' invasion route in proximity to her lair. She must have reckoned with the chance, however small, that some sharp K.N.A.V.E. would recognize her; she could be compromised, the Beanstalk could not. Therefore, this was the one spot in which no Giant would ever expect the Beanstalk to be raised. As Bulganova's absence might at any time be missed, only my bold action would save the day, as they would save

---

[3] Except, perhaps, what makes a really good barbecue.

*many other days. And though I would be called many
things during the course of my career—a rebel, a rene-
gade, and even a damned fool—I would never be called
a coward.*

From Chapter 7: "Jack of All Raids." *A Man Called Jack*

"Jack, what in the name of St. Ignatz' blessed balls
did you do?" The cow's head leaned in through the
window as far as it would go.

Jack awoke and knew he was dreaming, because
he'd sold Milky-White the day before, or at least he
must have, because he'd been going to. Things after
that were a bit fuzzy. But at any rate, cows didn't talk.

"Hello, Milky-White. Are you in cow heaven yet?"

"Cow heaven?" cried Milky-White. "Cow heaven?
I'm in Special Agent Ninth Circle of Bloody Hell! The
one with the Parliamentary Inquiry of Eternity and
the Expense Auditor With A Thousand Briefcases!
What have you been doing, Jack?"

Jack looked around. Yes, he was still in bed, and it
was still dark out. "Sleeping, Milky-White."

"Don't start that again! I'm Phil, remember?"

"No, Phil," said Jack.

"What were you doing before you went to sleep?"

Jack remembered that, a feat he thought he could
be quite proud of, considering that he was being awakened by an angry talking cow in the middle of the
night. "I hid the beans, Phil."

Jack couldn't see very well, but it occurred to him
that sunlight had never streamed through holes in the
roof while it was pitch dark out before.

"You hid the . . . ?" Phil broke off in a splutter.
"Oh, gods. You didn't. You did. This is all your fault.
It's all *my* fault! And you don't even remember be-
cause of my spell. You planted the beans right in their

top agent's safe house! I should have told you to *swallow* the bloody things! You might be dead, but I'd feel better!"

Slowly, Jack arose from bed and walked to where Phil's head poked through the window. The rest of the window was opaque blackness. He had heard of darkness so thick you could cut it, but he never had pictured the darkness as being green. Nor with little veins running up the side.

"Jack," said Phil, in tones of dead calm. "Come outside." She withdrew her head from the window, and sunlight burst through the space she had been. The green surface curved away from the spot.

Jack went out. The snores from the other room of the house told him his mother was still asleep, which Jack considered all for the best.

The Beanstalk obscured a great portion of Jack's personal sky before it disappeared into the clouds. Half the house's roof was missing, pushed aside by the lowest leaves. Jack stared in wonder, mouth hanging open.

"There's a bean sitting in the dungeons of the Emperor," said Phil in a dead voice. "It's being studied by archmages, alchemists, and the wisest of the wise. It could have been planted in secret, where the giants would never have known. Better still, we could have learned how to kill it, just in case they ever managed to plant one."

With a visible effort, she pulled herself together. "All right, Jack. Our one chance lies in surprise. You have to climb up there and see whether the Giants have assembled an invasion force."

"How will I know it's an invasion force?"

Phil was frothing at the mouth. "Because they'll be forty feet tall and have swords the size of castle gatehouse towers! An invasion force of bloody Giants is not a clan-bloody-destine operation!" Phil visibly calmed herself down. "If they have, then just get back down here; you can't do anything. I'll run back to town and see if I can raise the local garrison. We may be able to delay them." She sighed, then continued.

"But if they haven't, Jack, it's time for you to be a hero. Well, to try, at least. What makes the Giants really dangerous . . ."

"Besides being forty feet tall and having swords the size of gatehouse towers?"

"Yes, besides that. They have the Golden Harp."

"The Golden Harp?" Jack asked fearfully.[4]

"The Golden Harp unifies the Giants. Alone, they're dangerous brutes. Marching to the music of the Harp, they're actually an effective army. We don't know why."

Jack struggled for thought. "But why do the Giants want to invade us? Don't they have all the gold?"

"Food," Phil said, chillingly.

Jack thought about this. "But couldn't we just trade them, say, beef for gold?"

"Not if I have anything to say about it," said Phil. "Now climb up there."

"Climb? To the land of the Giants?" Jack was not completely familiar with the territory of fear, as the entrance requirements generally included more imagination than he possessed. But he was learning the lay of the land fast. "I don't think that's such a good idea. The roof will need fixing, you see; Mum's dead set on roofs for houses . . ."

Phil's horn struck so fast that Jack wasn't really aware of pain. Suddenly, he simply found that he'd levitated ten feet in the air and was grasping a vine

---

[4] Though not precisely bright, Jack had already figured out that nouns with audibly capital letters were dangerous things.

frantically with one hand and rubbing himself somewhat lower with the other.

Further down, he saw Phil, horns pointed skyward
and looking determined as only a cow can look. He
considered what loomed above. He considered what
waited below. He heard stirring from the house.

One thing was to be said for the Land of Giants,
Jack considered as he climbed. Mum wasn't in it.

The Giants were asleep, just as I had predicted they
would be; beings that massive could never shed enough
heat to function in daylight. No, they were creatures of
the night. It did not take long to spot their headquarters.
The problem of navigating the land of the Giants lies
not in the intellect, but in the sheer size. Pressing on
toward the castle, any room of which could have
housed a wing of the Imperial Palace, I stole through
the day.

From Chapter 9: "Robbing the Giants' Kingdom:
A Knight in their Fief." *A Man Called Jack*

To Jack's surprise, the only Giants he saw outside
the palace, the two doorwards, were asleep. Their
spears, each fashioned from a redwood tree, leaned
against the wall, and their snoring muffled any sounds
Jack might have made.

Jack had, in fact, been relieved not to find a Gi-
antish invasion force ready to cook *him* in lieu of all
the cows that roamed the plains below. So relieved
that he had almost slid down the vine to tell Phil the
joyous news. But the twinge in his left buttock told
him this might be unwise. He now found himself wandering through the courtyard of the castle, asking him-

self questions like, "If I were a Giant, where would I keep a Golden Harp?"[5]

There is a peculiar kind of fear that only happens to people in childhood, specifically during the part when they are ten years old and exploring, on a dare, the abandoned and almost certainly haunted house on the edge of town, thus risking parental hysteria, peer disapproval, and disembowelment by unspeakable evil. The explorer tiptoes cautiously around a corner, and suddenly feels his foot caught in a sticky, gelatinous mass, which sucks at his shoe. The sensation thus felt, upon discovery that the shoe is not in fact caught in the digestive pseudopodia of a hideous creature that will digest him slowly over millennia, but rather in the droppings of a nomadic and fairly ill dog, is a horror unique unto itself.

But it was a sensation much like this that Jack encountered when he entered the smaller courtyard of the central keep and, ready to be seized and eaten at any time by armed giants, found himself confronted by a large woman in a plaid dress.

"Are you lost, little boy?" said the woman.

Jack stared. She was hardly a Giant at all, no more than twice his size. Jack's rustic manners took over in the absence of conscious direction. "No, ma'am," he said, though his fright made it come out more like, "Nuh, mum."

"Well, I'm hardly your mum, little boy. But I imagine she must be worried. What are you doing wandering about the palace at this hour of the day? Don't you know that the King has set a curfew? Are you lost?"

---

[5]And trying not to ask himself questions like, "What if I have to use the lavatory?"

"Yes, mu . . . ma'a . . . milady."

"Oh, don't start that," said the woman. "It's bad enough going around all night hearing 'Your Majesty' this and 'Your Grace that,' just as if we were those ant-folk down below with their kings and such. 'Mathilda' will do, and I'll just call you 'lad,' as is proper for young Giants whose parents haven't been able to think up a name for them yet, which yours surely can't have done, as young as you are. Come along, and we'll have a midday snack together."

Jack followed Mathilda, who looked so much like his mother that he found it hard not to flinch respectfully in her presence, through the castle's deserted corridors until they came to a great room. The ceiling was sixty feet high, hung with an iron chandelier that could have enclosed an arena. A pair of small bonfires roared in the lamps, and the table was a long trestle, made from sequoia halves sanded flat. The benches along it were as high as Jack could reach. Mathilda reached down and lifted Jack up to one of them. "Now run along to my seat on the end there, and I'll bring you some nice bread and cheese."

It wasn't hard to find Mathilda's chair. It was set next to the biggest chair in the room, a great iron monstrosity that looked as though it had been made out of a thousand sword blades.[6] Mathilda's bronze chair was different. It was piled with cushions, and had steps leading up to it. Jack ascended the chair, and found it no great feat to stand on the table.

In the center of the table was a great bowl of fruit, with grapes the size of watermelons and an apple Jack might have used as a closet. Flanking the bowl, apparently asleep, sat two golden shapes.

---

[6]All carefully blunted. Unlike men, Giants have little use for either masochism or psychosis, even among their rulers.

The first was a great golden hen, with rose gold crest and yellow-gold feathers. She was about half the size of Phil.

The other shape could only be the Golden Harp.

Golden it was, a floor harp of the kind played at imperial banquets. Jack might have been able to lift it. To a Giant, it was a simple handharp. Or would have been had the Harp not already possessed hands. And feet. And the body between them.

The woman was not chained to the harp. She flowed into it, her golden skin blending into the gold of the harp until it was impossible to tell the two apart. Only her hair was not golden; a mass of ebony that curled around her body. She, too, was asleep.

Jack was not familiar with the term "exotic beauty," having been born and raised in the country, where heavy farm work meant that beards were the most reliable way of telling genders apart. But he was dimly aware that here was magic of a sort that sang in the blood. He felt a pounding in his chest.

It took him a moment to realize he also felt the pounding in the soles of his feet, in the planks of the table, and the very air around him. He just had time to sprint the length of the table and glimpse the harp and the hen come awake before he dived into the fruit bowl.

From his place under the grapes, Jack saw the Giant King. On his head was a crown of gold, crudely incised with Giant pictograms. His beard was long and black, and twice Jack's length.

"Queen," roared the Giant King. "What's that I smell? Are you having a man for a snack without me?"

"No, dear," answered Mathilda's voice. "It's just the perfume I'm wearing. Why don't you go back to sleep? It's still daylight."

"I must count my hen's golden eggs," declared the Giant King. The pounding footsteps came closer. Jack got a far more intimate experience with Giant morning breath than he ever wanted as the Giant King leaned over the hen and lifted her in one Jack-sized fist.

"Three, four, five, one!" He counted the golden eggs, each the size of Jack's head. Then he sniffed. "I smell the blood of an Englishman!" he roared.

"No, you don't, dear," said Mathilda as she reappeared with a plate of rolls and sliced cheese. "We don't do men the English way anymore; all that batter gives you heartburn."

"There is only one egg from this lazy hen, my queen," said the Giant King. He lifted a knife with a blade as long as Jack and fingered the edge, looking at the hen.

"That's four eggs, dear," said Mathilda. "I explained counting before. You always mix up the numbers."

The Giant King growled.

"Would you care to join me for cheese?" asked Mathilda. "If not, please go to bed. And don't shout; you'll wake up the troops and they'll be all cross for tomorrow's invasion."

At this the King scowled and stomped off to bed.

"You can come out now, lad," said Mathilda.

Jack climbed out of the bowl, and walked across the table to Mathilda's plate, where he picked up a cube of cheese half the size of his head.

"The invasion makes him grumpy. I figure that cow really sold him a bill of goods when she promised a beanstalk that would let him climb down to the Land of Men below and have all the cows he wanted if he'd only let her go." She shook her head. "Between that and the Golden Harp there, it's hardly been an easy time. Once that thing started playing, all of a sudden caves in the hillsides weren't good enough. No, we had to have palaces and armies and a foreign policy."

"What is a foreign policy?" asked Jack.

"If it's smaller than you and moves, squash it," said Mathilda promptly. "That's good enough for Giants. It's all this human cleverness that's gotten us in trouble. As if we need to compete with vermin. If we move down there, they'll be infesting everything in no time."

"What does the King need golden eggs for if all the mountains here are made of gold?"

"Gold?" laughed Mathilda. "You've been hearing a bit of Miss Harp's propaganda, there. Ask your parents when they last saw gold. Not bad enough giving my husband delusions of royalty," Mathilda sighed, flicking a lump of cheese at the quiescent harp, "she has to corrupt the young, too." Mathilda rose. "You wait here, lad, and I'll make us some tea to wash this down.

Mathilda left.

Behind him, Jack heard, "Hey. Hey, boy."

Jack turned, and found two pairs of eyes, one semi-human and one avian, regarding him expectantly.

"Time to go, boy," said the hen. "Take me and go. Now, while you've distracted her."

"Don't be ridiculous," said the Harp, her voice like honeyed thunder. "It is I who am your salvation. Carry me away from here, and you shall be king."

"Oh, I'd rather not, thanks," said Jack. "The King isn't very nice. But he likes you both. Why shouldn't you stay?"

"You thick or something, boy?" said the hen. "That monster loves my eggs. And he can't even count them. He thinks I'm drying up! Any day now he'll decide he can get them all by doing a bit of amateur surgery!"

"And the King loves only the power I grant him," said the harp darkly. "You would not be like him, I am sure." She smiled, and Jack felt himself go weak.[7]

"Phil said I was to take the Harp," he said, uncertainly.

"Harpy," said the hen. "He said Harpy, I'm sure. That's me!"

The Harp turned on the hen, discord in her voice. "You liar! You are not a harpy. A harpy is half-bird, half-woman!"

"Yep," cackled the hen. "So I am!"

"Which part is the woman, then?" asked Jack.

The hen slapped him across the face. "La. How dare you be fresh, sir."

"Boy," said the Harp, turning her voice sweet again. "Take me with you and I can command all men to your desire."

"But obviously not women," said the hen. "You never got Mathilda under your spell, did you?"

"Shut up!" snapped the Harp. "And what are you doing?"

"Part woman!" crowed the hen. "See?" There were two bulges just below her neckline.

"You've got two of those grapes stuffed under your feathers, you colossal pervert!" screamed the Harp.

Jack became uncomfortably aware of how loud the Harp's voice was.

"What's all the ruckus in there?" Mathilda's voice came from the kitchen.

"Look, boy," said the hen. "It's no secret to us you're here from the Land of Men. You can carry one of us. Now which is going to be better received by your people down there? Gold? Or a beautiful woman who can't charm other women worth a damn?"

---

[7] Well, most parts of him, at any rate.

Jack and the hen were accelerating through the main courtyard before the Harp even managed to get the soldiers stirring.

I confess that the run to the Beanstalk is now a blur in the haze of memory. Goldenharp, the first double agent I would ever turn, and the only one I would ever love, had stayed behind to undermine the Giants from within. But in drawing the wrath of the Giant King upon myself, I had run no small risk. However, I had judged my foe perfectly. Overheated by the chase in the strong sun of the afternoon, his judgment fatally compromised by his blinding rage, he plunged head-long onto the Beanstalk, where Phil's company of sappers waited with their Greataxe directional mines affixed to its stalk. The threat was ended; the Giant King no more than fertilizer strewn over that corner of the Empire.

Tragically, James would never recover from the venom Bulganova had dosed him with. It was a sad end to a great man's career, and it was my honor to have worked with him on his last mission. Until now, my oath of secrecy to the Empire has kept me from telling the true story of the Beanstalk, and the official record would always show that I did not truly become a K.N.A.V.E. agent for another three years.

Of course, the Land of the Giants would hold many more adventures, the rescue of Goldenharp not least among them, but that is a story for another time. And by then, the story of another man. The man code-named: Giantkiller.

From Epilogue: "The Giant's Leap." *A Man Called Jack*

DRINKER

Michael Jasper

The path itself remained the same, a trampled in-
dentation of ice and snow wending its way first
through black rocks and stubborn tufts of purpling
vegetation, then over featureless blue ice until it
reached the melted edge of the ocean. Its span, however, was always lengthening over time, like a hair-
tentacle attached to the head of an always-eating
foundling. At one end, our encampment of huts ringed
with caves remained static, while the vital salt water
at the other end of our march grew more distant with
each frozen cycle.

Before we went belowground countless cycles ago,
I, Iyannoloway, walked that long, frozen corridor with
my brethren. I journeyed to the edge of the iced-over
ocean, at first light-footed and brisk, returning trudging and achingly full. That was my role, the lowest
of all, determined for me by my unique, humiliating
physiology: wide shoulders, thick legs, strong finger-
toes. And an expansive belly. I was born to be a
Drinker for my People.

(But, I remind myself now, as we cut through space
and time, that role only existed back on our dying
world. A world my People and I have just departed,

forever. The ball of white, blue, and black slips farther from us with each shallow breath I exhale here on this resurrected ship of our Ancestors. I limp on old feet and bent finger-toes, passing cask after cask of my People, none of whom I can smell any longer. Many cycles have passed since I was a Drinker, but as degrading and demanding as that role was, it was fitting training for the role I have now.)

On my icy marches, I would lessen the drudgery and agony by singing songs of Uolloaway. I relived the songs inside my closed third eye, stories about how Uolloaway the young built the machines that allowed him to fly to distant lands and become the first to meet the other races on our world. How he braved the unknown to share his knowledge. How he came back a changed man—an Elder.

I sang Uolloaway's songs in silence as I walked. I sang them as I pulled deeply on the salty water of the ocean, my stomach and skin stretching, becoming taut with the lifeblood of my People. I sang as I drank and drank, as my throat burned with salt and my vision blurred from the growing pressure the water placed on my blood and in my gut. I drank until I was full, then I drank more for those waiting for us back home.

I could smell the courage and determination of my fellow Drinkers. It was a bittersweet odor.

Soon, the ocean ice would creak under the new-found weight of my fellow Drinkers and myself, but I was oblivious to the low bass sounds. Toward the end, I often would rise up to my full height, unsteady, responding to the tingling sensation in my stunted hair-tentacles. I was listening for the high-pitched cries of razorbeasts carrying over the stinging wind, afraid I would see the pale, three-legged creatures coming at us across the white-blue nothingness of the tundra.

(How my heart aches when I remember the above-

ground, in all its harshness. I can still see it inside my
third eye, even as we rush away from our world: the
black-treed forests, the viney caves, the huts of the
encampments, the forgotten towers, the tumbled bridges. I can sense our lost world as if I were right there,
plodding back home first on two feet, then on all four
feet as exhaustion set in, my belly scraping the slick
ice and sharp-crusted snow. You may not believe me,
but I miss it.)

Moving almost as slowly as water freezing, bellies
near bursting, we were near exhaustion as we marched
uphill, close enough to our encampment to smell the
rest of our People. The sun was a sliver of faded blue,
far above us, and it shed weak light on a stormy purple
sky. Inside the blackened trees of the forest next to
us were the bleached white bones of deformed creatures that made my spine ripple and crack with fear.

I imagined Uolloaway coasting on the air high
above us, looking down at our bent gray backs,
twitching hair-tentacles, and bulging bellies, and turning his air-skimmer away from us. Uolloaway's time
was far in the past, and we had been denied his flying
machines, now broken beyond fixing and hidden under
layers of snow. Even the red towers of the old cities
of the Ancestors were crumbling onto courtyards
abandoned and hollow.

I did not look at my fellow laborers waddling next
to me, giving off their odors of salt and excrement
and determination. I did not want to know if their
eyes were closed or open, if their finger-toes bled onto
the snow and ice like mine did, or if they passed their
time with their own quiet songs of the Ancestors, or
other Elders or even Drinkers.

So I sang of Uolloaway strapped into his skimmer
high in the air and wished idly for a fleet of his winged

machines to swoop down and shorten the long, mindless walk that cursed my fellow Drinkers and me. But a rescue from this unrelenting cold and the encroaching creatures made bold by hunger and desperation was never our destiny.

Unless we resolved to rescue ourselves.

Uolloaway was barely four full cycles past his time as a foundling when he built his first air skimmer. Strapped into his flying machine, standing atop the tallest of the red towers of the city where he'd lived all his short life, the songs claimed that he paused for only the slightest of moments before he kicked away from his perch.

I can imagine him laughing as his winged creation caught the first updrafts from the paved streets below him, his sturdy arms withstanding the violent tremors that buffeted the bar holding the single wing of his skimmer together. His black hair-tentacles writhing rhythmically above his third, vertical eye, as if tasting the cooling air high above the busy city.

The Elders had warned him away from displaying his simple devices and creations before the proper time, but Uolloaway scoffed at their words. Like the Stargazers, who worked only at night, the Elders preferred to work in secret, building their oversized machines, singing songs deep beneath the ground that bent rock and melted ore and consumed the very dirt itself, shaping all of it with their combined will into massive ships whose purpose Uolloaway was never told.

Hiding his curiosity and his inventions was not Uolloaway's way; he had to put his creations to use so he could explore. So he pushed himself into the air high above the green courtyards and mossy trees, aiming his air skimmer around the three other red towers of the busy city, narrowly missing the new tower currently under construction.

His first flight was painfully short, with a landing that was never set to rhyme in any heroic song. He had to rebuild most of his rudimentary air skimmer from scratch.

But he had *flown*.

Over time, his air skimmer gained a series of small engines; his single wing became two, then three; and he installed a pair of steering levers. With a pack of salted meat and a belly filled with four short-cycles of water (so little I have to laugh every time I envision this part of the song, for he was obviously not a Drinker), Uolloaway took his first flight over the yellow ocean.

The ocean was wider then, more open, instead of mostly frozen as it was in my time aboveground. The engines of Uolloaway's skimmer faded near the end of his flight, and he crashed into the icy waters just as the distant island came into sight. A clan of black-skinned People who lived next to the Widening Ocean rescued him. Giving off an odor sweet as new fruit, their eyes were slits and their skin darkened from being exposed to the sun, which he claimed was much brighter in that land year-round.

Uolloaway came to call them the People of the Yellow Sun. The cold of our world spread more slowly there, but even then the hints were there, in the details of their songs: chill breezes and dying vegetation and the unfamiliar smell of frost in the morning.

After four cycles in that other land, Uolloaway made an even longer trip, to the next continent, riding generous wind currents on his reinforced skimmer. There he met the People of the White Moon, a race with faded skin and bulging eyes who saw the light of our sun only as a small white bump on the horizon, if ever. They smelled like dust and fallen leaves.

Uolloaway exchanged food and stories with them, fathered a series of foundlings in his cycle there, and began work on the bridges that once connected the continents. Once the bridges were underway, he continued on across the world until he had circled it, reaching his homeland again. He came back with shorter hair-tentacles and a limp in his gait, and soon the air was constantly filled with the buzz of his air skimmer, along with a growing army of other winged ships he'd helped to design.

(I cannot tell you how many times I would begrudge the fact that Uolloaway never had to walk the ever-lengthening path we Drinkers walked from encampment to ocean and back. Each trip was slightly longer, as the ice spread from the growing, unabated cold falling onto our world. I would have given my third eye— and all its knowledge—for an air skimmer like his.)

One of the longstanding mysteries of our People was the final song of Uolloaway, which told of how almost all of the tools and machines from his time had been lost. When by chance some of the Ancestral tools were found buried in the frost, usually by an intrepid Digger, the tools were always broken, and not even our wisest Elders could decipher their uses. Somehow, the ways of the Ancestors had been lost, forgotten.

Though I, lowly Iyannoloway the Drinker, *did* remember their songs. They gave me hope that was sorely needed, for the world of *Wannoshay* had grown terribly, dangerously cold. And if songs could be remembered, then surely other skills could be recovered, or relearned. Couldn't they?

We almost lost one of our group on the worst march I'd experienced in four times three cycles since becoming a Drinker. If she had fallen to the iced-over rocks of the trail leading up to our encampment, we would have had to simply leave her, even though we were easily four times one hundred paces from the first ring of huts and fires of our home.

(I am haunted by the actions of my remembered self, passing her by with just a small, feeble touch instead of a supporting hand. I wish to think I would have done whatever I could to help her back to her feet had she fallen. But back then I'd feared we both would have died out there, our precious, filtered water spilling out of our bodies as we froze to death, in sight of the flickering orange cooking fires of our home.)

Waddling up the mountain trails leading to our encampment, I'd given up any pretense of gazing anywhere but at my bloodied feet. Looking down, of course, led me to stare not only at my finger-toes and the bits of stubborn mountain grass on the path, but also the brown and white droppings left by my siblings in front of me. Fortunately, my sense of smell had been diminished by the march.

Such indignities were unavoidable. I knew that I was also passing the extracted salt from the vast volume of ocean water in my belly, shitting out all waste and impurities from the water in a humiliating stream. If ever a body doubted what the lowest role on our world was, they need only look at a Drinker after a march, covered in a repellant coating of salt, excrement, and snow.

I was thinking of the blankets and shelter of my hut when I heard the dreaded sound of finger-toes scrabbling on ice ahead of me. I raised my head, middle eye still closed and reliving a song of the past, and saw one of my sisters slip. I am ashamed to admit my first movement was to steady myself, not to reach for her.

Fortunately, she managed to catch herself by digging all eight finger-toes into the sharp crust of snow and ice coating the path. She quivered there for long moments until she'd regained her balance, the ball of her belly sloshing loud enough for me to hear. Her hair-tentacles stood out from her oval head like a crown of gray fingers, but not a single sound came from her mouth. Her fear smelled like meat burning over a too-hot cooking fire.

I touched her shoulder as I passed, imbuing her with what energy I could spare. Four times two journeys back we *had* lost a Drinker in a fall, and the look on his panicked face as he fell back and began to roll down the incline still haunted me. But we'd been told to never stop to help; the rest of our People depended on us. He was as good as dead the moment he slipped to the ground.

I decided on that march that next time it happened—for surely there would be another incident—I would stop to help a fellow Drinker who stumbled.

The realization was as sharp and biting as the wind in my face: I was diminishing myself by not aiding my brethren. Calling my negligence *responsibility* was being untrue to myself; I imagined a piece of my soul curdling as a result. Never again.

Soon we came to the outlying caves, followed by the huts of our encampment. The other workers emerged from the caves and huts, waving their stubby arms at us, much to my humiliation. In my current soiled state, I did not want any sort of attention. I just wanted to be left alone in my suffering so I could complete my task.

I let my heavy head fall forward and kept my gaze low until I reached the well at the center of the encampment. My middle eye never opened, though the song had gone silent inside my head. At the lip of the black stone well, I inhaled a deep breath and leaned headfirst into the well. Clutching the rim with my shaking, battered finger-toes, I regurgitated my stored volumes of filtered water.

The emptying lasted four times twelve heartbeats. An eternity.

Utterly humiliated and deflated, I went back to my hut to sleep for close to three short-cycles as my belly returned—slowly, painfully—to its original shape. My dreams were as silent, odorless, and black as space, devoid of all scent or song.

Uolloaway was barely older than a foundling when he left for the other parts of *Wannoshay,* and most of his fellow People deemed him gone for good, doubting they'd ever get to share in his wild energy after his life ended prematurely. He made many friends in his journeys, a skill I found lacking in myself, though legend has it that his generosity with others also led to his downfall.

I listened and searched for stories of Uolloaway's demise, but the songs were few and vague. As best I could, I learned from his mistakes as well as from his victories and adventures. And thanks to the work of an old friend of mine with a different role, I found out the true history of my hero, Uolloaway.

(And that knowledge has made my relatively new role as an Elder somewhat easier to bear. For I know now what it means to make a hard, seemingly impossible decision. Twice.)

I woke from my rest after that march with fluid in all four of my lungs, a cough in my throat, and an itch to see my old friend, Oyallohawna the Digger. After devouring all of my missed rations of food at the cooking fires (I chose not to drink anything), I made my slow, sore-footed way out of the maze of viney huts in our encampment to the black caves where Oyallohawna and her fellow Diggers were working.

With their hardened hands and blade-like claws, the Diggers were expanding the caves and tunnels they'd cut into the ridge surrounding our encampment. Many People had moved from our aboveground huts into these caves, which were also covered in vines and roots. The Diggers were always hollowing out more, but I couldn't imagine living here; I'd miss the sun and the wind. The closed-in spaces made me lose my breath. As mad as it may sound, I feared I'd even miss the cold, open air of our marches.

Further, the caves held an unnatural warmth that never allowed me to fully enjoy my time down in them. Oyallohawna explained to me that the hot springs deeper down in the caves, along with the lichen stretching up from them toward the cave mouths like fingers, caused this warm humidity, but I'd never gone deep enough to see more than a few straggling vines inching toward our distant sun. I took her at her word.

I knew the strange minerals and unsalted waters of the belowground springs would be poison to our People, and I kept my distance from that water, as any good Drinker would. Little did I know that with one swallow, the true nature of that water would have ended my desolate life as a Drinker. But we were all convinced that any water other than the saltwater of the ocean, broken down on our long march inland by the enzymes of our Drinkers' bellies, would kill us outright. That was what the Elders had told us, and so, we believed.

(Had I relied on that blind faith in the good will of the Elders after I myself became an Elder? Had I taken advantage of the ignorance of those in lower roles to accomplish my purposes? I'd rather not contemplate such questions, not now, surrounded by my sleeping brethren in their casks on this journey through space devised by my fellow Elders and me, as well as the Ancestors, in their own way.)

On my way down the sloping cave to where my old friend was working, I passed a pair of hunched Gatherers, long gray arms filled with brown and green plants and glowing blue fungi from farther down in the caves. I gave them a bow of respect, but they ignored me. To them I was only a Drinker, a walking, shitting water barrel.

"Welcome back, Iyannoloway," Oyallohawna called out, her voice muffled by the piles of rock and dirt on either side of her. I inhaled her familiar, earthy scent while she remained bent over deep inside the hole she'd been digging. The gray skin of her bare back glistened with sweat down the knotted ridge of her backbone.

Diggers were born with stubborn bones in their hands, and the rock walls submit to them, allowing our People to tunnel. With their four-clawed hands they helped shape over four times ten times ten new caves deep into the rock of *Wannoshay*. This short-cycle of work had just begun for her, but already Oyallohawna had tunneled out a hole four times as deep and twice as wide as she was tall.

"Did you bring me something to drink?"

"Ah, I've forgotten, again." Our old joke made me smile, but barely. I kept seeing my sister-Drinker slipping, and recalling how my first reaction was to save myself. "How have you been?"

"Busy. More People are moving down here, out of the huts. I can't say that I blame them. The cold isn't

going to let up, Iyannoloway. It's the sun—I can tell
a difference in the light when I come up from down
here after a couple of short-cycles of working. Darker
each time, just a tiny bit, I can see it from right here."
She turned to me for a moment and touched her vertical middle eye, which was currently closed as she labored in the rock.

I nodded, about to say something, but Oyallohawna
continued after turning back to her digging.

"I think we should all move down here. That way
we'd stay warm. We'd have plenty to eat. The plants
and fungi living down here are plentiful, and quite
tasty. And some of the Gatherers have been trans-
planting food vines from aboveground, and they
spread like ice on the ocean. I say we seal up the cave
entrances to keep out the cold and live belowground
permanently."

My spine crackled at the thought. That felt too
much like being buried alive. I wiped fresh moisture
from my hair-tentacles.

"What about water? Are you going to open up the
caves every four times two short-cycles so we poor
Drinkers can make our marches to the ocean?"

"Iyannoloway, you fool. The water down here *can*
be filtered. I know it can. May not even need as much
filtering as the ocean water did. We've been ignoring
the obvious for too many cycles. Haven't we?"

I felt my spine shudder once more. Oyallohawna
was bordering on blasphemy against the Elders, and I
would not pursue that line of thought. They said the
water was undrinkable, and judging by its smell and
its unnatural heat, I had no reason to doubt their
knowledge. I tried a different tactic.

"But the caves just don't feel right to me. We don't
belong in the ground."

Oyallohawna snorted. "People said the same thing about the towers. 'We don't belong in the sky.' Didn't stop the Ancestors, did it?"

I moved out of her reach before responding. "And look at what happened to those towers now. Those that haven't fallen over are disintegrating more each short-cycle."

A shower of mud flew up out of the hole at me.

"You Drinkers hate change," Oyallohawna said, digging harder now, throwing out more mud and dirt and rocks. Then she stopped in mid-scoop, struck by a thought. "That reminds me. According to this, a tower once stood *here*." She threw a sheath of metal pages at my feet. The sharp edges cut into my already injured hands. "Found this earlier. Thought you might be interested."

"Is this one of theirs?" I forgot about the ache in my joints and the cuts on my hand-fingers. "An Ancestor?"

"Think so. I wish I knew how to work it, but . . ."

I didn't wait to hear what else Oyallohawna said. I was moving up and out of the claustrophobic caves, needing to feel the cold wind on my moist skin as I hurried back to my tiny, under-insulated Drinker's hut to unwrap this book left by the Ancestors.

I learned of Uolloaway's true history at the same time the combined herds of razorbeasts crossed the frozen ocean. The hulking animals were mad with hunger, and they attacked band after band of helpless Drinkers. The razorbeasts ran on three legs across the ice and blue freeze, seemingly unbalanced but surprisingly fast. They then moved closer and tore apart the Gatherers in the outlying caves and ambushed the Stargazers at night. The beasts even managed to kill many razor-handed Diggers before we could react

with fire and our own blades, most of them dull with
rust and lack of use.

Even if a band of Drinkers made it past the beasts
to the ocean, they never found the breaks. The ocean
had finally frozen solid. Half of the Drinkers died out
there, searching the ice, while the Gatherers could not
risk going out to find food in the forests or caves. We
would have to bring Diggers with us to help us break
through the ice so we could drink, but few of them
wanted to risk leaving the safety of the caves. Our
encampment reeked with the odors of desperation
and hunger.

(We were on the verge of extinction, living there
in the aboveground, susceptible to predators and the
unrelenting cold. We were dying off. I have to tell
myself that now. I just never imagined it could happen
so fast. I had no choice but to suggest what I did. I
had to convince the Elders and the rest of my People.
Just as I did four times four short-cycles ago, persuad-
ing the rest of my People that the recovered ships had
to be awakened. Such things always happen too fast.)

At the time, I kept wanting to ask myself how Uolloaway would have reacted to this situation, but I
could not dispel what I'd seen and experienced from
the book of metal pages my Digger friend had found
for me at the site of the Ancestors' tower.

Of course I knew how to use it. These metal pages
were created by Uolloaway's peers, and I knew their
songs as well. I began taking the flat pieces of metal
apart with tiny tugs and pops, disappointed that my
friend Oyallohawna was always too busy with her
head in the dirt to learn about the marvels of the
Ancestor technology.

When I placed the pages around me in my hut, according to the shape and patterns melted into each slice
of metal, the dim gray light of my hut was burned away

by a light so white it gave off heat. As the light coalesced into images in front of me from the collected pages of the book all around me, I saw what Uolloaway had done to his wondrous technology. And why.

In addition to his air skimmers, Uolloaway was known for his work on the towers as well as building the bridges that connected the landmasses of *Wannoshay*. The towers stored energy that was used, somehow, in the construction of the bridges as well as powering the engines of the air skimmers. His expertise not only with machinery but with all the People he'd encountered on our world made him a force to be reckoned with.

At least, that was my perception before I experienced the contents of this metal book left buried in the ruins of one of his red towers. The book's energy placed me inside his true history, starting at the base of one of the ancient towers.

I looked up and saw a fleet of air skimmers, sleek white wings and gray undercarriages disappearing into the noon sun as they rushed off into the distance. Many short-cycles flickered past as I watched, slack-jawed.

This city was magnificent: tamed razorbeasts pulled ornate carriages, while rushing men and women loped past on all fours, naked in the warm yellow light of the sun, their pinkish-gray skin painted in bright oranges and reds. Even their hair-tentacles were more colorful than the dull black of my People in my time. The towers all around me hummed with power that set my own hair-tentacles to quivering.

More short-cycles flickered past in this visual history, and the towers began to lean and the sun to gradually fade, while off in the distance, a tiny figure made his slow way toward me on a land bridge.

For the first time ever, I saw Uolloaway. He was

smaller and older than I'd imagined him. In spite of his limp and his age—his hair-tentacles were quite short and almost white—he returned like a violent wind belching forth thunder and devastation with each step he took.

Each step. That made me stop breathing, my spine crackling with fear. Uolloaway was coming back on *foot*, and the sky was empty of his fleets of skimmers. I was glad, watching this book from the safety of the future, that I could not smell him.

Uolloaway came back bearing his madness like a curse on his people and his descendants.

I watched, helpless, as Uolloaway stormed the red towers of his mother city. He began destroying every machine he'd ever created, followed by any other mechanism he could find. He triggered the devastation of the bridges connecting our land with that of the others across the water and ice, unhinging them with the removal of a double handful of pins from each end point. The bridges sank without a trace into the ocean, whose waters were impossibly close, unfrozen.

"Never will we let our People risk traveling to the other lands," he said over the din of his destruction. His voice was even more high-pitched than most of our People, and it was tinged with anger and something deeper. "Never again will we put ourselves at the mercy of others who only long to usurp our creations and belongings. I'd rather they never were created!"

He almost made his way down to the great black ships that were nearing completion deep belowground, but when he entered the secret tunnels, the other Elders fell upon him and smothered him in energy and light.

"Why?" I whispered, the light of the book's true history blinding me.

When I dared open just my middle eye, inhaling my own muddy, salty smell of fear, I saw the wonders of the rest of my world taking shape inside my hut as the history went farther back:

Uolloaway showing off his skimmer to the different Peoples of our world, in sandy, barren landscapes as well as dull gray lands untouched by sun, followed by the plush green and blue forests of the Ancestors' land, long before my own time. I marveled at the burnished skin and long fingers of the People of the Yellow Sun, then the hunched backs and wide, hungry eyes of the People of the White Moon.

My wonder dissipated when I saw our pale brothers placing their hands on Uolloaway's head, securing him by his hair-tentacles. Stubby fingers pressed against his head, denting his skull, and then breaking through the surface without spilling a drop of blood.

I understood immediately by the agony on Uolloaway's face that they were stealing his thoughts with their invasive touches.

I saw what the People of the White Moon planned to do with their stolen knowledge: skimmers filled the dark, weak-sunned air, which was now broken by red towers instead of black caves. They had built an armada and aimed it at our homeland; ships built to attack, not just to travel.

I felt a sickening moment of vertigo inside my third eye when I realized I was witnessing a possible future filtered through this book of the past. I was seeing the same future that Uolloaway saw, and prevented.

Breaking away before it was too late, before the last of his knowledge could be appropriated from him, Uolloaway fought his way back to his skimmer and escaped. But the loss of his stolen skills cut deeply. Already he was losing the ability to operate his skim-

mer, and he crashed it into a land bridge, another of
his inventions that he barely recognized now.

Walking back, furious now, aching with his amnesia
and loss, Uolloaway decided what had to be done. He
had to cut all ties to the other lands, as well as all ties
to his existing creations. I saw Uolloaway, mad with
rage, covered in bright white light that became so
bright I could not look anymore.

"The Wannoshay of our land were not meant to
travel, or to fly," a weary, quavering voice whispered
in the forefront of my mind. "Our place is here, and
here alone." And then the pages of the book fell
around me.

My history lesson ended there.

In his final act of anger and frustration and fear,
Uolloaway would curse his descendents with a life devoid of his mechanical wonders forever. Perhaps he
thought of himself as a hero because of this. I no
longer did.

Blinking all three of my eyes in succession, still reeling from the choices my hero had made, I realized
that my People and I had only one choice to save
ourselves.

We had to look elsewhere for our salvation. Not to
our heroes or legends, but within ourselves.

We could not travel far, not anymore. Without Uolloaway's air skimmers or the mythical ships of the
Ancestors, we lacked the ability to fly. So we had to
go belowground, where the heat gathered and kept
out the advancing cold.

I just had to make the rest of my People listen to
me, a lowly Drinker, before it was too late.

After the last cave entrance was sealed, my People
wanted to call me an Elder, but I refused to accept

the new role. Not after all I'd learned about Uolloaway and the choices he'd made.

(I still turn these thoughts around in my mind, behind my third eye: could we have remained on *Wannoshay* if Uolloaway's knowledge and machines had
survived and been passed down over the cycles, just
as the songs of the Navigators had been? Could our
People have continued growing and prospering instead
of stagnating and nearly freezing to death? Anger
fuels my long, slow walks through this sleeping ship,
with the Navigators the only others awake, singing
their songs of stars and fusion and momentum.)

"Call me an Elder later," I'd told the People gathered around me when the last entrance was sealed,
and my own painful adjustment to the belowground
began. The discussions and arguments about our move
down here had lasted half of an entire cycle, and as
we argued, many of our People had been lost to the
cold and to the predators closing in on us. We were
dying of thirst, we were starving, we were freezing.
And many of my People were afraid to leave the
aboveground.

During that painful half-cycle, unable to perform
my dùties as a Drinker (my belly tightening and my
finger-toes growing weak), I fought hard to make my
case.

I called in my friend Oyallohawna to demonstrate
how a cave could be sealed from the cold without
suffocating its inhabitants. I reminded my People of
our inability to protect ourselves from the razorbeasts.
I even showed my People the true history of Uolloaway, arranging the metal pages countless times for different audiences, but most of them were unmoved by
his tragedy, nor did they understand his choices the
way I did. But with each showing of this history, I

would see one or two members of the audience gaping at me sideways with their third eye.

They, at last, had remembered the melodies of Uolloaway's songs.

And, most compelling of all, I showed how I could imbibe the hot waters of the belowground springs with just a tiny bit of filtering, and—contrary to what generations of Elders had told us—I did not die of poisoning.

"Call me an Elder," I repeated, "after enough cycles have passed to ensure that our People are safe. Call me an Elder after we are certain that I have not doomed us all to a horrible fate here belowground."

I continued making my case for the move belowground long past all other voices in favor of the move had fallen hoarse. I simply forged on, one step after the other, still a Drinker in my own way, pushing myself until my task was complete. Until we sealed the cave entrances behind us, leaving the aboveground forever.

And to my amazement, though I never would feel the same belowground as I did in the open air (I always felt hunched over, as if waiting for the collected mass of rock and sediment to fall onto my ridged back), we thrived for many cycles belowground. The Diggers created endless tunnels and countless caves, while the Gatherers and Drinkers enjoyed an easier life of accumulating food and filtering spring water. The Stargazers found other roles, the Navigators practiced their songs to keep them committed to memory, while the Elders spent their short-cycles searching the deepest, oldest caves for traces of the Ancestors' mythic ships.

But in spite of all our best-laid plans, we still had to leave many cycles later, after the food supplies began to dwindle and the Diggers tunneled too deeply. Fortunately, a group of Elders and Drinkers led by Oyallohawna and myself managed to uncover the first of the buried ships of the Ancestors in time.

But that is another story altogether.

(I open my third eye and disperse the shadows of memory haunting my footsteps as I pace around the stacked sleep casks. As we continue chasing the Mother Ship through space, I know of no other way to help me relax other than walking. As I walk, I hope for the best on this green and blue planet the Stargazers found many cycles ahead of us. I pray it is neither too hot nor too cold, and that its People—if we find any—are not hostile to visitors.)

(I close my third eye and try to sleep, and as time becomes more and more fluid, I sink back into the welcoming black metal of this ship built by the Ancestors. Careful not to wake the others around me, I begin to sing the song of Uolloaway softly to myself. My old voice is too weak to distract the singing Navigators high above us, but it is strong enough, for now.)

(I will follow Uolloaway's song with that of all the Elders since his time, up to and including my own. With each word of the song, I slowly begin to discern the individual scents of my People gathered around me in their sleep casks. They smell of exhilaration, of relief, of hope.)

(I can only hope that these songs of the Wannoshay, unlike Uolloaway's, will end on a sweet note.)

KING HARROWHELM

Ed Greenwood

The dell filled with a sudden rustling of many disturbed leaves, as twoscore crossbows were thrust forward at once.

Griflet swallowed, staring at his death. Twoscore deaths, sharp and rusty-pointed, stared blindly right back at him.

"That, sirs, was the wrong answer," said the black knight barring the road, triumphal glee in his voice. A smirk came and went across his hard face like a ripple crossing a still pond. "Harrowhelm is king here now."

"Harrowhelm?" Sir Daergas growled, bushy gray brows drawing together. "And just who is 'Harrowhelm'?"

"Your doom," the knight snapped. The sudden slash of his hand heralded the uneven thunder of all the bows loosing at once.

Sir Galagars had already whirled in his saddle to glare at Griflet, sitting on his horse in the way of any retreat. Shield coming up, he shouted, "*Ride,* boy! Get gone!"

Gaping at him, Griflet had no time to obey, even if his mount had been willing. As things befell, it was too busy rearing and neighing.

Crossbow quarrels do not hiss like arrows. They snarl like eager wolves, in the instant before they thud home in shield or plate or flesh—and grunting, gasping men reel in their saddles and start to fall.

Horses screamed and bucked, hooves lashing out wildly. Lifeless bodies toppled, Daergas wearing a quarrel in one eye and Sir Nalorhands choking around the quarrel that had torn out his throat, as he went to the trampled earth in a long, wet gurgle.

Sir Baudwin of the Blue Hawk cursed and threw his sword—and the black knight clutched his own throat, made the same horrible wet sounds as Sir Nalorhands, and fell.

The road was suddenly clear, armsmen frantically cranking windlasses to ready their bows again. With a roar, Baudwin and Brastias spurred forward, plunging to freedom.

The surviving knights followed, the boy Griflet among them, pelting along the road, out of the trees into rolling farmland that should have been easternmost Northgalis, where Thaborn was king—or perhaps had until recently been king, if men were now guarding roads in the name of Harrowhelm.

The fields seemed deserted, and the knights slowed their frantic galloping.

"Dark devils take all kings!" Galagars raged to the skies. "And false knights, too!"

"Slowly!" the deep voice of Hervise de Revel boomed from behind them, standing in his saddle. "Slowly!"

Knights hauled on their reins in a brief, cursing confusion, and halted, ere he spoke again. "Not so harsh, Gars. The man may well have believed this road was safe; he came by way of it, not two days gone."

"Precisely," Sir Galagars snarled, wheeling his warmount. "Come to us from this Harrowhelm, no doubt,

with orders to lure knights hither! Daergas down, and Nalorhands—and Ulphonses, too!" He barked like a dog in sheer anger, and spat, "All these ten lawless winters since the death of Great Arthur have been better than this one summer of too many kings!"

"Aye," Sir Brastias agreed. "This Harrowhelm's not the first to seek the blood of passing knights! I heard—"

"Why?" Griflet blurted out, without thinking. His clear, high voice soared over the angry growls, and helmed heads turned to glare. He frowned back at furious faces in utter bewilderment, too excited in the wake of someone trying to slay him to know prudence. "Why kill knights?"

"To win regard," Galagars snapped.

"To become feared," Baudwin said more bluntly.

"To strike down champions knighted by another," old Hervise de Revel boomed, "and win their armor and blazons, to put on men loyal to you and claim them to be the men you've slain, now pledged to your cause. Knights seek men to lead them, and will rally to a leader—who'll then reach for a crown."

Griflet stared around at them all, informed but unenlightened. "So," he asked hesitantly, "what do we do now?"

Brastias laughed bitterly. "Do? Why, what we've always done, lad! Ride and fight and die, as our king bids us! That's what knights *do*."

"And the bidding is what kings do," Galagars added grimly. "Good and bad, bold and foolish, wicked and o'er-innocent. We are the dogs and wolves throned fools send into battle to save themselves the peril of swinging their own swords."

" 'Dogs and wolves'?" Griflet echoed. "Why both?"

"Some of us obey well," Sir Hervise rumbled, "and so are dogs. Some, loosed upon the land, savage and

chase as we please—or are swept away by our own
bloodlust: wolves."

"And you are—?"

"At this moment, Sir Squire of Many Questions,"
Baudwin snapped, "we are fast becoming wolves." He
swung in his saddle to point across the hills, and
added, "Let us ride behind yon stand of trees, and
there parley where Harrowhelm's eyes cannot so easily watch."

The sun was a flood of flame low in the western
sky, and the creakers had already begun their song. It
would be a warm night, and none of the knights had
bothered to gather wood for a fire. Griflet could not
keep his eyes off the distant dark line that marked the
edge of Harrowhelm's forest.

"Will they come for us?" he asked Baudwin, who
was nearest.

The knight smiled thinly, hefted his brush-axe in his
hand, and shook his head. "Nay. They'd have sent
men hence, creeping and peering, if it was in their
minds to come after us. Watch for any fires or lights,
lad; mayhap we'll go after them."

"We need bows," Griflet said, remembering the air
thrumming around him with death.

"Knights do not use bows," Baudwin snapped, giving him a dark look.

"But how—" Griflet began, and then remembered
the best tales he'd heard. "Merlin! He—"

"Nor spells," the knight replied, his voice even
colder. "Wizards are to be trusted even less than kings
and their sneak-knife knaves. True knights use the
lance, and the sword, and their fists."

Hervise de Revel chuckled as he lifted his dripping
face from the stream they'd found, and added, "Plus
the odd dagger and hurled tankard. 'Twas in my mind

to use such smaller fangs on this Harrowhelm, after a little stroll through the trees."

"No armor?" Galagars asked slowly, frowning. "That might be best, at that."

Griflet's heart leaped. "Can I go with you? And—and . . . how will you know King Harrowhelm when you've found him?"

Sir Brastias of the Green Shield and Sir Hervise chuckled in unison, this time, but it was not a sound that held much mirth.

"He'll be the one hiding behind everyone else so he need not fight us," Baudwin said darkly, "and no, Sir Tongueloose Squire, you'll *not* go with us. If this is lordless country, someone must stay with the horses."

"One lad with a knife to guard them?" Brastias murmured, shaking his head, but Galagars strode forward to stand with Griflet.

"We promised Mercel," he reminded Baudwin. "The lad is to be trained as a knight. So if knights go creeping through the night . . ."

Baudwin shook his head grimly, and gave Griflet a dark glare. Then he looked to the other knights.

Only to see slow nods of agreement with Galagars.

"Right, then," the Knight of the Blue Hawk said reluctantly, rounding on the squire, "but no screaming! Squeak and rouse them, and I'll slay you even before they do! Heed?"

Griflet swallowed, nodded, and managed to voice a reply that was not—quite—a squeak. "Y–yes. Sir."

"Heh. Settled. Now, we'd best hasten," Hervise growled, wrapping his cloak around the blade of his drawn sword and reaching for the buckles of his armor. "The moon will be up soon."

"They fear no nightly knightly attack," Galagars quipped in a wry murmur, as all that was left of the

Knights of the Table Round paced cautiously through the trees.

Ahead, the night danced with bright flame. A dozen blazes, or more, burned atop broken, crumbling watchtowers, along a broken, overgrown line that had once been stout battlements. A dark stone keep rose beyond the blazes. Aside from the fires, all seemed silent and deserted.

"Let's teach them a little fear, then," Baudwin muttered, peering this way and that through the dark tree-trunks, shaking his head in obvious disbelief at the lack of sentries.

The damp leaves were quiet underfoot, and Hervise had been firm that they should walk in pairs, a little way apart, with the lone squire following behind.

Griflet clutched his dagger so tightly that his fingers were burning and tried to keep silent, putting his feet just where Sir Hervise had trod. The knights seldom looked back, and when their heads did turn, Griflet sensed they were listening more than trying to see into the night.

The moon was reaching forth its first pale fingers, the trees casting inky shadows . . . and the knights were but silent black shapes moving among them, shadows among the shadows. Griflet glanced behind himself often, fearing prowling wolves more than men with crossbows.

They were very close to the fires, now, and he found his mouth very dry. Griflet swallowed, put his dagger into his other hand so he could wriggle fingers gone numb from clutching it too tight, and drew in a deep breath. Glancing back into the forest out of habit, he froze, heart suddenly hammering.

There was another black, moving shadow behind him. Close, and impossibly tall, gliding nearer in utter silence—nay; 'twas *flying*!

Griflet opened his mouth to shout, and so win his

own death under Sir Baudwin's blade—and discovered he was frozen with fear.

The shadow was very near, now. Griflet could see it was a man in a black robe, face hidden in its cowl, drifting along upright in the air, soft-booted feet not touching the ground. Closer it came, barely three trees away . . . and then seemed to sense or see his regard. It turned sharply aside, cloak swirling, and was gone behind thick trees.

The squire trembled, more terrified than he'd ever been in his life before—and that was when he heard a soft grunt of effort from the watchfire-lit battlements, a brief rustling, and then a queer sigh.

Griflet whirled around, dagger up and ready, in time to see a knight up on the line of tumbled stones let a dark form slump at his feet, and then straighten and move along the battlements.

A short, choked-off cry arose, several watchfires away, followed by a shout: " 'Ware! We're under *attack*! To arms!"

Ahead of Griflet, Hervise cursed softly and broke into a lumbering run, abandoning stealth. Shouldered-aside branches crackled and snapped.

A howling, agonized scream split the night, and a dark figure pitched past merrily leaping flames with steel glinting in its throat to thud heavily to the earth. There were more shouts, and the trees ahead of Griflet suddenly seemed alive with racing, leaping men, firelight gleaming on the helms of anxious armsmen.

"Throw some burning brands yonder!" someone ordered. "There, into the trees!"

Someone cried out at another place along the wall, and toppled—and behind the falling man, Griflet saw Sir Galagars wave a sword that glistened with dark blood. The knight spun away to lunge at someone else.

A horn sounded, loud in the night. Hervise de Revel cursed, and steel rang on steel, startlingly loud. There was a heavy thump and a shower of sparks as an armsman fell dead or dying into a fire, and the horn called again.

It was answered by many startled, sleepy shouts, and torches came bobbing along the ruined walls. In their light, Griflet saw the Knights of the Table Round hurrying here and there along the battlements, stabbing and hacking, swords flashing as they dealt death.

He trotted closer, afraid to go out of the trees to where crossbows could reach—but even more afraid to linger in the forest with the flying black shadow lurking somewhere close behind him.

The first crossbow cracked just as he rounded the last tree. The fires were burning like beacons along the old, tumbled wall—and in their leaping light he could see dark, wet ribbons of fresh blood descending the mossy stones.

Griflet swallowed, took a last look back into the dark trees, and then darted forward, into a gap in the old wall where no firelight reached.

Dead men were sprawled ahead of him, and he could *smell* blood. As Griflet swallowed, baring his teeth in distaste, a quarrel snarled overhead, to fall and shiver somewhere in the forest beyond the castle grounds. Griflet peered up; the bow had been fired from the keep, a lone tower rising into the moonlight. It commanded a small courtyard whose far wall rose high and unbroken, that held only the sagging remnants of a stable and a well where dead armsmen lay heaped thickly. King Harrowhelm was paying dearly for his harvest of three stranger-knights on the road.

More armsmen burst out of the keep, faces tight with fear and ready crossbows in their hands. Torches blazed in plenty, and there was much shouting and pointing and firing. Three quarrels met in one mailed figure and hurled it back from the well—but it was an armsman, already dead, raised up on the blade of a crouching Sir Galagars.

Furiously swung steel rang on clanging steel, hard by the keep door, and men whirled with startled curses. Crossbows bucked as they fired, someone screamed, and more men fell. Griflet saw Hervise de Revel staggering back along the wall with a quarrel through his arm, hacking at armsmen all the way and grimly shedding their bodies one by one.

Farther along the wall a knight threw up his hands, and Griflet ducked back through the wall to see better.

It was Sir Brastias, a quarrel standing out of his neck, as he staggered back out into the night, into the trees. As the sorely wounded knight stumbled through a tangle of branches, Griflet saw the black-robed shadow again, drifting out from behind a great oak to glide after the Knight of the Green Shield.

Two more crossbows fired—and missed, their quarrels humming far into the night before splintering amid faint, distant crashes. That must have left no bowman ready, because Sir Baudwin, Sir Galagars, and Sir Hervise roared wordless defiance and charged, hacking and chopping like madmen.

Armsmen fled or fell, hewn down like so much firewood, and then Baudwin was racing into the keep, Galagars on his heels. Hervise de Revel cut the throat of a wounded armsman who was feebly trying to unsheathe his blade, and then lurched after the other two knights, summoning Griflet with a level look and a beckoning jerk of his head.

The squire hastened across the courtyard and into the keep. Torches guttered along the walls of a high passage, and there was much light beyond—in a great hall where Galagars strode calmly over the bodies of armsmen even as Baudwin slew the last of them, to confront a masked, crowned figure sitting alone on a high-backed throne.

The room was cold and empty, dark tapestries rippling along the walls, as Galagars put his blade to the throat of the masked king.

There came a sob from behind that mask, and the figure on the throne cowered, weeping in earnest, its voice high and young.

Galagars twisted his blade, sweeping the mask away—and stared into the wide, dark eyes of a young lass white and trembling with terror. "*You* are King Harrowhelm?" he growled in disbelief.

A crossbow cracked, tapestries puffing out into the room in the wake of the quarrel that had taken Galagars in the back.

"No," a man's voice said coldly, as the knight Griflet loved the best of all sagged, dying. "*I* am Harrowhelm."

"Peladrus!" Baudwin gasped, raising his sword.

"Yes," that cold voice replied smugly, as a tapestry fell away in soft, billowing thunder to reveal a man in gleaming plate armor flanked by a dozen armsmen, cocked and loaded crossbows in all their hands. "Peladrus I was . . . but I am Harrowhelm now, and you stand in my realm. Small, aye, but swiftly growing. Thirty-four knights I've slain thus far—and before daybreak I'll add all of you to that muster. Quite a harvest, no?"

King Harrowhelm had eyes like two brown, rusty nailheads. His smile was wintry as he waved his hand—and crossbows lifted in unison for the second time that day. Griflet winced. He and Sir Baudwin and Sir Hervise were going to—

Quarrels snarled.

And then froze, to hang quivering in midair, half-way across the chamber.

The common gasp of astonishment was almost a shriek, and out of its noise a black-robed figure drifted out of the shadows like a cloak borne along by a lazy wind. It grew feet and a bearded head with great, dark eyes like black stars all a-twinkle. Those lips twisted wryly ere they parted to say in a mocking, lilting voice, "Quite a harvest, indeed."

"Merlin!" a dozen throats gasped. The tall, thin robed man made a little bow.

"The same," he replied almost lazily, waving one long-fingered hand. In the air, crossbow bolts spun around and then flashed back at their sources. "I fear even this pleasant land cannot flower if so bloody a harvest is allowed to continue," he added mildly, in the instant before the quarrels struck the doomed row of armsmen who'd loosed them. "Die now, Peladrus."

As the crossbowmen gasped and sobbed and died, Merlin waggled his fingers in a gesture that seemed both casual and incredibly intricate, and King Harrowhelm's face changed.

In an instant he went from furious defiance to slack-jawed terror, his eyes staring as he started to shiver. He staggered back, fetching up against a pillar, and threw up trembling hands. "Nay!" he shouted, stumbling blindly around the pillar and turning to flee. *"Nay!"*

The self-styled king took two frantic strides and then lurched to a halt, screaming wordlessly now, only to rush in another direction and then halt again. His screams rose to a frantic height—and then blood burst from his cheek, as if it had been raked by unseen claws. Sobbing and slapping vainly at the empty air, Peladrus staggered back as if he'd been struck, and blood fountained from his ear. Then another phantom blow rocked him back on his heels—and nothingness tore away his face in a bloody ruin.

The wizard Merlin turned his back on the gurgling, dying king and extended his hand like a courtier to the sobbing lass on the throne. "Wilt accompany me, fair lady? I have gentler uses for you than this."

She stared at him, terror stark in her eyes . . . but seemed to see something reassuring in his gaze, and nodded gently, tear-dewed face glimmering in the firelight. Hesitantly she lifted her hand to accept his.

There came another swirl of Merlin's dark cloak, and the throne was bare. The movement brought the wizard around to face the last Knights of the Table Round—but he looked past them, straight at Griflet.

The wizard's body was beginning to fade, as if he were in truth a shadow, but his eyes were as large and as dark as ever, stars seeming to sparkle in their depths. He spoke to the squire in a voice that was calm and quiet—and yet rang clear across that hall: "You will, of course, say nothing of what you saw earlier."

Something broke in Griflet then. He'd seen much bloody death this day, some of those passings men he'd liked and admired—and all men feared Merlin. Griflet could see why; there was something of the beast in those eyes, something dark that lurked and laughed at the world . . . before casually weaving magic that could halt crossbow quarrels in midflight, and doom men with things unseen.

Somehow he was out of the keep, shoulders bruised from crashing into stone walls, and running headlong into the forest, his own gasps loud and raw in his ears.

Full, bright moonlight made the woods seem magical, but Griflet could think only of fleeing as far and as fast as he could, to anywhere where he could hide from those dark, knowing, *smiling* eyes. He ran for a long time, stumbling on uneven places and roots, crashing through raking branches, and panting his way across open dells, until—

He caught one boot on something soft and yet solid, and went sprawling.

The fall drove his breath from him, and it was a long and gasping time ere Griflet ceased staring up at the stars and found his feet again. For the first time he dared to look back at the distant fires—and saw what he'd fallen over.

Sir Brastias lay on his back, staring endlessly up into the moonlight. His mouth was open, and there were ants and other small, wriggling things crawling into and out of it. The Knight of the Green Shield was quite dead, his stiff hands two frozen claws of pain reaching vainly into the air with a crossbow quarrel standing cruel between them.

Fresh terror rose to choke Griflet, strangling the scream he wanted so desperately to utter.

He spun around and ran on into the night, on and on he knew not where, racing as if every tree were a dead knight lurching upright to claw at him, until the moonlight grew brighter and brighter—and he was out into rolling fields, free of the forest at last, racing through tall grass to a line of stumps and trees, with more moonlit hills beyond. Run, Sir Squire of Many Questions, *run!* They're not far behind, they'll catch you yet!

Mewing in fear, Griflet raced to the stumps and clambered over them, slipping and sliding and— something large, dark, and very solid struck his head, and the moon overhead glimmered and slid away, down, down into waiting darkness . . .

By'r Lady, but it *hurt!*

Griflet growled and tried to claw at his head, which

seemed to be splitting apart. There was something preventing him moving, tugging at his wrists . . .

"He's coming awake. Don't struggle, lad."

The kindly voice and the hands firm on his own belonged to Sir Hervise. Griflet blinked at him in the sudden brightness. It was morning, in farm fields somewhere, and the paltry surviving handful of the Knights of the Table Round were taking to their saddles.

"I know this land well," Sir Brastias announced, "so I'll lead."

Sir Brastias? Alive?

Griflet struggled to sit upright in his saddle and speak, to—

The Knight of the Green Shield turned his head then, and Griflet found himself staring into the dark, starry gaze that had so scared him last night.

The whisper came deep in his head this time. *You will, of course, say nothing of what you saw earlier.*

The Squire of Many Questions swallowed, and then nodded his head as vigorously as he knew how. The movement made him groan with pain, red fire blossoming—and then Brastias lifted one gauntleted finger, his eyes changing to the wise, warm brown they should be. Something moonlit and soothing stirred in Griflet's head, and again he knew no more . . .

Bright sunlight greeted them as they rode over a bare rise and saw Castle Northgalis in the distance. In unspoken accord the knights and the fresh-awakened, drowsy squire halted their mounts to look out over the land ahead, although it was not the work of a wise warrior to halt in high places for all eyes to take note.

"I have a dream that I dream sometimes," Brastias said slowly. "I see a high castle, bright with many banners, wherein dwells a High King whose wise and just rule holds sway over all this land. A great knight that other knights reverence and fight for—a king of honor, who holds forth one code for all, great and lowly, and stands like a shield for all to take refuge behind. Under such a king, this fair land could rise at last out of the bloody toils of petty kings . . . and become great."

Sir Baudwin lifted his head, his eyes suddenly afire. "Have my thanks, Brastias," he said roughly. "Your dream won't be such a bad thing to live in my own head, late on cold nights." He shook his head. "Wouldn't it be a great thing, to see such a shining castle before we die, with a High King in it?"

"Aye," Hervise de Revel agreed wistfully. "Wouldn't it?"

They rode on in silence for some little time before he added softly, "I'd fight for that."

Brastias smiled and clapped spurs to his horse. It took him over a little rise well ahead of the others.

Where he made a tiny gesture that unleashed a magic to hurl all metal violently away from his advance, and so foil any attackers lurking in the trees ahead. His spell brought at least one startled cry out of that waiting gloom—and his smile acquired a wry quirk.

As he plunged down into the hollow, reaching for the still-unfamiliar sword he wore, the Knight of the Green Shield murmured so softly that only the passing breeze heard him, "I already do. Every day, until the fighting brings me to my last one, and snatches me away. There are worse things to die for."

I have a dream that I dream sometimes, that voice— Merlin's voice—said in the depths of Griflet's head suddenly, making him gasp and stiffen in his saddle, *and you're part of it. So guard yourself well, Sir Griflet Many-Answers.*

Oh, yes. Questions you have now, but your life shall be the finding of the answers. I need—all Albion needs—a High King who has answers.

As they rode down into the hollow and the Knight of the Green Shield turned smilingly in his saddle to greet them, he smiled at Griflet's silent, gaping face and added gruffly, in the young squire's mind.

You will, of course, say nothing of this to anyone. And always remember to say nothing of what you saw earlier, too. Even High Kings can be . . . replaced.

HONOR IS A GAME
MORTALS PLAY

Eugie Foster

Grandfather wished I had been a boy. He never spoke of it when he lived, but it was the same as when I scorched the rice porridge, or when I came home with the traps empty and dangling in my hands; the silent disappointment shone clear in his eyes. Now that he was dead, I didn't have to bear the heaviness of his frown or the disapproving shake of his head, but that brought no surcease.

His ghost whispered in my ear, poisonous words that had no place in a harmonious household.

"Ayame, your tears are as welcome to me as a drunkard's spittle," his ghost hissed. "What a sniveling weakling you have become."

The hem of my mourning-white kimono lifted, brushed by fingers of heat from Grandfather's funeral pyre. The ash spun into the air, stinging my face and blinding me, as a counterpoint to the ghostly tirade.

I didn't think less of Grandfather for his ghost's cruel outburst. The dead, after all, were renowned for their lack of decorum.

"I did not cry when your father left, dishonoring me with his defiance," his spirit continued. "Nor did I shed a tear when he returned destitute and sick with a baby in tow, or even when he died, leaving only a granddaughter to carry on my legacy. And now you weep at my funeral?"

Grandfather had reared and sheltered me, even named me. He had taught me to respect and understand the harmony of the cosmos, shown me how each tree, rock, and creature was an exquisite miracle, playing its individual melody in the great symphony of the universe. The words of an angry *yurei,* the manifestation of his unnatural death, would not change sixteen years of respect and love. But they did stem my tears.

"While my father chose to walk another path," I said, "my steps will follow yours, Grandfather. I will purge his dishonor."

I heard the clack of phantom teeth. "Honor! As though a girl could understand honor."

I bowed my head and intoned a prayer, one to mollify a newly dead spirit.

"Spare me your pious gibberish," Grandfather's *yurei* snarled. "I taught you those sacraments, spoke them at temples and altars before you were born."

"If my prayers are not to your taste, should I begin the *tsuina* ceremony?" I asked. "Have you become a hateful poltergeist, an *ara-mi-tama* that I must exorcise?"

"Disgraceful, wicked girl. You dare to threaten me? Do you think because you are my kin that I will not curse you?"

"Peace, Grandfather. I know my duty. I will slay the demon that murdered you. I swear upon the flames of your pyre and the ashes of your body that I shall avenge you. It will be my first act as a *taijiya,* my first demon hunt."

The *yurei* was silent for the space of several heartbeats. I wiped the tears and ashes from my cheeks with a corner of my sleeve and gazed clear-eyed into the dying flames.

"Very well," he said at last. "Honor your oath and I'll not trouble you again. But should you bring further shame upon this family, I will visit upon you all the horrors that are at the disposal of the dead."

"I will not fail."

"Then finish this. I am done."

I bowed to the now-embers of Grandfather's pyre and tossed handfuls of parched beans to the four corners of the world.

"Depart! Depart!" I called to the north and the east. "Depart," I cried to the south.

When I turned to the west, out of the edge of my eye, I saw a glimmering blue light rise from Grandfather's funeral altar. It flew into the sky, chasing after the last tendrils of smoke.

"Depart, Grandfather," I whispered. "The serenity you crave awaits you in the Pure Land."

I turned my back on the smoldering remains of what had been a magnificent bonfire and climbed the familiar path that led to the hut where I had grown up.

Without Grandfather, those walls no longer shaped my home. I wondered if that made the entirety of the world my home, for nothingness and fullness were but two sides of completeness.

I smiled at the thought. It was the sort of puzzle Grandfather might have posed. The notion buoyed me as I removed my mourning garments, folding the white kimono into a neat square and setting it atop Grandfather's rolled-up sleeping mat. But when I made to don Grandfather's red kimono, the badge and uniform of a demon queller, I felt the burden of my uncertainty return. I set the kimono aside and slipped into my

comfortable, colorless *yukata* instead. Tomorrow
would be soon enough to garb myself in red.

I knelt before our tiny house altar. Tomorrow I
must slay the demon that had stricken Grandfather
with the freezing sickness, a demon powerful enough
to overcome an experienced *taijiya*. And despite his
wrinkles and gray hairs, Grandfather had been strong
enough to carry two stone cauldrons upon his
shoulders.

Grandfather's *yurei* had been right. I was frightened
and unsure, a banquet of weakness for hungry ghosts
and demons to feast upon. And now I was alone, without anyone to rescue me should I falter. I beseeched
any benevolent *kami* deigning to listen for strength
and wisdom.

My meditations complete, I curled upon my straw
mat and clenched shut my eyes. Though my head was
empty, sleep was as elusive as a single minnow in a
burbling stream.

At the first glint of dawn's banner, I rose, no wiser
or stronger, and significantly less rested. And I still
could not bear to clothe myself in Grandfather's red
kimono. I draped my *yukata* about my shoulders once
more and tucked a rice cake into its worn sleeve,
bundling a wooden bowl and chopsticks alongside it.
I tied a pot of sake to my simple, unadorned *obi*,
and got Grandfather's satchel from the hook where it
always rested. Slipping his red uniform to the bottom,
I filled the rest with the tools and weapons of the
taijiya: a rustling packet of carefully inscribed spells,
vials of herbs, and bottles of ointments. At last, I took
up Grandfather's *shakujou*, a stout oak staff carved
with holy blessings. It contained a core of iron, and
two golden pins protruded like horns from its knotted crown.

Packed and provisioned, I turned my sandals to the

west, for that had been the direction I'd seen Grandfather's spirit go when it released its hold.

As I journeyed, I scanned the skies and studied the trees for signs of the demon's passage. Such a strong evil couldn't have passed without leaving certain indications, fluctuations of energy like footprints in the mud.

The forest's *ki* nudged me to the base of a spreading maple tree. I fingered a single red leaf, crisped with rime, on an otherwise verdant branch.

A rustling in the underbrush caused me to spin about, gripping the *shakujou* in both hands.

A russet face with a pointed muzzle and shining eyes regarded me from the knots of a bristly hawthorn bush. The creature stepped from her shelter, nimble as a cat, and waved a dark brush of tail in greeting— a fox.

I exhaled my relief.

"Hai!" she called. "Are you responsible for the chill in the air? If so, please desist. I haven't been able to catch anything to eat all morning."

"It's not my doing," I said, "but perhaps I can ease your empty belly." I offered her a corner of rice cake.

The fox eyed the morsel. "I'm sure that's tasty, but don't you have anything stronger, something to chase away the cold? I can barely feel my nose."

It was unwise to displease a fox, so I splashed some sake into my wooden bowl and set it down.

"That's more like it!" She lapped the wine, licking her whiskers to catch the last drops. "For your generosity, here's some friendly advice: turn back. There's trouble ahead."

I bowed. "I hope you don't think me ungrateful, but I regret I'm honor bound to press on."

"Oh? Well anyway, that's hardly an even trade, advice being free and not worth a drop of sake. I'll give you another bit of counsel: stay on the path. Don't vary your course."

I frowned. "Both turn back and go forward?"

The fox grinned, her tongue lolling from her muzzle. "If your yang is nourished and your yin starved, does that make you happy or miserable? Besides, what sort of advice do you expect a mouthful of sake to get you?" She barked, the fox equivalent of laughter, and bounded away.

I shook my head. Foxes. I would rather face a *tengu* demon than a friendly fox. With their riddles and pranks, they might ruin you even as they tried to help. At least with a *tengu,* I always knew what its teeth meant.

A puddle of ice-crusted mud caught my eye. It was a thick crimson. Over it, a copper tang hung like a shroud in the air. Several steps away, tiny red berries ornamented a young lilac tree—wet fruit that thawed into droplets of blood. A bloody icicle hung suspended from a twig like a red needle.

Perhaps because of my agitation from encountering the fox, I did not notice the man lying beneath it until he groaned.

In my defense, his kimono was dark—a chestnut brown with bands of deep ginger that blended into the crisscross shadows beneath the arching canopy. His hair also camouflaged him, a torrent of black that rooted him among the moldering verdure on the forest's floor. Still, his skin was whiter than milk, white as mourning. I should have seen him.

He watched me through half-lidded eyes. The source of the metallic bouquet suffusing the air was the seeping gash in his side. Even felled and half-conscious, I was struck by his beauty—the aristocratic lines of his face and the grace of his limbs. I'd never before seen such a nobly formed man.

When I stepped closer, he raised his arm, and I saw

the weapon gripped in his fist, a katana of folded steel, a samurai's sword.

"Come to finish me off, witch?" His voice was silver silk, frayed with pain. "Or merely to watch me die?" The katana wavered. How long had he lain there, bleeding in the dirt?

"I mean you no harm," I said.

He squinted. "What game are you playing now, Yuki-onna? How like you to turn my final moments into some farce." His words grew indistinct. "It's not a very good disguise in any case." His head drooped, and his arm slipped to his side, although he continued to cling to the katana.

I crept nearer and kneeled, counting upon his weakness to keep him from chopping me to bits. The icy mire of blood and soil soaked into my *yukata*.

I set the *shakujou* aside so I could open his kimono, noting as I did its sleek softness—not wool or even felt—luxurious as fur but thin as silk. His skin burned fever hot save for the bubbling hole—from a dart or arrow, perhaps—that poured frozen mist into the air. Whatever the cause of his injury, it was feeding upon his body's warmth, his vital *ki*. It wouldn't be enough to staunch the bleeding; I had to neutralize that poisonous cold or it would kill him.

I drew one of the pins from Grandfather's *shakujou*. I disliked these slim implements, so finely honed it seemed every time I handled one, I must pay for the privilege with blood. Grandfather had often despaired at my clumsiness, sighing as he wrapped my gold-scored fingers in linen. But they were thrice blessed and inscribed with prayers—*taijiya* tools to negate demon magic.

Moving fast as thought, the man snatched my wrist. I flinched, and the edge of his katana hovered at my throat.

"You're not *her*," he growled. "Did she send you to torment me?"

I spoke softly, as though to a frightened animal. "The dart that wounded you carried a curse, and I believe the point is still embedded." I tilted the sliver of gold so a wisp of sunlight could highlight the prayers etched along its length. "This is a *gofu*, a blessed amulet to counteract demon energy."

He studied me, his eyes creased with pain. "Not that," he rasped. "Use my *shoto* to dig it out."

"But—"

"Else plunge that thorn into my heart and have done with it." He closed his eyes and released me.

There was only one reason a creature would refuse the touch of a holy charm. I leaned close, searching. They had been concealed by the darkness of his hair and the lattice of shadows, the elegant pair of black horns that twisted from his temples.

I was a fool. Worse than a fool. This wasn't a hapless man but an *oni*, a malicious demon of brutal hungers. The drape of his kimono derided me, the tiger-stripe pattern evident now, clear indication of his true nature. I hovered in indecision, poised to drive the *gofu* into his heart, as he'd suggested.

But he was so defenseless. And so beautiful. Compassion, what grandfather had called the foundation of a *taijiya's* art, and also something else, something I did not wish to admit to, wouldn't let me finish him.

Instead, I tucked the *gofu* into my *obi* and pulled the wooden chopsticks from my sleeve. I found the demon's *shoto* sheathed at his hip, a long knife of gleaming steel, sharp and deadly as spite. It sheered into his flesh as easily as slicing water.

His cooled blood spilled over my hand. The sinews in his throat tightened, bowing his head back, but he didn't cry out. I cut again, widening the entry in order to insert the tips of my chopsticks within. His silent anguish continued, and I suffered with him.

His breath juddered through clenched jaws as I probed, searching with both blunt wood and also with that other awareness, the thrumming along my nerves that alerted me to *youki,* demon energy.

I touched the knot of cold with a chopstick at the same moment as I felt it, a contamination like a drop of tar in white tallow. I gripped it with the chopsticks and tugged. It resisted, slick and lodged tight, requiring me to dig it free with wood and steel.

The *oni* suffered my ministrations in silence.

At last I saw a pale bead peeping from the edge of his wound. Frozen blood encased it in a growing block of red. It wedged there, fouling my attempts to pry it loose. Despite his fortitude, I could not subject the *oni* (or myself) to another incision, so I used my fingertips to pluck it out.

As soon as I touched it, the bead slid into my palm.

The *oni* went limp, a ragged sigh slipping from his lips.

A bolt of winter hammered my hand, a numbness that sliced through muscle and bone. I dropped the *shoto* and drew the *gofu* from my sash. I stabbed the cursed pellet, and it shattered beneath the golden tip like brittle ice.

I thought the *oni* had finally slipped the yoke of consciousness, but when I pulled a length of linen from my satchel, I saw the glimmer of his eyes beneath his lashes, watching me.

In a rush, I remembered tales of *oni* who lusted after human women, violating helpless maidens before devouring their flesh. Fear sped my pulse, and also an intriguing thrill that brought guilt rushing after. I gripped the *gofu* tighter. It nicked my thumb, drawing a thread of blood from tip to meaty pad.

I swore and dropped the razor-edged metal. I immediately scrabbled after it, sifting the dirt with my fingers for the splinter of gold. Only after I'd found it and shoved it back into the *shakujou* did I recall the *oni*.

The demon had not moved during my antics, although his lips now wore a curve of mirth. I busied myself with herbs and bandages.

"That's not necessary," he murmured.

I glared at him, a swathe of linen hanging from one hand. "After all that, you don't expect me to let you bleed to death, do you?"

His smile mocked me as I inspected his side. I dabbed away the now-warm blood and discovered only a pinprick seam.

In a fluid motion, lithe as a dancer, he stood, towering over me. I scrambled to my feet, clutching the *shakujou* to my chest.

"As I said. Unnecessary." He pulled his kimono closed and knotted it with an *obi* striped orange and black like a tiger's tail. With skillful ease, he slid his katana into its scabbard.

He bent to collect his *shoto* from where I'd dropped it. I watched, bemused, as he twirled it in one hand. Would he now slash my throat, tear at my flesh and drink my blood?

It seemed not.

He wiped it clean with a tiger-pelt sleeve and sheathed it. His kimono possessed an unusual quality. Where it had been discolored by blood, it now gleamed, dry and unsoiled. The filth from his *shoto* rained from it in a gray dust.

In comparison, I felt grubby and unkempt with my *yukata* stained and damp, and my hair a tangled nest about my face.

"Do all *oni* heal as quickly as you?" I asked.

His eyes flitted to Grandfather's *shakujou*. "Not always," he said. "Some faster than others. That stick you're sporting has hewn down its share of *oni* by the look of it. The *taijiya* you stole it from is going to be eager to have it back."

"I didn't steal it," I said. "It's mine."

The *oni* arched an eyebrow. "Is it? Pardon my ignorance. I have not heard of a maiden *taijiya* so confident that she heals mortally wounded demons in order to defeat them in honorable battle."

I paled. "Are we to battle, then?"

He laughed, displaying straight, white teeth with only a suggestion of flesh-tearing serration. "Only if you demand it." He bowed, every line of his body distorting the salutation into a jest. "As you have saved me, I'm yours to command." His eyes—feral, tawny orbs like a tiger's—glinted a challenge. "What would you have of me?"

"I don't recall *oni* being so honorable," I said.

"May a demon not have honor? Would it suit you better if I fell upon you, slavering and rapacious?"

"Tell me your name," I demanded, doing my best to achieve Grandfather's authoritative boom. I straightened my shoulders.

"I'm called Ronin by those who care to address me." His amusement was obvious even without his muted laughter. As I feared, I sounded more like a puffed-up mouse squeaking at a wolf than a *taijiya*.

"What is your business here, and where is the demon who caused your hurt? I've a score to settle with him."

"Her. It was a woman's hand that threw the dart." Ronin's manner switched to bleak bitterness in the space of those words. "My mistress brooks no defiance

and no failure, she of the frozen heart, cruel Yuki-
onna." Ronin lifted his eyes to the white-rimmed
mountains behind us.

His wistfulness filled me with misery, a heartsick
desolation.

"It wasn't so great a thing she demanded. I've won
legendary prizes, magnificent and precious, for her,
razed whole villages at her whimsy, but at this, I
balked. All she required was a certain female infant,
with the only obstacle an old monk, her grandfather."

I started. "A girl and her grandfather?"

Ronin scowled, returned from whatever reverie he'd
fallen into. "I killed the old man. He was stronger
than I expected, but in the end, even his *ki* succumbed
to Yuki-onna's frozen death, delivered by the edge of
my katana." His laughter was harsh, dripping with
self-loathing. "But I could not bring myself to fetch
her some brat and told her so."

"W–what was the girl's name?"

Ronin shrugged. "Ayame or Ayemi, perhaps."

I felt as though I'd swallowed a lead ball. "It was
you," I gasped. "You're the demon that killed
Grandfather!"

His eyes widened. Faster than any man could move,
he sprang at me.

Rather than drawing a *gofu* or swinging the *shakujou* to ward him off, I screamed, cringing like a useless
fool. I expected to feel his teeth at my throat, but he
scooped me into his arms.

The earth fell away as he swept us aloft.

I struggled, but his arms were a cage of marble
and steel.

"A baby." His words were strangely fierce. "An *infant* girl."

Waves of heat throbbed through the dual layers of
our garments, smoldering hotter than an open forge.

The *youki* energy of an *oni* is akin to the *ki* of fire. It made me lightheaded and weak; I would have fainted but for the *shakujou* between us, radiating a soothing counterpoint. As dizzy as I was, I still noted that Ronin didn't care to touch it, buffering his skin with his tiger pelt where it pressed against him.

"Put me d–down!" I forced the words through chattering teeth.

"I regret I cannot. My mistress requires your presence." He flew, eyes fixed upon the summit of the tallest mountain. In the space of three breaths, the air grew chilly and thin, and whirling snowflakes powdered the sky. I writhed, half frozen by the piercing cold, half baking against Ronin.

"S–so much for a demon's honor."

He glanced at me. "You think honor is a game exclusive to mortals?"

"You s–seemed to tire of it quickly enough."

"Don't assume you know all the rules of this game, little *taijiya*." The resignation and sorrow in his voice were ancient as the mountain above us.

With a stomach-lurching maneuver, he deflected a gust of frigid wind with his back, sheltering me from the worst of it.

"By all the eight million *kami,* don't do that," I gasped. "Unless you intend to deliver me dead from fright."

"The cold will kill you faster than any distress I could provide."

"I wouldn't depend on that," I chattered.

"I could fly better if you carried your *shakujou*. It's awkward, wedged between us."

Ronin wanted me to keep the best weapon I had against demonkind? Why? He gazed over my head, intent on our journey.

"Very well, release my arms."

He adjusted his hold, cradling me beneath my knees
and shoulders, and allowed me to slide the *shakujou*
free. I wrapped one arm around it, and with the other,
I plucked out a *gofu*. Gripping it as tightly as I dared
in my numb fingers, I leveled the point over his heart.

Ronin tilted his head to regard first me and then
the gold skewer pressing into his kimono. "If you
don't put that away, you're liable to cut yourself
again," he said

"I have sworn to kill you, demon."

"We're quite high," he remarked. "If you stick me,
I may not be able to keep from dropping you." He
swooped at the distant crags below to illustrate.

I wrenched my eyes from the speeding ground.
"Death doubtless awaits me at your destination
anyway."

"Then perhaps I should do this before you send us
tumbling from the sky." I felt long fingers tangle in
my hair as he bent his neck, bringing his lips to mine.
At the touch of his mouth, an ember flared between
us, electrifying and sharp. I inhaled in astonishment,
taking the firestorm of his breath into my lungs. Ronin
tasted of smoke and hot steel, warm rain and summer
winds. His kiss chased away the chill of the frozen air
and left me breathless. Through the tiger pelt kimono,
I felt him trembling.

He buried his face in my hair, his lips brushing my
ear. "*Kami* of fire and light." I could barely hear him
over the screaming wind. He crushed me to him, so I
could not think.

"Ayame, I will be yours," he said, "to kill as you
wish. If you will not allow me *seppuku,* I swear I will
kneel to a blow from your *shakujou* or open myself
to the point of your *gofu*. Only free me first, little
taijiya. Please, free me first."

I had no more than a moment to splutter in astonishment.

He loosed his hold, and I cried out, expecting to plummet through a mountain's span of empty air. But my descent was brief; I sank not through the ether, but into snow, up to my ankles. My shout petered out, ending as a confused yip.

We had alighted during his kiss, and I had been too preoccupied to notice.

He kneeled.

I gaped, baffled, until I realized his obeisance was not to me. I turned, slow as a dream.

Behind me, not five strides away, stood the most exquisite maiden I had ever seen. Her skin was an ice blue so luminous she glowed against the backdrop of winter white. A curtain of raven-black hair cascaded to the ground, stray locks billowing in glossy streamers about her head. She wore a silk kimono—moonlight embroidered with clouds—and her eyes were dark as forever. There was a familiarity to her loveliness, like a forgotten memory, or a dream.

She didn't walk, but rather drifted to us, bare feet passing over the snow.

"You dare to return?" At odds with her visage, her voice was a knife of ice. "Do you love me so much, my samurai, that death means nothing to you?"

"Death has never meant anything to me, Yuki-onna." Ronin's words released me from my paralysis. I blinked, my eyes dry and chilled from staring.

She glanced at me. "And who's this?"

"She is Ayame. You charged me to fetch her."

"What nonsense are you babbling? You think I'll forgive your transgressions with a trick? I told you to bring me a girl child, an infant, not a maiden full grown."

"Girl children become maidens, my lady."

Her brow furrowed. "Could it be?" The edge of her voice softened. "Sixteen thaws and sixteen freezes. I'd forgotten how time affects those who bow to its passage." She caught my chin in her slender fingers and forced me to meet her gaze. "Do you remember me, child?"

Her touch sent tendrils of ice through me. "M–my apologies, l–lady, no," I stammered.

"You're shivering. Come closer. Let me wrap you in my kimono." She undid the knot of her *obi* and opened it, sweeping me into her embrace.

"No!" Ronin's shout floated to me, as though from a great distance.

Pressed against her skin, a glacial storm buffeted me—body and *ki*—tearing at my confusion, my unhappiness, and my lingering grief, even as it chilled me through. The *shakujou* slipped from my benumbed fingers.

Dimly, I heard the hiss of a katana leaving its scabbard.

I craned my neck so I could peer over Yuki-onna's white shoulder. Ronin whirled in a lethal dance, his katana a blur. Around him, white claws and fangs had sprouted, mindless snow *kami* whose only purpose was butchery. I saw his face as he parried, desperate and frantic—not for himself, but for me.

"Ayame."

So simply, with my name, she had me. A white mist—snowflakes and rime—billowed from her lips. It engulfed me and swept away everything that anchored my *ki* to my body: anger, compassion, and the resolve acquired through years as Grandfather's apprentice.

My shivering stopped; the cold no longer troubled me.

The folds of her kimono parted, leaving behind a memory of white silk whispering along my skin.

"Am I dead?" I asked.

She laughed, a delicate peal of ice crystals. "No, child, you are awake. The last sixteen years, that was the dream."

I heard Ronin cry out. Glancing back, I saw snow *kami* strewn in glittering shreds. He staggered and fell to his knees, clutching his side where crimson ribbons spilled through his fingers.

Yuki-onna leaned close. "In sixteen years, have you never wondered about your mother?" she whispered. "About me?"

I forgot Ronin.

Broken pieces of a puzzle I had not comprehended fell together: Ronin mistaking me in the forest, Yuki-onna's inexplicable familiarity, and her motive for wanting me in the first place. The answer was in the line of our limbs, the arch of our brows, the shared curve of our mouths—if only I'd known to look for it. She and I were forged from the same mold, mother and daughter.

"Let me share my secrets with you." Her voice was as mesmerizing as falling snow. "We shall explore frozen caverns where the bones of ancient animals lie glittering like jewels, and bathe in black pools, still as glass, that no man has ever seen. I'll weave you a kimono of spun pearls and teach you how to kill with a sigh. We'll rule the *kami* of blizzards and tempests, and you will never die."

"Never die—?"

"Never. Never suffer the ruin of old age. All you must do is discard that part of you which cleaves to time and the flimsy sentiments of mortality."

"I don't understand."

"Your name, daughter. Renounce Ayame, frail and filled with doubt, and become Yuki-onna."

"Grandfather gave me my name," I said. "I promised I wouldn't dishonor him."

"We are Women of the Snow!" Her voice rang over the mountaintop. "We are not bound by man or god!"

"Ayame, don't." Ronin had stumbled forward, but his way was barred by the *shakujou* lying between us. "It's not life she offers, but eternal death, an existence of inviolate cold. Her heart is a frozen rock. I know this better than anyone."

"Enough!" Yuki-onna gestured, and tiny darts flew from her outstretched fingers. They lodged in Ronin's chest with a sound like pattering hail. He crumpled without a sound, his blood a poem in the snow, red brushstrokes on white paper.

It was my voice that cried out, a wail of anguish. I would have run to him, but Yuki-onna caught me back with steely fingers on my shoulder.

"He's nothing," she hissed. "His kind hunger after the young and beautiful. Don't throw away eternity for love of him. No matter how tender or how devoted he seems, he will abandon you when you become stooped and gray."

Her touch extinguished the tantalizing yearning I'd felt from the moment I'd seen Ronin under the lilac tree. No longer anxious or conflicted, I could step aside and regard my feelings, like studying an insect caught in honey. It was a relief, a deliverance, to be free of them. Such peace was surely worth the trifle of a name.

It was on my lips, a glowing coal I could spit out and be rid of. But the heat in my mouth reminded me of Ronin's kiss. If I cast away my name, a kiss would mean no more than a breeze through my hair.

I rolled my name on my tongue, re-living the brief

thrill of Ronin's touch, the taste of his passion. Was death so terrible a price to pay for the likes of joy, for even the smallest chance of happiness? Death, after all, was nothing more than a change, the other side of living. Without it, there was no life and no love.

I swallowed.

"Even if love is fleeting, Mother, I want it."

Her face didn't change, but her eyes flashed with displeasure. "Fool. Love and death are the same."

She exhaled, and a cloud of sleet surged forth. Needles of ice blinded me, while a deeper, penetrating cold clamped me in a vise; I couldn't breathe, couldn't move.

My hand convulsed, and a new pain speared my arm, a pain that blazed. The *gofu*, I'd forgotten it. Forever eager to bite me—protesting my demonic lineage?—its keen edges sliced my fingers, thawing frozen nerves.

Calling upon every trick of will Grandfather had taught me, I stabbed that golden tooth at the arctic center, winter's heart.

Yuki-onna shrieked. Her scream became a howling snowstorm rushing to the sky. I covered my ears, but still I heard it. The sleet dissipated, and through stinging eyes, I saw her reel, her kimono whipping about like the edge of a blizzard. My mother grew indistinct as her *youki* fragmented, fading at last into nothingness. Quelled.

Overhead, the mountainside shuddered, throwing off its mantle of snow. An avalanche poured down, inexorable and inescapable.

My last thought before the frozen weight struck was that Yuki-onna was wrong. Love and death were not the same, even if knowing one meant embracing both.

*   *   *

"Ayame. Get up." Grandfather prodded me with a stiff finger, as he did every morning to wake me.

"How can it be dawn already?" I groaned.

"There's no dawn in death's Shadow Realm. Stop lazing about. I'm on my way to the Pure Land, and I'm in a hurry."

Memory lashed me alert. "The avalanche. Ronin!"

Grandfather smirked. "Didn't take you long to find yourself a young man, I see."

"But he's an *oni*," I moaned.

"So what? Your mother's a Snow Woman." His jovial grin turned solemn. "Do not fear the inevitable; destiny is best greeted with open arms. I always feared what would happen when she came back, but I should've had more faith in you. Your father loved her and though she destroyed him, he never regretted loving her. He was wise, just not strong enough. You, Ayame, are strong enough. Now be wise."

"Grandfather—"

"Must go now. Bye-bye." He patted my head. "Go have many daughters so you may be as proud of them as I am of you."

Then he vanished, leaving me in darkness. Cold, wet darkness. Snow. I was buried in snow. Waves of heat rose beneath me in a fluttering pulse. I was slumped over Ronin, sideways and crumpled, but whole.

I groped about until I could tell which end of him was up and wriggled through compacted snow until I reached his head. *Do not fear the inevitable.* Could I at least have qualms about the uncertain, Grandfather?

Destiny or no, I did what I'd longed to from my first glimpse of Ronin. I kissed him.

At first, there was nothing, and I was terrified he was gone. But then he inhaled. Like a spark touching rice paper, we ignited. He clamped me to him with one arm and fed from me, fierce and desperate, as though he would crawl down my throat. The heat we'd kindled erupted into a conflagration. I was overwhelmed, lost. There'd be nothing left of me, my *ki* sundered to ash and gone.

I didn't care. I met him, adding more fuel to the blaze.

We became molten steel, liquid fire, shining and white.

It was Ronin who broke away. I opened my eyes to see that the mountainside of snow had melted in a clearing around us. Tiger eyes, tawny as a summer afternoon, studied me.

"I thought she'd finished me," he said.

I sat in a puddle of slush, feeling both shy and defiant. And cold. "Rather, I finished her," I said.

He knelt awkwardly. "Will you allow me *seppuku,* mistress?"

I stared, disbelieving. "I will not!"

"I see. You would rather kill me?"

I propelled myself to my feet. "I would rather you had a brain, but it seems I might as well wish for wings." He already looked dry and sleek, even kneeling in melting snow, while I felt like a sodden lump. A *shivering* sodden lump.

I turned to storm off, not counting upon the drift of snow heaped to my waist.

"What of your vow?" Ronin stood at my back, close enough to caress my neck with his words.

I spoke over my shoulder. "My mother killed my father, and through you, my grandfather. By ending her, I have avenged my family."

I endeavored to contain my shivering so he wouldn't notice, but my efforts were futile. He wrapped his arms around me and I swayed, lulled by the warmth of him.

"Then what would you have of me?" he asked.

I held myself rigid. "Nothing. If you want to go, go."

His lips brushed my ear. "What if I want to stay?"

"Why would you want that? I'm not a beautiful immortal. I'll get old and wrinkled. I'll probably get a hump."

He laughed, a silken cord through my hair. "So?" He spun me about. His face was solemn, although his eyes twinkled. "While you are indeed quite beautiful, it's neither your creamy skin nor your lithe body which entices me. It is your spirit, endless and ageless. The fiery taste of your *ki* as it blazes against mine is more potent than a hundred barrels of wine."

He tipped my face up and kissed me. When he raised his head, I wasn't the least bit cold.

"So, what would you have of me?" he murmured.

I gazed into the amber glow of his eyes. "You. Just you," I whispered.

"Little *taijiya,* didn't I just say? I'm yours. To walk by your side and sleep in your arms, even to help you quell demons—other demons—if you insist."

An abrupt and enormous sneeze rocked me on my heels. "A way off this frigid mountain would also be appreciated," I sniffled. "And unless that fox has stolen my satchel, there's a certain red kimono I'd like back. I think it'll fit me, now."

"It is my honor to oblige you," Ronin said.

Then we were airborne. Despite his words, I knew it was not honor that cradled me, or honor that held me so tenderly. Honor was just a game, and I had already won the prize.

THE WIZARD'S LEGACY

Michael A. Burstein

"Call me Merlin," he said.

Jacob and I looked at each other. We were sitting in the Wizard's chambers, a spacious suite of rooms located in the top of the castle's tower. The Wizard had placed us in wooden chairs on the same side of a long, wooden table cluttered with books, candles, bottles, and other things I couldn't identify. Come to think of it, clutter filled the whole chamber. Every wall without a window had a cabinet or bookcases in front. The shelves were cluttered with the same assortment of objects as were on the table. And plenty of those unidentifiable objects littered the floor as well.

"Call you Merlin?" I asked. I heard a meowing from below and saw the Wizard's black cat pad over to him.

"I thought you only wanted to be called the Wizard," Jacob said.

The Wizard himself was an old man with a long gray beard. The few times I had seen him before now, he had always worn long, flowing robes. I didn't know his age, but as far back as I could recall lines had etched his face. He picked up his cat, petted it, and then put it back down.

"To others, I am the Wizard. But to my two new apprentices, I prefer to be called by a name."

"So Merlin's your true name, then," Jacob said with an odd smile.

The Wizard laughed. "No, it's not. It's the name of a wizard who protected the kingdom long ago, or so the myths say." His eyes twinkled. "You don't really think I would be so casual with something as valuable as my true name, do you?"

"Pardon me, sir," I said, "but what's a true name?"

Jacob turned to me and sneered. "If you don't know that, why are you here?"

I felt my face flush hot with embarrassment, but the Wizard ignored that and turned to Jacob. "Jacob. It is not your place to question Edmund's knowledge. After all, I have brought you both here to learn. There will doubtless be concepts new to you as well."

I heard Jacob mutter, "I doubt it," too softly for the Wizard to hear. The Wizard looked directly at me. "Edmund, an excellent question. Your true name is who you really are. It is the secret name that you were given at birth."

"I don't have a secret name," I said. "I've always been Edmund. My father named me for my grandfather."

"Nevertheless, you, along with everyone and everything in the world, have a true name. And true names have power. If you give your enemy your true name, then your enemy will have power over you."

Jacob leaned over and grinned at me. I didn't like the way his face looked. "How about that, *Edmund*?" Someone who knows your true name has power over you."

"Which is why," the Wizard said, "neither of you should tell anyone your true name."

"I can't tell someone something I don't even know," I said.

"But you can," the Wizard said. "Through your actions, through your deeds. That is why your first lesson will be on protective spells. You must know how to defend yourself—mind and body—from all attack before you start learning other spells."

He gestured at the bookcase, and two large tomes flew off the shelves. One landed in front of me, the other in front of Jacob. On their own, both books opened to what seemed the same page in each. But I had no way of telling.

I couldn't read.

My face began to feel hot with embarrassment. Jacob had been picking on me ever since we met, just a few minutes ago. He was a scion of one of the noble families, and in his presence I felt clumsy and uneducated.

"Jacob, would you please read aloud what it says on the page?" the Wizard asked.

Jacob glanced at the Wizard, then at me, and then back at the Wizard again. "Why?"

"Because I have asked you to."

Jacob crossed his arms. "I don't have to take orders from you."

The Wizard sighed. "As my apprentice, you do, but never mind that for now." He turned to me. "Edmund? If you would?"

I felt my eyes start to get wet with tears. "I would very much like to, sir, but . . . I can't read."

The Wizard raised his eyebrows. "Your father is an innkeeper. He would have taught you had to read."

"He's tried, sir, but I've never been able to get very far." I paused. "But I do know my numbers, though."

"I see," the Wizard said. "Let me think." He tapped his fingers on his chin for a moment, and then a gleam appeared in his eye. He walked over to one of his bookcases, grabbed a small, dark bottle off a shelf, and brought it over to me. He opened it with a pop.

"Drink this," he said.

I took it from him and sniffed. It smelled like pungent wine, and I grimaced. "What is it?"

"An elixir."

I sniffed it again. "It smells horrible."

"Trust me, Edmund."

I looked into the Wizard's eyes, shrugged, held my nose, and downed the drink in one gulp. It tasted vile.

"Now read aloud from the book," he said.

I looked at the page again, and my head buzzed with sudden understanding of the text. "Sir?" I said, looking up at the Wizard. "I can read this!"

"Of course you can. I gave you a learning potion. Now read aloud, please."

I looked back at the page and began, "A spell to defend oneself from magical attack," when Jacob interrupted.

"Sir," he said to the Wizard.

"Yes?"

I looked at Jacob; he was keeping his gaze on the table. "May I have some of that elixir as well?"

"No, you may not," the Wizard replied. His voice sounded harsher and firmer than it had before. "Let this be the first lesson to both of you. I am your new master. From now on, even above your parents, you are answerable to me. And you will keep no secrets from me, nor will you talk back, or I will punish you, and my punishments will be harsh." He paused. "Is that clear?"

"Yes, sir," we said in unison.

"Good. Edmund, continue to read. You will learn

your first spell today. And Jacob? If you want to learn it as well, you will have to pay close attention to Edmund and make sure to repeat exactly what he says. If you do, then perhaps I will grant you a taste of the learning potion tomorrow."

That was the first lesson we had with the Wizard. He had kept Jacob and me in his chambers all day, from the early morning until the sun had just begun to set. We learned how to defend ourselves from any sort of attack—physical, magical, or psychic—by building up a shield. But the Wizard was able to break through all our shields, and he did not teach us how to initiate attacks on that first day.

A member of the King's guard, the same one who had taken me from my home in a horse and carriage, brought me back after the lessons were over. My home on the edge of the capital was actually an inn that my parents had run since long before my birth. Since the Wizard lived and worked in the King's Castle at the center of the city, the trip home took over an hour. I dashed inside, knowing I still had my day's worth of chores to do.

But then I skidded to a halt. As always, the inn was filled with customers drinking and eating and laughing. Some I recognized, some I didn't, but I knew I didn't recognize the servant girl who was running about with trays of food.

I spotted my father in his usual place behind the bar just as he saw me. He was drying glass mugs with a towel. When he saw me, he stopped for a moment and waved me over to him.

"Who is that girl?" I asked.

He shrugged. "Her name's Julia. The Wizard sent her from the castle."

"He did?"

My father nodded. "I guess he must have been spying on me when I complained to your mother that he would be taking you away from your chores."

This was the first time I had ever heard my father say something bad about the Wizard. "Father, I don't understand. I thought you liked the Wizard."

Father took a deep breath. "I never really thought about it one way or the other. He keeps the kingdom safe."

"But you don't like him?"

"I don't know him." He sighed. "All I know is that he showed up here last week as an illusion and commanded me to send him to you. You know the rest."

"But he seems nice. Why don't you like him?"

Father looked at me and smiled. "You ask the question as if members of the royal court come to the inn every day. You know that they're not our clientele."

"But still."

"It's not that I don't like him. It's that I'm worried for you."

"Really?" Father hadn't said anything before. "Why?"

"Because of what this means."

"I thought you said that the Wizard was paying us well to have me take lessons from him."

"Edmund, have you ever heard of a teacher paying a student for the privilege of teaching him?"

I thought for a moment, and then shook my head.

"So why should the Wizard pay for a common innkeeper's son to take lessons from him?"

I considered the question, and then shrugged. "I have no idea."

"Well. Did you enjoy the lesson, at least?"

"I did, but—did you know about the other apprentice?"

He stopped drying the glass in his hand. "Other apprentice?"

"Yeah. His name's Jacob. He's the son of one of the nobles."

My father's face turned slightly pale. "A second apprentice . . ." he said.

"Yeah." I lowered my voice. "He's a bit of an annoying brat, if you want to know the truth."

"Never mind that. Did the Wizard say anything to you about there being two of you?"

I thought back over the day's lesson. "No. We went over defense spells, that's about it." I smiled. "He gave me a potion, and now I can read."

My father smiled back and said, "That's great, Edmund," but I thought I could see sadness behind his eyes.

"Father, what's the matter? I can tell something's troubling you."

"Edmund, have you heard the rumors?"

"No, sir. What rumors?"

"I probably shouldn't be discussing this with you, but—haven't you noticed how we've had a lot more business over the past few weeks than usual?"

"Of course. Late summer is over. We always get more people staying in the inn when the fall rolls around."

My father shook his head. "Don't compare to the months before, Edmund. How much business did we have *last* fall?"

Now I understood. "A lot, but not as much as we've been getting this year."

My father nodded. "When you compare one season to the next, usually you find that business stays the same. But this year . . . we're getting a lot more people coming from the outskirts of the kingdom, looking to the capital for safety."

"Safety?"

"People don't travel to the capital unless they've got business here. We usually get a regular clientele of traveling merchants, and the occasional adventurer. But we've been seeing a lot of families coming, fathers bringing their wives and children and looking for any work they can find."

"What does this have to do with me?"

He leaned forward. "History, Edmund. The kingdom needs a Wizard, and the old Wizard always finds an apprentice to take over near—well, he always does. From what I understand, the Wizard's magic allows him to choose the only appropriate candidate for the job. But for the past five hundred years, the Wizard's next apprentice has always been chosen from among the fifteen-year-old boys living in the kingdom."

"I'm thirteen," I said. "So is Jacob."

He nodded. "I know. And assuming that what I know about magic is correct, that means that you are the most appropriate candidate for the job. But he should have waited two years before summoning you to the castle."

"What does that all mean?"

"It means he felt obliged to start training a new apprentice two years early. And that's what worries me."

He stood up, smiled, and picked up another glass to clean. "Go upstairs. Tell your mother about your day, and then get some rest. I have a feeling you're going to need it more than ever before."

My father was right. For the entire fall, I had lessons with the Wizard that lasted from just after sunrise to well after sunset. I would come home yawning with exhaustion, and I would wake up barely rested when the call of the King's guard came to my window from the outer darkness.

I would arrive at the Wizard's chambers just as a sliver of the sun appeared in the east. Jacob was always there too.

The Wizard had a collection of grimoires, he called them, large tomes filled with spells. We learned all sorts of magic in the mornings. He forced us to memorize arcane words and bizarre recipes for casting spells, and he didn't have an elixir to help. We had to rely on our own minds to retain everything we learned.

In the afternoons, we put the magic to the test. The Wizard took us out to an empty field within the environs of the castle, and we would practice throwing fireballs, summoning lightning, inducing sleep—all sorts of spells. And when I told my father about them, he would shake his head and ask me when I was going to learn how to turn water into wine, or something else innocuous.

What I didn't tell my father was that the Wizard had Jacob and me learn our spells by practicing these attacks upon each other. I didn't want to upset him. As it is, the Wizard always kept an eye on us as we practiced, and if our own defensive spells weren't up to the task of repelling an attack, he would lend us a little of his own magic for our protection.

Lessons progressed like this, as I said before, for the entire fall. And then one winter morning, when a light snow had left frost on the windows but the Wizard's chambers were warm through a magical, unending fire, a knock at his door interrupted our studies. Jacob and I both jerked our heads up from the grimoires in surprise; our lessons had never been interrupted before.

The Wizard looked surprised too. He pushed him-

self out of his leather-covered chair and walked over
to the door, his face showing a combination of curiosity and annoyance. I caught a glimpse of a King's
guardsman when the Wizard opened the door, but
then he pushed the guard into the hall and spoke so
quietly I couldn't hear what they were saying.

I returned to my reading, but Jacob interrupted me.
"Want to know what they're talking about?"

I leaned a little bit away from him. "What do you
mean?"

He grinned and flipped the pages in his book.
"There's a spell in here for eavesdropping," he said.

"I don't think that's such a good idea," I said.

He rolled his eyes. "Well, I'm going to do it. My
father says never let anyone keep secrets from you."

He flipped a few more pages and then stopped.
"Ah, here it is. Sure you don't want to join me in
casting it?"

I shook my head. "I really think we should stick to
the lesson."

"Suit yourself," Jacob said. He put his fingers on
the page and began the incantation. *"Audio sanus pro-
cul—"*

And then he stopped, because the door opened and
the Wizard ran back into the chamber.

"Edmund, Jacob, I apologize for this interruption,"
he said, as he dashed to his cabinet. He opened it and
began grabbing various arcane items. "But I must
rush."

"Sir? What's going on?" I asked.

"No time to explain," he said. "There's a threat to
the capital that only I can deal with. Keep learning
your spells, and I'll check on you when I'm able to
return."

He stuffed a variety of bottles and skins into the
pockets of his robes. And then, with a loud bang and

puff of smoke that made me flinch, the Wizard vanished.

And I suddenly realized that for the first time, I had been left alone with Jacob.

I glanced at him briefly, then looked back at the book and concentrated on reading. But just as I expected, Jacob wouldn't let me. He got out of his seat, walked over to me, and said, "Come on, Edmund."

"What?"

He gave me a haughty look, as if he wanted me to know that he thought me stupid. "Don't you get it? Merlin's gone. Now's our chance to find out what he's got hidden away in his inner sanctum."

"His what?"

Jacob rolled his eyes. "Haven't you taken a look around this place at all? There's one door Merlin leaves closed no matter what. I bet he's got a ton of magical artifacts hidden inside."

"So what? We'll get to them eventually."

"Are you so sure about that?" He leaned closer. "You know that no wizard in the history of the kingdom has ever taken on two apprentices? I bet he's going to leave one of us behind and only finish training the other." He paused. "My father told me always to take advantage of my opportunities. I want to see what he's got now, in case I don't get to later. You might want to do the same."

Now, had I been a smarter thirteen-year-old, I probably would have realized why Jacob really wanted me working with him. If the Wizard discovered us, Jacob could pin the blame on me, setting himself up as the trustworthy apprentice. I guess I still didn't see it as a competition, despite the clues.

But Jacob's argument convinced me. I pushed myself out of my chair and said, "Fine, I'm in. Where's this door?"

"Follow me."

We walked around the chamber, past the piles of clutter to a rounded alcove I had never spotted before. At the back of the alcove stood a door painted with runes I couldn't decipher.

Jacob stepped towards it, grabbed the doorknob, and pulled. But the door didn't budge.

"Hm," he said. "Maybe there's a spell I can use to pry open the door."

I heard a sudden movement from behind and turned around to discover the Wizard's cat staring at us.

"Um, Jacob?"

"Don't bother me. I'm trying to figure out the runes."

"I'm starting to think that we shouldn't be doing this."

"What?" He turned away from the door. "Why?"

I jabbed my finger twice, pointing at the cat. "We're being watched."

Jacob looked over his shoulder and saw the cat. "So? It's just Merlin's cat."

"I know, but I've read that wizard's cats are smarter than regular cats."

Edmund gave me a disparaging look. "What's the problem, Edmund? Are you scared of a little cat?"

"I just think—"

The Wizard's cat jumped onto a pile of books in the alcove, arched its back, and then hissed. It leaned back as if about to pounce.

"Jacob, what do we do?" I whispered.

He whispered back, "We use our magic, idiot." He stepped forward and gestured with his hands. "Freeze, feline," he said.

The cat leaped forward and then suddenly froze in midair, its mouth wide open and its teeth bared. I flinched and then recovered.

"It's not going to last," Jacob said. "Hurry."

"Hurry and do what?"

"Let's get the door open."

Jacob started pounding on the door with his fists and muttering words under his breath.

"Jacob, that's not going to work. We'd better go back to our seats."

"And how will you explain the cat? Come on, help me out!"

Unsure of what to do, I ducked under the frozen cat and walked closer to the door. I lifted my fists, about to help Jacob—

"WHAT ARE THE TWO OF YOU DOING?" The Wizard's voice thundered through the chamber.

We both stopped and turned around. The Wizard stood just outside the alcove, frowning. I suddenly remembered a saying about how quickly wizards became angry, and I froze, cold with fear.

Jacob, on the other hand, jolted forward and pointed back at me. "It was Edmund, sir! It's his fault! He urged me on."

The Wizard raised his hand with all his fingers extended, like a claw. "You lie!" he shouted, and blue lightning crackled from his hand. It hit Jacob, and he shuddered and then fell forward.

I swallowed hard, and somehow found my voice. "Is he—"

"He will be fine," the Wizard said as he looked over Jacob's unconscious form. "But I will have a long talk with his father." He glanced at me. "As for you . . . I expected more from you, Edmund."

I felt ashamed. "I'm sorry, sir."

He nodded, and looked suddenly weary. "I'll have the guardsman take you home. Lessons are over for the day."

*   *   *

But lessons weren't over for good. The next morning, the guardsman came for me as usual. During the trip to the castle, I thought a lot about what had happened, and I came to a decision. I asked the guardsman to pass a message to the Wizard, asking if he would be willing to meet with me privately during the hour we took for luncheon.

During our morning lessons, there was no talk about what had happened the day before. I mean none. Neither the Wizard nor Jacob mentioned our attempt to break through the door or the Wizard's blast. So I said nothing either. The morning stretched on, as we sat quietly, reading a history of magical attacks on the kingdom that earlier wizards had repelled.

Finally, the time came for lunch. Jacob closed his book and dashed away, presumably to join his family as he usually did. I was about to get up myself when the Wizard put his hand upon my shoulder.

"You wanted to talk," he said. "Come, we will eat together today." He had the guard bring us some bread and cold meats, and we sat at the table, with a magical, heatless candle illuminating our meal.

"So what did you want to meet about?" the Wizard asked just as I had taken a large bite of food.

I swallowed and murmured, "I wanted to ask you about Jacob."

"What about him?"

I knew the Wizard couldn't be so unobservant, but still, I went on. "His behavior. Yesterday wasn't an exception. Haven't you noticed that he's almost gleeful when we practice attacks? He doesn't like me."

"You shouldn't allow his actions to bother you, Edmund."

"I can't decide what bothers me and what doesn't. And Jacob's attitude—surely you can see that he's only learning magic to benefit himself? I doubt he has any interest in defending the kingdom. He's too young. So am I." I paused. "I'm forced finally to ask you. Why the two of us? Why now, when we're younger than the usual apprentice?"

The Wizard had been nibbling at his food while I spoke. He put his food down onto his plate, took a sip of water, and shook his head.

"You have shown me how little I truly know. A teacher of mine once said that the only real test of your knowledge is your ability to teach it to others. I see I have much to learn."

"I don't understand."

"What I mean is, I should have taken you into my confidence from the beginning. About you, and about Jacob."

"So tell me now."

He sighed. "Edmund, I'm sorry to say that I had no choice when inviting you and Jacob to become my apprentices."

"I don't understand."

"Magic has rules, just like science. But magic's rules are capricious. She can be a cruel mistress." He looked into the distance. "Last year, a prophecy was brought to my attention."

"What sort of prophecy, sir?"

For a brief moment, the corners of his mouth turned down and his eyes looked sad. "I'm getting old, Edmund. I feel it in my bones. I'm not long for this world."

I shook my head. "No."

He nodded. "I'm sorry, but it's true. When I realized that the weariness I felt was more than just simple exhaustion, I cast a spell to help me find my new apprentice. And the magic revealed to me the faces of not one but *two* boys."

"Me and Jacob."

He nodded again. "You and Jacob. As far as I knew, this had never happened before in the history of the kingdom. But the magic is never wrong. It forced me to take on both of you, because if I only took on one . . ." He trailed off.

"If you only took on one, what?"

"Then the other wouldn't be ready."

"Ready for what, sir?"

"For what's about to come." He stood up and took his plate and cup. "In case I am wrong, that is all I can tell you for now. But rest assured I will keep a close eye on Jacob and make sure he does not, er, bother you again."

The Wizard walked away and disappeared behind the alcove. I heard a door creak open and then slam shut. I finished my meal in silence and resolved to practice my magic well enough to be prepared for anything.

And I ignored the chill in my bones.

Winter melted into spring, and then the summer came. Things had become quite busy at the inn, and the capital itself was filled with strangers from all corners of the kingdom. At the time, though, I had barely noticed, since I was far too occupied with my studies of magic.

But fate and destiny played their parts. On a blazing hot morning, when I arrived at the Wizard's chambers, he ushered Jacob and me into his sanctum. It was a bit of a letdown after our little winter adventure, as the room contained very little: just a table and chairs. Somehow, though, the Wizard managed to keep the room dark and cool, and I thought I could feel powerful magic radiating from the walls. But I kept my suspicions to myself.

The Wizard had us take our seats, and then he

spoke. "Jacob, Edmund. I'm sorry to have to tell you this, but today is the day you put your learning to the test."

"What do you mean, sir?" I asked.

"Have either of you been following the news of the kingdom over the past year?"

"We've been under attack, haven't we?" Jacob said.

He nodded. "Yes. By an enemy that we know very little about. All we know for sure is what he's sent after us."

"And what would that be?"

"A demonic dragon."

I held my breath for a moment, and I was pleased to see that Jacob had turned pale as well. We had studied the different kinds of magical creatures over the spring, and of them all, the demonic dragon was the one I feared the most.

"Impossible," I said. "I would have heard."

The Wizard shook his head. "No, you wouldn't have. First of all, I've kept you too busy training with magic to take such note of the world around you. And secondly, I've been using powerful magic to keep the populace from remembering what's been attacking. We've had people from the outlying areas of the kingdom flocking to the cities. But the last thing we needed was a total panic, so I made people think that they had been fleeing nothing more than a human army." He sighed. "It has been quite a strain. But the battle is almost over."

"What do you mean?" I asked.

"The demonic dragon is coming here, to the capital. I've scried its goal. It plans to burn down the castle, presumably to scare our citizens into accepting its master as their new ruler. And as the defenders of the kingdom, we can't let that happen." He paused. "So today, we're going to stop it."

I gulped. "We can't fight a dragon. That's what the King has knights for."

The Wizard grimaced and shook his head. "Knights are useful for many tasks," he said. "If we were under attack by an army, I would agree that they would be equal to the fight. But dragons—especially demonic dragons—are creatures of magic, and so only magic will stop them."

"This isn't what you've been training us for, is it?"

The Wizard put a hand on my shoulder. "Are you afraid, Edmund?"

I swallowed hard. "Yes, sir, I am. I'm not ready to take on a demonic dragon."

"Listen carefully. Perhaps one of us would be overwhelmed by the creature's magic. But three wizards are more than enough to defeat it."

Jacob surprised me by speaking up softly. "But, sir, we're not three wizards. We're one wizard and two—two children."

The Wizard smiled. "No, Jacob. Today, we are all wizards together."

We left the chamber armed with magic wands, climbed the stairs to the castle's highest turret, and stood behind the battlement. Open holes alternated with walls, but unfortunately, the walls weren't high enough to block out the sun.

"What now?" I asked.

"You both know the vanquishing spell I taught you. Keep your wands at the ready, and wait."

We didn't have to wait long. The demonic dragon arrived quickly, almost as if it knew we were ready for battle. It appeared as a dot in the east, which got larger and larger as it approached.

A regular dragon is a large beast, with silver-red scales, humungous wings, and breath of fire. But a demonic dragon is all that combined with fiery glowing eyes, a stench of months-old garbage, and a chilling scream like the sound of fingernails across slate. Despite the intense heat of the day, I shivered as it came close.

I could hear the people of the city screaming as well, as they ran for protection. But I could have told them that their running was both useless and unnecessary. The demonic dragon knew where its true enemy waited for it and came toward us with an unrelenting fury.

"Now, boys!" the Wizard shouted. The three of us lifted our wands and chanted the vanquishing spell. As the Wizard had instructed, we recited it three times and then ended by shouting with the true name owned by all demonic dragons: *"Draconus!"*

Tongues of flame and lightning flew out of our wands and smashed into the demonic dragon. He recoiled in pain and emitted the loudest moan I had ever heard.

And then just like that, he recovered. The dragon fixed its gaze on us and accelerated.

"Something has gone wrong with the spell," the Wizard said. "Jacob, Edmund, get ready to try again."

We lifted our wands, but the dragon left us no time. It swooped down toward us. Jacob and I ducked away to either side, but the Wizard was not so nimble. It grabbed him with its talons and flew off, leaving behind a windstorm.

The Wizard's screams turned my blood cold. For a moment, I froze. But then I realized that the safety of the kingdom depended on us.

"Jacob, come on!" I shouted over the wind. "Let's try this again."

He shook his head and shouted back, "It's useless!"

"The Wizard is depending on us!"

Jacob stared at me, and for a moment, it looked

like he was about to nod. But I heard an odd whisper drift past, and suddenly an eerie smile appeared on Jacob's face. "Ah, Father," he said. "I understand."

I felt confused. "You understand what?"

Jacob didn't answer me. Instead, he jumped back, pointed his wand at me and shouted *"Fulguris!"* A crackling bolt of lightning emerged from his wand directly toward my heart. Fortunately, I had been practicing attacks with Jacob for almost a year. I raised a shield around me just in time, and the lightning dissipated.

I lowered the shield, pointed the wand at Jacob, and steadied myself. "Jacob, stop it! What are you doing?"

"I'm doing what my father is asking of me," he said.

I glanced quickly to either side. "Your father?"

"Yes. Fulguris!"

"Flammare!" I shouted without thinking. *"Flammare! Infere! Succendo!"*

A ball of fire, hotter and brighter than any I had ever created before, formed at the tip of my wand. Jacob's lightning bolt hit it and was instantly absorbed, and the ball grew larger.

"Jacob, don't make me do this," I said.

He just flashed that eerie smile and once more raised his wand against me. *"Ful—"*

Before he could summon the lightning again, I twisted my wrist and sent the fireball straight into Jacob's chest. It burned straight through him, singeing his robes, but it didn't leave a hole. A shocked look appeared on his face. He grimaced, and then his features relaxed and he stared at me once more with that eerie smile.

"Thank you, Edmund," he said. "You have given me just what I need."

And then he collapsed to the ground, and I thought saw something phantasmal fly away from his body.

Out of some instinct, I jumped over to Jacob to see if he was all right, but I couldn't get close. A shield had been raised around his body, protecting it and keeping me from approaching any closer than a few feet. Again, I was confused; as far as I knew, Jacob was dead and I had just killed him, and yet here was powerful magic, still protecting him.

The demonic dragon roared louder than it had before, and I ceased my pondering. I turned around to see it heading right toward me, a murderous look in its glowing eyes.

And suddenly I thought I knew what was going on. Jacob had used me. My fireball had freed his spirit to occupy the dragon, and now he was coming to finish me off. My only hope would be to use the vanquishing spell again, and I prayed that Jacob's transformation had left him weak and susceptible.

Reaching deep within me, I pointed my wand at the dragon to focus my magic. I cast the same vanquishing spell that had failed the three of us before, but this time I ended it by shouting "Jacob!"

Flame emerged from my wand, and then sputtered into smoke. I had failed. I closed my eyes, bracing myself against what would come next when the dragon grabbed me.

And then I heard an odd whisper again, but this time, it was the Wizard's voice inside my head. "Edmund, listen," he said. "The true name you want is Greenwald."

I felt confused for a moment, until I remembered that Jacob was the inheritor to the title Duke of Greenwald.

The dragon swooped back down, its screams echoing all around me. I ducked behind a wall just in time and cast the vanquishing spell again, substituting the name Greenwald for Jacob.

The effect was immediate. A look of terror appeared on the dragon's face, and within seconds it exploded into a shower of fireworks. With my right arm, I covered my eyes against the brightness that filled the sky. When the light faded, I saw a small figure falling in the distance. It was the Wizard. Quickly, I cast a levitation spell on him, and he flew back to the turret. I pointed my wand, and he gently floated onto the ground.

I slipped my wand beneath my robes and ran over to the Wizard. He looked pale and weak, and I knew that this was the end for him.

"Now you know why I trained you so hard," he rasped.

"You trained Jacob too."

"Jacob would have come to magic on his own. Dark magic."

I looked behind me, and realized that Jacob's body had vanished. "He was the dragon, wasn't he? That's why he's gone. But I don't understand why he helped us out at first."

The Wizard shook his head. "No. Jacob wasn't the dragon. It was Jacob's father occupying the demon at first."

"I still don't understand."

"The Duke of Greenwald wanted to wrest the kingdom from the King, and the magic was within their family's blood. In truth, neither Jacob nor the Duke knew what the Duke's unconscious desires were doing until this very hour. Once the Duke realized that the demonic dragon was coming from his own mind, he sent his spirit into it to give it even more power."

"That odd whisper I heard. That was the Duke, asking Jacob for help."

He nodded. "And now you know the full story. I had to take Jacob on as an apprentice in order to bring out the Duke's magic as soon as possible. Had I waited two years, the Duke and Jacob would have become too powerful for us to defeat. So I had to accelerate the Duke's attack on the kingdom so that I and the next true Wizard could defeat him."

" 'The next true Wizard'—you mean me?"

"Yes, you." He coughed. "It was the prophecy. I was destined to die. It is your job to take over and protect the kingdom."

My eyes became wet with tears. "I'm not ready."

He coughed again and shook his head. "On the contrary, you have proved that you are."

"But—"

With his last bit of strength, he reached out and grabbed my arm. "Edmund, listen. My time is up. The demonic dragon has emboldened our other enemies. The kingdom is about to face its most dire threat, an invasion from the east. You *are* up to the challenge."

And suddenly I realized that I was. Because I had to be.

"There is just one thing more," the Wizard said. He released my arm and crooked his finger.

I leaned forward, and with his last breath, the Wizard who had asked to be called Merlin whispered my true name into my ear.

I had finished my story. My apprentice, a fifteen-year-old boy named Harold, looked into my eyes, past my wrinkled face and wizened body, and for the first time he saw me for who I truly was.

"I had thought your name was Merlin," he said.

I smiled and shook my head. "Merlin's only the name that we pass along from Wizard to apprentice," I told him. "But my true name, and yours, is this: Defensor.*"*

He nodded. "Protector."

"Yes."

"Will I have to face a threat as dire as the one you faced?" he asked me. "The demonic dragon? The armies of magical creatures? The Sorcerers Guild?"

"I don't know," I admitted. "The prophecies have not been that clear for me. But they have shown me this. Threats come in cycles. The kingdom will never be completely safe. It may be attacked from without, or it may degrade from within. Which is why there must always be a Wizard."

And, knowing that the kingdom would once more be in safe hands, that the line of succession of its protectors would continue unbroken, I lay down upon my bed and fell asleep for the last time.

A TOUCH OF BLUE
A Web Shifters Story

Julie E. Czerneda

Ersh, Senior Assimilator and center of my personal universe, had firm ideas about what I should do with my time. These ideas doubtless stemmed from my being the most Recent of my kind and, to be honest, an unprecedented accident, but I hardly viewed them as fair. After all, was it my fault I'd been born instead of properly budded from Ersh's flesh as the rest of our Web?

I plopped another seedling into its pot and straightened it morosely. One such idea was this morning drudgery in the greenhouse.

My education was another.

Ersh had decided I was to receive the wealth of knowledge gained by our kind of the biology and cultures of more ephemeral races only after she herself had sorted that knowledge through her own flesh. *Doubtless leaving out the good bits.*

My toes snapped the seedling at the stem. I hastily shoved the remaining piece deeper into the soil. It might not wilt until after I'd left. Despite centuries of practice, I wasn't good with plants.

I wasn't good with anything.

I sighed heavily, my tail sliding between my legs. Enjoying the melancholy, I sighed again.

"Esen."

I straightened in haste, the movement sending the tray of transplanted seedlings flying off the table in a spectacular spray of dirt, tiny green stems, and pots— pots that shattered noisily on impact with the stone floor. Well, except for the one that arced through the air all the way to the wall, which produced more of a smash and slither.

"Esen-alit-Quar!"

At least she wouldn't notice the broken seedling, I consoled myself as I warily turned to face Ersh.

I was Esen-alit-Quar when in trouble, Esen for short, Es in a hurry or between friends, not that I felt warmed by friendship at this moment. Ersh's massive crystalline Tumbler-self had an ominous tilt forward. I tried to unobtrusively tilt backwards—not easy in my current form, that of the canid-like Lanivarian. This was my birth shape, the one I preferred for the value of its useful hands and still the easiest for me to hold.

For we were Web-beings, creatures of energy and matter and transitions between, able to spend some of our mass to bind our remaining molecules in a different, memorized form until choosing to release and return to the flawless teardrop of blue that was our heritage.

I was still working on that part.

"Hi Esen." A dark eye peered around the side of Ersh.

My jaw dropped in a grin. "Lesy! Welcome home!"

My web-kin didn't come out any further. I wasn't surprised. We were six in the known universe: Ersh, Skalet, Mixs, Ansky—my birth mother, Lesy, and myself. Lesy and I shared one other characteristic. We both did our utmost to avoid facing Ersh when she was annoyed.

Ersh herself, likely taking my grin and greeting as signs I wasn't suitably grief-stricken about her dying seedlings—which wasn't entirely true, since being the one who'd have to clean up and repot fresh ones all afternoon, I felt significant anguish at my fate—chimed a note of distinct temper. Lesy's eye disappeared.

I spread my arms in appeasement, which helped hide pots. "You wanted me, Ersh?" this brightly, with a deliberate lift of my ears.

"Not on any level," she muttered, but not loudly enough to expect a reply. She did expect me to hear, being fully aware of the capabilities of my current ears. In more normal tones, "Lesy does. You're going with her, Youngest."

I blinked. "Going where?"

The immense greenhouse was the deepest portion of Ersh's house, that house a series of rooms quarried into the side of a cliff almost as old as she. The cliff was part of Picco's Moon, a world of rock and rock-based life, its surface stained by the lurid orange and purple reflection of Picco except during Eclipse. Lesy didn't come here unless summoned by Ersh; she kept to her windowless room when here, other than occasional conquests of the kitchen. She wouldn't go outside unless forced by Ersh.

Why? Because Picco's exact shade of orange, as she frequently reminded everyone but Ersh, drained her creativity.

As creativity was something Ersh insisted I avoid at all costs, I judged Lesy's claim as another concept I'd be taught when I was older. *If that ever happened.* Though I suspected this one fell within the category of what Skalet called "Lesy's idiotic prattle."

We were the closest of kin, together forming the Web of Ersh. *Didn't mean we were always kind to one another.*

"Go where?" I repeated, ears heading back down. A kitchen summons was likeliest. Lesy could clean up after herself. Well, she could, but rarely did. I'd take refuge in planting if necessary.

I hated wet paws.

One, then three dark eyes, each the size of my clenched fist, peered at me from behind the crystal form of Ersh, reflecting in gleaming facets until there might have been thirty. The glowing green ring encircling each signaled unusual excitement. Or a fever. Lesy's middle-aged Dokeci-self was prone to stress-related illness if she persisted in using it within significant gravity. Which she did. "Dokeci-Na, Youngest! The western continent. I'm holding my first exhibit in the capital!"

"Pardon?" Our kind might possess perfect recall; that didn't mean we couldn't confuse one another. Portula Colony was Lesy's preferred home. I'd been there before: a quiet, self-contained environment inhabited by, at most, forty self-absorbed artists. It wasn't Picco's Moon, but the next best thing for a young web-being of uncertain parentage—so Ersh had proclaimed. *Boring.* Though there was, I recalled fondly, a remarkable pool. But Dokeci-Na?

An entire planet teeming with life—life that had evolved there? Life that wasn't rock?

There would be restaurants, I thought, charmed beyond reason. I tipped a questioning ear towards Ersh, hardly daring to believe my good fortune.

"After you finish here," Ersh said with remarkable restraint, considering, "pack and be ready. The shuttle's on its way. I need not remind you of the Prime Laws or what I expect from your behavior offworld, Youngest."

"No, Ersh." Her expectations consisted of my staying out of sight and out of mind, which basically translated into "don't talk to ephemerals." One day I
would, *if I lived that long.* Right now, I wasn't trained
for such interaction. Wouldn't be a problem; Dokecians didn't believe anyone my age could hold a
conversation.

But if behaving meant I'd get my first-ever visit to
a world without opinionated crystal?

My tail swung wildly, knocking the surviving pots
to the floor.

"Esen-alit-Quar!"

I possessed Lesy's memories of Portula Colony—
those Ersh deemed fit for me to have, anyway. A private space station, it lay within view of the famous
Jeopardy Nebula, said view the source of inspiration
for the colony's artistically-minded population. Portula
was the place Lesy currently favored when not on a
mission for our Web. Since she went on fewer missions
than any of web-kin but me—for no reason Ersh
deemed fit for me to know—Lesy had had time to
become well established within her isolated home. We
were to head there first, to finalize the shipping of her
art, then accompany that art to Dokeci-Na.

The closer our transport drew to Portula Colony,
however, the more worried Lesy became. *And not
about her art.*

"You're sure you can maintain this form on the
planet, Youngest?"

This being the fourteenth time she'd lifted the top
of my crate and peered within to inquire, I wrapped
my arms over my face and wiggled the now-black fin-
gerlike tips at her.

"Don't do that!" she gasped. "That's—it's not done.
Do you hear me, Esen-alit-Quar? That's very rude!"

If Lesy was trying to sound like Ersh, I didn't have the tubal pumps to tell her how infinitely far from the mark her soft, anxious complaint registered. I did lower my arms and sent an apologetic ripple of pink through my skin. "Sorry, Lesy," I added aloud, though Dokecians relied more on appearance.

Hers? More flustered than ever, judging by the welts rising over her round face. "Don't call me that!"

We were alone and she'd used my birthname first, but I'd learned over a century ago never to correct my elders. *Where they could hear me, at any rate.* "I'm sorry, Riosolesy-ki." My name in this form, Ses-ki, lacked respectful prefixes, a prejudice against callow youth I'd noticed crossed species' boundaries. "Are we there yet?" I tried to shift position.

"Don't do that!"

I was truly trying to behave, but this was one too many don'ts. *Especially before we'd even arrived.* "You try sitting on—what am I sitting on?" My box, while padded on all sides, held more than over-compressed Esen. Lesy had slipped in a few packages at the last minute. None, she assured me, edible, or I'd have been rid of them during the preceding hours.

"Those are art supplies. Important secret art supplies."

I squirmed. "They feel like rocks."

The welts acquired a mottled red. A frown. "You peeked!"

"I sat," I corrected, shifting again. The Dokeci form consisted of a round head with a handsome rubbery beak and those three massive eyes. The head sat on a thick neck from which the five long flexible arms sprang like a collar above a pair of sturdy hips. The rest of the body was a boneless abdomen that swung like a pendulum between the triple-jointed legs. Mine, though compact and firm, now had distinct sore points.

This form wasn't designed for sitting, let alone being pressed against rocks, artistic or otherwise. "Can't I come out?"

"We're almost there," my web-kin promised, slamming the lid down.

I put my arms over my face and wiggled my fingertips.

Free at last. *In more ways than one.* I stretched my arms, after carefully checking the placement of fragile objects, kicked myself from the floor, and let myself drift back down in a slow spin. Not quite null-gee, but close enough for fun. Portula's operators balanced the physiological preference of older Dokeci with the practicality of keeping paint on brushes and out of the air scrubbers. The Dokeci were a species who lost significant musculature with age; to make it worse, their abdomens enlarged and sagged floorwards. By the middle of their lifespan they depended on the strong limbs of younger kin.

Those like Lesy who wanted to remain independently active had a choice of donning support devices—none, she confided, in the least fashionable— or cheat by living on low gravity stations like Portula. Personally, I'd have abandoned the form by her age, not that she'd asked my opinion. I'd noticed that about my Elders before now.

Spin done, I poked around Lesy's quarters. Nothing had changed. The pillows, carpet, and cupboards of supplies were in my memories along with the way to the station galley, its menu, short cuts to the common areas—including that remarkable pool—and, for some reason, the completely unremarkable aft shipping hold.

Where I didn't plan to waste my time. "Will we have time to use the pool?" I asked.

Lesy's topmost eye sent me a vague, preoccupied glance, the rest of her attention on the packages of rocks she was removing from my crate. "Yes, yes. Let me put these away first."

"I'll help." I bounded towards the crate, abdomen swinging.

Unfortunately, it was somewhat more difficult than I'd anticipated to lose all that wonderful momentum.

I crashed into both crate and web-kin.

We fell together in a slow motion grapple of writhing arms and packages, packages that spilled out over the lovely finger-knotted carpets, packages that cooperatively rolled free of their wrappings to expose the deep glitter of gemstones.

I extricated myself from Lesy, whose skin flickered with alarmed pseudolightning and rising splots of violet. "Sorry," I said. *Already a habit.* I picked up the nearest stone, being helpful, only to stare at what I held in disbelief.

"Pretty, isn't it?"

Pretty was an understatement. The gem had a fiery inner glow that could come from only one source. *Biology.* "This," I scowled, "isn't a rock." It was a Tumbler excretion.

Or worse—I dropped it and wiped my fingertip vigorously on the carpet, the rest of my arms stretched as far away as possible. "It's not one of—"

"Waste not, want not."

Smuggling excretions was the only persistent non-Tumbler enterprise on Picco's Moon, an enterprise involving clandestine landings and distressingly noisy responses by those who claimed to be in charge—not that Tumblers noticed either, considering soft-fleshed beings to be, at best, implausible. Ersh herself took precautions to discourage prospectors, licensed or otherwise; namely she sent me out every few nights to collect any deposits made by wandering neighbors—not to mention the piles from those who visited Ersh for those month-long chimings over rare salts. I'd almost filled a deep cleft in the cliff over the years.

Ersh's own? Suffice to say I'd never asked nor wanted to know, and viewed that ignorance as one of the bright spots of my short existence.

I rose from the floor, my own skin flaring with outrage. "You've been stealing from Ersh!?"

"There's no need to raise your voice." Lesy somehow managed to pout adorably without lips. "She lets me take the prettiest. For my creations. You know how highly Ersh values my art."

I was beginning to get the idea. Elder or not, Lesy was a worse liar than I was.

As for her art? I remembered innumerable lectures from Ersh. I wasn't to ask about Lesy's creations, or Lesy's dreams for that matter. When either topic arose during our rare meals together, those decidedly unweblike aspects of our web-kin's nature made Skalet twitch, Mixs grumble, and Ansky offer more food.

While they made me curious. And, I realized abruptly, Ersh wasn't here. That she'd inevitably find out wasn't something I need worry about now.

A great many of my decisions were made on that basis.

"What do you do with them?" I asked, unable to stop myself.

Her skin ridged and developed a faint flush of pink. "They're part of my newest creation. An entirely new art. Would you like to try? I'll teach you. What a wonderful idea, Esen!"

Where had that come from? My epidermis did its best to turn inside out. "Try?" I echoed weakly. "I really don't think we have time for—this isn't—"

Lesy was ignoring me. I was used to that. But what she was doing while ignoring me offered sufficient novelty that I closed my mouth and watched with all eyes.

Two hands opened cupboard doors, while the other three reached in to pull out, with blinding speed— Lesy could move when motivated—a bucket, several narrow white tubes, an assortment of hammers and pointed tools, and, last and requiring all five hands, what appeared to be a large nondescript mold of, yes, it was a face.

Ersh's face, to be exact. Even as a Dokecian of considerable age, features reversed and made of puce-toned plas, I'd know that expression anywhere. Lesy might have thrown molten plas over the Senior Assimilator while she was mid-argument with me.

Lesy must have mistaken my stunned silence for approval, for her blush deepened and she thrust the face mold at me. "Beautiful, isn't it? It's the very same image they used in the 44th Dynasty coins. Not the same, really. Bigger." This with small spots of worry. Her arms twisted, rotating Ersh's frozen scowl. "Too big? It's 155% life-size. I like big eyes, but one never knows—"

" 'Coins?' " I echoed.

"Some shields did survive, a statue or two. Coins were the main—you should know this."

"A certain person doesn't," I said testily, "share everything with me." While it was quite reasonable Ersh had lived within Dokeci society in a time known only through the earliest—that I did know—remains yet uncovered by that species' archaeologists, it went against everything I knew that the center of our Web, the being who ruled caution above all, *who insisted I travel in a crate* . . . that she'd be . . . "She was famous?"

"Infamous," Lesy giggled. "Legendary. Teganersha-Ki. Rose to power on the severed arms of her enemies. United the western continent against the east and north. Brought in plumbing."

The plumbing I could believe. Ersh regularly cited the hallmarks of a successful technological society. Sanitation was top on her list. "Does—" There was no safe way to ask, so I went for blunt. "Does she know about this?" I flailed a finger at the face.

Lesy faded to a smooth, nonplussed beige.

While I flushed abashed purple. *Of course Ersh knew.* There were no secrets from the sharing of memories held within our flesh. Well, there were plenty of secrets within Ersh's flesh, but only because she alone had the ability to pick and chose what to include per bite.

The rest of us? Doomed to reveal every memorized instant of our lives. However dull or personally mortifying.

I stared at Ersh's reversed face—presumably shortly to be coated in pulverized Ersh excretion with the result sold to the locals for use as pots or doorstops—and felt an unexpected twinge.

How often did we disappoint her?

As a Web-being, I had intimate access to the aesthetics of all more ephemeral species my kind had yet explored. That didn't mean I knew good art from bad—just how to fake it in the appropriate company. At the moment, I would have gladly traded all the memories in my flesh for a clue how to tell the three glittering heads on the shelf apart.

"Don't you want to take yours home, Youngest?" Lesy's skin was beginning to spot.

I tried not to look obvious as I examined the results of our labors. The molding process had reminded me of putting soil into pots, though wetter. The final finishing—that had been more challenging. Lesy's instructions consisted of "follow your dreams" as she herself used all five arms to quickly glue bits from a box to Ersh's thunderous face at seeming random. While singing, which I hadn't attempted.

Glue I could and did. *Not that I'd anything to follow.* Only Lesy claimed to remember dreams. The rest of us? Memories lasted, intact and detailed; whatever might visit our sleeping minds did not. After first learning of ephemeral nightmares, I'd decided that was fine with me.

Without guidance—and to be honest, some coordination issues with five arms—an embarrassing number of my small bits were also glued to carpet and furnishings. Lesy forgave my lack of control once I'd helped pull off the pieces somehow glued to her skin. All three busts now stared back at me, looking as if they'd rolled down a garbage heap after dunking themselves in syrup. The leftmost one had only one eye exposed, giving it a baleful look. The centermost was blinded by strings of cheap plas beads. The right—I looked away, hoping in vain Ersh wouldn't taste the memory of her heads.

"Shouldn't I leave it here, Lesy?" I suggested. "This is a place of artists." *I had no shame.*

She almost glowed. "We'll do better than that. We'll put your first work of art on exhibit with mine!" Her arms swept up the leftmost lump as if it were precious. "I'm proud of you, Es."

Which made no sense. We had no possessions. There were no physical manifestations of a Web culture. We were, that was all. Was this Lesy's difference? A compulsion to make things without purpose or value?

Then what were dreams?

My troubling thoughts might have manifested in

stripes on my skin for all my web-kin noticed. After tucking all three heads into a fresh shipping crate with great care—a procedure which required privacy for no reason I could imagine, but I was used to climbing into cupboards on command—Lesy grabbed the nearest of my arms. "I'll show you the rest." She towed me towards the door with frightening enthusiasm, her abdomen bouncing up and down. "My best work is in aft shipping already." She halted our forward motion with a quick grab by two arms at a convenient handhold. "I think it's my best. Oh dear. What if it isn't? And where are you going?"

I'd have thought it obvious, since she'd let go of me in order to grab said handholds. I thus sailed onward, arms flailing as if that would help, tumbling in midair until the lower part of my anatomy met the corridor wall with a *smack* and I slid, slowly, to the floor. "Who knows?" I muttered.

"Know? I can't. Can I know my best?" Lesy could fuss without pause for breath. She hurried forward and took my arm again, hauling me to my feet. "Cureceo-ki says it's my best work. He'd know, wouldn't he?"

I blinked at her, something three eyes did quite well. "Who is Cureceo-ki?"

"You remember, Ses-ki!"

"No one told me," I stressed the second last word. In this alien environment, no web-being would be more specific. *Or ought to be,* I thought, worried by Lesy's now-distraught posture. Upset, a Dokeci's forward-facing arms became rigid and unusable, aimed outward to fend off trouble. Which was me, in this instance. As she continued to hold onto me with an arm over her hip, the rest were fending off my abdomen. "Who is she?" I asked more gently. The pronoun was the accepted neutral, since the species had an astounding variety of reproductive forms. It took birth or an autopsy, Ersh had told me, to sort out who was pregnant.

"He," Lesy insisted, either knowing more than I did about the individual in question—*presumably*—or imposing her own pronoun—*likely*. Since my arrival, those in the "family way" made her uncomfortable, Skalet admitting the same reaction. "The museum's curator. Cureceo-ki personally arranged the exhibit." Her third eye widened, its aim somewhere behind me. "Oh dear." The surface of her skin wrinkled, the crevices lime-green. "He looks upset. Hush."

"Greetings, Riosolesy-ki," the approaching Dokecian said, ignoring me. His skin was lumpy and dark, arms almost stiff. *Not a happy being.* "What's the delay? We've been waiting for the rest of the shipment."

Compared to Ersh's ability to obliterate my existence when preoccupied, this corpulent and aging being was an amateur. However, he did have species-mores on his side. Dokeci my age were considered little more than obstacles to traffic. So I did my best to be inconspicuous, though I'd have preferred to bristle. With aquamarine highlights. *And a pithy comment or two.*

"Why the haste, Curator?" Lesy surprised me by protesting. "I've yet to pick which cloak I'll wear to the gala. You did promise a gala for the opening of my exhibit."

Trust personal adornment to stiffen her arms. Lesy loved anything she could add to her form's sake. Otherwise, in any form, her reaction to conflict was distress and flight. None of us, not even Ersh, would speak harshly to her. Unlike this curator.

So different was Lesy from our siblings, so frail and uncertain, that I often wondered if Ersh had somehow

robbed her at birth—if birth was what you called sort-
ing which parts of your own flesh would leave you
and become opinionated.

*Or had Ersh chosen to discard with Lesy's flesh
every shred of weakness from her own?*

Some curiosities I knew better than pursue.

"Some haste would be useful, my lovely Riosolesy-
ki. There are precautions to be taken—much to complete!" Cureceo-ki's tone eased only slightly, but he
held out a gracious arm, eye rings aglow. "I will take
care of everything while you prepare yourself. I
merely need—" His lower two eyes seemed to search
Lesy for something. Sure enough, he asked sharply:
"The rest of the supplies—for the demonstration.
Where are they! Don't tell me you forgot them!"

If I'd been Lanivarian, my lip would have curled
over a fang, rude or not. My fingers itched to wiggle
at him.

But Lesy's skin swelled into a glorious mottling of
amber and ultraviolet. *Triumph?* "We've created three
new works for the exhibit! The crate's waiting in my
room. You will take care of them, won't you?"

"But . . ." I'd never seen a Dokeci completely pale
before. *Not attractive.* "What about the supplies?"
Cureceo-ki squeaked. "Don't tell me you rui—used
them all?"

"I don't think so." Lesy took a moment to think
deeply. I could have answered for her; under the circumstances, I couldn't imagine why. "Why yes.
There's quite a few left."

The curator's skin flushed with smooth whorls of
elated rose. "With more of your exquisite art,
Riosolesy-ki. How splendid! Splendid. Come now, you
must rest and prepare yourself while we finish our
tasks. Your audience awaits."

I kept my third eye locked on the curator. Dokeci

vision was extraordinary, quite reasonable in a species that relied on the morphing of skin to provide emotional context, though such cues could mislead, depending on the intentions and skill of the owner of that skin. Dokeci dialects were laced with wisdoms such as "wrinkles don't lie" and "never buy from a smoothie."

Needless to say, by this point, I didn't trust a patch of Cureceo-ki's hide.

"You should try on your cloak for the gala, Ses-ki. We won't have access to the wardrobe bags in transit, I'm quite sure. Space travel is so inconvenient. I've always thought so. Did I mention the gala?"

With every other breath. "We know mine fits," I reminded her. "Are you sure we shouldn't go down to shipping and check on your work?"

"You may be fine." The pout was back. "I'm still in turmoil. Turmoil!"

I relented. What Lesy didn't mention was that whatever cloak she wore would have to hide the supports her more mature Dokeci-self would need on the planet. Here, on the station, she could enjoy swirling the fabric around. Her arms swept up the next option, a green gauzy mass that resembled a "cloak" only by virtue of being wrapped first about her neck. It gave her a striking resemblance to an overripe seed pod.

Cureceo-ki had taken the crates, including the one with Ersh's heads. If his arms were tighter around the crate containing the remaining excretions, that wasn't my business. Ephemeral greed, as Ersh would say, was their curse, not ours.

The door chime sounded. Lesy swirled her way to it, clearly thrilled to show her cloak to someone of better taste than her youngest web-kin. But it was only a delivery. She turned back into the room, arms wrapped around a bouquet of flowers and a slim twisted bottle filled with a copper liquid. "Look, Seski! Welcoming gifts from the gallery!"

"You haven't left yet," I pointed out.

Lesy ignored this, busy pouring the liquid into two glasses. She looked at me, her skin mottled pink, then returned the liquid from one of the glasses to the bottle. "When you're older," she clucked at me. She took a sip. "Wonderful vintage."

As I was at least 400 years more vintage than any living Dokeci, I opened my mouth to complain.

The glass slipped from Lesy's finger. She let out a surprised moan and her skin went flaccid, its color draining away. She slumped to the floor, the gauzy green cloak settling around her.

I desperately firmed my hold on my Dokeci-form as Lesy abandoned hers, cycling to that perfect teardrop of blue, her surface glistening with drops of moisture. *Poison.*

There wasn't much time. The Prime Law. *Never reveal web-form to aliens.* I lunged for the bouquet of flowers and tossed them at her. The leaves, stems, and flowers touched and became her, their living matter assimilated into web-mass. *It should be enough.*

It was. She was back as Riosolesy-ki, sprawled on top of her gauzy cloak, a copper stain spreading from the dropped glass.

I waited expectantly.

She didn't move.

Not good. It was impossible to poison a web-being—our instinct to cycle was too quick for that. When Lesy returned to her Dokeci-self, her memory would have rebuilt everything about her forms' sake, not unmetabolized drugs. A web-being remembered broken bone, not any painkiller still in her blood.

My tubal pumps were protesting. I eased closer, careful to avoid the stain, and poked Lesy firmly in the abdomen. *Nothing.* I laid the first portion of one arm over her skin. Warmth, overlapped pulses, a rise and fall that signaled respiration.

I moved away, far away, finally huddling in the furthest corner from my web-kin's unconscious self.

I was alone.

I'd never been alone before.

How was I to know what to do?

Portula Colony was a cluster of spheres, the centermost and largest containing both gravity generators and living quarters, the outer being studios and communal space. The pool, with its view of the nebula, was to one end. To the other was a slowly growing tangle of warehouse pods. Most were for Lesy's previous creations—she was, if nothing else, productive. I shuddered at the image of corridors jammed with junk-coated Ersh heads.

But I had other concerns. Lesy was still unconscious. There was nothing to eat in her room. *Panic made me hungry.* Help for her and food for me could be summoned. There was also a criminal curator to be caught, preferably in the act.

All of which would be easy—for an adult. There was a com panel—visual, given Dokeci self-expression. There were neighbors. Probably five-armed station security patrolling the outer corridors, eyes vigilant.

And there was me, alone, trapped by this form. Young Dokeci became clever mimics before developing an understanding of language. Lesy's "idiotic prattle" just about covered it. No adult on this station could believe a word I said. The sudden inexplicable appearance of a non-Dokecian on Portula would likely be noticed.

Ersh would not approve.

That left me one alternative. I went to the art supply cupboards. "I'll show you nonverbal," I muttered to myself, pulling out supplies.

"My work's been stolen? Are you sure?"

I could only gaze, mute, at my web-kin. I'd never seen Lesy happier.

I wasn't alone. The station manager rumpled in confused distress. "You authorized the shipping request, Riosolesy-ki," she repeated, as if this might help, "but the destination wasn't the gallery on Dokeci-Na. I'm deeply sorry, Riosolesy-ki. The entire affair appears to have been a hoax. The gallery hasn't—there's no exhibition of your work scheduled. Cureceo-ki falsified her credentials. You were sedated." A neat sidestep around "nearly murdered," I decided.

"Altogether an elaborate, well-planned theft, I fear. Portula Station will of course pursue a full investigation."

"Oh, I couldn't possibly press charges." Lesy sparkled. "No need for an investigation. They loved my work. They had to have it. What artist could want more?"

I felt sorry for the perplexed station manager as Lesy almost pushed her out the door.

There was something less happy about my web-kin as she looked at me. "You've done it now, haven't you?" In a low voice. "I can't hide what happened."

"What do you think happened?" I asked innocently.

"You called for medics, security personnel. Set the station on alert! She'll have to know. She will know. This will be bad, Ses-ki." Lesy sank on a cushion, her skin mottled with distress, only to bounce up again. "What—?" She reached underneath and pulled out the head of the infamous Teganersha-Ki. "This isn't mine," she announced. She plucked at the gauzy green fabric covering most of the face "This is. What have you done to my cloak, Ses-ki?"

I took the head and put it over mine. "Help! Help! This is Riosolesy-ki. I think I've been poi—poi—poisoned!! Ahhhhharggghhhhhh." My voice echoed within the cavity, coming out deeper and nicely desperate. I pulled off the head and grinned.

"That's—" One of the things I loved most about Lesy was her laugh in any form. Now, she dropped on her abdomen and rocked back and forth, her beaked mouthparts clicking together in a blur, her skin rising in welts of purple that drew the same response from my own.

Ersh might not like being imitated, but she'd have to admit I'd followed her rules.

Well, she didn't have to admit anything, but there could be a volume reduction in the inevitable lecture.

Once we'd both calmed, Lesy sighed. "My only regret, Youngest, is we won't be going to Dokeci-Na. I know you were counting on it. I'm sorry."

I shrugged with all five arms. "There's the pool."

Lesy smiled. "Wonderful idea. Just what we need. Let's go!" She surged to her feet.

It felt odd to feel the Elder. "What about your art?" Cureceo-ki might have been after Tumbler excretions, but the end result was the same. All of Lesy's "best"—or at least her newest—work was gone. "What if it's never found?"

My web-kin lifted her arms and spun around. "I will always have it in my tubal pumps." *Which made no sense.* Then she stopped and winked her uppermost eye at me. "Besides, each piece is marked. Long after the current owners pass into dust, I'll be able to find every one."

"How?"

"My creations are part of me; I am part of them."

Was this more idiotic prattle?

Looking at my triumphant, ever-mysterious web-kin, I wondered suddenly if any of us took her as seriously as we should. "What do you mean?" I asked.

Lesy winked again. "A touch of blue, Youngest. That's all. Signed work is more precious, don't you think? Now, shall we go?"

I followed my Elder to the pool.

But I kept wondering . . .

Where was the first Ersh-head I'd made?

And why hadn't I seen blue paint in Lesy's cupboards?

SIR APROPOS OF NOTHING
AND
THE ADVENTURE OF THE
RECEDING HEIR

Peter David

I, Apropos, spawn of rape, bastard son of a tavern whore, lame of leg and quick of wit, Apropos the one-eared, short-lived knight, bearer of strange rings, slaughterer of thousands, known and unknown through lands far and wide, master of all I survey, king of kings, and once known with barely concealed sneers of contempt as "Sir Apropos of Nothing," had everything.

Naturally I knew it wasn't going to last.

I have been through a good deal in what I laughingly refer to as "my life." If you had asked me at any time during my existence, I would certainly have told you that my life was a pathetic, useless and valueless thing . . . which was odd when one considered the number of people who had tried to take the damned thing from me. Kings and commoners, warlords and ladies, sorcerers and monsters seemingly without end have endeavored at different times to snatch permanently the breath from my lungs. Perhaps I just have a way with people.

I never expected to be a king. Never wanted it, nor desired it. In my youth, I had been presented with a wall-hanging created by a Farweaver—a mage who foresaw the future by creating elaborate tapestries that depicted said futures. I was amazed to see on that tapestry an unmistakable rendering of me, much older than I thought I had any right to be. I was seated upon a throne, looking as dyspeptic as I typically do, and missing an ear.

I considered it to be a mistake. But that didn't stop me from keeping the tapestry with me in all my many travels.

But I didn't believe.

Then I lost the ear, in a brutal mishap during my tragic sojourn in the far off land of Chinpan.

After that, I believed.

My path to becoming a king was a long and torturous one, and I shall no doubt write about it one day. Gods know there were many bumps and bruises along the way, and not a little peril, and the literal falling out I had with the bastard son of my loins was so heart-wrenching that, to this day, I still find it impossible to put it down in narrative form. Odd, I know, considering all he wanted to do was kill me, that I should still feel that degree of attachment to him. Perhaps it boils down to the simple notion that none of us asks to be born. Since I was conceived under rather indelicate conditions, I'm probably more aware of that truism than just about anyone, and thus would have preferred a more charitable fate for my own son. So that tale will also be told, if at all, another time.

Instead I find myself moved to discuss matters of far more recent vintage.

The land over which I was the king was a small and unassuming realm called Ahl-Meedya, tucked away in an outer eastern region. As king of Ahl-Meedya, I was stern, but I endeavored to be just in my dealings with the people. After all, my own beginnings were humbler than most any others, and so I felt sympathy toward peasants who had difficulties. When disputes involved peasant against peasant, I was evenhanded, and likewise with man of privilege against his peer. But I must admit that, in mediating those disputes that arose from peasant against nobleman—a man deprived of wages, say, or a nobleman who had swooped into a wedding because he felt like availing himself of the new bride—my biases leaned in the direction of the less privileged.

The conspicuous downside of such an attitude was that peasants—save when they're armed with torches and pitchforks—rarely exert any influence or have any power in society. The major areas of support for my kingship came from the nobility. It was they who would have, and should have, been my true allies. I didn't break bread with butchers and bakers; I spent time in the company of lords and ladies.

All right, that's actually a bit of an exaggeration. The truth is that I spent very little time with anyone.

My decision to minimize my interaction with others was facilitated by my fundamental dislike for, and distrust of, people in general and . . . well . . . people in specific, now that I think about it. I spent most of my time working on my memoirs, or sometimes I'd do something as simplistic as stare into mirrors. I would search the lined and careworn face for some hint of the young man I once was. My red hair was now dark and infested with gray. My eyes, once so filled with cunning and a tendency to despise the world around me, now simply looked haggard, with crow's feet crinkling the edges.

Occasionally I longed for the caress of a woman's hand to ease the wrinkled brow, and it wasn't as if I couldn't have had my choice of such wenches. But I trusted none of them. A lifetime of being betrayed by females will do that to one, and so the fires of a young man's passion had long ago dimmed.

My advisors kept me advised. My courtiers kept me courted. And so passed each day, one much like the next. My sole counselor expressed concern over the noblemen whose collective noses I might be putting out of joint with my tendency to tend to the needs of the masses rather than stepping on their throats. He went so far as to tell me that he was convinced I was sowing the seeds of my own destruction by angering powerful men.

Mayhap he was right. I couldn't say. This was odd, I know, considering I've always prided myself on being self-aware enough to know exactly why I do what I do. But in these recent times of slow, downward spiral, my motives were a mystery even to me.

With the lack of a queen, though, other concerns began to present themselves.

This was made abundantly clear to me during one of my occasional chess games with the aforementioned counselor, more about whom I shall tell you now.

My counselor was the only man in the kingdom of Ahl-Meedya that I trusted. Trust was not something that came easily to me, and certainly counselors would be the last individuals that any king could trust. Why? Because as much as they might have purported to keep secrets, that often wasn't the case at all. Counselors were by definition wise men, and wise men knew that one of the fundamental rules of the universe is that nothing is forever. Not even kings. Especially kings. So counselors typically kept their eyes upon, not the king's best interests, but their own. Consequently, there was every reason to assume that nothing you told them stayed between you, and it was always possible the advice they gave you was coming

from other sources that were trying to manipulate you
through means of a cat's-paw (namely the counselor.)
Counselors frequently had other allies, other sources
of income, and other concerns that outweighed any
questions of loyalty to their king.

Not my counselor. No, no. He was my man and
mine alone. Again, why? Because no one wanted a
piece of him in any sense.

He was a leper . . . Schlepper, by name. Schlepper
the leper. I had encountered the poor bastard some
years before, being tormented by local children. Old
I may be, but the vivid memories of torture I endured
as a youngster at the hands of other children had not
diminished with the passage of time. With a single
shouted command and a threatening swing of my staff,
I sent the children running and put out a hand to him.
He stared at the outstretched hand, gaping. "Un-
clean!" he cried out, and jingled some bells on a short
staff to warn me back.

"The gods have rendered me immune," I said, and
I knew this to be true. Some years earlier, sick and
half-starved and on the run from implacable pursuers,
I had wound up taking refuge in a leper colony. The
lepers nursed me back to health. I spent a year there
and never contracted the disease, so I had no reason
to fear it now. "I extend you my hospitality." Of
course, I was not in the habit of being generous. My
motives, as always, were selfish: there were simply too
many damned people hanging around the court in
those days to keep a misanthrope such as myself
happy, and I figured the moment they saw a leper
mingling among them, they'd clear out.

I was right. For three solid months people left me
the hell alone, probably waiting for me to die. It was
bliss. When I didn't, they slowly came filtering back, but
by that time I'd become genuinely fond of the bastard.

Because of his various scars and running sores, it was hard to tell how old Schlepper truly was. All he ever admitted to was being middle-aged. He had a thatch of scraggly, curly brown hair that somehow was still in residence on his head, and his ears were shriveled at the lobes. Once I got past his looks, I discovered him to be one of the most erudite, well-informed and savvy individuals I'd ever encountered. He never talked about his background, even though I asked him about it many a time. All he said was that I wouldn't have liked him back before he was a leper; he claimed he was far less interesting.

The advantage of having a leper as a confidante is that no one else is going to want to have anything to do with him. The courtiers kept their distance from him at all times, and the mere tinkling of his bells was enough to clear out a room well before he entered. My keeping him at the court kept people away from me, and his nature kept him away from them, so it was a win-win proposition as far as I was concerned.

This particular rainy day, Schlepper was looking at me with more than his typical amount of concern as we engaged in a game of chess. He had been silent for much of the time since he'd first sat down opposite me and we began our play, but finally he said, "Majesty . . . have you given thought to an heir?"

"Well, I'm not planning on producing a son anytime soon, if that's what you're hoping for. Why would I need one, anyway?"

"Because," he said reasonably, "you're vulnerable."

"Nonsense." I moved a piece. "I always know if I'm vulnerable."

He moved a piece in response and said, "Checkmate."

I stared at the concluded game. We both knew I hadn't seen it coming, putting the lie to my previous boast. "All right," I said, unable to keep the annoyance out of my voice. "You've got my attention. What does my not having an heir make me vulnerable to?"

"It makes you a bigger target."

I began to understand what he meant.

If there is a direct line of inheritance firmly established, then there was far less incentive for power seekers to make a move against whoever was in charge. But if there was no line for transfer of power, that meant that the current possessor of the throne in Ahl-Meedya—namely me—had a problem. Saying I was a target was an understatement. If someone decided to engage in a bit of regicide, that would create an instant power vacuum. People would be vying with each other to be sucked into it. An heir would help cover my back against those who were eager to stick a knife in it. To kill a king, when there was no one to avenge him and power was up for grabs, was tempting. To kill a king when power would pass directly to an heir, who would then be looking to dole out punishment, was discouraging.

Of course, there was always the possibility that the heir would himself try to grab power. But I'd learned long ago that there was no perfect solution to any problem.

I looked at Schlepper thoughtfully. "Are you vying for the position, leper?"

Schlepper wheezed at that, which was the closest he ever came to a laugh. "I have heard tell of the occasional leper king, majesty, but I've no interest in being one. It's far too much work for a Schlepper."

I leaned back in my chair and sighed heavily. "I'm not really in the market for a queen. For one thing, I have this problem with women . . ."

"You're not attracted to them?" he asked with an air of surprise.

"No, I'm attracted. But the women I meet, sooner or later, they want to kill me."

"Yes, well . . . a lot of men share that desire."

"True, but they don't share my bed. You see the problem."

Schlepper nodded, scratching thoughtfully at his chin. Some skin fell off, leaving some puss oozing out. Both of us were polite enough to ignore it. "I suppose so. Still . . . getting married, with the woman and the wedding and the cake and the whole thing. You don't need all that *tsuris* to have an heir. You just, whattaya call it . . . adopt."

"Adopt?"

"It's certainly a lot easier to bring in an artificial heir instead of growing your own."

"I suppose." I was still doubtful about the entire proposition. "But . . . where would I find one? And how do I know he'd be loyal to me?"

Schlepper shrugged. "You'd have to take a chance or two."

"I don't like to take chances. You know that."

"Oh, right, right. The whole cowardice thing." He sighed heavily, like a disapproving mother. "That doesn't bother you? Being a coward?"

"Should it?"

"Well, you know . . . a hero dies but one death, while the coward dies many."

"Mayhap. But that also means the coward has many lives to go with the many deaths. I'll take all the lives I can get."

He gave off that wheezing laugh of his again, and let the matter drop, along with a piece of his scalp. "Tell you what, your majesty," he said as he slapped the piece of stray skin back in place as best he could, "ask the gods for guidance. They'll help."

Now it was my turn to laugh. "You don't know the

gods the way I do, my dear leper. The only ones the gods help is themselves."

"Well, we are in their image. Or they're in ours. That part, it's always a little confusing. Never know which is which . . . and sometimes it's both."

I disdained the notion of turning to the gods for help, considering the way they had routinely slapped me around for their amusement over the years. But Schlepper's words stayed with me, and over the next days I gave a good deal of thought as to where I could possibly find an heir. Producing one with a queen was, for reasons aforementioned, not going to happen. That meant finding one. Probably the best source was orphanages . . . but orphans tended to be on the young side. Did I want a young heir? If I were seeking someone to act on my behalf, and to help keep me safe, I couldn't very well lay that responsibility on some child and wait for him to grow into the role. But if I took on an older fellow, what guarantee had I that he was going to be loyal to me at all? He might fall in league with people plotting against me. Not that I knew for certain there *were* people plotting against me, but for someone in my position, it was always preferable to assume the worst.

And then, after some weeks, the matter of the heir apparent to the throne of the King of Ahl-Meedya seemed to resolve itself.

I had opted to take some time to go out into the nearby, rather copious woods and get some hunting in. Lame of leg I might have been, but my ability for woodcraft had remained impeccable, even after all these years. I had developed some facility with bow and arrow over the years, and so had brought that with me along with an assortment of snares. I was looking for small game only; I had no desire to go head to head with something that could have done me injury.

The air was crisp that particular day, and I could see the mist from my breath hanging in front of me. I was dressed warmly, mostly in wools. I had brought a cloak to serve as protection if the weather turned foul, but at that moment it was in my pack since I didn't need it snagging stray branches and brambles. As much as I was able to still move silently through the forest, I cursed the aging that made me strain to hear that which once had come so easily. Nor was my sense of smell what it once was. Then again, part of me cautioned against the notion of being angry over aging since the alternative to aging wasn't particularly attractive.

I had taken up a station at what seemed a particularly advantageous area, down by a watering hole. I was certain that it would provide an attractive lure for various forest creatures, and all I needed to do was sit and wait for some attractive target to wander by. My patience was rewarded after half an hour, when I heard a faint rustling and saw a magnificent buck emerge from the brush. Its nostrils flared, trying to determine whether it was alone or not, but I had taken care to sit downwind from it so that I would elude its formidable olfactory skills.

It remained unmoving for what seemed hours but was probably less than a minute. The arrow was already nocked into the bow, but I had not drawn the shaft back. I knew the creaking of the bow would alert the animal, so I was going to have to accomplish the feat as quickly as I could lest it scamper away. Satisfied that it was alone, the buck slowly approached the pond. I didn't move a muscle. The creature drew closer and closer to the water; I couldn't have been more then fifteen feet from it. I was waiting for it to lower its head to drink, at which point I would draw and release in one smooth motion, sending the shaft zipping through the air and—with any luck—straight into the creature's heart.

I waited . . . waited . . . trying to prevent my hands from trembling in anticipation of the swift move that would be necessary . . .

And suddenly there was an unholy ruckus from a short distance away. My gaze shifted for a heartbeat in the direction of it, and then I quickly looked back at the buck. Except there was nothing to look back at; the creature had instantly taken flight. All I saw was a quick flash of its tail before it vanished back into the brush.

I uttered an extremely loud curse, since subtlety was no longer a requirement, and shoved the arrow back into the quiver that was hanging from my hip. Determined to see who and what had made such a bloody racket in my damned forest (it was part of the royal woods and thus, technically, indeed my forest), I hauled myself to my feet with my staff, shook the circulation back into my numb legs, and made my way in the direction of the noise I'd heard.

I could tell even before I got there that it was far more than just a single outcry. There was some sort of battle going on. Curious to see what was transpiring—not that I was intending to lend a hand, you understand—I tossed aside any concerns about quietly proceeding through the forest since whatever noise I myself might have made would have been drowned out by the ruckus I was hearing.

I heard the clang of swords, shouts, curses, the pounding of feet. And then it all ceased before I could get close enough to see who was fighting whom about what. I got to a safe vantage point, a very large boulder, and looked down to see what I could see.

There was a pack of what looked to be robbers, all right. Or at least, from what I could tell of the back of them. That was all I was able to make out, for they were running and laughing and waving contemptuously to the one survivor of the carnage they had left behind. Within seconds they had vanished from sight down the road.

There was a woman lying on the ground, with an obviously fatal stab wound to her chest. So striking was her beauty that even death could do little to diminish it; there was still a hint of blush upon her cheeks. She had thick black hair that framed her face in peaceful repose. Kneeling next to her, his face in his hands, was an adolescent I took to be her son, for she was of sufficient age to be someone's mother. He had hair that was not dissimilar from hers, although it was cut somewhat shorter. He wore a blue jerkin that was far too light for the chill of the air. His grief was monumental, for he was slamming his fists on the ground and crying, "No! No! No!" over and over again. Actually, not both fists; he was still gripping a sword in one hand, apparently having been employed against his attackers.

I eased myself down from the rock and approached carefully. He heard me, which he never would have been able to do if I'd been trying to cover my approach, and instantly he gripped the sword and pointed it at me. The tip was wavering, no doubt thanks to the trembling of his hand. *"Now who?!?"* he shouted. *"I'll kill you, don't think that I won't!"*

"Oh, I think that you won't," I said easily, stepping more fully into view, "unless one of your ambitions is regicide."

"Regi—?" He stopped and looked at me suspiciously. "That's . . . killing a king."

"Very good. And what with my being a king, then killing me would certainly qualify."

He realized who I was at that point, and instantly dropped to one knee. "Majesty . . . !"

"Get up, get up," I gestured impatiently, having no patience for groveling. He did so, but continued to keep his gaze lowered. I studied the scene for a moment and then pointed at the corpse. "Is that your mother?"

"My . . . my mother?" He was still in shock, not understanding the question.

"Yes. She. Your mother. She seems a bit old to be your wife, although perhaps an older sister . . ."

"No . . . I mean, yes, she's my mother, no, she's not an older sister or . . . yes. She's my mother," he said again, stammering with his words tripping all over themselves. I couldn't bring myself to judge him too harshly, despite his inept presentation. The poor teen had just lost his mother. I could certainly relate to that; my own mother's demise had been under less than delicate circumstances. Indeed, everything about my life was less than delicate.

"So what happened here? Some sort of ambush—robbers, perhaps, or rapists, or gods-only-knew what—and you did your best to protect your mother and . . . well, it didn't work out so well for you, did it." His face was a picture of misery. "Where's your father?"

He shook his head and shrugged. The gesture said it all: Either the father had left them, or the lad had no idea who his father was.

I knelt down next to the mother, whose eyes were open. I reached over and, as gently as I could, closed them. Then I noticed a small leather pouch attached to her belt. I slid my hand under it, tested the heft. It felt like an impressive amount of coins. "What did your mother do for a living, boy?"

"She . . . taught dance."

"Is that what she told you?" He continued to nod in such a way that I was sure his head was going to tumble off his neck. "Did you ever actually see her teach anyone?" This time, to break up the monotony, he shook his head.

That told me all I needed to know. When a woman was making her way around with a considerable amount of coinage, the chances were huge that she was selling herself. I should know; that was certainly the case with my mother. This boy, though, seemed unaware of his mother's occupation. I was beginning to think that the attackers had done him a disservice. They should have dispatched him handily since he was clearly too stupid to live.

And yet . . . there was something about him. He looked up into my eyes and there burned such cold, dark fury. And why not? He'd just lost his mother, the only thing in the world that meant anything to him. It was clear he now had nothing. If I, of all people, could not relate to that, what was I?

"You'll come with me," I said firmly. "The castle is not far distant. We shall go there, have your mother's body retrieved, and give her a proper funeral."

"What of me?" the boy practically wailed. "What will become of me?"

How about we leave you to fend for yourself? That's what I did for decades.

I couldn't bring myself to say that, however, because I knew what that time had done to me. I knew the man it had made me, and although I wouldn't have changed any aspect of me for all the world, I was not especially enamored of the thought of inflicting that life upon someone else.

"If you wish," I said, "you'll be well-employed and taken care of at the castle. And you'll be trained."

"Trained for what? I . . . I have no real skills. I've spent my life attending to my mother's wishes. I've never trained to do anything or be anything."

"Never? You're totally useless?"

He looked crestfallen. "I . . . I guess."

I clapped a hand on his shoulder and smiled. "What's your name?"

"Hedgeworth, sir. 'Hedge' to my friends, if I had any."

"Tell me, Hedge . . . do you think you could tell other people what to do?"

"You mean be a leader?"

"No. Just tell them what to do."

"Oh. Well . . . I guess."

"Can you make decisions and stick to them without regard as to whether they're right or wrong? Can you fail to learn from your mistakes, or never admit that you made any in the first place? Do you think you're capable of launching a war without having the faintest idea of what you're doing?"

"I . . . I suppose."

"Good. You're qualified to be a king."

My decision may seem precipitous to you, but consider: when one has far more of his life behind him than ahead of him, one tends to see the patterns all the more clearly. The patterns that keep certain people down while others are elevated beyond their deserving or their worth. Every so often, one is seized by the desire to undo those patterns. To try and make things turn out in such a way that others don't have to undergo the same tortured existence. This is especially true if one believes that we are helplessly dancing to the tunes played by the gods, and we want to show off by changing the music.

I was as good as my word. Actually, considering the

number of times I had broken my word, I was in fact better than my word. I brought young Hedge to the castle and offered up a proper funeral pyre for his mother. The service was held just outside the towering Temple Meads, the stately and many-spired building that served as both a house of worship and brewery. Then I announced that the young man was officially the king's ward, and immediately embarked upon a program of education, scholarship, and the manly arts of warfare.

In my youth, I had wound up coming to a king's palace and being made a squire. But it was a far different circumstance. In my case, my heart burned for revenge against the knights of that court, one of whom I was certain was the bastard who had raped my mother and conceived me. So everything that I learned was colored by my distrust for the house of chivalry that I perceived as being built upon a foundation of sand.

Hedge, however, had no such problems.

He took to the classes, the training, all of it with alacrity and excitement. He was a virtual knowledge sponge. I delighted in the eagerness he displayed. He was all over the castle, talking with anyone and everyone whom he could approach. Naturally, being my ward, he was entitled to approach anyone. Most of the time he didn't have much to say, but that was perfectly all right. You'll find that the favorite topic of most people is themselves. Given half a chance, they would talk about their views on damn near anything for hours on end, and Hedge was perfectly happy to listen for as long as they felt like talking. This prompted many a person to come up to me and tell me "what a superb conversationalist" my ward was, which amused the hell out of me for obvious reasons.

On those occasions when Hedge did choose to open his mouth, he exhibited a folksy charm that, remarkably, worked for both the high- and lowborn alike. The nobility, usually so eager to freeze out those who were not born to the purple such as themselves, quickly recognized his potential as heir apparent and were happy to cozy up to him. The peasantry, at the same time, felt that he was one of them, thanks to the well-publicized humble nature of his origins and his self-effacing manner.

I started showing up in court more, mingling with the high and mighty and low and not-so-mighty, and even started doing the unthinkable and throwing the occasional social galas. Most of the time I did so in order to watch Hedge go about his interactions. No one worked a room quite the same way he did.

Most impressive of all was his development in weapons training. Initially he seemed hopeless. My master-at-arms claimed he'd never seen such ineptitude. But within a month's time the master-at-arms had completely reversed his opinion. Facility with swords both long and short, daggers, maces . . . Hedge learned his way around all weapons with speed that bordered on the inexplicable. The master-at-arms, once the lad's harshest critic, decided that he was, in fact, a natural.

Schlepper kept a close watch on the lad as well.

Schlepper didn't like him.

"There's something about him," Schlepper told me. "He's too perfect. He's too good at getting near people."

"Couldn't he simply have infinite capacity for charm?" I asked.

"You want I should tell you what you want to hear?" demanded the leper. He spoke in a rapturous tone. "He's wonderful! He's marvelous! He's the most wonderful thing to happen to mankind since . . .

since . . ." He paused, thought, and then asked, "What would you think if we started slicing bread?"

"Slicing it?" I considered. "How?"

"Vertically. Take a loaf, make about, oh, twenty, thirty slices."

"Instead of just pulling it off in chunks, you mean."

"Right."

"Hunh. That's a good idea. That's a really good idea. But . . . why did you bring that up?"

"So I could have a comparison. Hedge is the most wonderful thing to happen to mankind since that idea I had just now."

"Ah. I see," I said, although I didn't entirely. I half-smiled. "Tell me, Schlepper . . . is it possible that perhaps you're just a little jealous because he can mingle with people so easily, whereas others back away from you whenever they see you coming?"

"You think what you want, highness," he said, shrugging and—in doing so—breaking open a large pustule on his neck. He dabbed at it carelessly with a cloth. "I just call them like I see them."

"I thought you were half-blind."

"I make up for it by looking twice as hard as everybody else."

So popular did Hedge become that, when I announced at a spring gala that I had officially decided he would be my heir, there was thunderous applause from everyone in attendance. Hedge beamed at me, glowing with pride, and the women of the court began reassessing him as potential husband material.

And then, one day, long after Hedge had taken up residence in the castle, I was making one of my occasional sojourns in and around the immediate hamlets. As always, I did so in disguise, dressed as a lame beggar—which, frankly, is far closer to the truth of me than I like to think about. Even with the refreshing presence of Hedge, the castle and my kingly duties could be occasionally suffocating. I had considered taking Hedge with me; he had been particularly demanding of late, hoping that he and I could go hunting, just the two of us. I was reluctant to, for the weather had been getting colder once more, and I was feeling it more in my joints these days. So I had demurred, and he had seemed disappointed but understanding. Still, inclement weather or no, the urge for time by myself out and about had grown to the point where I simply had to hie myself away under cover of disguise and darkness.

So there I sat in a pub, off to one side, nursing a drink, watching the little people going on about their lives, having their discussions, their disagreements, and their drunken encounters.

And I was getting concerned with what I was hearing.

There was much discussion of matters that I was woefully uninformed about. That was as much my fault as anything else, for despite my recent efforts to make myself more accessible, I still tended to keep to myself.

Rumors were swirling, it turned out, concerning war. Impending war with enemies foreign and domestic. Servants of nobles loved to gossip, and servants heard everything. The economy had been fallow, and the nobles were anxious to prey upon weaker nations in the hopes of expanding their own coffers.

They spoke of me as a warmonger, which was interesting considering this was the first I knew of it. They talked about my secret plans, my lust for power. Certainly no mentions of any of these concerns had been made by any of the peasants seeking my aid in various adjudications . . . but then again, they wouldn't have mentioned them, would they? Not if they wanted to get on my good side and have me rule in their favor.

I would have considered it an isolated aberration, save that this was the third tavern I'd gone to that night, and I had heard much similar rumblings at other places. It seemed as if matters were reaching a tipping point, and I was concerned about what might be the final straw to push it over.

Then I saw a man making his way around the tavern. He was showing people what appeared to be a drawing, a small portrait, and asking them questions. Each of them shook their heads. Clearly he was asking about the individual on the portrait. I was curious, but didn't have to make any endeavor to approach him since he was heading in my direction. He came up to me with a concerned air and said, "Excuse me, sir . . . I wouldn't be bothering you, would I?" Beneath my hood, I shook my head and gestured for him to sit. He did so. His accent was unfamiliar to me; clearly he wasn't from the immediate area.

"My name is Tucker. I am . . . or I should say, I was . . . a wealthy merchant. Last year I fell in love with a gorgeous woman. She married me, and then, not too long after that, she disappeared. I thought she was a woman of means herself, for she had considerable funds of her own and the look of a fine lady about her. But she vanished like a thief into the night, taking all my money, my valuables, anything small and easily transportable . . ."

"I can sympathize," I said. "Something not too dissimilar happened to me, back when a far younger man's visage peered at me from mirrors. You are looking for her?"

He nodded and passed the drawing over. "I rendered it myself. I don't pretend to be an artist, but it is the best I could do."

You may find it difficult to believe, but I knew whose picture would be on it even before he handed it to me. Sure enough: the image of Hedge's mother stared at me.

I said nothing for a long moment. Then, very quietly, I asked, "Would she have been traveling with anyone?"

"Not that I am aware of."

"Is it . . ." I licked my lips, my mind racing. "Is it possible that another man, a young man, might have been looking for her?"

"Why . . . yes!" He seemed surprised. "Within a day of her disappearance, a young man came seeking her out. I didn't know it was she that he was seeking at first, for he asked for her by a different name. But his description of her was such that I knew it was my lovely Janna he was looking for."

"Your lovely Janna." I shook my head, and moaned softly to myself. Pieces were already clicking together in my head. "Fellow . . . I want you to listen carefully. I want you to go home. You will not find her. Ever."

"But I . . ." He choked slightly. "I still love her."

"Even after what she has done."

"Yes. I could never just . . ."

I reached into the folds of my cloak. He flinched slightly, perhaps thinking that I was going to pull out a knife. Instead I put a medium-sized bag on the table, glancing around to make certain no one was noticing it. "This will help you to forget her."

"Sir," said the merchant, prying open the bag with a reluctant air, as if he were greatly put upon. "I could never forget my glorious . . ." Then his eyes widened as the sizable amount of gold sovs within worked their magic upon him.

"Is she forgotten now?" I asked.

"She's dead to me."

I nodded and watched as he walked out of the tavern, taking care not to move the bag around too much lest the coins jingle in a way that would entice thieves.

I decided I needed some distance from the castle that night, and so rented a small room in the tavern. With sounds of the tavern wench cleaning up downstairs, I lay in the small bed, feeling oddly far more comfortable and at peace there than in the vast, luxurious bed that was mine to enjoy back in the castle. Staring up at the darkened ceiling, I ran possibilities through my head, considering and weighing options, putting pieces together.

Life is patterns. Life is seeing the same things over and over. Life is realizing how little of anything is new, and what passes for wisdom in the aged is not truly insight, but simply remembering that which has already occurred and realizing how it can be applied to the here and now.

I drifted off to sleep and was awakened by screams.

I rolled out of bed and immediately hit the floor. I lay there with my head buried under my arms, hoping that if there was some sort of danger—particularly danger involving armed men trying to kill people—I would remain undetected and be able to ride it out. Never once did I give any thought to rushing down and saving frightened women or innkeepers. Anyone who believes that crossed my mind for an instant simply doesn't know me very well.

But then I heard cries of "fire!" and I smelled the smoke. I realized that smoke was drifting in from the north, in the general direction of the castle. I hauled myself to my feet, grabbed my staff, and quickly made my way out of the room, down the stairs, and out into the dirt streets. The sun was just coming up over the horizon, and I easily blended in with the crowd of people who were running in the direction of the thick plume of black smoke.

Temple Meads was burning.

I mentioned it in passing earlier, but I now wish to make clear that it was a towering, glorious structure, dedicated to worshipping the many gods, and all denominations in Ahl-Meedya had found common ground there. People had been born there, married there, buried there. The mysterious priests who oversaw it had settled great disputes, and it was truly believed by many that the gods themselves looked with favor upon it and dwelt within. Furthermore, as the premier brewery in the area, it had easily paid for its own upkeep, and its product was widely celebrated in taverns local and abroad.

Now, as the citizenry gathered and tried tossing buckets of water upon it in utter futility, I watched in helpless frustration as, one by one, the spires of the church collapsed one upon the other, crashing to the ground with a thunderous roar that was almost immediately drowned out by the horrified, anguished roars of the onlookers. These were followed by deafening explosions as the fire made its way to the distillery equipment and vats of aging alcohol that only fed the conflagration.

It might have continued to burn for hours upon end, but apparently the gods looked down upon the destruction and were moved to pity. Dark, fearsome clouds came rolling in, blotting out the sun and sending torrents of rain down upon the now smoldering ruins.

I watched it all, never moving from the spot. People ran about like headless fowl all around me, but I continued simply to gaze upon it in rapt fascination. I felt as if I were seeing it all from outside myself.

All was hazy, and yet all was clear.

When I returned to the castle, I was so covered in grime and soot that my own guards almost didn't let me in. They were greatly chagrined to realize belatedly my identity, and clearly they feared remonstration. I didn't bother; I had other things on my mind. My various courtiers and would-be advisors clamored for my ear—my only remaining good one—but I stalked right past them, opting to bathe and change. As I finished putting on new clothes, there was an insistent pounding upon my door. I knew who it was going to be before I even opened it.

Hedge stood there, bristling, anxious. "Let me take the war to them!" he said as he stalked into the room without even asking to be invited. "This is what you've been training me for!"

"The war? To them? What them?" I asked calmly.

"The enemy who did this!"

"We know who it was?" I continued to towel off my hair. "I've heard a number of names bandied about. Different city states, different kings, all accused of this act. Do we know for certain it wasn't simply an accident?"

"Oh yes," Hedge said with conviction. "We know that of a certainty. I've been speaking to people. They're furious. They thirst for vengeance. They will not allow the perpetrators of terror who did this to get away with it."

"And they look to you to lead them?"

He paused and then said quickly, "You are their ruler, highness. You are Apropos, the King of Ahl-Meedya."

I stared at him for a long moment. "And I've been training you for this, have I? It seems not for so very long. You wish to . . . what? Lead the charge?"

"In the glory of your name, highness."

"Indeed." I limped over to my staff, which was leaning against the wall, took it, and settled my weight on it. After all these years it felt as normal as if I had a fully functioning right leg. If the gods came down and restored health to my leg, I'd probably have kept falling over. "My boy . . . you've wanted to go hunting for a while now. We go this very evening."

He looked startled. "Sire, the . . . the people are busy craving vengeance." He pointed as if they were massing outside the door. "Is this evening the appropriate time for . . . ?"

"Yes. Yes, I believe it is," I told him.

He stared at me, and there was much going on behind his eyes.

He thought I didn't know. He probably took some measure of security in that. And when he nodded and thanked me and said he was looking forward to it, he probably still thought he was safe inside his head. He had no idea I was already well insinuated within.

I spent the balance of the day talking with various nobles, men of power. They echoed Hedge's sentiments. There was a general agreement that some devious foreign government must have been responsible for the horrible misdeed, perhaps issued as some sort of preemptive warning against us. The feeling was that if they were going to try and instill fear into us, that they were sadly ill advised in the endeavor. Instead of beating us down into submission, we were going to rise up in the face of our foes, whoever they might be, and respond in kind or even worse.

Never had I seen such uniformity of intent, purpose and anger.

All right . . . actually, that is not remotely true. My long career as a liar has made it second nature for me. Even in these memoirs, which I resolved would be the truth and nothing but, I tend to fall reflexively upon the untruth from time to time.

The fact was that I had seen such uniformity of intent in my time. Quite a few times, in fact.

And I knew where it would lead, and what would happen as a result.

Only Schlepper advised caution and seeking out facts before making precipitous decisions based upon misinformation. Consequently, it was to Schlepper whom I ultimately turned for all my needs in the matter of the war . . . and of my heir.

Hedge and I went hunting that early evening, as planned. The rain had long passed, and the ground had dried out. We slipped out unnoticed through corridors generally reserved for menials. In short order, we were in the forest, well armed and prepared for anything that we might encounter.

We made our way, looking for game, and quite silent. Hedge appeared thoughtful. Perhaps he was wondering about the odd timing of our little hunting excursion.

I didn't keep him in suspense.

"You realize where we are?" I asked.

He looked around, seemingly indifferent. "Isn't this . . . where we first met?"

"Yes. Where you were ambushed. Funny. You didn't seek vengeance."

Looking puzzled, Hedge said, "I . . . don't understand."

"My mother was killed. I thirsted for vengeance upon those who did it. I would have crawled naked across shards of wood to accomplish it. But you haven't spoken of such desires. Why is that?"

"I . . ." He looked confused. "I . . . figured that when the time was right, we . . . I could—"

"And your skill with weapons seemed to develop almost overnight. As if you were covering your facility with them before getting bored with doing so and instead allowing your teacher to take credit for your 'progress.' "

"Highness, I don't understand wh—"

"When were you planning to kill me?"

I asked the question so calmly, so indifferently, that at first he didn't quite register that I had asked it. "I . . . what?"

"Now would probably be the best time," I said so casually that we might have been discussing the weather. "You can blame it on unseen enemies. You, as my heir, will be able to give the noblemen what they want. And you will be in a remarkable position of power. Not bad . . . for an assassin, eh?"

The look of confusion slowly dissolved from his face, and there—unguarded, undiluted—was the look of cold assessment that I'd seen so fleetingly that first day.

"*Apprentice* assassin," he corrected me. "In training."

"And the woman . . . Janna . . . she was your target."

"Yes." His expression twisted in quiet fury. He seemed far older than his years. "The head of our guild gave me a great honor. The bitch had pretended she loved him. Had married him. And then looted him and fled."

"A confidence woman conned an assassin . . . and a chief at that," I said wonderingly. "Was she brave or merely foolhardy?"

"She didn't know what he was. She thought he was a weapons maker. She had no idea that he supplied them to the entire Guild. When she departed and he realized he'd been taken advantage of, his wrath was towering. I was his foremost pupil. He gave me the honor of finding her, killing her, and retrieving as much as possible of what she'd stolen. It took me many months, but I tracked her down."

"But displayed abominable timing. She departed

shortly before you arrived . . . and then, just before you caught up with her, highwaymen found her first." My mouth twisted in a grimace of a smile. "We are the playthings of the gods, are we not?"

Hedge nodded. "True. The bastards robbed her of most of the riches she had on her, save for that one small bag of coins they missed. I caught up with her just as they fled. I was furious at my luck."

"And you killed her. It was her blood on the sword. They merely robbed her. You slew her."

"Yes. And you found me," he said, his anger rising, "bathed in womanish tears because I had failed to recoup my master's losses. That, and because I was going to have to cut off the bitch's head and bring it back to prove she was dead, instead of simply returning my master's treasures. I wasn't looking forward to that, I can tell you. So when you came upon me, I was mortified, I nearly killed you on the spot . . . until I realized who you were."

"And how you could use me."

"As you intended to use me!" Hedge snapped. "Making me your heir, in order to . . . what? Deter those who might seek to overthrow you by making sure there would be no power vacuum, but instead one who would seek justice for anything that happened to you? To serve as a breaker against waves of treachery?"

"More or less," I admitted.

"And did you consider," he asked, "what would happen if your breaker decided to unleash the waves of treachery upon you . . . himself!"

He came straight at me, his dagger out and clearly intended to be driven straight into my heart.

The metal-jawed trap, hidden thoroughly in the undergrowth between us, snapped tight on his left leg.

Hedge screamed and went down. He clutched at the

ruined leg, sobbing and cursing my name in a string of very colorful profanities. He tried and failed to pry the jaws of the trap apart, and blood poured down the leg where the metal jaws were biting deeply.

"As a matter of fact," I said calmly, "I did consider exactly that."

There was a rustling of brush nearby and Schlepper the leper emerged. He had his hood drawn up to cover his head. I heard something *splut* to the ground and wondered briefly what piece of him that might have been. "Nicely set," I said.

"I know," said the leper, never one to undervalue his own handiwork.

Hedge was still endeavoring to pull the jaws apart. I walked over to him and said calmly, "Here. Let me help you," and—balancing with my staff—I shoved my left foot down as hard as I could. Obviously this didn't do much to alleviate his pain. The howls were deafening. But it did provide me with a few moments of amusement.

"Stop it! Stop it!!" he screamed the moment I let up on the pressure.

"Did you set fire to the temple?" I asked.

"No!"

I stepped on the trap once more and he screamed even more loudly. I repeated the question. Again he denied it, even though he was making himself hoarse in his howls. Impressed, I eased up once more.

"So you think it's true?" asked Schlepper. "That an enemy did it? Or do you think he's just lying again?"

"Who cares? I just like doing this." I made as if to step on the trap and he cried out in anticipation. But I withheld my foot and instead laughed at him.

He glared at me with as much hatred as he could muster. But I'd received hateful stares from everything from damsels to gods, so it took more than a crippled apprentice assassin to leave me feeling daunted. "I'll kill you," he snarled, gasping for breath. "I'll kill you."

"You won't need to. I'll already be dead," I told him.

He stared uncomprehending. "What . . . what do you—?"

"Eventually," I said, "you're going to free yourself of that trap, I've no doubt. And you will limp your way back to the castle, and tell a very pretty story of enemies springing upon you and me. How you tried to defend me. How you saw me cut down and my body hauled away. They left you for dead because they didn't realize who you were: the next King of Ahl-Meedya."

"But . . ." He shook his head as if trying to dispel a cloud of confusion. "But . . . why?"

"Because," I said matter-of-factly, "I am a coward. I have always been, and always will be. And in my life, I have seen too many times the steady drumbeat of war being sounded. I've seen its beginning, and I watched it continue steadily, louder and louder, until the inevitable becomes the reality. People who are believed enemies, become enemies. Words of war supersede words of peace. And there will be much fighting, and much dying, and I have no wish to be any part of it. You have . . ." My voice caught a moment, and to my annoyance, I felt my eyes beginning to tear up. I wiped them away angrily with the back of my sleeve. "You have no idea," I said, my voice becoming strained and husky, "how many people there are who live on only in my mind. Countless souls deprived of their bodies, their livelihoods, their dreams—all that they ever wished to be or could be or would be— because of me. Because of my machinations, or my base cowardice, or my desire to sacrifice anyone and anything just so I could continue to live. I have enough blood on my hands to paint the forest red and have plenty left over. And now I'll be called upon to lead another war? More blood? More souls? More lives destroyed? More women sobbing for their men, children crying out for their fathers? No more. Let it be on your head, my dear Hedge. Take up the gauntlet that I throw to you. Gladly do I leave it behind, and depart with nothing, for to have nothing remains, as always, my natural state of being."

I leaned forward on my staff and, very softly, I added, "And don't get any ideas about seeking out members of your . . . association . . . to hunt me down. Should that happen, I assure you, I will outwit them. I always do. And then I, the king, will return, and paint a very different story for the masses from what you have told them. And by the next crow of the cock, you'll be dancing on air with a stretched neck. Do you understand?" He didn't answer immediately. "I said, do you understan—"

"Yes," he fairly snarled.

"Say that you understand."

"I understand . . . you bastard."

"I am that."

"Son of a bitch."

"As well," I replied unperturbed.

With that, I . . . along with Schlepper the Leper, the only individual whom I could recall having called "friend" . . . walked away. "Where are we going?" inquired the leper.

"Haven't the faintest idea."

"Oy," moaned Schlepper, but offered no protest other than that.

And as we headed off, we heard from behind us continued thrashing and muttering from Hedge, who was going to lead a nation in the completely wrong direction, and they would undoubtedly thank him for it until they finally realized, at which point they would probably kill him. So it would all work out. Just before we vanished from his sight, he screamed, *"You didn't have to ruin my leg!"*

I turned to him and tipped a hand in a mocking salute. "If you are to rule in my stead . . . then you will walk in my tread. I have shared so much of the benefits of my life with you; I thought that sharing one of the primary handicaps would likewise be . . . oh, what's the word . . . oh yes . . ." and I smiled, ". . . apropos."

I bowed deeply, his curses serving as my "bravos," and vanished with my companion into the deep of the forest.

About the Authors

Robin Wayne Bailey is the author of fifteen novels, including the Dragonkin series, *Night's Angel* and *Shadowdance*. His short fiction has appeared in *2001: The Best Science Fiction of the Year, Thieves World,* and many other anthologies and magazines. He's also edited *Architects of Dreams: The SFWA Author Emeritus Anthology,* as well as the critically acclaimed *Through My Glasses Darkly: Five Stories by Frank M. Robinson.* He serves on the Board of Advisors of the Science Fiction Museum and Hall of Fame and is the current president of the Science Fiction and Fantasy Writers of America. He lives in North Kansas City, Missouri.

Michael A. Burstein, winner of the 1997 Campbell Award for Best New Writer, has earned ten Hugo nominations and two Nebula nominations for his short fiction, which appears mostly in *Analog*. Burstein lives with his wife Nomi in the town of Brookline, Massachusetts, where he is an elected town meeting member and library trustee. When not writing, he edits middle and high school science textbooks. He has two degrees in physics and attended the Clarion Workshop. More information on Burstein and his work can be found on his webpage, *www.mabfan.com*.

Award-winning author and editor **Julie E. Czerneda** recently published her eleventh science fiction novel from DAW, *Reap the Wild Wind*, Stratification #1, along with two new anthologies: *Polaris: A Celebration of Polar Science* and *Under Cover of Darkness*, edited with Jana Paniccia. Meanwhile, Julie is keeping busy, returning to the Trade Pact with the next in her Stratification trilogy and editing two more anthologies, *Misspelled* and *Ages of Wonder* with Rob St. Martin. When not canoeing out of reach of phone or email, that is.

Peter David has had over sixty novels published, including numerous appearances on the New York Times Bestsellers List. His novels include *Sir Apropos of Nothing, Knight Life, Howling Mad,* and the *Psi-Man* adventure series. He is the co-creator and author of the bestselling *Star Trek: New Frontier* series and has also written such Trek novels as *Q-Squared, The Siege, Q-in-Law, Vendetta, I, Q* (with John deLancie), *A Rock and a Hard Place* and *Imzadi.* He produced the three Babylon 5 *Centauri Prime* novels, and has also had his short fiction published in such collections as *Shock Rock, Shock Rock II,* and *Otherwere,* as well as *Isaac Asimov's Science Fiction Magazine* and the *Magazine of Fantasy and Science Fiction.*

Eugie Foster calls home a mildly haunted, fey-infested house in metro Atlanta that she shares with her husband, Matthew, and her pet skunk, Hobkin. She is an active member of the SFWA, winner of the Phobos Award, and Managing Editor of *Tangent.* Her fiction has been translated into Greek, Hungarian, Polish, and French, and has been nominated for the

British Fantasy and Pushcart awards. Her publication credits include stories in *Realms of Fantasy, The Third Alternative, Paradox, Cricket, Fantasy Magazine, Cicada,* and anthologies *Hitting the Skids in Pixeltown,* edited by Orson Scott Card; *Best New Fantasy: 2005,* edited by Sean Wallace; and *Writers for Relief,* edited by Davey Beauchamp—a charity anthology to benefit the survivors of Hurricane Katrina. Visit her online at www.eugiefoster.com.

Esther M. Friesner is the author of thirty-one novels and over one hundred fifty short stories, in addition to being the editor of seven popular anthologies. Her works have been published in the United States, the United Kingdom, Japan, Germany, Russia, France, Poland and Italy. She is also a published poet, a produced playwright, and once wrote an advice column, "Ask Auntie Esther." Besides winning two Nebula Awards in succession for Best Short Story, she was a Nebula finalist three times and a Hugo finalist once. Her latest publications include *Tempting Fate,* a short story collection, *Death and the Librarian and Other Stories,* and *Turn the Other Chick,* fifth in the popular "Chicks in Chainmail" series that she created and edits. She is married, the mother of two, harbors cats, and lives in Connecticut.

Ed Greenwood has published over one hundred eighty fantasy novels and Dungeons & Dragons game products, and is the award-winning creator of the famous Forgotten Realms fantasy world. His novels include the bestselling *Spellfire* and *Elminster: The Making of a Mage* and their many sequels, the Band of Four saga, and his current Knights of Myth Drannor trilogy, (thus far: *Swords of Eveningstar* and *Swords of Dragonfire.*)

Jim C. Hines is the author of the goblin trilogy from DAW Books. *Goblin Quest* was published in 2006, followed by *Goblin Hero* earlier this year. The third and final book, *Goblin War*, should be out in early 2008 . . . assumimg he gets his revisions turned in on time. After that, he'll be starting all over with *The Stepsister Scheme*, the first of what will hopefully be a series of butt-kicking princess novels. His short fiction has appeared in over thirty magazines and anthologies. This is his first time editing an anthology, but he hopes it will not be his last. Jim lives in Michigan with his wife and two children, all of whom have been extremely understanding and supportive of his bizarre writing obsession.

G. Scott Huggins was born in California but was raised in Kansas, which may explain not only his profound personality conflicts, but also his tendency to punch people who make Wizard of Oz references around him. He currently lives in Wisconsin with his wife and far too many cats. His works have appeared in the anthology series *Writers of the Future* and *MOTA*. He has also appeared in *Amazing Stories* in the States and in *Andromeda Spaceways' Inflight Magazine* in Australia.

Michael Jasper gets by on not enough sleep and too much caffeine in Wake Forest, North Carolina, where he lives with his lovely wife Elizabeth and their amazing young son Drew. Michael's fiction has appeared in *Asimov's, Strange Horizons, Interzone, Fantasy Gone Wrong, Aeon,* and *Polyphony,* among many other fine venues. His story collection *Gunning for the Buddha* came out in 2005, his paranormal romance *Heart's Revenge* (writing as Julia C. Porter) came out in 2006, and *The Wannoshay Cycle*, featuring the aliens from his story "Drinker," is due out in January of 2008.

James Lowder has worked extensively on both sides of the editorial blotter. His novels include *Knight of the Black Rose* and *Prince of Lies,* and his short fiction has appeared in such anthologies as *Shadows Over Baker Street* and *The Repentant.* As an editor, he's directed fiction lines or series for several different publishers. He's also helmed ten anthologies, some of them not about zombies.

Vera Nazarian emigrated to the USA from the USSR as a kid, sold her first story at the age of 17, and since then has published numerous works in anthologies and magazines, and has been translated into eight languages. She made her novelist debut with the critically acclaimed *Dreams of the Compass Rose,* followed by an epic fantasy about a world without color, *Lords of Rainbow.* Her novella *The Clock King and the Queen of the Hourglass* with an introduction by Charles de Lint is available. Forthcoming work includes her first collection *Salt of the Air,* with an introduction by Gene Wolfe, and a novella *The Duke in His Castle.*

Catherine H. Shaffer lives and works in the Detroit area. She is a regular contributor to *Analog Science Fiction Magazine,* and has published stories in a number of other magazines and anthologies. She also works as a science writer specializing in the field of biotechnology. She shares her home with a husband, a child, and a number of varmints. When not writing, Catherine enjoys running, cycling, and playing the violin. (The varmints particularly appreciate the last.)

Sherwood Smith's day job is dodging raining accordions and battling flying squids, otherwise known as junior high teacher. Her most popular YA book is a fantasy called *Crown Duel*. She published *Inda*, her first fantasy for adult readers, with DAW Books in 2006, followed by its sequel, *The Fox*, in 2007. She has one spouse, two kids, and two dogs.